Also by Murray Smith

THE DEVIL'S JUGGLER

STONE DANCER

STONE DANCER

Murray Smith

MICHAEL JOSEPH
LONDON

For Jane

MICHAEL JOSEPH LTD

Published by the Penguin Group
Penguin Books Ltd, 27 Wrights Lane, London W8 5TZ
Penguin Books USA Inc., 375 Hudson Street, New York, New York 10014, USA
Penguin Books Australia Ltd, Ringwood, Victoria, Australia
Penguin Books Canada Ltd, 10 Alcorn Avenue, Toronto, Ontario, Canada M4V 3B2
Penguin Books (NZ) Ltd, 182–190 Wairau Road, Auckland 10, New Zealand

Penguin Books Ltd, Registered Offices: Harmondsworth, Middlesex, England

First published in Great Britain 1994

Typeset in 12/14pt Plantin Medium by
Datix International Limited, Bungay, Suffolk
Printed in England by Clays Ltd, St Ives plc

ISBN 0 7181 3645 4

Acknowledgements

FOR THEIR good-natured patience and for their unselfish and valued advice, the author wishes to thank Oleg Gordievsky, formerly Colonel, First Chief Directorate, KGB and invaluable agent of the British Intelligence Service, who risked all in his fight to free Russia from its totalitarian nightmare; Tom Beattie, CMG, formerly of the British Foreign Service; Clair E. George, American patriot, who has received no thanks for taking the rap for his masters' mistakes; Sid Telford, formerly of the US State Department; the late Wolfgang Lotz, Mossad hero, who fooled most people right to the end, and those members of the US, British and Israeli intelligence communities who must remain nameless.

Also grateful thanks to the very many hospitable people of Beirut, who took time from their struggle back to normality, to help a simple storyteller.

I

The Rape of the Lock

IN THE RUSSIAN city of St Petersburg, until just recently known as Leningrad, it was twenty minutes before midnight.

Two men strolled past the Hermitage, home of some of Russia's finest art treasures, looking cool and collected on the outside, but with pulses raised and adrenalin high, for the stakes they were playing for equalled, say, the national debt of some minor nation, like Bulgaria. Just to take an example.

The sky was a pale yellowish grey in the moonlight. A few large flakes of crisp white snow descended lazily. But the sidewalks were dry. Street-lamps lined the broad avenue.

'I can smell shashlik. Roasting,' said the shorter of the two, in Russian. They both wore grey topcoats over the uniforms of Aeroflot pilots.

'No. It's just charcoal.'

'I know, from shashlik. Come on. Mmm, smell it. I know that smell.' The short man stuck his nose up like a hound-dog and inhaled deeply.

'It's charcoal. You got the digital key?'

'Check.'

'And the C-30 400?'

'Of course.'

'Just remember. You have thirty-four seconds, once I access the computer. I'll be counting and when I touch the glass, that means get ready to quit.'

'Sure, sure, and when you touch it again I come out of the system.'

'And you must exit with the code, zero, backslash, then the dollar symbol and four hash signs.'

'It'll be fine. And that *is* shashlik.'

'*Mozhet byt,*' replied the taller one. 'Maybe you're right.'

'Of course I am. This nose has a prodigious memory . . .'

They reached the corner of Ulitsa Kormoranskaya, and paused. A couple of slender girls approached, one wearing a trenchcoat, the other a fur-trimmed green jacket, tailored to flatter her shapely figure. Maybe just a bit too much rouge on her aristocratic cheekbones.

'Hi boys,' said the fair-haired girl in the trenchcoat. 'What hotel are you staying at?'

The shorter of the two men, who was using the name of Arkady, smiled and raised his shoulders, in a gesture of regret. The taller, calling himself Yevgeny on this particular evening, stuck his hands deep into his coat pockets and gazed through the eyes of each girl in turn, in a way that they both agreed later had made them suddenly afraid.

'Aeroflot does not pay enough for us to afford the likes of you,' he said, and the penetrating gaze altered, perceptibly, to something approaching sadness.

The younger girl touched her shoulder-length hair. 'We're not expensive,' she announced, matter-of-fact. She let her deep brown almond eyes linger on Yevgeny's.

'You bloody well should be,' he said, softly. 'Your pimp must be blind . . .' And he hunched his shoulders and moved on, crossing the street. Arkady glanced at each girl, shrugged – a briefer, goodbye shrug – and hurried after his companion.

'Sentimental old fool,' he said, shaking his head, amused.

'Poor kids. What kind of a way is that to earn a living?'

'I didn't see you give them any money.' Arkady glanced up at his colleague.

'I earn mine the hard way . . .' This from a man who at that particular time, on that particular night in St Petersburg, was worth twenty-eight million dollars in hard cash, bullion and transferable bearer bonds. All of it stolen. All stolen by a series of immaculate frauds and deceptions, always involving counterfeit and forgery, of one form or another. And after this night's work, that figure was going to look like a pittance.

The two men strode in off the street, off Ulitsa Kormoranskaya, into the lobby of the Hotel Nevsky. A splendidly furnished, spacious place, the Nevsky was soon to be awarded two stars in the first Michelin guide to Russia, a thin book, as Michelin guides go. It had once been a palace, built in the seventeenth century by a descendant of Aleksander Nevsky, made famous by Sergei Eisenstein in his epic and eponymous movie. After the Revolution of 1917, Felix Dzerzhinsky, founder of the Cheka, direct forerunner of the KGB, had it turned into his Leningrad headquarters and secret police prison and interrogation centre.

In the time of Brezhnev, the Nevsky building, with its onion domes and minarets, was declared a Soviet Treasure, and it was handed over to the administrators of the Hermitage Museum and Art Gallery, to be refurbished. The building had stood in considerable disrepair in the final decade of the Cold War, until, in 1987, Mikhail Gorbachev had forced through a deal between the City Mayor of Leningrad and Armand Hammer, the American Russophile and billionaire entrepreneur, whereby Hammer's company would throw money at the Nevsky, employing the finest Russian craftsmen, and restore the palace to its former glory.

The USSR fell. Hammer died. Nobody in his corporate maze could find any documents relating to the Nevsky. Funds were frozen. And the half-restored old palace was in danger of falling into a kind of unfinished limbo when the new city mayor bowed to a referendum to change the name of Leningrad back to the old Tsarist St Petersburg and completed a deal with a multinational US credit bank whose plastic cards were a household name around the world. He would lease them the Nevsky, provided they took over where Hammer left off, and provided it was converted into a first-class hotel, capable of comparison with the Georges Cinq in Paris, the Plaza in New York or the Connaught in London.

The US bank had been as good as its word, and now the Nevsky was one of *the* places to stay in St Petersburg. Its chefs were French and Russian, trained in the best hotels in Europe. It was amazing what had been accomplished in the four years since the fall of the USSR.

'I used to work here,' confided Yevgeny, as they strode across the vast lobby and lounge area, shrugging off their topcoats, revealing the white braid of Aeroflot captains on their epaulettes.

A small orchestra were playing muted Tchaikovsky on a low stage, surrounded by potted plants. They looked slightly jaded.

'That must've been fun.' Arkady was tense. This was the seventh operation he and the man using the name Yevgeny had carried out. The law of averages told him their luck would not run for ever.

Inside the polished, rosewood-panelled elevator, with a brass plaque in Cyrillic script informing readers of Russian of the manufacturer's name – Otis Pifre – the two men stood silent. An American businessman leaned in a back corner, smiling encouragingly and squeezing the slender hand of a waiflike girl, not dissimilar to the two who had provoked, from Yevgeny, words of uncharacteristic gentleness.

The long ride upwards finally sighed imperceptibly to a stop. Seventh floor. The cage doors heaved themselves open, with a rattling that made nonsense of the hitherto silent journey.

'Dobry vecher,' said the American politely to the two pilots, as they left the elevator's polished cabin.

'Spokoinoy notchi,' replied Arkady, without looking back. There was no doubt, from the rattling and metallic crash, that the elevator gates had closed.

The two men followed a plum-carpeted corridor to a tall, solid door. *Komnata Chetyrye*, in Cyrillic script, informed them that this was Room Four. Arkady noted it was not Room Seven Zero Four, as it would normally have been, being room number four on the seventh floor. This numbering system applied not only in the West, but in places like Moscow's Hotel Metropole as well.

But this was just plain Room Four. *Komnata Chetyrye.*

Yevgeny tapped his knuckles softly on the door. It was opened by a fit-looking man of about thirty-four. He wore a Giorgio Armani suit, in dark navy, a white Versace shirt and a handpainted silk tie by YSL. On his wrist was a stainless-steel Rolex. It was the Makarov in the shoulder-holster that blew it, thought Arkady. Why could KGB – correction, Russian Security Department – correction, Russian Security Department pretending to be ex-KGB working the private sector – hoods not find themselves decent heaters? The Makarov was a thug's, an assassin's pistol.

Arkady shrugged to himself, meeting the security guard's professional glance, as the guy gave him the once-over. Maybe he was just biased. He still had a shard of lead from a Makarov lodged inside his pelvis. From the days when he went by another name and had existed, quite contentedly, on the salary of a Grade Four officer in the best espionage service in the world.

But that was before his life of crime . . .

The guard studied the two identity cards Yevgeny and Arkady held at shoulder-height for his inspection.

'Why the uniforms?' he asked, his eyes flicking from the men's ID to their faces and back.

'You know we're expected. Time is passing,' said Yevgeny, and his cool eyes narrowed a little, taking on the same ice-penetrating stare that had chilled the two young hookers on the street outside.

'Okay . . .' The guard stood aside to let them in, closing the door behind them. Arkady heard its electronic locks clunk shut.

Inside, it was not a room but a corridor. The floor was carpeted in grey-blue, the walls tiled with grey soundproofing slabs. After two turns to the left, one to the right, a silent walk of about forty-three feet and another right-hand corner, they came to another door. When Arkady glanced behind him, he saw that the first security guard had been replaced by two others. Both wore expensive European suits, spoiled by the ubiquitous Makarovs stuck into cheap shoulder-holsters made of thick leather.

'You might be wondering why we're dressed as Aeroflot pilots,' said Arkady, slightly unnerved by their ominous silence.

'I couldn't give a shit,' replied the one with the Tartar cheekbones and the maniac's moustache.

In front of them, the corridor ended in a blank wall. As they reached it, the wall slid open, revealing an armoured glass door. Behind it stood a man in Levi's and a sweatshirt with 'Nervous Records of New York' emblazoned across the front, wearing a big grin, steel-rimmed glasses and a ponytail.

The armoured glass door slid upwards, disappearing into the ceiling. Beyond was a series of open-plan offices partitioned by glass walls. Much pricey electronic hardware.

'*Gavaritye pa-Angliyski?*' asked the big grin, in an American accent.

'Sure,' replied Arkady, who had spent many years in New York City. 'I do. He doesn't.'

'*Nemnozhko . . .*' said Yevgeny, looking hurt. He meant he spoke a little English.

'Maybe a little. My partner says he speaks a little.'

They stood still, just inside the open-plan office area, which was very dimly lit, the tiny, flickering lights of the computer hardware making the place seem like a city viewed from an approaching airplane.

'Are you sure you can fix this thing?' asked the American, after telling them his name was Mike and asking how they were doing.

'Mike, I don't know. The bank flew us in from Paris, as you know. We were setting up Narodny's new security systems.'

'No seats on plane,' Yevgeny interjected helpfully, and pointed to the lapels and wings of his uniform jacket, grinning broadly.

'You devils. Hence the uniforms. Jeez, bank security really knows how to pull strings.' Mike led them into the office area, scratching his head in wonderment. This troubled Arkady, for he knew that US Credit Express did not employ klutzes in the heart of its international electronic money-transfer business. So what was troubling this Mike guy, that he was coming on as some kind of amiable dumbfuck?

Arkady smiled and gazed around, as if he had not spent the past three weeks in a perfect replica of this place, in a mock-up, identical down to the wrinkles in the imperfectly laid carpet.

The two goons were in the room, leaning against the wall. Bored. But with those fucking Makarovs. Arkady felt a twinge inside his pelvis.

'This is the problem area.' Mike led them through a sliding-glass door, into a room with eight serious IBM master computers, a number of VDU terminals and humming, flickering electronic equipment.

'Run through it one more time for me, Mike. Would you do that?'

Mike leaned against a desk. Coloured indicator lights from the machines reflected on his glasses. 'Tell you what, Arkady. You just run through what your understanding of the situation is . . .'

Arkady smiled coldly. This Mike was nobody's fool.

'Essentially, we seem to be looking at an interface

malfunction. The equipment translating satellite emissions into Intertel Nine grammar is interpreting one particular sound bite as a signal to lock down the system. Which is a bitch, because each time it does that, you have to get the originating source to run a full security ident, in order to unlock this office's electronic fund transfer paths.' Arkady gazed around the room and beyond the glass partitions into seven other similar rooms. 'And that source could be in Los Angeles, Hong Kong, London or . . . anywhere.'

'And your task?' Mike's steel-rimmed glasses glinted, reflected pinpoints of light alternately changing colour.

'My partner and me, we will enter the program here, where the trouble has been located, and . . . hopefully, repair it.'

'You think you can?' Mike had relaxed, thank God. 'I mean, the traps in the Intertel program might just close down the entire US Credit Express system, and that would cost us millions.' He smiled apologetically. 'And I'm the guy on duty.'

'Bummer,' sympathized Arkady. He turned to Yevgeny and spoke in Russian. 'This should not take long. Provided what we have here is not the Korean virus.'

It was obvious, from Mike's eyes, that he understood Russian perfectly. Which figured, reflected Arkady, otherwise the guy would not be working nights in St Petersburg.

'Okay,' he said, 'let's get started.' He took off his Aeroflot jacket and dropped it casually over a chair. Then he sat down at a desk and, with practised speed, opened up a complex program directory on the computer screen.

Yevgeny unbuttoned his jacket and loosed his necktie. He drew a thick, triple-folded set of notes from his inside pocket and opened them, spreading them on the desktop. The letterhead announced *US Credit Express, Office of Security Investigations* and was overstamped SECRET – OSI EYES ONLY. It was there for Mike to glimpse, in order to put any remaining qualms at rest. Yevgeny noted, by watching the American in one of the glass partitions, that the move had probably worked. He was aware of cool perspiration running down the small of his back, and deliberately controlled his breathing, the way he had been taught so many years before, at the GRU training school at Ulitsa Dolgobrodskaya, in Minsk.

Silence.

Only the muted hum of state-of-the-art electronic machines. The flickering of hundreds of tiny coloured lights.

Arkady worked with calm professionalism, opening up the complex security program called Intertel 9, tailored to prevent anyone penetrating the US Credit Express bank's innermost secrets, including how to access major fund-holdings. Major funds were those which held sums in excess of thirty million dollars, often just for a few hours, before being moved on, to take advantage of the world's ever-changing markets.

One of the ex-KGB guards sighed, out in the corridor beyond the glass room. So tense were Arkady and Yevgeny that the sound was like a rush of wind in a tunnel. Mike Berkowitz, the American manager of USCE's St Petersburg office, put their controlled tension down to the fact that they believed something called the Korean virus might be lurking inside the Intertel program. Computer viruses, planted sometimes by hackers, other times by competitors or extortionists, were the scourge of the industry. They could wipe man-years of work from a system's memory in seconds, often mocking the victims with obscene or droll messages on the VDU screens.

No wonder, considered Berkowitz, the two experts were tense.

In was part of his duty to watch the screen and observe what the man called Arkady Paninov was doing. For Mike was a highly trained computer user, as opposed to systems analysis expert. But quite frankly, the speed with which the short technician was going about his work made it difficult to follow events on the ever-changing screen. Also, Mike Berkowitz had been up since 6.30. His baby son was cutting his first tooth, and wanted the whole of western Russia to hear about it. Berkowitz glanced at a clock on the wall, beyond a couple of glass partitions: the hands stood at 12.18 a.m. He realized he was pretty damn bushed. The constantly, rapidly changing screen display made little sense to him.

No big deal. The electronic proceedings were being recorded by a special security tape.

'I think I've found it,' grunted Arkady, in Russian. Yevgeny leaned forward. 'This is not a software problem,' the shorter of the two went on. 'Where is the main frame? Is it in here?'

Yevgeny turned to Mike. 'Where is main frame? For international transactions?'

'Through there. Next room.'

'Show Yevgeny, would you, Mike? This might be easier to solve than we thought.'

'My God, if it's a piece of dust . . .' Mike shook his head ruefully and led Yevgeny through a sliding-glass partition to the next room, which housed rather more solid items of electronic hardware.

Thirty-four seconds. Oi, thought Arkady as he worked calmly and meticulously. But fast. Aware of nothing but the screen in front of him. Thirty-four seconds, while Mike was away from the screen. Thirty-six seconds before Intertel 9's security failsafe lock would realize the Fund Transfer System had been illegally penetrated. Raped. Shafted. His lips parted in a mirthless grin as he reproduced the digital access key from memory and entered the international system's Tokyo terminal, informing, by counterfeiting its own failsafe codes, that it was perfectly in order to close down Holding Account number 0011357.

Arkady, like a concert pianist, a maestro, his fingers racing over the keyboard, put that instruction on Pause and accessed the Intertel 9 Failsafe Trap, using a highly secret maintenance code to pause the device for twenty-eight seconds. Back into Holding Account 0011357, held in the Tokyo Main Office.

And like a trusting child, Holding Account 0011357 allowed 157 million US dollars to be lifted away in a millisecond and transferred into Account M-142 in Palermo, Sicily, home of the Italian Mafia.

With four seconds to go, the man calling himself Arkady obliterated any possibility of tracing the Palermo recipient of US Credit Express's money and exited the program with .5 of a second before Intertel 9 started to shout Stop Thief! His face was wet with perspiration as Mike and Yevgeny came back in.

'*Tam vsyo normalno . . . Shto budem delat?*' Yevgeny's face was a mask of casual self-control. It's okay in there, he had said. What's to be done?

'I think I've found it,' replied Arkady, leaning back in his seat and forcing his body to announce, Look, I'm really relaxed.

'You're sweating,' said Mike, his high-IQ eyes glinting behind the steel-framed glasses.

'Yeah, so would you be.' Arkady casually watched the two ex-KGB guards in the reflecting glass. They seemed quite bored. Disinterested. 'I don't suppose you have a beer in here?'

'No, but I can send one of the guards for one, if you like . . .'

Yevgeny and Arkady both said No at precisely the same time. Very definitely with a capital 'n'

'Okay, let's check it,' said Arkady.

This was the worst part. They had just irrevocably relieved the biggest international credit card franchise of 157 million dollars. And now they had to sit here in front of the St Petersburg manager and two Makarov-toting goons and prove that the bank's computer security system was working much better than before. Than before its rape. Its grand shafting.

Well, of course Arkady – the man using the name Arkady Paninov, with exquisitely counterfeited ID to prove it – did just that. And at three minutes before one in the morning, he and the taller man were standing in the silent elevator, the one with the noisy gates, stuffing their hastily folded Aeroflot pilots' jackets into a plastic bag bearing the logo of the GUM store in Moscow.

The orchestra were pulling on coats and placing their instruments in battered instrument cases, as Arkady and Yevgeny ambled across the stunning, marble-pillared lobby. The two men wore light-coloured coats (the coats had been reversible) over white shirts without neckties.

As they paused on the steps of the Nevsky Palace Hotel, a blue Volga taxi pulled up, and two slightly harassed-looking men climbed out, the shorter of the two pausing to pay the driver. Arkady and Yevgeny stepped aside courteously as the two men hurried up the four shallow steps and went into the hotel. Under their raincoats, they had clearly been wearing the uniforms of Aeroflot pilots.

Arkady and Yevgeny exchanged glances. The warm glances of, say, bullfighters who have just done fairly magnificently. Expressions of *hidalgo*, a fierce, elite pride.

In a final act of outrageous style, the shafters of Intertel 9 caught the same taxi and instructed the driver to take them to the docks. Unknown to them, the two girls who had propositioned them loitered at the end of Ulitsa Kormoranskaya, observing their departure.

The hookers strolled away into the broad avenue beside the Hermitage Museum and, it would seem to any casual or not so casual observer, were importuned by a man driving a seven-year-old blue BMW Five Series. They climbed in, after settling a price for anyone watching to hear, and the car moved away.

Inside, the one with rouge on her aristocratic cheekbones shook her hair free.

'Well . . .?' asked the driver. A man of about forty, with thinning brown hair, a serious expression and two small scars on his right forehead.

'They just made it,' replied the girl with aristocratic cheekbones.

'I admire their . . . impertinence,' said the driver. And he dropped the two girls off a couple of blocks further on.

2

A Lifebelt from Zion

THERE IS A restaurant in Washington, DC called Le Palm. It's on P Street and is a scruffily chic kind of place, much frequented by political bit-part players hoping to rub shoulders with the real movers and shakers in the power-hub of the USA.

A craggy Englishman sat alone at a table near the door. He was about six foot three, with a crooked bridge to a badly repaired nose and the faintest trace of a scar from his right cheekbone to just beside his mouth. His name was David Jardine and as he sipped from a glass of iced tea and toyed with a Caesar salad, he browsed through the *Washington Post*, bringing himself up to speed on matters of moment with regard to the view from Capitol Hill.

As a waiter cleared away the remains of his lunch Jardine shoved the slice of lemon around his glass with a long spoon and let his lazy eyes wander around the room. The *Washington Post* was running a series of stories on the city's drug menace, but the real drug in DC, he knew, was one that made cocaine seem as powerful as caffeine-free cola. You couldn't buy it in plastic sachets on some unlit street corner. Nor was it available on prescription. For the real drug here in the capital of the USA was political muscle. Power. It was almost tangible and it made fools and tyrants of many of its junkies.

The P-word. He imagined it stamped on every forehead in town, for nobody in DC escaped its influence, bootboy and President alike, its acolytes. Its lackeys.

And secret power . . . well, that was the most powerful drug of all.

As David Jardine gazed idly at the cartoons of two generations of Capitol Hill inside trackers, which just about papered the walls, he came to realize – and he was to remember this moment precisely, because it was probably the instant when every catastrophic thing that was soon to take place became almost inevitable – that for the first time in his life, he was not totally immersed in his job.

For the first time in twenty-one years and ten months, the Englishman was no longer engaged in the aggressive, clandestine filching of secrets from hostile targets. Denied Areas, was the Office euphemism. Which is to say, where his operators and agents had the task of obtaining seriously protected information from Britain's enemies (and one or two of her friends). And where if caught, in certain circumstances, the lucky ones were executed. Eventually.

But since his promotion, which he had struggled against until the Top Floor's limited sense of humour evaporated, Jardine had become one of the Firm's less shadowy figures, liaising with foreign agencies and sitting on a variety of self-perpetuating committees, not one of which was ever going to have the slightest effect on international events or the course of history. Which were the two things that had sold him on the idea of spying for a living, when he had been recruited from Reuters all those years before.

You can make a difference, David, the Scotsman who had recruited him, had promised. How many jobs can offer that?

And he had believed it. And just maybe, once upon a recent time, he had.

Jardine shrugged to himself and, catching the waiter's eye, indicated he would like a coffee and the check.

Outside Le Palm, as he debated whether to walk the half-mile to the Old Vietnamese Embassy, where the Agency was hosting the sixteenth meeting of J-WISC, or grab a taxi, David Jardine noticed, hovering on the sidewalk, a perplexed young man with the look of a slightly daft gundog, maybe an English setter, who couldn't quite remember what he had been commanded to do.

This was Tom Crawford and he was a fledgling officer in Her Majesty's Secret Intelligence Service, working out of the British Embassy with the cover of Third Secretary in the consular section.

The boy watched with something approaching apprehension as Jardine strolled over to him. 'You look worried.'

Crawford almost blushed. 'It's just . . . I wasn't sure whether or not to, um . . .'

He meant he had not been sure whether he and Jardine should be seen together. The callow youth had clearly been brought up on a diet of John le Carré.

'Tom, this is Washington. It's not a bus station in Prague, you know . . .' And Jardine realized he had just dated himself, for a clandestine meeting in Prague was not, these days, particularly dangerous.

Poor Tom Crawford looked crushed. David Jardine wondered what was happening to him. Only weeks ago one of his considerable skills had been the ability to put young officers at their ease.

'Come on. Let's walk a little.'

Jardine strolled with Crawford to the corner of P Street and Wisconsin, waiting for a truck with Miller Lite on the side to rumble past, before crossing to the other side.

'How's your sister, these days?' he asked, refusing the opportunity to give a dollar bill to a vagrant who had lurched close, a cardboard notice around his neck announcing 'Viet Vet $1 will help me stay alive'. A quick guestimate of the man's age would have made him about six years old when the last helicopter left the US Embassy roof in Saigon.

'She's fine, thanks.' Even the most junior of the Firm's probationers were conditioned not to call their seniors 'sir'. Such a reflex could prove fatal in the wrong environment.

'Still in Jakarta?'

'Still there.' They strolled on in silence.

'So what's the problem?'

The Washington Station would not send someone, not even Tom Crawford, out looking for Jardine, unless there was some kind of problem.

'Um. Pomegranate.'

Jardine felt his heart skip. The way a young man's does when the name of a secret love is mentioned. For Pomegranate was the codename of a spy, in a dangerous environment light years from the comfortable in-crowd of Washington intelligence-broking. One who had insisted on being run by David Jardine, or no one at all.

Her identity was known only to Jardine and his two most trusted . . . accomplices. Daughter of a murdered Beirut newspaper editor, an Islamic moderate, she was an agent of influence recruited by David Jardine just over eight years before. A legal secretary at that time, Pomegranate had risen to a position of some influence in the latest Lebanese government, as political adviser to the Foreign Minister.

Somewhere along the route, this trusted agent of Jardine's had allowed herself, upon Jardine's advice, to be recruited by the Iraqi Mukhabarat, Sadaam's efficient intelligence service. Thus through Pomegranate, Jardine had an ear not only to the Beirut administration, but also to certain activities of the Iraqis. Particularly where Abu Nidal and his terror group were concerned.

Of course, young Crawford was aware of none of this. In company with the most senior, most highly cleared members of SIS, he did not even know that Pomegranate was a woman.

'What about him?' asked Jardine. Meaning her. What about her?

'He needs to receive some guidance. Urgently.'

Jardine knew – and a draught of cold fluttered around his back, around his ribs – all too precisely the circumstances which could have forced Pomegranate to send an unscheduled signal, asking for 'guidance'.

'Anything else?'

'Direct radio link seven this evening our time.'

'I'll be there.'

'That's it, then . . .' Crawford chanced a quick glance at the tall man walking beside him. He knew the legend about the two slugs in the left lung and the knife fight in some Berlin back-alley. David Jardine would have been mortally embarrassed to learn that, to Tom Crawford, he was as close to a hero as the young man had ever met. And to be passing him a secret, clandestine message, while strolling in a Washington street . . . well, gosh.

'Thanks, Tom.'

'Okay . . .'

And Tom Crawford turned away with studied nonchalance, and stepped off the kerb to cross the road. It was only the lightning reactions of a nearby bag lady, with a grip of steel, that saved him from being turned into salami by a passing fire engine. Its throaty bellow completely unheard by the young spy, so enthralled had he been by the moment . . .

The fact that the CIA had not hosted the four-day seminar of J-WISC at its Langley headquarters was not unusual and implied no snub. It was simply that the Old Vietnamese Embassy, which the Agency sometimes shared with its principal inhabitants, the Diplomatic Security Service, was central and accessible, and saved the participants the inconvenience of a morning and evening slog through the traffic to Langley, Virginia, across the Potomac and some miles outside town.

J-WISC stood for Joint Western Intelligence Steering Committee. As far as Jardine was concerned, it was just another stepping-stone to oblivion. He wondered if he was becoming menopausal.

The conference chamber had been converted to a room inside a room. Transparent plastic screens, mounted on fibreglass stands, were placed along the walls and windows, rendering microwave eavesdropping impossible.

Electronics security teams worked from a room next

door, and from an unmarked panel truck in the street outside.

The committee members sat around a long cherrywood table.

The CIA, the British Secret Intelligence Service, the German Bundesnachrichtendienst, the French DGSE and the Israeli Mossad were each represented. As well as the new Russian Intelligence Service and one or two former Soviet satellites. But the latter were not invited to every session, for reasons of security. Just in case the march of history took one step backwards.

Being a realist, David Jardine did not envisage J-WISC providing much that any seminar of senior journalists and academics could not. For he could not imagine that any of the assembled master cynics of espionage would divulge anything remotely resembling a real secret, from the arcane bowels of each country's service.

Not here. Not at this table.

He listened to each speaker say his or her piece, and began to draw the Bermudan sloop of his dreams on the back of a top secret CIA paper on Russian nationalist organizations, who were sending selected members to fight with Serbian irregulars in Bosnia. Ideally, she would be about twenty-six feet long. Anything longer was difficult to manage, single-handed.

As the minutes became quarter- and half-hours, the droning of successive representatives engendered a feeling of claustrophobia, and Jardine wondered if it was clinically possible to expire from such sublime and endless tedium.

Three months earlier, he had been an SIS Sphere Controller, running the outfit's West 8 Division, responsible for clandestine operations in Denied Areas of Central and South America and the Caribbean. Travelling the globe. Using other identities so familiar they fitted like favourite clothes. Getting into danger. Defending his life.

Ah, yes . . .

Defending his life.

By killing a man who had trusted him.

'You bastard . . .!' he heard a voice crying from a cemetery in Bogota. It was a voice he did not pass a day without hearing.

Or a night.

Jardine shuddered. He shook off a clutch of dreadful memories and smoothly sketched a long, deep line for the keel, wondering if it should have stabilizers, like on the Americas Cup yachts, at which instant he became aware of seventeen pairs of eyes focused, politely, intently, upon him.

'. . . in respect of a *jihad*?' Stefan Wydwiroslav, the Polish representative on the committee, was gazing at Jardine, an expectant and quizzical expression on his face.

Jardine stared back, thoughtfully.

'A *jihad*, Stefan,' he replied smoothly, and everyone hung on his words of wisdom, 'like beauty, is very much in the eye of the beholder.'

Not so long ago, chum, he mused, gazing levelly into the Pole's pale blue eyes, since you were double-crossing your people by working for the old Soviet GRU.

'However, in this instance . . . and your point is so well made, I really wonder if you have disclosed your full deck of cards . . .'

Amused chuckles. It was hardly the work of a James Jesus Angleton to suggest that a spy, in a roomful of strangers and recent enemies, was keeping things close to his chest.

'In this instance, I believe we could be looking at the first genuine, twenty-four-carat *jihad* since the start of this century.' Jardine tapped his pen against the table-top, leaning back in his seat and gazing shrewdly round the table. The others nodded gravely.

He continued, with an expression conveying he wished he could divulge more, 'So perhaps we should look to each other for a frank exchange of product in that area. For have we not a joint and mutual interest? Correct me if I'm wrong . . .'

And there was a buzz of agreement. Only poor Stefan,

who must have expected a more specific reply, looked slightly mystified.

At which point, ruddy-cheeked, former Olympic rower Bob Summers, the Canadian representative, started to drone on and on about Iran's plans to acquire a nuclear warhead. It was close to embarrassing to hear him divulge how little his service was aware of the real facts.

Bored to the point of narcolepsy, Jardine amused himself by identifying those members of J-WISC who were actively betraying the countries they represented on this committee to other, 'friendly', intelligence services sitting round the same table.

It was then that he became aware that Avriam Eitels, the senior Mossad man present, was quietly watching him and, judging from his amused expression, no doubt reading his every thought.

Jardine met Eitels' gaze and the two men smiled. They had not always been on the same side in the ruthless secret wars each man had spent his life fighting, but they were both cold professionals and they shared a mutual regard which transcended mere things like lying to each other and destroying each other's agents' networks when their interests differed.

At 4.10 the meeting broke for a respite.

Eitels and Jardine left the room and found themselves standing together in the corridor, where CIA security men discreetly guarded the environment.

'How about a cup of coffee? In the Willard,' murmured Eitels, lighting a cigarette, cupping the flame of his Zippo from habit.

Jardine glanced at his wristwatch. Just under three hours till Pomegranate's radio communication from Beirut.

'Anything to get out of this place,' he accepted, stepping towards the elevator as its doors slid open, debouching two brow-furrowed Langley ladies who had arrived to relieve the duty stenographers of J-WISC, whose torpid deliberations had to be on the desks of a dozen intelligence supremos by the weekend. God help the future of suffering humanity, if they were acted upon without question.

The coffee shop in the Willard Hotel is off a broad corridor which leads from the elegant and spacious foyer to an arcade of shops mostly offering designer clothes and jewellery. It is designed in a California-functional style, with shades of New Mexico. The staff are pleasant, and there are booths where food or drinks can be enjoyed in privacy.

David Jardine and Eitels sat in a booth at the back, to the left of the entrance, and down a couple of steps. They did not have a particularly good view of the doorway, or of the comings and goings of the other diners. But on the plus side, not many people could see them. It was the same table Jardine had sat at many times, with other intelligence contacts. He remembered sitting there with the CIA's Director of Covert Operations during the Iran–Contra hysteria, and mentally shook his head at the way the US system really went for its spymasters if they got caught, doing the very jobs they had been paid to do, often at great personal risk.

'So,' said Eitels, removing his thick, steel-rimmed spectacles and breathing on the lenses.

'Two coffees, regular. And two glasses of iced tea,' Jardine replied to the waitress, who had asked how he was doing, in that way American waitresses and store assistants and people in hotel elevators have.

He relaxed in his seat and watched Avriam Eitels. The Israeli smiled. 'You got a good memory . . .'

'It's only two years, Avvy.'

Eitels shook his head sadly. Disappointed by the passage of time.

'What's new at Century House?'

Jardine frowned, as if he had just been asked how much money he had. 'We're moving,' he replied carefully. 'New monstrosity. Bottle-green and sand-coloured. Sort of late Bauhaus. Enormous bloody great pile. Still on the south side of the river. Terrific views. Costing a fortune.'

'How's Ronnie?'

'Which Ronnie's that?' But they both knew Eitels meant a man who had been a fifteen-year-old freedom fighter when he fled Budapest in 1956 after an unequal battle against Russian tanks and Mongol infantry. Ten years later, by that time working for SIS, Ronnie Szabodo had saved Jardine's life in Berlin.

Since then, the squat Hungarian had never been too far from David Jardine's orbit. Unkind comments included the sobriquet 'Renfield', after Dracula's manservant, who was reported to have picked up the more distasteful remains.

'You know which Ronnie . . .'

Jardine gazed around the coffee shop in the Willard Hotel. Was it a sign of his age that casual conversations evoked so many memories?

Tonight, Szabodo would be arranging the Pomegranate link from Beirut, through Century House in London, to the British Embassy's secure cipher room in Washington.

'Oh, Ronnie's fine. Something of a survivor,' he replied.

The waitress served the iced tea and coffee and told them to enjoy, before departing, smoothing her apron.

Eitels emptied a sachet of sugar into his glass. 'Has it come to your notice, your people,' he asked, 'a series of major international frauds, all involving . . . counterfeiting, forgery, of some kind?'

'Well, Avvy, that's not really my territory.'

'Unless it's big enough to pose a political, a strategic threat. And that, David, is what I'm talking about.'

Jardine's mind was 4000 miles away. He wondered what her problem was. Pomegranate. He wished he could have been across the Atlantic. In Beirut. Or Cyprus. The poor girl probably believed there was a whole section at Century monitoring her every move. Listening to her phones. Ready at a moment's notice to step in and extend the big, safe paw of omnipresent British Intelligence. Instant succour from whatever threatened her.

For that was what he had led her to believe, as the slim,

always smiling young woman had risked her life daily for the last eight years. What a total bastard. In the service of . . . what? His country? Democracy? The office? Survival?

'Big, big numbers,' Eitels was saying. 'Major league, David. Millions, tens of. All around the world. Each time a different country. Each time the target could be totally wrecked. Ruined. But each time they take just enough to get seriously rich. Wealthy. Like footprints.'

Jardine frowned. Unless some foreign government was behind those crimes, there was nothing here for the office.

'Different countries,' the Israeli went on. 'Every continent. And each time it gets bigger. Larger stakes. All around the world.'

'Footprints. . . .?'

'As if they want to bring themselves to our attention.'

'Whose attention?'

'People like us, you and me. Who advise our governments. Come on. Whadda you say? You guys must know what I'm talking about . . .'

Jardine considered this. Eitels sipped at his tea, watching the Englishman like a poker player.

'Avvy. I know it works differently in Israel. You're a small nation. Everyone knows everyone else. That's why you're all so good at this business. But I'm not a policeman. I wouldn't have heard of that unless it affected our foreign policy in some way. Or threatened British interests.'

Eitels frowned, adjusting the glasses on the bridge of his nose. It occurred to Jardine he was not unlike a younger version of Woody Allen.

'So how'd you ever get things done?' The Israeli seemed genuinely concerned.

Jardine smiled. 'I really don't know. We have so much information we don't need. And never enough of the stuff we do. A score of different clients, too many . . . product-gathering – um – organizations. Right hand, left hand. You know what I mean.'

'David, let me tell you – you have a moment . . .?'

'I just don't see how international fraud might concern SIS . . .'

'Well, I'm gonna try and persuade you.'

Jardine sipped his coffee and sat back in his seat. 'Why not . . .?'

Eitels thought for a moment. Choosing his words. 'Okay. Even now, in some part of this globe, they will be working on crime number eight. And of one thing we can be sure.'

'What's that?'

'It will be bigger than the last time. Which lifted one fifty-seven mil out of US Credit Express, using a contrived computer fault in St Petersburg. It will definitely involve some form of counterfeiting, from plastic to people. So we're talking gigantic stakes. The modus will be immaculate. Professional. And it will be totally non-violent.'

'Actually, that's three things,' said Jardine. But as it happened, Avriam Eitels was absolutely right in all of his predictions. Except for onc . . .

Some street-lamps were still on, pale necklaces of bluish white in the dawn light. Sections of the Corniche were thus palely illuminated, the gaps somehow ominous, like whole sections of missing teeth.

David Jardine allowed his head to nestle into the pillow supplied to Executive Class passengers and gazed past the inner perspex window and the outer armoured-glass window at the Mediterranean waters around Beirut's Corniche and the ruins of the once beautiful Phoenicia Hotel, hanging suspended 600 feet below, as the Middle East Airlines DC9 banked steeply, lining up for its landing approach at Beirut International Airport.

The airframe creaked and groaned while the landing gear was lowered. A bit on the late side, thought Jardine, with only 500 or 600 feet of clear air between his comfortable seat and the stone shells and newly risen office blocks below.

A light pinged on, on the bulkhead above, showing a cigarette with a red bar across it. The seat-belt sign had been on for some minutes.

The Green Line, separating Christian East Beirut from the Islamic quarter, dominated still by the fanatics of Hezbollah, suddenly dropped away as the port wingtip rose and the plane righted itself, accompanied by a drop, then a surge, of engine noise.

Two women in Arab dress, their fingers glinting with gold and gems, half-closed their eyes and held on tightly to their seat arms. As if they anticipated a crash-landing to add to the sullen detritus of twenty years of civil war in the broken streets and boulevards just 200 feet below.

Jardine relaxed. Flying was a pleasure to him. It was one of the few times nobody could intrude on his peace. He was looking forward to seeing Alisha. Alisha Abdul-Fetteh was the thirty-one-year-old political secretary to George Channam, Foreign Secretary in the Lebanese Government of National Unity. Her codename for the last eight years had been Pomegranate. Anyone watching CNN reports when the new government had come to power would have been struck by the slender beauty of the poised girl hovering near Channam, ready with all kinds of documents in the assembly chamber as the TV cameras recorded the shattered Lebanon's return to self-rule and what passed in that country for normalcy.

'For what purpose is your visit to the Lebanon, Monsieur Ramseyer?' The immigration official carefully studied Jardine's photograph on the Swiss passport in the name of Jean-Pierre Ramseyer, occupation archivist. He had spoken in French.

'I have been asked to advise the University library on a number of Byzantine documents.'

'Where will you be staying?'

'It's on the landing card.'

Slight pause. The official was a neatly dressed man in the uniform of a Lebanese police lieutenant. He peered at the landing card. It occurred to Jardine that the officer probably needed reading glasses.

'Twenty-one B, Rue du Bac. It's the home of a friend. He teaches at the University.'

The official seemed not to have heard. Then he stamped an entry visa on the much-stamped passport, scribbled something over the stamp, smiled and handed the document to Jardine.

'Enjoy your stay in Beirut, *monsieur*.'

'*Merci bien*.' Jardine picked up his soft leather bag, which he had bought at the craft centre in Bogota about 10,000 years before, and strolled past Customs, which seemed a fairly haphazard routine, towards the Arrivals Hall exit and the taxi rank.

It was a mere nineteen hours since he had flown from Washington to New York's LaGuardia airport, then by helicopter to JFK, in time for the morning Concorde to Paris, where sixty-two-year-old Jake Douglas (a retired operator who made a somewhat racy living showing wealthy American widows around the Latin Quarter) had given him an envelope with passport, driving licence, credit cards, Zurich ephemera like matchbooks, café receipts and a used cinema ticket, along with two Swiss newspapers and a magazine detailing the restaurant and entertainment scene in Zurich. Also a pair of gold-rimmed spectacles and a Patek Philippe wristwatch made in 1955, which was a present to Jean-Pierre Ramseyer from his father.

Jardine had given Douglas a similar envelope containing everything that might have identified him as anyone other than the Swiss archivist he had now become.

He felt happy with the persona. It was one he knew well, and it had served him for six years without a hitch. The firm's Section Twelve, also known as CLD and working out of an Edwardian building in Buckingham Gate, handled the continuous establishment and maintenance of Clandestine Logistics in Depth, in other words, deep-cover stories. CLD even had an accommodation address for

Ramseyer, and a phone number in Zurich which had a record of in and out calls, from and to the sort of contacts an academic archivist might have.

Indeed, several people in Switzerland and Europe had received telephone inquiries over the years from Monsieur Ramseyer and they would happily have testified to his existence. For David Jardine's firm left nothing to chance.

The room had not changed. Morning shafts of sunlight, not yet fierce, probed the rosewood table, the old leather couch, draped with colourful rugs, the winged armchair David had given to her when she graduated from the American University, and fell across an old upright grand piano on which Alisha's father used to play 'Mood Indigo' and 'I Can't Get Started'. The slatted wooden blinds split the shafts of sun so that the effect was like something out of an old Humphrey Bogart movie.

Jardine moved gently on to the big Berber carpet, sidestepping the brass coffee-table on cedarwood legs. Taking delicate care, breathing carefully, as if he were in a small chapel.

There was the hookah, on top of an untidy set of shelves, white-painted and crammed with books of every description from travel guides, phrasebooks in a dozen languages, to fiction, history and cookbooks.

Her smell, her aroma, hung in the air. Guiltily, Jardine accepted that he had forgotten the magic of Alisha's tantalizing aura, her gleaming hair just after she had washed it. Her natural good health and youth.

Stepping on through the room, pausing to listen to the lazy bustle of the Beirut streets outside, Jardine's heart tugged with a longing for times past and gone for good. The bedroom was empty. Bed, as always, unmade, the top sheet turned down, thrown down, over the counterpane. Some form of prudishness, or just plain decency, made him reluctant to look too closely at the sheets. But he did, for it was part of his job. He was annoyed with himself for feeling relieved that there was no evidence she had slept with anyone the night before. I mean, he thought, what the hell business is it of mine? Thirty-six hours before, David Jardine had forgotten Alisha Abdul-Fetteh even existed.

Now, the intimacy of her flat had seduced him. Christ, those glistening flanks. The arc of her neck as she met his eyes, reflected in the wall mirror, the gleam of triumph as she bucked against him, taking him far too far along pleasure's path for an Englishman who preferred to remain in control.

The cat on top of the dressing-table watched him, all-knowing. Some bloody spy, thought Jardine. He had not even realized it was there. He glanced at his wristwatch.

Where the hell was she? Alisha, Pomegranate, was never this late.

Two days before, after coffee at the Willard with Avriam Eitels, Jardine had returned to the Old Vietnamese Embassy for yet another session of J-WISC.

At 6.10, he had taken a taxi to the British Embassy and gone directly to the SIS offices, which they shared with three officers from the Security Service, popularly known as MI5.

Tom Crawford was waiting (he had missed the final rehearsal of the Embassy choir's performance of *The Mikado*, much to the disgust of his young wife) and at seven on the dot, cipher links had been established with Pomegranate, via Century House in London, on a secure satellite frequency.

By 7.04, David Jardine had been standing in a corner of the windowless basement cipher room, digesting the contents of Pomegranate's signal.

POMEGRANATE to AJAX, it had read. Ajax was Jardine's codename, as far as Alisha was concerned . . .

POMEGRANATE to AJAX. 0200 1102

1. Receiving overtures from Egyptian name of Salim Jaddeh (SJ).

2. IBEX informs this source SJ is agent of HALCYON

3. SJ visiting Beirut as private banker. Living in house leased by Egyptian Embassy at Junieh.

4. Lebanese security office file on SJ has gone missing but Rif Daoud (chief clerk in Sy Office) says he is listed as banker for Abu Nidal.

5. Something about all this is not good.

6. Need urgent advice.

7. Ends P 078805

IBEX was the codename for her Iraqi 'controller', a Baghdad-born doctor who worked in Beirut.

HALCYON was the codename for SIS. Talk about misnomers, thought Jardine.

The closing serial indicated that Pomegranate was not acting under duress.

Young Tom had watched the big man carefully. He had kept out of the way as Jardine had sat and scribbled four communications, before crumpling them all up and tossing them on to the floor.

Century House's Director, Forward Plans, as David Jardine had become since his unwelcome promotion, then made a decision which with the benefit of hindsight would appear rash, but he had been ready to seize any reasonable opportunity to escape the claustrophobic tedium of J-WISC.

'How soon can I be in Beirut?' he had asked the room, empty except for Crawford and Jimmy Bonnar, the SIS cipher clerk on duty.

'Um . . .' said Tom Crawford, and Bonnar had opened a drawer and passed over, without a word, a well-thumbed airline timetable, not a classified document, but prepared by Miss Gresham, the office's indispensable – and unfortunately detestable – resident senior clerical grade and self-indentured 'treasure'.

'Jimmy,' Jardine had said to Bonnar, 'tell Pomegranate I'll be in Beirut tomorrow at . . .' He had glanced across to Crawford, not exactly impatiently. But not in his most laid-back mode either.

'I'm routing you through Paris,' Tom Crawford had announced with an authority that stunned both Jardine and Jimmy Bonnar. 'You'll not be travelling as yourself, obviously. So Paris Station will have time, while you're airborne, to arrange the necessary legend.'

'Quite,' Jardine had replied, readjusting his opinion of the young man.

'So it's fly from here to LaGuardia – you can take the 5 a.m. shuttle. There's absolutely no point in racing off before we set everything up efficiently. You can sleep here, I'll get you a change of shirt and linen. Presumably you do have your passport with you?'

Tom had glanced at Jardine brusquely and the senior man had nodded meekly.

'Then it's helicopter from LaGuardia to JFK. Concorde to Paris. Meet our man for new documents. Paris–Rome. Rome–Beirut. Al Italia and Middle East Airlines do it alternate days, tomorrow's MEA. So' – this to Jimmy Bonnar – 'there's no possibility of Ajax reaching Beirut, able to operate with his full complement of brain cells, until any time after say, 8 o'clock on Thursday morning.'

Tom had passed his neat timetable to Bonnar and swivelled his chair to gaze at Jardine.

'Questions, David . . .?'

'Um. No. No, that sounds just about right.'

And Jimmy Bonnar had signalled Pomegranate, via London, where the squat Hungarian, Ronnie Szabodo, was handling the exchange. Her signal had come back within forty seconds. Decoded, it had told Jardine to make his way to her apartment and under no circumstances to travel under a UK passport.

David Jardine watched the cat, absentmindedly, his senses

alert to every sound. Once, he heard footsteps approaching, on the street outside. But it was not her.

There was a coffee pot on the electric stove. It was lukewarm.

When she was two hours late, he started to search the apartment.

3

The Man Who Was Nice to His Mother

AFTER THE GRAND shafting of the Credex secure banking system, the two men calling themselves Arkady and Yevgeny had taken a taxi to St Petersburg docks, paid the driver and strolled for another half-hour, checking most comprehensively for surveillance, before climbing the gangplank of the SS *Sumaru*, registered in Glasgow. It was a cargo ship, a mere 240 feet, just a few thousand tons. But it was known to the coastal authorities all around the Baltic Sea as an innocent vessel, with a decent skipper and innocuous cargoes. In this case, Stolichnaya vodka and 100,000 Russian dolls inside dolls within dolls.

The *Sumaru* was in fact the property of the two men, going under entirely different names. Not that anyone paid much attention to them for they were quite forgettable types, so perfect had been their training in earlier days, when they had not yet embraced a life of private enterprise.

In the intervening couple of weeks, the *Sumaru* had unloaded some of the vodka and all of the dolls, hoisted on board a cargo of Dutch tobacco, copper plumbers' fittings and thirty-one tons of building nails, brackets, girders and angle-irons.

The broad-beamed, sturdy rust-bucket now rose and fell on a mercury-smooth Atlantic swell, off the small harbour of St John's, on the Caribbean Leeward Island of Antigua.

Danny Davidov, who had called himself Arkady in St Petersburg, rubbed some Piz Bruin sun factor 8 on to his bald crown. He made a mental note not to touch his reading glasses until he had cleaned his greasy hands.

Sometimes he preferred to wear a hat. But today he felt in a festive, carefree mood. The Atlantic crossing had been a bitch, without the additional ferocity of the previous night's gale (Danny was essentially a landlubber, although his pride would never allow him to admit it). But now, anchored in more gentle Caribbean waters, with the ruins of an old British fort on the starboard beam and the quaint, mint-green, pink and yellowing, once-white colonial buildings strung haphazard, along the waterfront, he watched a pelican haul itself lazily past and sighed with something approaching contentment.

The funds looted electronically from St Petersburg had indeed been transferred to their account with the Banca di Calabria in Sicily, without a millisecond's hitch. One hundred and fifty-seven million dollars. In a couple of days' time, he and the man who had called himself Yevgeny would fly there and sign the necessary papers, transferring the money in bearer bonds to three safety deposit boxes. Seventy-five million each, and the balance for operational funding.

The safety deposit boxes would be in the underground vault of one of the safest banks in the world, in the Sicilian capital, Palermo.

It was a small concrete fortress near the Piazza di Quattro Canti. Everyone from secret police generals to politicians, to fine-art collectors, to the wealthiest (and therefore most ruthless) members of the Italian Mafia, the Cosa Nostra, kept their fortunes with this bank, whose name was in no phone book, and whose fiscal existence was noted at Palermo's Chamber of Commerce with the minimum information required by law – which was its name, the Banca di Calabria, and its board of directors, which consisted of ladies in their seventies who lived in a villa in the hills above Corleone, a town where even the local Carabinieri did not venture out after dark.

The strongrooms of the Banca di Calabria were as close to a safe haven as one could find, in an island ravaged by Mafia vendettas and the wars between Cosa Nostra and the Italian State. They were neutral territory. And rumour had it that one day, when the then Minister for the Interior had paid a visit, to withdraw a priceless diamond and emerald necklace for his daughter to wear at her wedding, he had found himself in the same heavily guarded waiting room as the most wanted man in Italy, Giovanni Favorito Noto, waiting patiently to deposit bank drafts worth 500 million, the proceeds of some deal involving cocaine from Colombia.

Who knows what transpired, what passed between the two men? But they had both conducted their business and gone their separate ways. That was the legend, anyway.

So Danny Davidov, sitting on the afterdeck of his far from luxury vessel, basking in the Antiguan sun, felt something relatively close to contentment. But life could be cruel. Why the hell did he have to languish on board a tramp-steamer instead of one of those luxury yachts which dotted the island's turquoise-watered sandy bays?

Life in fact had never been easy for Dan Davidov. It had not been easy being the fourth son of a Tel Aviv cop, even when the old man rose to be Chief of Detectives in the Anti-Corruption detail. It had not been easy when Rita Goldblat, eldest daughter of a millionaire hotelier, had fallen for him, proposed marriage (yes, she had proposed, that was Rita's way, for she was used to getting everything she ever wanted), and introduced him to a life of water-skiing at Eilat and Taittinger Blanc de Blancs and designer underwear.

It had gotten tougher when old man Goldblat had given him the Mount Carmel Hotel in Haifa to run, as a wedding present. For Dan had no wish to spend the rest of his life in the hotel trade. As a matter of fact, the Israeli hated hotels. They had always made him feel uncomfortable, with their impersonal staff and wiseacre barmen.

Then Rita, the lovely Rita let's be fair, twice voted Miss Personality at Tel Aviv Senior High, had turned out to be sexually insatiable. Not that Dan had anything against conjugal bliss, it was just that she turned it into a (usually fruitless) quest for the ultimate multiple orgasm. He had lost ten pounds in the first four weeks of their marriage and was going down at the rate of a couple more each month when hallelujah, as the goyim would say, the blessed Egyptian Army had launched an attack across the supposedly impregnable Suez Canal and made a passable impersonation of a *blitzkrieg* over the Sinai Desert, directly towards the Israeli border, with Tel Aviv and Jerusalem reputedly the principal targets.

Dan had been a reservist in the Infantry, and he had grabbed his kit and gotten the hotel driver, Wally Cohen, to take him directly to his mobilization location in an office over a grapefruit warehouse near the waterfront at Port Haifa.

Another of life's tough breaks was that Rita's father the hotel millionaire had arranged for his new son-in-law to be attached, with the rank of corporal, to the local Press Liaison and Censorship Centre in Haifa. A military posting which would ensure that Rita's exhausted partner would be in about as much danger from an Arab–Egyptian attack as his cousin Boaz who worked in the garment trade in downtown New York, 5000 miles away. And designed, of course, so that Danny would never be far from his beloved and the Mount Carmel Hotel.

However, Danny the *nebesch* (a sobriquet arising from Rita's amusing descriptions of his attire pre-Armani and her decision to improve his taste for him) was not about to permit this God-given opportunity provided by Cairo's unleashing of the dogs of war to slip away. He got in touch with his father, the Chief of Detectives in Tel Aviv, and managed to persuade him to arrange a transfer to a tank unit, as a radio operator – his original qualification from compulsory military service. Within twenty-four hours, he was rocking across the Sinai in an IDF Chieftain tank, as part of the delayed counter-attack.

It had not been easy finding himself part of General Sharon's daring, fast, brutal, noisy flanking assault, the reek of cordite and diesel oil and burning flesh permeating hair and combat fatigues. But it effectively cut off the Egyptian Army from its native land, severing its supply-lines and pounding it into surrender.

Dan had been wounded – a couple of minor lacerations from shrapnel – and the way things sometimes fall into place, he was sitting in the sand, leaning against a wrecked T-62 of the Egyptian 173rd Tank Regiment, his shoulder and hand bandaged, when who should come loping past, looking for his driver, but the Divisional Commander himself, Ariel Sharon.

The General had stopped and asked Dan how he got wounded. Dan had told him and at that moment a medic major had arrived to inform Sharon that his driver had just received a battlefield amputation of his right leg and was being casevac-ed from the front line.

So Dan became the General's driver and the two had got on like a house on fire. He made Sharon laugh with his gripes about the millionaire father-in-law, the Mount Carmel Hotel and Miss Personality, his insatiable bride.

The upshot of all this was that after the Yom Kippur War, Sergeant Dan Davidov was offered a regular enlistment with the 23rd Parachute Regiment. He seized the moment, although he had never thought of himself as a professional soldier. Two years later, Rita had divorced him for a member of the Israeli Olympic marathon team and four months after that, Sergeant-Major Davidov had been invited to try for the elite and secretive Unit 101, a Special Paratroop detachment which was, unknown to most of Israel, the hard cutting-edge of the Israeli Intelligence Service – the Institute or, in Hebrew, *Mossad*.

By 1983, ten years after that wonderful Egyptian invasion, Dan was thirty-seven and a major in Unit 101. He had graduated, on an army scholarship, in political history at Tel Aviv University and had just returned from a four-month operation in Europe, codenamed 'Yayin a Dom', or Red Wine, as part of a Mossad move to liquidate extremist Palestinian terrorist leaders in Paris, Rome and London. He had not, at this time, been allowed into the most sensitive heart of Mossad's most secret intelligence operations and planning.

Then one evening, as Major Dan Davidov was sitting at a pavement café in old Jerusalem, waiting for his date, a pretty girl in the Israeli Foreign Service, whom he had met at a barbecue the weekend before, two men sat down at his table.

One he recognized – Marty Effriam, Deputy Director of Mossad's Active Measures Department. The other was unknown to him.

'Dan,' Effriam had said, putting a fatherly hand on his arm, 'you're a good boy and we think it's time you came into the business . . .'

So with a glowing career like that, a patriot and reluctant hero, and a man who, whatever faults he had, had always been kind to his mother, how come Danny Davidov found himself sitting on this rust-bucket anchored off the island of Antigua, where the Atlantic Ocean meets the Caribbean?

The answer was that the Israeli intelligence officer – former intelligence officer – was wanted these days by the law enforcement agencies of a dozen countries. Along with his partner in crime, who had gone ashore to arrange for a couple of girls. And they would be no great lookers at that. For passengers on a tramp-steamer did not have all that much *mazulla* to throw around. Which was crazy. For either Danny or the man who, in St Petersburg, had called himself Yevgeny, could probably have bought up Antigua and every hotel and bimbo and fancy yacht moored in its idyllic marinas.

But low profile, Yevgeny had kept insisting. Low profile and we don't attract attention. Profile schmofile, thought

Danny, why should I listen an ex-KGB hood who got thrown on the scrapheap just for being Polish?

The answer was simple. Yevgeny Zemskov, real name Nikolai Serafimovich Kolosov, was no hood. The man was a genius. And without each other, the greatest *vozmozhnost* in the history of crime would not have been possible.

Vozmozhnost was the Russian word for possibility. But in the underworld, around the districts of Moscow where the black markets flourished, it was used as a dry understatement, to indicate a stinging criminal victory. A coup.

And with a joint fortune of 323 million dollars, US, scattered prudently among a number of discreet banks, the possibility of going down in the history of crime as the most successful, the grandest masters of the sting, was becoming more of a sure thing with every operation they performed.

If it seems an odd ambition for two grown men, neither of whom had turned to crime until the onset of middle age – and Danny had often chewed this question over in his mind – the best explanation is that both were uncomplicated high-achievers. And both had been rejected by the establishments whose approval had meant a lot to them.

So there was a 'We'll show them' aspect to their unique new careers. Coupled with a cold, aesthetic, egotistical . . . satisfaction in doing what they were among the best at, not for government or country, but for themselves.

Danny blinked his eyes against the fierce, comforting warmth of the sun. A radio on the bridge was playing some East Caribbean station. A song about rum and swaying hips. Hips swaying like palm trees.

He hoped Nikolai would remember the rum.

It was the kitchen Jardine kept going back to.

He was relieved it had not been the bedroom – the kitchen did not revive the same memories, but there was something about it. Even after he had come to terms with the warm coffee pot and the toast in the pop-up toaster (which had indeed popped up, for two pieces of hand-sliced bread were sitting hard and stale in the machine).

He checked his watch. Two hours, nineteen minutes since he had let himself in. That was another thing. The door had four serious locks on it, to complement the apartment's other devices against burglars or snoopers. But they had not been used. The last person to leave the flat had merely pulled it shut.

Jardine had locked the thick iroko-wood door from the inside. To allow him time to get out, should someone try to enter during his search. He had forced a locked window in the bedroom, which looked on to the pink-tiled roof of a building in the bullet-pocked alley below. Just in case. Just in case he had to leave in a hurry.

He had examined the contents of every jar, bottle and carton in the place. Salt, olive oil, tea, herbs, lentils, chick-peas, rice, peppers, wine, Haig's Dimple, raki, Stolichnaya vodka, Williams Pear schnapps (the only liquor bottle unopened), coffee and flour. The kitchen was a mess.

As were the bedroom, the bathroom and the sitting room.

The big cat sat on a high wooden stool in the kitchen, beside the phone which was attached to the wall, by the door which led into a small, ascetically uncluttered lobby. It watched Jardine, occasionally blinking solemnly, as if, somehow, it trusted him to divine from all this chaos a way to bring her back.

The breadknife, how could she have cut the bread without a breadknife? There was the wooden chopping board. Crumbs of varying sizes going stale in the morning heat. There were the untouched slices of bread in the toaster. Perhaps they had popped up to an empty kitchen.

Ah.

It had fallen on to the polished wood floor, half-hidden by the overhang of the freezer.

David Jardine stooped slightly, about to pick up the knife. The telephone rang shrilly. He jumped, straightening his head and twisting a muscle or a tendon or something in his neck that was to hurt for two or three days.

The cat almost shook her head in doleful despair. If this was the best help at hand . . . she seemed to be thinking.

After six rings, Alisha's voice was clear. The clarity was somehow disturbing.

'I'm not available to come to the phone,' she was saying, in French. 'If you have a message, please speak after the bleeps. *Au revoir*. And have a nice day . . .'

The last part was in English.

Jardine stared at the freezer door, listening as a man's voice spoke rapidly in Arabic. In his file, it stated quite clearly that David Jardine spoke an immoderate number of languages quite fluently. By fluently, the Firm meant he could be deployed in any region where one of those languages was spoken, and pass for, if not a native, at least someone who had lived there for a long time. He was also listed as having a fairly 'agricultural' (q.v.) grasp of one or two others.

Arabic, in its several forms and dialects, was one of those marked 'fluent' in his office records, but the speed, and accent, of the caller rendered it difficult for Jardine to understand what was being said. The sounds were more than averagely guttural, suggesting a Gulf influence, maybe Yemeni. But the few words he recognized clearly were from the classical Arabic found in the educated circles of Cairo and Alexandria. The two did not combine elegantly.

The caller was asking Alisha why she had not made a lunch date. The Arabic word he used meant appointment or, more accurately, informal appointment.

And yet . . . hard though it was to follow what the voice on the telephone was saying, there was something vaguely familiar about it.

'*Shukran*,' the man's message ended. Thank you.

Was this the voice of SJ? The Salim Jaddeh of Alisha's urgent signal to Ajax in Washington?

What was it she had communicated? 'SJ is agent of Halcyon' . . .? Which in plain English meant Salim Jaddeh is alleged to be an SIS agent.

At this stage, there was no way of ascertaining the weight

of such an allegation. The way the Firm's sections, cells and network runners operated, the identity of totally deniable, illegally recruited assets – known in the business as 'black' agents – would be known only to a minimal number of SIS officers. On occasions, that number might be just the one.

So whether or not SJ was an agent of some section, or individual operator, from Century House, might never be discovered. Not even by David Jardine.

After all, only three people knew the identity of Pomegranate.

Jardine had not moved during these deliberations. His eyes remained fixed on the freezer door, his hearing acutely tuned, for halfway through the telephone message his senses had been triggered by the thump of the cat's four paws landing softly on the polished wooden floor. And now that the answering-machine had stopped, and the cat was gone, he breathed carefully and . . . listened.

Someone walking in the street outside. Coarse laughter from a team of workmen he had seen on the rubble of a bombed building, at the intersection between Rue du Bac and Avenue Balbek. The altering pitch of distant airliner engines, as it started its landing approach. The hum of the freezer motor. A faint, tinny transistor radio, playing Fat'mah Baloush, a singer popular in the Lebanon and North Africa. Muted rumble of cars and trucks, horns sounding. Children playing, about a block and a half away.

In other words, what passes to the untrained ear for almost total silence.

And there was not a sound from the person in the bedroom. Who had entered so quietly, so delicately, using the voice amplified by the phone machine to cover any infinitely gentle, unavoidable sounds. Who now stood, absolutely still. About twelve feet from Jardine, who wondered if the intruder knew he was there. Not sure if it was a serious threat, or a curious neighbour – some friend of Alisha's, Alisha herself, or a thief, seizing the opportunity of the open window . . . the police, a passing detective . . .

Time passed with infinite slowness.

Nothing stirred.

There was no sign of the cat.

Jardine could hear his every silent breath.

Dare he turn? Did he imagine it?

Well, David, he said to himself, we can stand here like a constipated orang-utan or do we initiate some kind of action? He had declined the opportunity to acquire a firearm from the Office's Beirut Station, to avoid the necessary contact being observed. For nowhere in the world were there more observers than in Beirut, and either a brush contact (in which neither operator overtly acknowledges the existence of the other) or a dead drop (where the object for collection is left in an unremarkable, secret location – like a toilet cistern, or a trashcan) might have collected a tail so professional that even Jardine might not have noticed, thus compromising Pomegranate. Wherever the hell she was . . .

The sudden, close sound of the cat purring was as loud as a chainsaw, to his stretched senses.

It came from the bedroom. Just through the wall.

The only weapon available was the breadknife on the floor at his feet. Dear God, he thought. I really am getting too old for this. Maybe I should have stayed with that bloody committee.

Then he smiled (only slightly, to be accurate). Well, sport, David Jardine said to God, for that was the appalling way he communed with his Maker, I prayed for some action but I hope you haven't gone to extremes . . .

Then he dropped to one knee with remarkable agility, scooping up the knife, and as he straightened, came face to face with a cold, handsome face. Young. A young face. So close he smelled the garlic on the youth's breath. As Jardine slid his left foot lightly back, the sole brushing the floor, his left wrist blocking instinctively the knife thrust he could only have sensed in the millisecond available, and as his right hand travelled up with the speed of light, breadknife dropping away, the heel of the hand his weapon, the searing hot, unnatural, gasping rip of cold, honed steel sliced into his left abdomen, just below the lowest rib, and absolutely simultaneously his right-hand heel jarred against the attacker's jaw and kept on going, lifting the young man's very toes off the floor. And he followed the blow through with that same hand clamping round the back of the young neck and his right knee coming up hard to contact the assailant's head, forced floorwards by that quick and remorseless right fist.

The result was an unconscious youth of about eighteen lying on the wooden floor, half-sitting against the door jamb, his head lolling in a way that made Jardine wonder if he had killed the boy until he felt a rapid, irregular, but strong pulse from the carotid artery on the loser's neck. It gave him no moral problems. In any engagement of this nature, there had to be a winner and there had to be a loser.

David Jardine, breathless with adrenalin, glanced up and mentally said Thank you. Thanks, Lord.

Truth to tell, certain events of the last couple of years had robbed him of that close and comfortable, comforting . . . propinquity he had felt since his conversion, at the hands of a wise old priest at Farm Street Church, headquarters of the Society of Jesus in England.

God was more distant now. The loving informality of their earlier relationship had soured. Had *been* soured, by Jardine's own actions. Worse than sins. For God would forgive those. But the English spy had committed a wrong against his own surprisingly strict personal code. And he knew that even the passage of time would not allow him to forgive himself. And not even his erstwhile Chum's absolution would make any difference. And he apologized to the Man upstairs for the heresy of that thought.

Jardine shrugged away the moment and took a well-worn Bowie knife from the unconscious young hand. He removed the boy's belt from his faded blue jeans and swiftly and none too gently tied his wrists tightly together.

Only then did he become aware that his own side and left trouser leg were saturated in warm blood.

Trembling now, with shock from the adrenalin and fear at what he might find, Jardine ripped off his shirt, not bothering to fumble for buttons, and rammed a tea-towel from the washboard beside the sink hard against the wound.

The boy on the floor had a chunky swelling rising on his left cheek and brow, all but closing his left eye.

Silence.

No sign of the cat.

No sign of anyone else. No back-up for the Arab youth.

His heart thumping, gasping like a sprinter, Jardine eased the fierce pressure on the tea-towel pressed hard against his left abdomen. There is nothing like a knife wound to awaken intimations of mortality.

Very, very delicately, as if the ripped flesh had been that of an infant, he let the tea-towel lift clear, and waited for the spurting of an arterial wound – Don't be stupid, you big sissy, he thought to himself, hands trembling, there are no arteries there, or are there? – or worse, the deep, dark red offal of some part of his vitals. Or the grey-blue of intestines.

Gradually, his fright eased. The knife thrust had sliced horizontally, opening about four inches of flesh, revealing a comfortable half-inch of subcutaneous layer. He chuckled with relief, pleased for once that the middle years had made him a fatter bastard than he once had been.

The boy started to groan. That wild, unnerving wail which often precedes a return from enforced unconsciousness.

Annoyed at having a double problem – keeping the youth harmless, and attending to his wound – David Jardine folded a fresh tea-towel and poured half the contents of the Haig's Dimple scotch whisky bottle on to it, letting it saturate the cotton, which he then held tightly along the length of the wound.

Ah – ah – ah, his breath was taken away by a searing stinging, almost like a second knife thrust.

The Arab youth's groaning had stopped.

As Jardine pressed the towel to his side, he leaned against the kitchen's cedar work-surface and watched his vanquished attacker gradually recover consciousness. This was the moment when a stupid interrogator would move in hard and cruel, thus so completely confusing the already bewildered patient that he would be extremely unlikely to extract any remotely useful information. For the first thing a person returning to consciousness needs is reassurance. The brain is not in a position to think along anything but the most primaeval lines. Sometimes for minutes, sometimes for days, sometimes for longer.

This was David Jardine rationalizing to himself. He knew the truth was that he felt a bit too shaken to play the hard interrogator. Jardine gazed at the still stunned boy slumped on the floor, and looked around for an empty saucepan which he filled with water from the tap and threw over him.

For a moment, the youth seemed to be working out what had just happened. Then he opened his one good eye and, with some discomfort, turned his head to look up at Jardine. He seemed bewildered. But his gaze took in the big man's bloody shirt, then dropped to the floor and his wounded side.

Jardine knew he would have to find some way to suture the sliced flesh, but it was clean enough now and his breathing had returned to normal.

Time passed. The sounds of Beirut came back into his perception. He wondered if Alisha kept any cigarettes in the kitchen. But he had searched it, hadn't he? And he knew there were none.

Maybe the youth had some. The youth with the impressive and worsening black eye.

'There's steak in the fridge,' Jardine said. In Arabic.

'What?' said the boy, his good eye rolling in astonishment.

'Steak. A nice slab of raw steak. In the freezer.'

The Arab boy rocked his head painfully from side to side.

'But I am not hungry . . .'

Jardine watched him, surprised to feel compassion for the kid. 'It's for your eye,' he said. 'Raw steak will reduce the swelling . . .'

He opened the freezer door and lifted a pound of fresh sirloin from a bloody plate. And as he turned round, holding the piece of meat in one hand, the other clutching a whisky-sodden, bloodstained tea-towel to his left side, his eyes met the boy's one good eye and for a moment, for the merest blip in time, the world stood still.

The youth's mouth moved lopsidedly. At first Jardine thought it was the pain, but he was actually laughing. Trying to laugh. Not very loud, and not very hard. But he was clearly amused at the absurdity of the sight before him, and Jardine smiled slowly. Jesus Christ. Was this how grown men earned their living?

The cat padded in from the hall, and sanity was restored.

'Where did you learn to do this?' asked Jardine, his teeth almost clenched, looking away casually after first ascertaining that the youth actually knew what he was about.

'This is Beirut, *monsieur*,' Hassan replied.

They had switched from Arabic to French, for after the application of the raw steak and the cleaning and closer examination of Jardine's wound, mutual introductions had been made. And it was learned that the youth was Hassan Abdul-Latif Rashdan, aged eighteen and a young friend of Alisha's. Jardine, of course, was Jean-Pierre Ramseyer.

The Englishman had boiled a pan of water and had dropped a long needle, the kind used for sewing linen, along with a reel of thick, black thread, into it.

Then they had both scrubbed their hands and poured

vodka over them, and with Hassan's assistance, Jardine holding the flaps of sliced flesh back together, they had used long Band-Aid strips to keep the wound tightly closed.

Now, Hassan was suturing the cut with the sterilized needle and thread. Going past each strip of plaster, then removing them, one at a time, and going back with a neat stitch to seal the gap. It was clearly not the first time he had done amateur surgery.

The youth worked with breathless concentration, using his one functioning eye. The slab of raw steak was held, surreally, in position over his left eye and cheek, with a bandage made from yet another tea-towel torn down the middle.

Conversation until now had been limited to a guarded exchange of identities and the information that Hassan had mistaken Monsieur Ramseyer for someone else.

Neither man nor boy seemed to have contemplated calling for the police. Or even for an ambulance. This unspoken acceptance of conspiracy engendered a grudging, delicate, mutual truce.

Jardine gasped in some pain.

'Sorry.'

Hassan worked on in silence. Somewhere outside a truck's horn sounded, about three blocks away.

'Was she expecting to see you?'

'What do you mean?' Hassan's expression was difficult to read.

'Did Alisha know you were coming?'

'I often look in.' The youth avoided Jardine's sudden glance. He was certainly a good-looking young man, with intelligent, almost feminine, dark eyes. Eye. Jardine presumed the left eye was similarly dark and intelligent. Before it came into contact with a Century House knee.

'But not specially today . . .'

Silence.

Jardine shrugged. Why was it stitches took for ever?

'And you, Monsieur Ramseyer?'

'I was not expected.'

Silence.

'Who did you think I was, Hassan?' Jardine went on. 'This person whom you wanted to kill . . .?'

Hassan had almost finished. Jardine realized it was, if nothing else, unconventional to be interrogating someone who was shoving a needle in and out of his abdomen.

When it became clear that no answer was forthcoming, Jardine tried another tack.

'Alisha's father and I were close friends.'

Hassan looked up involuntarily, jabbing the needle painfully but unintentionally into a tender part of the gash.

'Aw, *merde*!'

'*Pardon*.'

'It was a tragedy, his murder . . .'

This gambit was known in the trade as getting off the bloody fence, at least that was the way Ronnie Szabodo had described it in the training sessions a million and six years ago, in the Firm's Operational Conduct course, which had taken place at a refurbished seaside holiday camp. Operational Conduct was about how you behaved on clandestine assignments in Denied Areas and had nothing to do with Conduct of Operations, which was an altogether more academic study.

Hassan squinted at Jardine. Thoughtful. More experience written on his injured eighteen-year-old face than on that of many men of forty.

'I never knew him,' he replied. Noncommittal and wise.

'He was a brave man. Even if one did not agree with his politics . . .' Jardine eased back away from the faster course he had just set.

The cat licked one paw, and gazed sideways at Jardine. Dearie me, it seemed to be thinking. Dear oh dear.

'It was my brother who killed him,' Hassan said, matter-of-factly. 'With a point two-two modified Colt. Reduced charge.'

David Jardine nodded, as if such information verged on the banal. 'To make it look like the Israelis . . .?'

'Just so, *monsieur*. There. What do you think?'

The knife slash was now a four-inch, deep red line, dark blood oozing along its sutured length. The twelve black knotted stitches as neat as any casualty nurse's.

'Very nice, thank you,' said David Jardine, as if he had just been shown his haircut by a barber.

While Hassan washed his hands, Jardine went through to the ransacked bathroom and the opened first-aid box which, as in most war-weary Beirut households, would not have disgraced a paramedic's inventory.

He stripped, discarding his bloodsoaked trousers, underwear and socks. Then he stood in the bath and cleaned the blood from himself, using the opportunity to soap away the sweat and staleness of nineteen hours of travel and a swift but shattering fight for survival.

Jardine dried himself on a big bathtowel emblazoned with the crest of the Gritti Palace Hotel, Venice. He smiled, remembering that Alisha, Pomegranate, was a compulsive thief of artefacts from classy establishments.

He swabbed the sutured wound, the flesh swollen now into livid welts drawn together along that dark line, and dabbed it dry with clean lint. Then Jardine laid an eight-inch-by-four-inch melolin pad over the wound, and placed a field dressing on top of it. Only then did it sink in that just a couple of inches more to the right would have meant a punctured pancreas or kidney.

He used strong three-inch-wide plaster strips to hold the dressing firmly in place. He glanced at his face in the mirror. His eyes were dark-shadowed and strained, his face close to being haggard, and David Jardine realized that on top of everything else, he was enduring the rubber-legged, gritty-eyed, slightly dislocated sensations of jet-lag.

'What are you going to wear?' asked the youth, appearing at the door of the bathroom, unwinding the torn dish-cloth which held the raw steak over his injured eye.

He removed the meat and gazed, unmoved, into the same mirror.

David Jardine splashed some water on his face and dried it on a towel that had been folded over an expensive steel and white fake-ivory towel rail, with the crest of Shepheard's Hotel in Cairo.

Jesus, she must have removed it lock, stock and barrel. He imagined Alisha, doubtless on some official diplomatic jaunt, painstakingly unscrewing the fixture from a bathroom wall in one of the oldest and, once again, most expensive, hotels in Egypt. And as he pressed that towel to his wet face, there was her smell. Her young, insouciant fragrance.

'I have a pair of jeans and a spare shirt in my bag,' he replied.

'Ah.'

Which was just as well, for there were no men's clothes in the apartment. Jardine's search had found an unused Gillette Sensor pack, with two spare blades, in the wall cupboard beside the washbasin, along with three new toothbrushes still in their plastic wrappers. In a carved chest of cypress wood, with a flat top and a sliding drawer, beside the unmade bed, were a packet of Beecham's Powder capsules, a carton of Actifed sinus decongestant tablets, an ivory snuffbox with about a half-ounce of hashish resin wrapped in tinfoil, a pack of Camel Lites, a couple of foil strips with contraceptive pills, in use until the day before, and four male condoms sealed in plastic wrappers.

But nothing to indicate anyone was welcome there on a permanent basis.

Jardine gazed round the bathroom. The problem of the warm coffee, the unlocked front door, the abandoned toast in the pop-up toaster . . . and that telephone message in guttural Arabic. All those things were returning to puzzle him, now that the business of the stranger in the next room had resolved itself . . . the young stranger with the Bowie knife and a mean line in battlefield first aid.

He pressed the towel once more to his face, almost nuzzling it, as if this vestigial contact with her could somehow help divine what had happened. What was it she had signalled? Something about all this is not good.

Well, you were dead right, Pomegranate old girl. But what? That, he mused, to quote the Prince of Denmark, is the problem.

Jardine handed the towel to Hassan, who had splashed water, tentatively, against his face, and went through to the sitting room. The sun had moved around, casting its slatted rays across the wall and door where he had let himself in. And of course, like every other place in the apartment, the room had been ransacked.

The Director, Forward Plans, opened his battered leather Colombian travelling bag and after rummaging around lifted out a pair of boxer shorts with a Donald Duck motif and a Cash's name-tag sewn into the waistband, stating 'Andrew Jardine'.

Oh, wonderful. That just makes my bloody day, he thought. For Andrew Jardine was his beloved son, in his last year at boarding school in Dorset. The ace spy must have packed the wrong linen – Andrew had zoomed up in the last eighteen months to equal his father's six foot three – with a bloody name-tag on it.

So much for the Firm's immaculate efficiency in furnishing Jardine with Jean-Pierre Ramseyer's immaculate legend.

For a brief moment, the mundane school name-tag flooded his mind with pictures of safe England and school rugby pitches, and the farmhouse and Dorothy's kitchen. And Andrew and Carol, his Cambridge undergraduate daughter, watching *The Blues Brothers* for the umpteenth time. They knew all the dialogue by heart.

But you don't last long in this game with thoughts like those, and Jardine shrugged. Just as he was pulling on the faded, well-pressed blue jeans, the telephone started to ring.

David Jardine and Hassan exchanged glances. They waited until the ringing was interrupted and Alisha's calm and attractive voice once again explained that she was not available – well, we do know that, Pomegranate old sport, reflected Jardine – and please speak and have a nice day . . .

'This is Jaddeh,' said a quiet, authoritative voice, and a flicker on the boy's face told Jardine quite a lot. 'Mam'selle Abdul-Fetteh has had to leave on urgent business. The Deuxième Bureau are on their way to the apartment. I suggest, Monsieur Ramseyer, that you leave right now. You have about four minutes, unless the place is already under surveillance.'

Click.

End of message.

Hassan retrieved his Bowie knife from the kitchen floor, wiped the blood – David Jardine's blood – from the blade and slid it back under his belt.

They stared at each other in silence. Somewhere in the distance, a dog started to bark.

'Him,' said the boy.

Jardine nodded, understanding.

'I thought you were him.'

'And you wanted to kill him . . .'

Hassan's good eye narrowed. He nodded. 'Sure. We should go.'

And he turned, crossed to the bedroom and leaned carefully out of the window.

David Jardine picked up his Colombian bag and followed, alert.

The boy glanced back. 'It's okay, I think.'

Well, you couldn't ask for more, in Beirut.

'Come on,' Hassan urged.

But the Englishman held back. 'If your brother killed her father . . . how is it you are her friend?'

'*Allons, sidi*, let's go!'

'I think you're probably a little bit in love with her.'

The boy leaned outside the window, listening, like the cat. For a moment David Jardine thought he had not heard. Then Hassan turned his bruised face to study Jardine.

'I think she affects people like that.'

Silence.

Jardine nodded slowly, meeting the young man's gaze. 'Yes. I think she probably does.'

'And *sidi* . . .' *Sidi* was Arabic for mister.

'What?'

'I also think we should get the hell out of here.'

'That might be prudent.'

So by the time the Lebanese Interior Ministry's Deuxième Bureau, which is to say their Security Service, had broken down the iroko-wood door, all that greeted them was a ransacked apartment. With blood on the kitchen floor, and no towels in the bathroom.

There was no tape in the telephone answering-machine.

4

The Other Tennessee Williams

THE SUN WAS FIERCE. Even the steel hull near the waterline was hot to the touch. Ex-KGB Colonel Nikolai Kolosov held on to the companionway platform as the motorboat moved with the waves. He watched as the man who had flown into Antigua from Caracas, on a regular flight of LIAT, the Caribbean airline, made his way cautiously over the wooden thwarts, picking his way through baskets of fresh fruit and cases of Carib beer, towards the gunwale.

It occurred to Kolosov that the broad-shouldered, lean and fit-looking visitor, whose immaculately groomed hair was longer than was fashionable in Europe at that time, was actually quite uncomfortable with boats and waves and things nautical. This suited the Russian, for in any other circumstances, his Sicilian guest – his and the Israeli's – had a pretty formidable reputation.

The two hard-faced, olive-skinned men who accompanied the visitor, who called himself Cagliaro, showed no such unease. One of them wore a loose jacket over a plain blue T-shirt. He swarmed nimbly over the side and on to the platform, revealing, in the process, a short Mini-Uzi machine-pistol. His colleague, a stone-eyed descendant of the Moorish bandits of southern Sicily, waited patiently, his gaze watchful but relaxed.

Cagliaro handed his leather shoulder-bag to Kolosov and steadied himself, before scrambling awkwardly on to the platform, about two feet above the gentle waves, and moving close to the hull for protection, only to glance down and instinctively step away from the space between companionway and warm, looming, rusting metal. The bodyguard in the blue T-shirt and loose jacket steadied him, all the time watching someone at the top of the stairs.

'*Buon giorno, signor,*' called Danny Davidov from the ship's deck at the top of the companionway steps. 'Welcome on board . . .'

Cagliaro nodded and pulled himself, hand tight on the guardrail, up the steps. Preceded by Joe Messina, the one with the Mini-Uzi.

Kolosov smiled grimly and followed.

The second bodyguard, Vito Menfi, glanced at the skipper of the motorboat, as if disappointed there had been no trouble, and swung himself on to the companionway.

Danny Davidov closed the heavy steel door, leaving the two Sicilian bodyguards reluctant and unhappy on the outside. Kolosov and Cagliaro sat down at a polished teak table, on the comfortable leather squab couch that ran round three sides of the steamer's wardroom, which was about the size of a regular sitting room in an average apartment. Except the ceiling was much lower, and made of hard iron. The smell of engine oil, polished wood and brass, and cooking from the galley, no longer affected Davidov or Kolosov, after two weeks at sea. But the Mafia lawyer's face had turned a shade paler.

'So,' said Danny, pouring from a jug of iced tea, 'this is quite an honour. Don Giovanni's *consigliere* in person. Don't think we don't appreciate it. Right, Nikky?'

Nikolai Kolosov half-closed his killer's eyes and inclined his head infinitesimally. He really wished the little asshole, his partner in crime, would not call him Nikky.

'Let's get down to business,' he said.

'That would be good,' replied Cagliaro, accepting a glass

of tea. *'Grazie,'* he thanked Danny, holding Kolosov's cold gaze.

'We're looking to hire, rent, purchase, the two best counterfeiters in the world.' Danny had no intention of being left out of the negotiations.

'And who would that be?' Cagliaro laid his glass on the saloon table. He had been around a couple of times. You did not accept drinks from dangerous strangers.

'Couple of Vietnamese. Grandfather and grandson. Name of Nghi, pardon me if I don't say it right.'

'And what makes you think I can help you?'

'Signor Cagliaro. Gimme a break. What you doing all this way from Palermo if you can't deliver the goods?'

Kolosov listened as the two men circled around the subject. Beneath the almost oriental politeness there was real menace. He was constantly surprised by the very different way the Israeli went about his business. That Davidov was good, there was no question. If he had not been, former KGB Colonel Nikolai Kolosov would not be sitting there. But where a *kontora* man, Moscow-trained, would be blunt and, if necessary, threatening, this little guy would smile and say what was to be said without ever raising his voice. It was actually much more effective. On occasions.

Cagliaro had just asked where Danny had gotten his information.

'Hey, hey,' said Davidov. 'Don't make me lie to you. Let's just forget you asked me that. So, up till last October these two little slant-eyed forgers were the property of one Pablo Escobar, am I right? But his luck is running out and a Bogota lawyer called Restrepo sold a whole bunch of experts to the Sicilian family. I hear the price was one hundred million cash, am I right or what?' Danny touched his short ponytail. That was another thing about him that irritated Kolosov. A ponytail. Jesus.

'What do you want them for?' Cagliaro looked like he might need something to be sick in. Ships made some people like that. But that he was one very tough hombre there was no doubt. Ruthless and sadistic, his KGB file had recorded, back in 1979. Could go far. And here he was, right-hand man to the *capo di tutti capi*, the very Prince of the Cosa Nostra–Camora Mafia alliance, Don Giovanni Favorito Noto. A man who, it was rumoured, had tentacles reaching into the Vatican and the Italian Secret Service, not to mention the very judiciary which was instructed to find evidence against him and put him inside.

But right now the Prince of the Mafia's right-hand man looked distinctly green about the gills.

'Counterfeit US dollars,' replied Danny Davidov with such unhesitating honesty that even the Russian wondered for a second if there had been a change of plan. That's how convincing the little Israeli with the ponytail could be. 'Four different denominations. And each denomination running to one hundred different, and random, serial numbers.'

Cagliaro did not blink. 'Have you a ballpark figure? Concerning the cost of an operation like that?'

'The plates are the biggest expense.' Kolosov lit a cigarette. He meant that each currency bill would require a separate pair of brass plates, individually and painstakingly engraved, to duplicate to within a millionth of an inch the real thing. This meant at least 800 counterfeit engraved brass plates.

'Your people, your experts . . .' He exhaled, smoke curling from his nostrils, his gaze fixed on the Sicilian. 'If Don Giovanni agreed to let us use them. Plus the materials. Even without your fee, we have to be talking . . . thirty million dollars?'

'More than that.' The Sicilian lawyer watched for reaction. He seemed to relax slightly. 'But maybe not too much more.'

'And your fee?'

'Come to Palermo. We can discuss it.'

Danny and Kolosov exchanged glances.

'Hey, hey.' Danny spread his hands. 'Palermo is your home territory. For us it's too dangerous.'

Cagliaro studied his glass of iced tea for a long moment. A cockroach moved slowly across the polished wood table. He gently lifted the ashtray, with Kolosov's smouldering cigarette resting on it, and just as gently squashed the cockroach.

'But you gentlemen bank there . . .' He gazed into each man's eyes without hostility, aware that he had just shattered any illusion they might have harboured that their most private financial arrangements remained a secret. 'So why not make it a social occasion? I believe you will be visiting the Banca di Calabria in two days' time. Unless my information is wrong.'

Danny Davidov watched the Sicilian lawyer with amused respect. This was going to be a game and a half.

'Sure. We'll be staying at the Palazzo,' he lied. 'What do you suggest?'

'Oh, I'll be in touch.' And the man who called himself Cagliaro put his glass on the table, stood up, and inclined his head politely as the other two got to their feet.

'*Arrivederci,*' he said. '*Piu tarde* . . .' meaning, See you in Palermo.

After David Jardine and the Arab youth, Hassan, had left Alisha's apartment by the bedroom window, they had strolled down the bullet-pocked alley past an aged knife-grinder sharpening blades on an antique round stone with a wooden axle, mounted upon a precarious kind of barrow and operated by a wooden foot-pedal. Hassan had said that the old man had continued to ply his trade all through the troubled city's civil wars and the Syrian and Israeli occupations.

There is a café at the junction of the Rue Balbek and Rue Wadi Sabra, between the desolate ruins of a once immaculate office block and a shopping mall, wrecked by Soviet D-24 heavy artillery fired from Moslem West Beirut, Israeli mortar rounds and a stray shell from the USS *Wisconsin*. The café is called Le Camel and it operates from a ground floor salvaged from the devastated Banque de Crédit mercantile building, which looms above like a blackened, burned-out fortress.

Inside, it was bustling with chic Lebanese women and men in business suits and crisp white shirts. There were young students from the nearby University, in jeans and sweatshirts with legends like 'Bob Marley' and 'Harvard'. A radio was playing more Fat'mah Baloush.

'*Sidi*,' said Hassan, 'this is a good place for us.'

Is he kidding? wondered Jardine. I need urgent medical attention, and so does he. Plus, somebody called Salim Jaddeh knows my workname and in all probability set the local sleuths on me while I was turning over Alisha's place. In the name of God, this is no time for coffee.

'Hassan, we should get off the streets, there are one or two things going on outside our control here.'

The boy looked really frustrated, the way Andrew did when told he couldn't borrow the car, or go to an all-night rave at Popham airfield. The way he raised his shoulders and cocked his head to one side made the English spy feel quite middle-aged.

'This is Beirut, *monsieur*, not Geneva.' He gazed wonderingly at Jardine. 'Things are always out of control.'

David Jardine met the young man's good eye. He shook his head, grinning. 'Sure. *Allons*. I'm getting old . . .'

And they strolled into Le Camel, unnoticed by the clientele, past the rococo fifties jukebox and under the broad arch beside the serving counter, and chose a table in the right-hand corner. A bead curtain behind them led, Hassan assured him, to the washrooms and a side-door to the Rue Chamoun.

'*Keh fahlik*.' A white-shirted waiter appeared. How's it going, in other words. He flicked the red and white checked tablecloth in a ritual movement he was probably unaware he had made, gazing past them at two very pretty girls from the local television station. Jardine had seen one of them read the news bulletins, in tapes the local Station sent to Century House.

Hassan ordered two cups of the delicious thick black

sludge that was the local coffee. And two glasses of iced water.

'So, who is the man you wanted to kill?' asked Jardine quietly, when the waiter had gone.

'His name is Salim Jaddeh.'

This is Jaddeh, the voice on the telephone had said.

'Tell me about him.'

The youth glanced around the café. Nobody seemed interested in them. 'Who are you, *'fendi . . .?*'

'Like you. A friend of Alisha's.'

The youth looked thoughtful. Slowly, he raised a hand and touched his badly swollen face. Jardine felt dreadful. For God's sake, David, he thought, the little bastard tried to kill you. Well, yes, but he believed it was somebody else. Oh. Oh, that's okay then. It is? Sweet Jesus, senility is really setting in.

'Alisha's family put out the word on my brother, after he killed Monsieur Abdul-Fetteh. Her father.'

'Well, they would. This is Beirut . . .'

'Also on me and our two brothers. Also my father and his three brothers. We were with a rival clan, you see.'

'No kidding, that's a surprise,' said David Jardine drily.

'When they came for me, I was at school. The American marines had just been blown up. The town was as bad as it's ever been, people going crazy. Hezbollah hitting on Danny Chamoun's soldiers. Arafat's people seizing the opportunity to hit Hezbollah and blame the Israelis. One more schoolboy was no big deal . . .'

'How old were you?'

'Eight. They took me in a car, along the Corniche. It was like Mad Max, *'fendi*. Me was in the trunk. But it had four bullet-holes and I could see.'

And breathe, reflected Jardine, and his heart tugged as he realized that the recollection of that awful day was taking Hassan back to his appalling childhood in the most violent city on earth – until Sarajevo happened along.

'There was a viaduct that the boulevard went over. And underneath it were arches, like vaults. It was there the

Christians used to dump the bodies. You should have seen them, we used to peek, on our way home from school. After a while they became like wax. They melted, you know. Into the earth. And into each other. It was kind of beautiful. As if there was some sort of . . . continuity.'

Holy Mother of God. What have we done to children like this . . .? And I am a Christian. Jardine stared into the boy's good eye.

'What happened . . .?' he asked quietly.

'A motorcycle. I heard a motorcycle.' Hassan was there, back in that car trunk. With four – not three, not five – with four bullet-holes. 'It was her. She was furious. She screamed at them, "Call yourselves men!" She had a piece. A Skorpion. God knows where she got it. "That child is eight years old! You big, brave bastards. Why don't you rape him while you're at it? Come on, get your dicks out! Show me what brave fighters you are. But make sure the child is tied up first. In case he tries to struggle. Jesus Christ, you make me sick." That is exactly what she said . . .'

And David Jardine could just hear Alisha, Pomegranate, yelling it. There was nothing to say. He watched the boy and waited.

Hassan was breathing more shortly. Back in that trunk. His eyes on the past. '"Well, you kill me first," she said to them. "For I could not live with the memory of my murdered father, who was so good, so honourable, so fucking brave . . . I can't be around when his memory has been pissed on like this . . ."'

A tear ran down Hassan's cheek. He shook his head. The waiter deposited two cups of coffee and two glasses of water. He seemed used to seeing men cry.

'So they didn't kill you,' said Jardine, simply.

'No . . .' Hassan sighed, a long, deep, shivering sigh. David Jardine had no need to ask what had happened to his older brothers.

'And you will defend her with your life.'

'Of course.'

Jardine laid a hand on the youth's arm. Hassan was about a year younger than Andrew. Who liked the Blues Brothers and had a rather endearing crush on a girl at a nearby girls' boarding school, who was unofficially engaged to an England Rugby International in his final year at Cambridge.

'That is as it should be,' he said. 'As one man to another.'

Then, before he got sentimental, David Jardine laughed shortly. 'So I forgive you for shoving that goddam knife into me.'

Hassan brightened and smiled, his eye bright. '*Sidi*, you moved real fast. Will you teach me such things?'

'Listen, pal, we are ships that pass in the night, you and me. I don't plan on being around long enough to teach you anything.'

'Of course.'

'So tell me about Salim Jaddeh . . .'

And over several cups of restoring, sweet black sludge, Hassan Abdul-Latif Rashdan did exactly that.

The beat was insistent and infectious. Three Jamaicans, wearing baggy pants, outsize tank-tops, rat's-tails, caps worn back to front and enormous, ankle-high trainers, sunglasses and wide grins, were taking up the sidewalk, moving rhythmically and in step to the ground-shaking beat from a ghetto-blaster playing Bob Marley's 'Exodus'.

They did not move much, just a basic left foot across right foot, right foot back, left foot stomping down, back where it came from, right foot across left, and so on and like that. Over and over. It was hypnotic and it made folk passing, stepping off the sidewalk, smile and visibly relax. Even the two uniformed cops from the 17th Precinct, who strolled by on the other side of Mercer Street, past Popolino's spaghetti joint, on their way to Washington Square, seemed to boogie a little bit, ignoring the breach of a half-dozen minor street laws regarding keeping the sidewalk clear for pedestrians and so forth.

A taller than average, granite-faced man, whose great-grandfather, a freed man, had been a stone-cutter in the Mississippi Delta, sat at a window table inside Popolino's, pushing a spoon around his cup of cappuccino and watching the Jamaicans on the sidewalk. He couldn't help admiring the nerve of those guys who worked the street for NYPD's Narcotics Task Force. Plus they could dance. That was more than Elmore Williams could do in the days he used to work undercover. Out of the 14th, further up Manhattan, in Midtown South.

Williams could remember like it was yesterday, the stake outs on crack dealers, the long, cold waiting in unmarked vans and trucks. The chestnut stand he used to man on West 43rd, with that big Wop cop, what was his name? Yeah, Lucco. Eddie Lucco. Before Eddie had made Sergeant of Detectives and got into Homicide. Boy, oh boy, was that a long time ago. Before Elmore Williams had quit the Force.

And just look at him now. He wondered what that bear-strong stone-cutter would think of it all.

Elmore sipped his coffee and continued to gaze through the window at the sidewalk. A kid, presumably one of the students – for this Washington Square neighbourhood housed many students from New York University – suddenly dashed out from somewhere and started to run round the square, frenetically touching all different kinds of things, lamp-posts, fire hydrants, stuff like that. Who knew what he was doing; maybe it was a bet, or some form of hazing, or the guy was doped up. What the hell, New York, this was it.

The slate-green Oldsmobile slid, sharklike, along the street and stopped just across the junction with Waverley.

Elmore's pulse kicked into a different gear. Instinctively, he arched his back and raised his shoulders, cracking the tension that had gripped him. He placed two five-dollar bills on the table and sauntered out, nodding to the Italian girl on the cash desk in a tight, partitioned corridor near the door. His 9-mm Smith & Wesson pistol felt snug and available in his right-hand back trouser pocket, under a loose jacket. He resisted the temptation to pat it as he stepped onto the street.

'What kept ya?' Harry Cardona eased the car towards Washington Square, away from the three undercover cops still hip-hopping to their ghetto-blaster.

'Nothing kept me, man. A guy can take a coffee, right?'

Cardona did not reply. He cruised towards East Broadway and made a right, heading uptown.

'So where's the merchandise?' inquired Williams.

'In the trunk. Sammy the Nose is at the place. I sent him there early.'

'No kidding? Now, why the fuck did you do that?'

'Because I call the fuckin' shots, that's why.' Cardona sounded his car horn and swerved past a Lincoln Town Car that seemed to have lost its way.

Elmore Williams gazed morosely out at the traffic. It was three in the afternoon. If Cardona was telling the truth, and you never knew in this business, in the Oldsmobile's trunk were two Samsonite valises with ten million counterfeit dollars, in hundreds and fifties. The price on the street, for high-quality forgeries, was about 400,000 dollars real money. And that was the day's business.

'Tell me about Reynolds and Trupiano.' He fumbled for a cigarette. The names he had mentioned were the buyers, if they could raise the 400 grand.

'The deal in Atlantic City went right,' replied Cardona. 'Tino Lucchese knows them from Vegas.'

'No shit . . .'

'So take it easy, will ya?'

Greed is a terrible thing, reflected Elmore. This Harry Cardona was down to put twenty big ones in his pocket as soon as the deal was done. Elmore's own share was to be twelve grand, for putting Cardona together with Sammy Hubbard, otherwise known as Sammy the Nose on account of it got bitten off in a fight on B Landing at Joliet, and sewn back on in the prison sanatorium. Never looked the same, but Sammy was slightly crazy and the trick was not to stare.

Sammy, in the way things sometimes go down, had landed on his feet during his time in the slammer, and he was in good with a serious counterfeit operation run by persons unknown, but who were flooding Florida and New York City with a ton, probably literally, of almost perfect funny money.

Harry Cardona's part had been to find a buyer. This turned out to be Joe Reynolds and Angelo Trupiano, two partners in a business that sold marked playing cards to certain casinos, mainly in Atlantic City and on the West Coast. Four meetings had been painstakingly and clandestinely arranged, three in Las Vegas and one, just the night before, in Atlantic City in which the players had sniffed each other out, dropping names of wiseguys they had in common, figuring out if it was safe to proceed to each new step in the deal.

Cardona had met Elmore Williams in Miami, a couple of years back, when Williams had been running with some Colombian mobsters, using the name Jake T. Harry Cardona believed him to be an ex-NYPD cop, kicked off the force for graft and extortion. Then he had run into the guy again in Las Vegas just two weeks ago and he had recruited this Jake T. to act as minder and use his police contacts to check for any undercover operators trying to penetrate the counterfeit game. Harry Cardona felt he had been quite smart in taking on this Jake T, it would indicate to Mister Big, whoever he was, that Harry meant serious business.

'So what's Sammy doin' there? Exactly?' inquired Elmore.

Cardona glanced sideways at Jake as he made a right off Broadway. 'Just taking care, Jake. Just taking fuckin' good care we don't walk into somethin', okay? You approve? As if I give a fuck.' But he grinned, winningly. You had to admit it, the forty-year-old wiseguy could turn on the charm. Likeable, even.

Elmore Williams' heartbeat was about 120 as the Oldsmobile pulled up behind a Michelob beer truck on West 43rd, across the street from the Algonquin Hotel.

This was serious business, by any standards. Four hundred thousand dollars and eight mil in loony tunes up for grabs and nobody really knew each other and it could go any which way.

'You can't leave it here,' he said, meaning the car.

'Wise up, my brother. I got a St Pat's sticker.' Cardona meant that on the windshield was a hexagonal sticker with a green shamrock and the figure 10 stamped on top of it. This meant the driver allegedly had contributed 1000 dollars to the NYPD Widows and Orphans last St Patrick's Day. Like everything else about Harry, it was fake.

Elmore's eyes narrowed. He did not approve of his peers calling each other 'ma brother', even if they felt it was cool, a bonding gesture. But for a white man like Harry Cardona to call him that . . . He ignored the remark and climbed out, automatically glancing around the street, checking out the environment.

Apart from the beer truck, there were two yellow taxicabs, a couple of guys selling hot doughnuts from a stand, a couple of panel trucks, one from a flower shop, the other old and beat-up. And a provision van unloading at a nearby delicatessen.

'Whadda you think . . .?' asked Harry anxiously. For he trusted Jake's judgement.

After a moment's consideration, Elmore nodded. 'Let's do it, man,' he said, and without looking back at Cardona, crossed the street and walked purposefully towards a ramshackle building that had a barber's shop and an office equipment place on the ground floor.

Cardona shrugged, opened up the trunk and hefted out two Samsonite suitcases. He glanced around, one last time, and followed.

The fifth floor of 1246 West 43rd Street had a bare, linoleum-covered landing that smelled of dust and worse. The rickety elevator had returned to the ground floor. There were three doors off the hallway. One claimed to be the office of a theatrical agency, one had just the number 23 on the door and the third bore the legend, 'M & T Gaming Ancillaries' on a wooden plaque.

Inside, a cramped waiting room led into an inner office. There was a washroom off the narrow passage between them. The furniture was sparse and cheap. In the office, there were two desks, two two-seater sofas and three wooden chairs.

Elmore and Cardona stood by the door. A lean, long-faced man, in loose-fitting Italian jacket and baggy pants, white shirt and necktie worn loose at the collar, was sitting on one of the sofas. The purple line around the base of his pointed proboscis, like a faint tattoo, identified him as Samuel L. Hubbard, Sammy the Nose. Who had gone on ahead to see if the atmosphere was okay for the transaction to proceed.

The two heavy Samsonite cases, with eight million in counterfeit hundreds and fifties, had been placed on wooden chairs in a kind of no-man's-land between the three men and their hosts, their customers.

One of those customers, Reynolds, stood back of one of the two desks, leaning against the peeling wall, one shoulder against a grimy window. He was a big man, wearing an expensive grey silk and wool jacket and a sunbed tan that just shouted Las Vegas.

Trupiano was short and wiry, with cool eyes that had seen it all before. He wore a white shirt buttoned to the neck, with no necktie, and an Italian designer topcoat, open all the way and maybe too long for him.

'You gentlemen want a beer or something?' asked O'Dowd. 'Maybe a cup of coffee?'

'The coffee's shit,' remarked Trupiano, without smiling.

'I'll pass on the shit,' said Harry, and they all laughed, to break the awkward tension.

Silence. Then, way down on the Avenue of the Americas, the throaty bellow of a fire engine.

'So you wanna count it?' Trupiano lifted a briefcase from beside the desk and laid it on the sofa beside Sammy the Nose. If events were proceeding according to plan, it would contain 400 grand in real money.

Sammy glanced at Elmore. 'Elmore . . .?' He meant, You're the ex-cop, whadda you think?

Elmore nodded. 'Sure.'

Sammy opened the briefcase and swiftly and professionally counted out the thick wads of 100-dollar bills.

As they waited, a phone started to ring in some other part of the building.

Satisfied the full amount was there, Sammy extracted five bills at random and laid them out on the top of one of the Samsonite cases. He slipped a jeweller's eyepiece against one eye, like a monocle, and took three small eyedrop bottles from his right pocket.

The phone stopped ringing.

Sammy dropped drops from each of the three bottles on to each of the five randomly selected currency bills, checking, as any prudent criminal would, that he was not being paid for his counterfeit money with counterfeit dollars.

Trupiano and Reynolds exchanged glances. A millisecond of amusement seemed to pass between them, as if to say, 'Can you believe this guy?' What a fuckin' mistake, thought Elmore.

Then Sammy's right foot started to tap gently on the floor, as if in time to some silent beat.

Cardona and Elmore deliberately did not look at each other. For this was the signal that something was badly wrong.

And if Sammy was to follow the agreed procedure, he would now announce the deal was off. He was to push the real money back to the two buyers and Elmore was to produce his piece and cover their swift exit. That was how they had rehearsed it. So when Sammy the Nose nodded calmly and announced, 'This is fine,' laid the attaché case on the floor, in neutral space, and casually pulled one of the Samsonite valises round so that he could open it, Elmore, forcing himself to look really relaxed as hell, nodded, smiling slightly, and stepped back so that he could cover the room and block the door.

Sammy the Nose flicked the case open and lifted the lid a couple of inches. There was something about the look in his eyes that troubled Elmore. For Sammy had a serious history of violence and Elmore's instinct told him the guy just might have flipped.

'I think you'll find this is in order, gents,' he said, and the BRRARP!! of a dozen 9-mm bullets took even Elmore by surprise and *he* was half-expecting it. The back of the Samsonite case lid erupted in holes and O'Dowd shuddered as the rounds whacked him and his right arm flung out and splattered red against the shattering window.

Elmore Williams was not the fastest gun in the east and it seemed like a thousand years getting his piece out and joining in the shooting. But his reflexes were probably better than his anxious, adrenalin-bursting heart imagined, and BLAM-BLAM-BLAM! BLAM-BLAM! Even as he fired he became aware of hot, ejected shells from Sammy's Mini-Uzi pinging against his hands, and Sammy Hubbard was suddenly a mess of hair and bramble jelly, because every one of Elmore's five rapid shots had hit him in the head and he just kinda sat there for a moment. Stone-dead.

BOOM! Tagliatelli or whatever his fuckin' name was was crouched in a classic two-handed stance, and whatever he was holding, its noise deafened everybody and plaster sprayed out from the dingy wall – Elmore was so hyped, like in an auto accident, things were happening like it was all underwater, in slow motion. The pieces of plaster were individually recognizable – oh, SHIT!

Trupiano had swung just a tab to his left, and Jake could actually see the copper bullet glinting down the barrel of what had to be a .44 magnum revolver. As the next BOOM! happened Elmore dived at Harry Cardona and the two men crashed against the wall, Elmore's left arm locked around the hoodlum's neck, using Cardona's body as a shield.

Trupiano's .44 followed, so that Elmore was still looking at the muzzle and yet another horrible copper slug deep inside.

But Elmore Williams was calm now. This was what he did for a goddam living. Ducking behind Cardona's head, which smelled of hair and some kinda cheap gel, and of sweat, he checked out Reynolds, who was slumped in the corner, protruding from behind a desk, his blood seeping on to the cheap linoleum in broad swathes, where he had slithered down the wall like in a Tom and Jerry cartoon. But his eyes were watching the action and he was trying to reach his shoulder-holster with his good left hand.

Okay. This was it.

Elmore took a deep breath and yelled out, real loud but with a certain cold authority, 'Federal agent! Federal agent! Hold your fire!'

'Federal agent my ass, drop the piece, asshole!' Trupiano was still trying hard to get a bead on Elmore, intent on slamming that copper slug right into him.

'Tony di Corvo!' yelled Elmore. 'Tony di Corvo and Frank Clancy! Jack of Hearts, for fuck's sake, Jack of fuckin' Hearts . . .!'

Now this certainly stopped events in their tracks. For Trupiano and Reynolds were in fact Special Agents Tony di Corvo and Frank Clancy of the US Secret Service's New York Field Office, engaged on an operation to trap those three counterfeiters. And naturally they were momentarily thrown when one of the wiseguys started calling out their real names, and the codename for the operation, which was Jack of Hearts.

Elmore took a deep breath, said a prayer to whoever looked after undercover agents investigating other undercover agents, and holding his 9-mm piece up, open-handed, he dropped it on to the floor beside the couch where, bizarrely, Sammy the Nose had failed to topple over, like they do in the movies, so he was just sitting there, Mini-Uzi resting almost primly across his knee. Only what was left of his head was like a scene from *Nightmare on Elm Street*.

Trupiano kept the piece trained on Elmore and Harry Cardona, clearly not a trusting soul.

Elmore kept a tight grip on the struggling Cardona. 'This is no kidding, gentlemen. My name is Elmore Williams. United States Secret Service, just like yourselves.

Your codename for this is Jack of Hearts, am I right or what . . .?'

'Fuck you, pal!' gasped Harry Cardona, realizing maybe he had made a mistake to believe Elmore's story about being a failed cop.

'And fuck you sideways, greaseball.' Elmore kept Cardona in a necklock.

'You have ID?' Trupiano was cool as ice. Very definitely the man in control. From the floor above, sounds of feet and doors opening. That must have been where they had been taping and recording the bust the two New York agents were engaged on. When the bullets started.

'Inside my sock.'

Silence.

Trupiano was in no hurry to give up the high ground, or allow Elmore to make even the slightest move. It was Special Agent Frank Clancy, who had called himself O'Dowd, bleeding badly on the floor, who resolved matters. Even as footsteps clattered on the stairs to the landing on the fifth floor.

'Who's SAIC in Seattle . . .?' he grunted. SAIC meant Special Agent in Charge.

'Tom Harrison,' replied Elmore.

'What was his last job?'

'New Orleans. Deputy to Bobby Delaware. Bobby has a daughter called Ginny who has just passed outa Training.'

'No kidding? What's her first assignment?' Clancy, badly wounded, seemed actually to be interested. Maybe it was shock.

'I can't tell you that.'

The traffic outside was hotting up. Car horns sounded angrier. It must be getting near five, thought Elmore. Trupiano nodded, slowly. He eased the hammer down on his Colt 44, his hostility, if anything, more lethal than before. Elmore realized his shirt was wet with sweat, front, back, and sleeves.

'Just who the fuck are you?' asked Trupiano.

'Elmore Williams,' Elmore repeated, and Harry Cardona

twitched with anger. 'Dee-Sac. Office of Inspections.' Dee-Sac meant Deputy Special Agent in Charge.

'Well, that's just dandy.' Trupiano stepped forward, reached out for Harry Cardona and yanked him free from Williams' grip, which was freely surrendered.

Trupiano dropped a set of handcuffs on the floor. 'Okay, Elmore, do the honours . . .'

Williams knelt and jerked Cardona's wrists behind his back, expertly handcuffing them together. He got to his feet, ignoring the revolver still held ready in Trupiano's right hand, and opened his ID wallet, which he had retrieved from his ankle while kneeling.

'There you go. No hard feelings . . .'

'Fuck you,' replied Trupiano.

Now all this confusion was because an undercover operation, a 'sting', by the New York Field Office of the US Secret Service, had gone bad, and one of the three wiseguys had turned out to be another undercover agent, working out of Washington and – no two ways about it – trespassing on their patch which was in violation of the Service's rules of procedure and discipline.

The United States Secret Service was a division of the US Treasury. Its task was to protect the President's life and safeguard the American dollar from counterfeiting, forgery or fraud. It was divided into Field Offices around the United States, and had attachés working out of embassies abroad. Its Office of Inspections was like Internal Affairs to a police department and its personnel were tasked with probing the efficiency and honesty of individual Special Agents and entire Field Offices, sometimes routinely and sometimes as the result of information received.

It was not the most popular assignment in law enforcement.

Trupiano took the ID wallet from Williams and made a point of checking its authenticity. Then he threw it back, just as the door to the outer waiting room burst open and a number of New York Field Office agents came in fast,

Glock 9 mm automatic pistols and Ingram Mac-10 machine-pistols at the ready. They wore flak jackets with FEDERAL AGENT on the front and back.

First in was Joe Pearce, a big, burly man in his early fifties, his sandy hair and Celtic face the hallmark of so many men in US law enforcement. He stared hard at Williams, then shook his head. Life was still full of surprises.

'Fuckin' Elmore . . .'

'Hi, Joe,' said Williams. He had always known that this awkward moment was inevitable, from the start of a decision he had made the previous night, to accompany Sammy and Harry to New York.

'I saw you on the screen. Fuckin' Elmore, I said to myself. It can't be . . .' Joe Pearce glanced around, noting that Trupiano was calling in medical aid, while two trained agents attended to the wounded man on the floor.

'Frank, what's the damage?' Pearce covered his concern with gruffness, bending over Clancy.

'Fuckin' arm, chief. Coupla slugs.'

'Wearing a vest?'

'Sure, I'll be bruised but the arm's broken. Maybe now I'll get some time off.'

'Bullshit,' replied Pearce. 'You can work in the office like the rest of the walking wounded.'

Joe Pearce turned to study the grotesque corpse of Sammy the Nose. 'Jesus and the little star of Bethlehem, you sure as hell took a dislike to this fellow's physog . . . and you know what? You've shot off the poor man's nose.'

'Maybe they never sewed it on right in the first place,' remarked one of the agents, and everyone in the room started to laugh grimly, just to show they were not fazed by this half-headless monster on the couch. Everyone except Harry Cardona, and Elmore Williams, who understood he had no right to be there amongst this group of trusted companions.

And at this point drama cooled. There is a routine to be

followed when Federal agents (which is to say, not just the FBI, but agents of any government law enforcement division) become involved in violent death, that immediately and automatically becomes the responsibility of the local police Homicide Department. In this case, operating out of the 14th Precinct, which is to say, Midtown South, in Manhattan.

Elmore Williams, being the Secret Service agent who had killed Sammy the Nose Hubbard, had already surrendered his weapon, which was correct procedure.

The first person on the scene was the Crime Scene Supervisor from the 14th – a Sergeant of Detectives, name of Eugene Wharton. He was soon joined by a doctor who had a mild aroma of Kentucky sour-mash bourbon on his breath. Dr Henry Grace.

Williams failed to recognize Grace but Grace remembered him.

'Why, Tennessee,' he remarked, stooping slightly and peering at the deceased as if it were a sculpture in the Museum of Modern Art, 'what in heck are you doing here . . .?'

The other Secret Service men stopped what they were doing and turned to stare at Elmore Williams and their gaze was not at all friendly.

'That's what we used to call him,' explained Grace. 'Tennessee was with Narcotics, in the 14th. This very precinct. What, ten years ago . . .?'

Williams became aware of the hostility in that room.

'Tennessee . . .' said Joe Pearce, softly.

'Williams, you see. After the playwright.' The doctor tugged a pair of steel-rimmed glasses from his top pocket, the frame askew, and fixed them on.

'Tennessee Williams . . .'

'Just so.' Dr Henry Grace stooped even lower and gazed with professional interest at that bloody part of Samuel L. Hubbard where his nasal organ had been.

'This man lost his nose once before,' he mused, to nobody in particular. 'Sure. The other Tennessee Williams, we used to call him. Boy oh boy. Of course, that was in the days when I had a sense of humour . . .'

The New York agents exchanged cold glances, ignoring Elmore, and went back to work.

Joe Pearce put a fatherly arm on his elbow and steered Williams through to the outer office. An ambulance team had by then removed the wounded agent, Frank Clancy.

'Get outa here,' Pearce remarked benevolently to a couple of agents in the room. Then he closed both doors and sat on top of the reception desk. He nodded to a couch. 'Take the weight off . . .'

Williams flopped down and realized he was completely drained of energy. And his hands were trembling.

'You want something? Coffee? Something stronger?'

'In good time, Joe. Say what you have to say.'

Joe Pearce scratched his big, sandy-haired Irish head. 'Elmore, I gotta tell you, what is the procedure here? If you were an agent of mine, I would have to suspend you, temporarily, you know the score. Pending the outcome of an investigation into the homicide through there. But you are not an agent of mine. As a matter of fact, nobody in NY Field Office even knew you were in town, much less working deep with Harry Cardona.'

He paused and drummed his fingers on the desk he was sitting on. Despite his amiable self-control, it was obvious that the Special Agent in charge of the US Secret Service's New York Field Office was hog-tie mad at Williams' transgression.

'Joe, number one, this is your town . . .'

'Why, thank you, Elmore.' Pearce did not try to keep the sarcasm from his voice.

'So you should go ahead and recommend my suspension to Washington. Sid Longstreet's Assistant Director, Office of Inspections, these days.'

'No kidding? Well, I must confess I did not know that. You know why? Because I am happy to say that my Field Office has never suffered an internal investigation. Not in my time.'

The two men stared at each other. It was times like these Elmore Williams wished devoutly he had been given another assignment.

'You recommend my suspension, Joe. And I'll cooperate with NYPD, make a statement. There are two – correction, three – witnesses. Counting Harry Cardona. And like, take it from there.'

'Then, Elmore,' Pearce went on, ignoring all that, 'we have the problem of internal discipline. So now I am required to ask you, are you working here in New York officially, or unofficially? If it's not official – say you got so closely involved with the case you were working in deep cover, you had no time to go through the proper channels and info my Field Office of your presence – okay, I guess we could cover for you. After all, you did probably save my two agents' lives.'

Williams reached into his jacket and tugged out a pack of Camel Filters, trying to keep his hand steady. The adrenalin rush had wrecked his system, in the short term at least. He let Pearce light the cigarette for him, with a Zippo presented by the President himself, and inhaled deeply.

As the smoke drifted out, Elmore Williams met the big Irishman's gaze. 'Joe, I'm real sorry. This is official. It's an investigation I started some weeks back.

The big, honest, reliable Joe Pearce looked winded. Pole-axed was the expression that came to Williams' mind.

'Joe, what can I say, man? Goddam job . . . I had planned full team cover from outa town.' He shrugged. 'Then last night, Atlantic City, ten before midnight. Things changed.'

'The way they do.' Pearce did not take his eyes off Williams.

'Sure. Like that. They advanced the deal by three days. I chose to info DC and stay on the case.'

This was a severe blow to everything Joe Pearce thought he had going right in his domain. After a long silence he asked, 'Is this routine? A kind of routine thing?'

'I can't discuss it.' Elmore knew he had received no authority to attend the funny money deal on his own. It was an absolute rule that no undercover agent, and certainly not one from the whiter-than-white Office of Inspections, would work that close to danger (and temptation) without back-up.

But Joe Pearce was more concerned about his own team's reputation. 'Okay. Is it . . . ? Uh, aw, shit. Is it . . . procedure, some failings of procedure? Or,' Pearce forced himself to say the words, 'is it graft?'

'Gimme a break, Joe. Please.'

'And have you come to a conclusion?'

'Yessir, I have . . .'

And by rights, Elmore Williams was obliged to say not another word on the subject, until he had filed a report to his boss in Washington.

'Is it a bad result? Is it bad news for us here?'

A clock ticked on a cheap table beside the desk. Joe Pearce looked so forlorn. And Elmore Williams had already concluded, over the past few weeks, that the Field Office was clean, that the information against it had been wrong, or worse. So he studied the smoke rising from his cigarette and met Pearce's anxious gaze.

Without saying a word, the investigating agent from Washington lifted his right thumb from a clenched fist. And smiled.

Joe Pearce let out a long sigh of relief.

'Gimme one of them cigarettes,' he said.

'Sure.' Williams grinned and passed the pack. 'When did you quit?'

'Nineteen seventy-five,' replied the big man, and he brushed an arm over his forehead, wiping off cold sweat.

5

Salim Jaddeh

DAVID JARDINE HAD listened carefully to Hassan Abdul-Latif Rashdan as the youth told him what he knew about Salim Jaddeh. Or what he was prepared to tell, to be more accurate. For information is currency. It should not all be spent at once.

Customers in Le Camel café came and went, each one noted and evaluated by the Englishman. And as he listened, it did not leave his mind for a moment that Hassan might have led him into a trap.

Two women came in, carefree and elegant, behaving as if the Beirut outside was the same. And of course it had been, in the days before the madness had destroyed a city that for centuries was the cultural, economic and military link between South-east Europe and Asia on the one hand, and Egypt, Arabia and Africa on the other.

Jardine remembered a Beirut of souks and cafés, museums and sophisticated restaurants, a bustling seaport with stunning architecture reflecting influences from the ornate Byzantine and Moorish to the languid military elegance of the French colonial. With dashes of New York and Beverly Hills glitz liberally scattered in between.

And the most wonderful women in any of the aforementioned continents.

He did not know who was the one with the Hermès

headscarf and the dark blue leather Gucci shoulder-bag. But as the two new arrivals found a table and sat down, he was relieved that the other elegant, olive-skinned girl, aged about twenty-five, had her back to him. For she was – he couldn't remember her name – the daughter of a one-time waiter at a marvellous little restaurant in Souk Tawileh. Blasted to rubble by Phalangist shelling. Jardine struggled to remember what it had been called. Something beginning with 'A' . . . Al Ajami, that was it. And now here she was, a survivor of the constant and appalling dangers and dressed by some expensive designer. She has the unmistakable bearing of somebody who was in with somebody who could look after her, in Beirut. And that took some looking after. Some clout.

Maybe her father, that pleasant waiter with the sincere smile and tired eyes, who would be about fifty now, had survived the hideous waves of mayhem and torture and had emerged as a man to be reckoned with.

Or, of course, she could have acquired a lover. A member of one of the several clan families who continued to rule parts of the city and the Lebanon's fertile coastal region like feudal warlords. She had been only fourteen or fifteen when David Jardine had been SIS Head of Station in Beirut and she had helped in the restaurant, clearing tables and adding up the checks.

And if he remembered her, so changed as she now was, there was no reason why she might not remember him. And that would have been problematical, because at that time Jardine had used the workname Jeffries, and he was accredited to a British bank, doing business with the many Lebanese banks who not only had continued to trade throughout the entire rape and evisceration of the nation, but who had actually raised the value of Lebanon's currency by 40 per cent.

'So that is who he is, *'fendi* . . . In the name of God, who is merciful, that is exactly all I know.'

David Jardine knew that Hassan was using the Arab word *'fendi* (short for *effendi*, meaning master) because of the recent unpleasantness when Jardine had not only prevented the boy from killing him, but helped repair the kid's damaged face and treated the event as nothing more than a fairly routine occurrence.

'Thank you for telling me,' he said gravely, raising a palm to stop the waiter from putting down yet more thick Arab coffee. Three cups were more than enough for him.

He sipped from a glass of iced water and listened to the strains of an Algerian singer on the jukebox. It was a male voice singing in French, 'If you don't want me, that's fine by me . . .' And for some reason, he found himself thinking, as he had been constantly, about the missing Alisha. Pomegranate.

Hassan had told him that Salim Jaddeh was a cold man, with cruel eyes and the mouth of a torturer. Nothing that might stand up in a court of law, mused David Jardine, but coming from an eighteen-year-old youth, who himself had the eyes of a man of forty, who had seen his mother and sister raped and mutilated by the heroes of the PLO, and his father and brothers murdered by the brave men of the Christian Phalange . . . this Salim Jaddeh must have something, to have made such an impression.

Hassan had also told him that Alisha seemed uncomfortable in the man's presence. As if, although they had lunched together, and had gone to clear out the apartment of a friend of hers, and had sat up listening to jazz records in her apartment (Jardine just knew, without anything being said, that Hassan had probably been standing very near them – if not actually in the next room, then certainly nearby), and although they seemed to be getting closer, in a non-romantic way, there was something about him that . . . well, frightened her.

Jardine put down the tumbler and tugged out his pack of freshly acquired Winston cigarettes, then automatically put it away. He was trying to limit himself to three a day.

'You followed him, didn't you?'

After a moment, the youth nodded.

'So where did he go?'

Hassan knew he was in possession of good information. The entrepreneur in him made him reluctant to share it without some benefit. But David Jardine's profession was the acquisition of protected information, by whatever means seemed to be appropriate.

'Listen, Hassan. How would you like to work for me? Just for a day or two?' Jardine slipped into gear, his reaction intuitive, like a whore's at the rustle of a 100-dollar bill.

'Doing what, *sidi*?'

'Keep an eye on her place. Let me know who comes and goes. Check out if Jaddeh is still at his office . . .'

'But you don't know where it is . . .' Hassan was nobody's fool.

David Jardine smiled. This boy showed promise.

'But you do,' he replied. And placed four 100-dollar bills on the table.

It was 9.18 a.m. in the East Caribbean, and Danny Davidov was at Antigua International Airport, waiting patiently amidst the state of perpetual chaos to purchase two return tickets on the 10.45 British Airways flight to London Heathrow. He would be paying cash, US dollars, and he had no intention of either himself, or Nikolai Kolosov, using the return halves. But experience had taught him that no opportunity to confuse the opposition should be missed.

As he watched two local families sort out their various offspring and untidy baggage, creating an impassable obstacle between himself and the ticket desk, two tall policemen in immaculately pressed, pale mud-coloured uniforms, with black peaked caps, sauntered among the teeming passengers.

Outside, a propeller-driven LIAT aircraft roared down the runway, aiming for the sky. A bit like myself, ruminated the Israeli. And for the thousandth time, wondered why he was continuing with this odyssey. Surely he had proved his point? He had enjoyed the eight capers he and the

Russian had pulled off without a hitch. He had millions, but then he had started this game with quite a few millions – but that was another story – and a feeling of outrage at the system and, in particular, at Mossad. But the pain had eased. The sheer . . . disbelief that his own people could have banished him, casting him out into the Diaspora, that had passed.

Almost.

No, it bloody well had not. The memory of his last meeting with the Memouneh, the Chief of Mossad, and Avriam Eitels, at that time Director of Security, rose crystal-clear in his consciousness, and suddenly he felt the outrage all over again. The only Sabra, to his definite knowledge, ever to have been kicked out of Israel and warned, on pain of death, never to return, and never to use his own name, the name he had been born with, in Tel Aviv, forty-three years before.

Danny Davidov realized he was actually blushing with the shame of that recollection. By God, he would teach them. And to think that, just a few seconds before, he had almost gone soft.

'Excuse me,' he said to the disorganized families between himself and the ticket desk, 'but some of us have planes to catch.' And he pushed his way through.

Finding out why Hassan wanted to kill Salim Jaddeh had been tougher than David Jardine had anticipated. But in the course of eighty-seven minutes in Le Camel, his not inconsiderable skills as an oblique, patient and quietly relentless interrogator had led him to divine that the boy had identified Jaddeh as one of two men who had visited his father and older brothers, six years previously, at the family apartment in the shattered Rue Georges Picot – and who had quietly and urgently explained to them why the editor of a certain Beirut daily newspaper should be murdered.

Hassan's family, the Rashdani, were Druze Moslems. The Druze were among the most stable and, at the same time, the most feared of the players in the Lebanon's macabre dance of death. The two most powerful factions, or clan families, were the so-called 'socialist' Druze, led by Wahlid Jumblatt (they were probably less left-wing than the average US Democrat), and the 'conservatives', led by the Arselan clan.

The two men who had called late one night had letters from Karim Jumblatt, commander of Druze militia intelligence operations, authorizing them to issue orders on his behalf. It was a time of secret meetings and passwords, coded, clandestine letters of introduction and routine killings – some random, by long-range artillery; some careless, by car bombs; and others quite specific, by targeted assassination.

Young Hassan, aged eight, had been asleep on a couch in the next room. He had heard enough to know that his oldest brother was to kill some newspaper editor, for reasons of politics that were beyond him. But on specific orders from a senior and respected Druze militia leader.

His father had been particularly perturbed, and had questioned them over and over, asking precisely why somebody so clearly honourable, and with the Lebanon's best interests at heart, had to die.

Then voices had been lowered, and strain as he might, he could not make out the words. But there was no mistaking the smooth reason with which the man he now knew to be Salim Jaddeh had countered his father's protests.

The two secret visitors had left. One week later, Youssef Abdul-Fetteh, newspaper editor and father of Alisha, had been shot dead as he strolled from a game of squash at the Laban Squash Court, near the bomb-blasted shell of the Fakhoury Pharmacy.

The consequences of that act had already been recounted to Jardine. The axiomatic revenge visited on his father and brothers by the murdered man's family and supporters, and the saving of Hassan by the editor's own daughter, Alisha. Pomegranate.

Now, if none of this seemed good enough reason for Hassan Abdul-Latif Rashdan to want to kill the messenger, the Druze persuader who was now up to some business with Alisha, who seemed afraid of him, the clincher was that when Hassan had confronted Karim Jumblatt with the accusation that his orders to kill that newspaper editor had decimated Hassan's family, Karim had sworn on the Koran that, far from wishing the man dead, he had admired his fearless editorials and had issued orders that he was not to be harmed. Even when his skilful arguments came down hard on the Druze, who were no more safe from his pen than anyone else in the orgy of self-destruction that passed for civil war in Beirut.

So, if Hassan was to be believed, Salim Jaddeh had been an *agent provocateur*, posing as a secret agent of the socialist Druze. With perfectly forged letters of credence and equipped with all the correct passwords and code-phrases. Just one more of the everyday occurrences in the excitement of the times. His aim? To cause confusion and bloody conflict between former allies.

Not badly accomplished, mused David Jardine, thinking as a professional. The 64,000-dollar question now was, who the hell is Salim Jaddeh, and who does he really work for?

Jardine paid his check and told the boy to leave and go about the business he had been paid 400 dollars for.

Hassan had understood when Jardine had explained it would be better if Jaddeh was permitted to live a while yet. So that together they might both learn who he was. And who he worked for, thus possibly enabling them to damage the organ-grinder rather than the monkey.

Of course David Jardine had not the slightest interest in furthering the youth's vow of vengeance, but he would cross that bridge when he came to it. The business of running a Joe, as poor Hassan Rashdan had become – that is to say, a paid agent of Jardine, and therefore, unwittingly, of SIS – involved allowing them to know only the very minimum that was required for them to function efficiently.

Jardine, whose wounded abdomen was by now causing him considerable pain, had prepared himself for a half-hour education of his latest recruit into the business of clandestine communication, dead drops, brush contacts, five-second phone calls from one pay-phone to another, and so on.

But he had not reckoned on the streetwise Hassan, who already knew so much that Jardine's instructions not to communicate but to make himself available at specific times and in specific locations, for a few brief minutes over the next forty-eight hours, and the other stuff of an agent's work, were assimilated and understood in under five minutes.

David Jardine waited a while, then casually strolled to the men's room. On emerging, he turned left to go through the store-room and out into the Rue Wadi Sabra, where a truck was unloading cartons of fresh vegetables and rice on to the sidewalk.

For a moment he wondered if he was hallucinating, for out of an alley, a souk, flanked by the shells, the cadavers of buildings where God knew what horrors had transpired over the last eighteen years, appeared four immaculately groomed and tacked thoroughbred racehorses, and on each one sat a jockey in full racing livery, complete with a satin blouse of brilliant crimson, sky-blue, yellow and white or apple-green. With a jockey's cap of matching colour.

The horses clip-clopped sedately out of the souk and along the street, heading in no particular hurry for the Corniche Mazraa.

A ragged beggar limping along in front of him did not deign to notice this surreal vision, and David Jardine shook his head. Jesus, this town. It was a lesson in survival.

The sun was hot and bright, and as he walked under a red and white awning, the shuffling beggar turned round and, with a grin that revealed surprisingly clean and healthy teeth, raised his grubby burnous, his shawl, to reveal a silenced Czech Skorpion 7.65-mm machine-pistol.

'Good day to you, Mr Jardine. I am Salim Jaddeh, perhaps you have heard of me . . .'

And the muzzle of something metal and indubitably life-threatening pressed hard into Jardine's back. The BMW 750, which had whispered to a stop alongside a parked Fiat van, was attracting outraged hooting from the traffic behind. Its rear door opened, revealing another armed man inside.

'Please hurry,' said the beggar, 'I'm double-parked . . .'

The BMW was driven by a lean, tanned young man with a wispy, jet-black beard and hard eyes that missed nothing. He wore a white shirt, well laundered but with no collar, black trousers and a stainless-steel Rolex. The butt of a .45 Colt automatic protruded from his belt, on his left side.

In the back, beside Jardine, was an older man, thicker-set, with grey, close-cropped hair and wearing a dark grey linen jacket over a white shirt, again with no necktie. He wore a heavy gold signet ring on the third finger of his right hand. Across his lap rested a Polish AKS assault rifle with no stock, just a pistol grip, the muzzle pointing impersonally in the direction of David Jardine.

As the car moved through the Place Dunant and headed east along the Rue Beni Marouf, Salim Jaddeh shrugged off his ragged burnous and unwrapped the filthy kaffieh from his head. He picked up a tan polo shirt from the floor and pulled it on, smoothing his hair flat again. Jardine noted that he was in his mid-forties, with not a trace of fat on his torso or neck. His face had the lean, smooth skin of a man who worked hard at staying in shape. Perhaps Hassan had been lucky not to have confronted him, even armed with a Bowie knife.

Jardine winced as the knife wound jabbed at his abdomen. He watched the streets pass and, not for the first time, wondered at the sheer resilience of this shattered city's inhabitants, of all religions and political allegiances. For reconstruction was under way here on a major scale, and fresh concrete multi-storey office blocks and hotels were rising out of the rubble. It was as if someone had superimposed a holograph of Manhattan on the ruins of post-war Berlin.

He felt, perhaps bizarrely, relaxed and composed, except for the discomfort of the knife's gash. It was not the first time he had been in a carload of armed strangers, and it would probably not be the last. He wondered if such an attitude was not irresponsible, and realized just how out of things he had become during his months on that bloody committee.

Nobody spoke. And as the driver turned south on Bechara el Khoury, then east again, heading for the shell- and bullet-pocked Place du Musée and the Green Line, David Jardine was not inclined to utter a word.

In a way, the four men were more comfortable in each other's company than they would have been in a bus or a plane. For they were four of a kind. Four operators in the business of espionage. At the sharp end.

Once over the Green Line and in that part of Beirut which was ruled by the Phalange, the BMW drove on through the suburbs of the damaged city and thirty-five minutes later was climbing along winding roads, through woods of pines and cedars, into the Metn Hills. Then through Brummana, where before the madness there used to be truly splendid international tennis tournaments, and on for another nine kilometres to a quiet and idyllic little town called Dhouer El-chouer.

Two kilometres beyond the town, approached by a narrow track through the pines, was a cluster of villas, each with its own high wall and security cameras. This was typical of the mountain retreats where the bankers and the power-brokers of Lebanon had their lairs.

The BMW swept into one such property and the iron and wood gates slid shut behind it. With quiet authority, Jaddeh told the driver he would not be required until later. They spoke educated Arabic in the accents of Cairo.

'Please get out, Mr Jardine,' said Salim Jaddeh, in mildly accented English. 'I hope you enjoy surprises . . .'

The villa was spacious, with thick walls and polished wood floors, scattered with many rugs, in the traditional style of the region. The walls were mostly white and the furniture was of cedar wood and soft leather. Antique maps and oil paintings of the village of Dhouer El-chouer, of the Metn region with its ravines and pine groves, and of various coastal towns around Junieh and Beirut, along with a collection of prayer mats and camel rugs, hung on the walls.

The general impression David Jardine had was of good taste and a degree of learning. For in addition to the works of art there were books on the region, and on the history of the Lebanon, in Arabic, French and English, as well as collections of literature and poetry going back to Phoenician times.

There were no clocks, however, and no photographs. So whether this was merely an expensive and well-chosen safe house, or someone's home, was not immediately apparent. Jardine recalled Pomegranate's signal to him at the Office's Washington Station, when she had mentioned that SJ – Salim Jaddeh – was living in a house lent to him by the Egyptian Embassy. But that had been in Junieh, a coastal town, far from this hideaway in the hills.

He ignored the man with the AKS rifle who sat by the teak-framed door. From another room, he could hear Jaddeh's voice, maybe speaking on the phone. It had a calm air of authority about it.

A slender woman in her forties entered and placed a tray with a silver and glass flask of sweet mint tea on a low table beside him. She inclined her head and left, backing towards the door.

Well, if this is me kidnapped, mused Jardine, it's not too disagreeable . . . Yet.

And still he did not feel any serious degree of apprehension. What's wrong with me? he wondered. Why is this more interesting than anything that's happened in the last four months? I mean, who is this man Jaddeh, who arranged the death of Alisha's father? Of my agent's father. And by so doing, knew that the killers themselves would be wiped out. Who was able to pass himself off most convincingly to seriously suspicious Druze underground fighters.

And was Pomegranate, Alisha Abdul-Fetteh, not aware that this was the very man who had brought about her own father's murder? And if she had been, surely she would have mentioned that in her signal. The signal which had persuaded David Jardine to fly at once from the meeting of J-WISC in Washington to Beirut, and into a world of violence, betrayal and double-cross.

'I am so sorry to have kept you waiting, Mr Jardine . . .' Salim Jaddeh had changed into a pair of comfortable old grey trousers and a faded blue cotton shirt. On his feet were a pair of ancient slippers. He padded across the room and curled up on a couch under a Shi'ite prayer rug hanging on the white wall.

And as he did so, the man with the AKS rose and left the room, quietly pulling the two carved wood doors shut behind him.

The aroma of sweet mint tea haunted David Jardine. And he realized he badly needed its refreshing wetness, its warmth, its quintessentially . . . Arabian sweetness.

Jaddeh observed him for a moment, composed, relaxed and with just a hint of friendly amusement. Who did he remind Jardine of so strongly? The Englishman was very tired. It had been one hell of a day. And outside it was only just getting dark.

'Look, please forgive me. But I'm going to call you David. Is that okay . . .?'

David Jardine gazed coldly at his abductor, his face devoid of expression. He had no intention of playing this man's game, whatever it was. Salim Jaddeh raised his shoulders a fraction. As if to say, how tedious. But the look in his eyes suggested, we'll see . . .

Jardine inclined his head, and leaning forward, the pain from his wound searing across his left side, poured a small cupful of mint tea with a steady hand. So you're still a tough old bastard, he thought to himself.

'Well, David, let me play you something. It's a tape-recording and you have, I believe, a right to hear it.'

Jaddeh reached for a remote wand and pointed it at the jet-black and silver Bang & Olufson sound system nestling in a carved set of shelves.

The voice was unmistakable. And David Jardine immediately knew why his abductor had asked if he enjoyed surprises.

For the voice was that of Steven McCrae, his boss. Sir Steven. Director-General of Her Majesty's Secret Intelligence Service. And he was clearly talking in the belief that his conversation was secure. The slight tinniness of the too-clear recording indicated to Jardine that it had been obtained by microwave, low-frequency, electronic eavesdropping.

'David . . .?' McCrae was saying. 'I really don't see any future for David in the new order of things. I mean, he *was* screwing the man's wife.'

'You're not suggesting,' this was the voice of Tim Lewin, the firm's Director of Personnel, '*that* persuaded him to send her husband on Corrida . . .?'

Operation Corrida had been the most appalling experience of David Jardine's life. He had fallen in love with the wife of an officer in Britain's SAS, who had been persuaded to resign his commission and take on a contract job for the Firm. The job had been to infiltrate Pablo Escobar's Colombian cocaine cartel.

Harry Ford, the officer concerned, had performed brilliantly. Half-Argentinian, bilingual South American Spanish, he had succeeded in getting himself recruited by Pablo, and as a result of saving the drug baron's life in a bloody ambush, had found himself appointed security boss of El Grupo, as the cartel was known in Colombia.

Sadly, the boy had then become corrupted. And David Jardine had flown out to Bogota to resolve the situation.

'You bastard! You wanton whore . . .! That was my *wife*!' Even in this mountain lair in the hills above Beirut, Jardine could not rid himself of the memory of that awful day. In a graveyard in Bogota. Four thousand, eight hundred miles to the west. At times, it seemed about 4000 years ago. And sometimes, just yesterday.

He betrayed no emotion as Salim Jaddeh, relaxed and very much in control of the situation, watched his every movement.

'Let's not go over the Corrida business again.' Steven McCrae's urbane, corridors-of-power voice. Jardine could just see him, probably in his office on the Top Floor at Century House. Not the absolute top floor, which had the penthouse and all kinds of electronic and communications gadgetry. The Top Floor, with the boss's office, was in fact the floor below that.

Steven had rejected advice from the Office's Counter-Surveillance Section to move his rooms into the windowless centre of the Great Glass Box, eighteen floors high, at St George's Circus in south London. The building had been designed by a long-forgotten fifties architect presumably out to make some kind of idiosyncratic statement.

If he had moved the offices of C, as the Chief of SIS was termed, into the heart of the building, he would have surrendered a fairly impressive view over the rooftops of Lambeth towards Big Ben, Whitehall and the Houses of Parliament. And that would never do. For Steven McCrae was very much aware of the importance of an agreeable and harmonious space in which to work. After all, he had been Head of Station in Hong Kong, and he had been made aware of such things, even to the extent of the precise location of his desk, his potted ficus trees, his framed photographs and the chairs for his guests.

This abstract science was called *fung shaou* in Cantonese, and there were many cases where hardened, practical round-eyes had found complete changes of fortune by calling in the services of a *fung shaou* man.

Thus Sir Steven had insisted on keeping his office with its splendid and harmonious view. And, in the process, had failed to avoid being eavesdropped upon by sophisticated, expensive, microwave, low-frequency listening devices. Devices which the Office's own technical wizards, working with the best brains of the Government Communications Headquarters from their London base in the Post Office Tower, had gone to equally sophisticated and expensive pains to render useless.

David Jardine was not really surprised.

'I accept that David has been a considerable . . . asset to the Office. Over the years.' God, McCrae could be a pompous ass when he put his mind to it.

'Whatever he was up to with the man's wife, Steven, he certainly pulled Corrida out of the fire. The way he placed his back-up operator into the heart of the cartel was, um . . .'

'Brilliant. Absolutcly. No, no, I quite agree.'

There followed a silence during which – Jardine knew from similar conversations with the Chief – Steven McCrae was waiting to see how big a pit Tim Lewin would dig for himself. In his defence of David Arbuthnot Jardine, CMG.

Jaddeh met his gaze, reading his thoughts, it seemed, and once again raised his shoulders. This time as if to say, it's the same the world over, believe me.

'In fact of course, Steven, the decision was made, you said at the time . . .' Sound of a chair scraping. A glass being filled. It would be Buchanan's. McCrae made a big thing about not having any time for those malt concoctions. In fact, his sister had married into a whisky distillery dynasty and Jardine knew he received Buchanan's by the case, two or three times a year. Lewin's voice went on, '. . . in order to lift David up a rung. So that he might eventually be able to see the view from the bridge. That's the way you put it. I do seem to recall.'

Well, well. Tim was actually fighting Jardine's corner.

'Did I say that? My word. A nautical metaphor.'

Nautical my arse, you illiterate twerp. Arthur Miller wrote *A View from the Bridge*, what *did* they teach you at Cambridge? Ah, yes. The Peloponnesian Wars. What else?

'A view from the bridge, eh?' McCrae's slightly tinny voice went on. 'Well, we'll see. Let's not make a federal case out of it, Tim. I did not say I was not open to alternatives.'

Silence.

David Jardine sipped his mint tea. His side felt as if it had been kicked by a horse.

'I just feel he's, um . . .' This was Lewin.

'Wasted . . .?'

'On J-WISC.'

'Wasted, Timothy? Or perhaps not giving it the full shilling.' This last was a statement and of course Jardine knew, guiltily, that Steven McCrae was right. The whole business of J-WISC was not an enterprise for serious men, for serious, top-echelon intelligence executives. But even those tasks which bored one to tears (this was the teaching of Alice Hanson, a sixty-year-old and divine heroine from Infiltration and Pipelines, who had taught a twenty-eight-year-old David Jardine how to become a spy, how to think like one), even those required one to deliver, to concentrate, to participate. Alice's words. She had died of a fall while walking near Gornergrat, on the Matterhorn, only four years ago. Aged seventy-nine. Her little satchel of sandwiches, beer, sketching pad, brushes and paints, spilled out across the edelweiss. It was the way she would have wanted to go, thought Jardine. And even in his present, quite urgent predicament, he still felt the old lump in his throat when he remembered Alice.

'I just feel we owe him. The man is the best agent-runner in the business. If you'll forgive me for saying so, Chief, I can't really imagine why you gave him J-WISC. It would have been ideal for young Kate Howard. You're always saying we should skip a generation and give the young blood a chance.'

'She's going to replace Alan Prendergast.'

Jesus Christ on a one-wheeled bike. Alan Prendergast ran the SIS Security Section. The school prefects. It was not an ideal career move for a serious Operations Officer – in fact, a bit like J-WISC, in a more minor key – but young Kate had entered the Firm from Oxford and, with a ruthless dedication worthy of Machiavelli himself, had clambered into the most important (and most highly secret) job in Personnel, helping to select 'black' operators, before landing a choice job in the Operations Section of the Office's London Station. Admittedly it was only arranging the security and protection of safe houses, and the welfare of debriefed defectors who had chosen to settle in the UK, but Jardine had no doubt that by this time Kate would have made that fairly menial job into something mysterious and seriously meaningful.

And now Security. It was an Assistant Director's job. Equivalent in rank to an army colonel. And Kate Howard could not be a day more than thirty-one.

David Jardine found himself raising his shoulders. And as his eyes met Salim Jaddeh's, he smiled, ruefully.

'So you finally decided to communicate . . .' said Jaddeh, with a twinkle of humour.

He switched off the tape-recording and laid down the wand.

'My real name is Reuven Arieh. I don't know if that means anything to you.'

Well, this certainly was more interesting than bloody Washington.

Reuven Arieh was a name known only to someone with intimate professional knowledge of the Israeli Intelligence Service's innermost secrets. To someone who, if not a senior Mossad official, could only have acquired the information illicitly. And that, of course, was the nature of David Jardine's employment.

Reuven Arieh was one of Mossad's prize black operators.

That much the Englishman knew. The Israeli was credited with some profoundly impressive coups in the aggressive intelligence war against his country's enemies. He too had the equivalent rank of colonel. What a funny old world. Arieh had first come to the notice of SIS around the time of the 1972 Munich Olympics massacre of eleven Israeli sportsmen by terrorists in Yasser Arafat's Al-Fatah faction of the Palestinian Liberation Organization. The killers had claimed the slaughter on behalf of Black September, which referred to the month two years before in which the PLO had been driven out of Jordan by King Hussein's tough and professional army.

The Mossad had been directed by Prime Minister Golda Meir to seek out those responsible for the atrocity and, by hunting them down and killing them, wherever they were in the world, to make it ruthlessly clear what the State of Israel's response would be to any future acts of terror against its nationals.

And it was about then that the name of Reuven Arieh had come to the attention of the Office's Political Action and Special Projects desks. In 1972, there had been no specific Counter-Terror Directorate at SIS. But that had soon come into being as a result of increased international cooperation in the wake of the Munich affair, along with the rise of the Baader-Meinhof Group in Germany, the Red Brigades in Italy, the Japanese Red Army and a plethora of pro-Palestinian gangs with a penchant for hijacking airplanes and machine-gunning airport departures halls.

Four years later, in 1976, Jardine had led several deniable and illegal operations for a section of the Firm's Counter-Terror Directorate, which involved the deployment of seconded, and lethal, noncoms from the British Army's Special Air Service, and it was in the course of this business that he had become personally aware, in detail, of the intricate and patient skill of Mossad's work in the same field.

Oh, yes. The name Reuven Arieh did mean something to

him. But – and this was a tribute to Mossad and to the man – even with deeply buried, secret assets of its own inside the Israeli Service, SIS did not really know much more than that.

And here he was. David Jardine's captor, playing him tapes of Jardine's boss discussing a career plan which did not, on the face of it, sound at all promising.

Time, perhaps, to end his silence.

'I'm afraid the name Arieh means absolutely nothing to me. Except, of course, that it would appear to be, um, not an everyday name for an Egyptian.'

Jaddeh gazed at Jardine. A cool, not unfriendly gaze. More, appraising.

'Well, of course I am not an Egyptian, sir. I am an employee of the Institute.'

'Anyone in your position, sitting here in this room, could say that,' Jardine replied, in Hebrew.

'Interesting.' Jaddeh smiled and continued in comfortable Israeli Hebrew. 'Nowhere in your file does it say you speak our language.'

'The point is,' Jardine went on, rapidly running out of the 180 words of Hebrew he had taught himself, as a very junior spook stationed in Tel Aviv, about four million years before, 'you can say anything you like and I would not be able to believe you . . .'

'No kidding. Try this for size.' To Jardine's relief, Jaddeh had reverted to English. 'Two days ago, you drank coffee with a colleague of mine in the Willard Hotel coffee shop, in Washington, DC. His name is Avriam Eitels. You are joint members of an intelligence steering committee called J-WISC. Avvie says you were bored shitless.'

Well, this just might become interesting.

'As I recall,' said Jardine, 'Eitels complimented me on something. What was it?'

Jaddeh frowned. Searching his memory. 'I don't know. I can find out. We'll ask him.'

Jardine considered. Either the man was ducking the question, or it was an honest answer. 'Fine. You're a pro.

That much is clear from the tape-recording. Which could only have been obtained by a seriously able service. But anything you say to me to try to convince me you're with Mossad would very probably be information my own firm has acquired, illegally or through diligent . . . research.

'And any good service, likewise. So you could sing and dance Hava Neguila all evening, and recite the Torah backwards, and all it could mean is you're good at faking it. And for what? Israeli or Egyptian, Syrian, Iranian or Seventh Day Adventist, here we are. I'm held against my will and you've got the guns. So spit it out, Salim or Ruben or whatever your bloody name is. What's the ante?'

'I'm sorry?'

'What's your game? What do you want with me?'

Jaddeh met David Jardine's hostile stare. 'David, we have not gone to all this trouble for nothing. Avvy told you a story about a series of criminal acts around the world. All of them involving counterfeiting. Forgery of some kind. Forgive me, the answer to your last question is, what I want with you right now is to . . . just go along with me. Let's pretend I really am Reuven Arieh . . .'

Jardine inclined his head. He was beginning to believe it.

The man who called himself Salim Jaddeh, or rather the man who had called himself Salim Jaddeh and now claimed to be Reuven Arieh, seemed to sense the quietening of David Jardine's professional scepticism. His relief was undisguised and he rose from his couch and crossed to an ancient carved dark wood dresser, which had three panels, each with a shield carved on it. The device on each shield was the same: a chevron separating the shield into two halves, with two five-pointed stars in the upper part and a bird in the lower. If one looked closely, it was just about apparent that at one time the wood had been painted in bright colours.

There was a collection of bottles of spirits on the dresser, and about ten tumblers of varying sizes.

'You know what this is?' asked Jaddeh.

'To my untutored eye, it appears to be a knight's chest

from the Crusades. The wood's certainly old and this is the right part of the world for it.' Such priceless antiques could still be found in the Lebanon. Along with the detritus of more recent conflict. Wrecked Israeli and Syrian tanks, jeeps, civilian trucks and once gleaming automobiles. And the occasional blackened, twisted child's perambulator.

'It's a reproduction.'

'Well, there you go,' said Jardine. 'I'm no expert.' This from a man who had read medieval history at Magdalen, who had won a respectable First for his dissertation on the Crusades.

Jaddeh smiled. He poured two healthy shots of Lagavullin malt whisky into two chunky crystal tumblers.

David Jardine wondered if it was mere coincidence that Lagavullin, a fairly rare brand, not to say esoteric, was his own favourite. Taken with just a smidgen of Highland Spring mineral water. Which released the zesters. He wanted to believe it was coincidence.

Salim Jaddeh opened one of the panels to reveal an ice-box inside, an off-white, plastic box, with Coke bottles, cans of orange, bottles of Kronenbourg and Sol beer. And an ice-cold bottle of Highland Spring mineral water.

So much for coincidence.

Jardine's captor carefully poured an equal amount of mineral water into each tumbler. Precisely the correct amount. Of course.

'It was copied in the sixteenth century by a Lebanese carpenter called Daoud. He's mentioned in several works of literature.' Jaddeh crossed to David Jardine and offered one of the tumblers. 'The original chest was the property of a knight called de Caumont . . .' He raised his glass in a silent toast to his prisoner.

'Spare me,' said David Jardine. 'I think you'll find the age of chivalry is past.' And he sipped at the whisky.

Thank you, dear Lord. This is just what the doctor ordered. If I'd remembered to pray, this is probably precisely what I should have prayed for. Failing the arrival of the Seventh Cavalry, but of course you would know that, being omni-something. So, cheers, old bean.

And David Jardine swilled the wonderful smoky liquid around his mouth and, with some reluctance, swallowed it.

He raised his eyes and saw a look of pleasure, of pleased relief, on Salim Jaddeh's face.

'*L'chaim* . . . sport.' Jardine met Jaddeh's eye. 'You pour a reasonable dram.'

Jaddeh toasted Jardine with his tumbler and sipped. 'I wanted to offer you our best . . . hospitality.' And he flopped back on to the soft leather couch, cradling his own drink.

There was nothing David Jardine would have liked more than to have drained the glass and stretched out his hand for another. But business was business and he had a feeling that it was going to be a long night. So he sniffed at the zesters at the rim of the tumbler and at that moment one of the dark teak doors opened and in she walked, glancing at him shyly, her one-time lover and present case officer, then chose a scattering of big cushions piled against the wall under a camel rug, hung to display its intricate russet and purple and deep blue design.

She wore a cotton dress of some neutral colour. Jardine could never remember, subsequently, what colour exactly, for at the moment, Alisha Abdul-Fetteh, Agent Pomegranate of the British SIS, gazed directly and impersonally at him and said, 'He congratulated you on your memory, David. I've just spoken to Avriam, in Washington . . .'

'My memory . . .' Jesus, Mary and Mahatma Gandhi, what's going on here? Jardine exercised all his training to keep any sign of surprise from his expression or his body movement. There will be moments of astonishing shocks, Alice had warned all those years before, when the fledgling Jardine had been learning the profession of espionage. That, she had said, is what separates the men from the boys, the quick from the dead, and the serious operator from the guy on his way to the gadget with the electrodes and a small but nasty electric generator.

So David Jardine contrived to look as if it was fairly everyday, mundane even, a matter of no importance, to discover at the end of an appalling day, when he had been stabbed, kidnapped and was swooning from jet-lag, that his prized and admired agent, the jewel in his Lebanon network, so secret that only three people in Century House knew her true identity, so vital that he had flown from Washington, DC at the drop of a hint of a problem, his treasured and supposedly vulnerable agent Pomegranate, whose sheets he had only this morning been so tacky as to examine for traces of semen, was quite clearly a fully paid-up member of a Mossad cell, run by the man who, according to the boy Hassan, had brought about the murder of her own father.

Well, Alice, he mused. So this is what you meant, all those years ago . . .

'In the coffee shop at the Willard. I've just spoken to Avvy Eitels on the phone. He says he congratulated you on remembering he liked to order iced tea. And coffee together. He drinks the iced tea first. Then lingers over the coffee.' Then she turned to Reuven Arieh and said in rapid Hebrew, 'Avvy says if you want anything else, you should signal the Embassy. He didn't like me phoning DC direct.'

There followed a long silence, during which she tried to stare him out. Not aggressively. More defensively. Like a favourite daughter who is just daring her father to criticize her most recent outrageous act.

After some time, her gaze faltered, and David Jardine drained his glass of Lagavullin and held it out for more.

'Not so much water this time,' he said to Salim Jaddeh or Reuven Arieh or whatever his bloody name was.

At which point the day's events overtook the British master spy, and to his eternal embarrassment, he fainted, spilling the empty tumbler across an antique Ottoman rug and revealing, as he toppled from the couch, a bloodsoaked shirt, for several of the stitches had torn loose.

What he never did learn was that Alisha cried out his name and ran to him, even before he had hit the floor.

This was something Reuven Arieh never forgot. And he was annoyed to have suffered a most unusual emotion, hitherto foreign to his personal experience.

It was jealousy.

6

Mambo Hat

PALERMO CAN BE every bit as dangerous as its reputation. And yet there is a lazy vitality about the place. Maybe the ever-present possibility of violent calamity acts as a spur on the adrenal gland. Life there is enjoyed with a quiet urgency, not to be found in more prosaic urban environments like Manhattan or Milan.

Danny Davidov lit a cigarette and observed the street activity around him. He was standing in the shade of the Church of La Martorana, in the Via Maqueda, which was part of the principal artery leading from the busy, modern town centre, the Piazza Castelnuovo, to the old city and the port, by way of the centuries-old Piazza di Quattro Canti.

He watched the tall, lean figure of his partner amble easily along the far side of the street. His vision was obscured from time to time by passing cars and trucks, gaily painted in primary colours, with the name of a special saint on the front, above the cab, like the destination sign on a bus. There were occasional, ominous, stop-for-nothing mini-convoys of armoured Lancia sedans and four-wheel-drives, windows blacked and flanked by buzzing Japanese trail-bikes, ridden by young men in jeans and leather jackets, with varying makes of sub-machine-guns slung over their shoulders, or jammed into special brackets on the bikes.

Davidov knew that some of those convoys were speeding Polizia and Ministry of Justice officials on anti-Mafia business. Others carried Secret Police bosses, or leading members of the Cosa Nostra, wanted men whom nobody was going to risk certain death by apprehending. Not here. Not in the Via Maqueda. Not at this time.

None of this seemed to perturb Danny's partner, Nikolai Kolosov, who glanced, comfortable with himself, into shop windows and nodded to the occasional beautiful Sicilian girl as their paths crossed.

Danny Davidov wondered, for the thousandth time, just what it was that made Kolosov tick. The man was a stunning professional. He had that vital attribute, which marked the genius operator, of complete intuition coupled with an ability to react instantly to changed circumstances with, thus far, infallible precision.

But still . . . although Danny had chosen Kolosov with all the care and background investigation he had learned – and indeed, had taught – during twenty years with the Institute, there were still so many parts of his accomplice's mind that were somehow impregnable to the Israeli's every, and considerably able, attempt to peel more layers off that onion, the enigma that was Nikolai Sergeyevich Kolosov.

The unlikely alliance between the two men stemmed directly from that awful day when Davidov had received his marching orders from the Institute. One fateful September morning in Tel Aviv, he had been arrested in his own office, in front of his staff, and taken to the apartment used for interrogation of traitors to the State.

There, the Memouneh himself had given him twenty-four hours to return some money, a small matter of a few million pounds sterling, which he had secreted in private bank accounts all around the world – except in Israel – and told him to hand over his passport and sign a top secret, but legal and binding, document swearing never to return to the land of his birth, the land to which his grandfather had brought the Davidovs from Kiev, in 1928. And he was not permitted to spend even a moment in the bathroom without an escort from Mossad's Security Department, during his last day in the country he loved and to whose secure future he had contributed so much.

It was a day he relived every day thereafter. And in his sleep, he had nightmares about it. And that was the day on which he had understood with an intense clarity (he called it his Damascus Road experience) precisely what he was going to do with the rest of his life.

In order to fulfil his new destiny, Danny Davidov knew he would need to recruit a partner, reliable, capable and sane. A person with experience of deception and infiltration operations in the world of espionage. Someone whose personal psychological profile would probably equal his own. A top operator, in some foreign service, similarly hurt and angry at having been cast out by the very people he had devoted his life to. Probably risked it, too.

And Danny Davidov, furnished with a new identity as a South African businessman (which he discarded the moment he got off the plane that had transported him into the Diaspora), was glad he had secreted, during his years of loyal service, a little 'insurance'. A collection of forty-one 3.5-inch computer discs, which gave him access to most of the Tel Aviv Institute's top secret files. These he kept deep-frozen inside packets of pork dinners in the freezer of an apartment he rented, on a cash basis, from the widow of a movie producer in Milan.

It had taken the Israeli – former Israeli – eight weeks of painstaking research seeking out potential recruits, at first on his IBM in the Milan apartment, then in a number of European countries, before he found his ideal accomplice.

And at the swimming pool in the sports complex just off Prospekt Michurinsky, in what had been the Olympic Village for the 1980 Moscow Olympics, Danny Davidov had made contact with Colonel Nikolai Kolosov. Deputy Head of Service A, of the First Chief Directorate.

And here they were, some two years on, in a street in Palermo, still comparative strangers. But getting bizarrely wealthy, on their joint odyssey towards the ultimate objective. The one that would go down in history as the grandest shafting ever delivered by two *nebishes*, two nobodies, to the most powerful nation on earth.

It did, on occasion, occur to Danny Davidov that his mind had maybe flipped. That the shame and anger of being rejected by his beloved country, over a paltry few million English pounds, had deranged him. But after deep and thoughtful, and essentially Hebraic, introspection, he had appreciated that the truth was much simpler: Daniel Davidov, son of the Tel Aviv Chief of Detectives, was a born criminal. It was more than an aberration of character. For Danny, it was a calling. A vocation, even.

And as he watched two priests in shallow black hats, missing only the black ringlets of orthodoxy to make him feel truly at home – God, how he missed Jerusalem – glide like black-robed Chinese courtesans towards the church steps, he noted that Kolosov had reached the door to a dark stone, important-looking building. Just four storeys high, with polished aluminium, slightly curved doors, exactly fifteen feet by twelve.

There was no plaque or identifying sign on the outside of this building, which would have been number 623 Via Maqueda, had anyone been counting. But this was the repository of the 157 million dollars which Danny Davidov and Nikolai Kolosov had so sublimely lifted from under the nose of the Intertel 9 security failsafe computer system, in St Petersburg, just three weeks before.

This was the Banca di Calabria, Palermo mercantile branch.

'*Buon giorno*, Signor Muhler,' greeted the deputy manager of the bank. His grey woven silk necktie, crisp white shirt, dark suit, highly polished black moccasins and discreet pearl tiepin combined to lend him an air of . . . menace, which was quite contrary to their presumably desired effect. Maybe it was the jet-black moustache, or the cool, smiling eyes, which sent out a very clear signal – I have seen it all. I have served the richest men and women in Italy with discretion. I am valued. And protected. So don't mess with me.

He smiled politely and spoke in Italian-accented German. 'All the necessary documents have been drawn up. Perhaps I can offer you something first? A glass of sherry? *Un petit coup de champagne . . .*'

'No, thanks,' replied Nikolai Kolosov, glancing somewhat gracelessly at his watch.

'I wouldn't mind a cup of coffee,' said Danny, whom the deputy manager believed, or more cynically accepted, to be one Bernard Muhler, using the passport of a Luxemburg businessman.

'Then coffee it shall be.' The deputy manager, one Alfreddo Buonatempora, indicated two seats on the far side of the polished eighteenth-century table and sat down. He briefly examined a series of documents bearing the embossed stamp of the bank, with ornate scroll copperplate lettering in dark blue ink along the top.

Satisfied, Buonatempora pushed the documents across the table, turning them for Davidov and Kolosov to read.

Thirty-one bearer bonds, drawn on the First National Bank of Boston, each worth five million US dollars. And one for two million dollars. Such bonds were exactly like cash and, say you dropped one in the street, anyone finding it and presenting it at a reputable bank would be entitled to the full amount in regular currency.

'Thirty-two bearer bonds, gentlemen. Worth one hundred and fifty-seven million dollars, as you have requested. It merely remains for you to pay for them . . . He inclined his head towards a solitary cheque, drawn on the Banca di Calabria. In elegant copperplate penmanship, a clerk had carefully written the words 'one hundred and fifty seven million US dollars', and in the box for figures, had neatly entered '$157,000,000'. The account number was M–142.

Danny Davidov gazed at the cheque with a degree of humility, and pride. He remembered the adrenalin of that night in St Petersburg, when he and Nikolai had burglarized the most elaborate failsafe computer security program the world's major international credit card bank had been able to devise.

Account M–142 at the Banca di Calabria, mercantile branch, Palermo, was in the joint names of Bernard Muhler and Pierre Jacques-Stiguer. And their signatures were on file. In fact, they were on two white papers, bonded in clear, laminated plastic, at the deputy manager's right hand.

Davidov glanced at the Russian. Even Kolosov seemed to be impressed. Quietly he nodded and lifted his eyes to gaze at Buonatempora.

'If everything is in order, gentlemen . . .' Buonatempora indicated two quill pens, resting on ivory racks beside two ink pots.

'What about your percentage? The bank's charge for this transaction, Herr Buonatempora?' Kolosov's German was excellent. It was more educated than Danny Davidov's, and he had worked in Germany as an illegal for four years, in the early eighties.

The deputy manager smiled, as if a small child had just asked if God was always merciful. 'There is our usual handling fee. In the nature of the facilities we offer, we accept only cash.'

'How much?' asked Danny.

'A mere five per cent. Do you take milk with your coffee?'

A man wearing a spotless white jacket and white gloves had entered, pushing a trolley with pots of coffee, milk, sugar and a jug of lemonade.

'That's nearly eight million dollars.' Nikolai Kolosov did not like this one bit.

'Seven point eight five,' smiled Buonatempora. 'Just another form of robbery, I can see your point of view . . .'

The servant, who had the high cheekbones and dark, merciless eyes of the most ancient up-country Sicilians, poured coffee for all three men, then retreated to a corner by the door. Clearly in no hurry to leave. Davidov noted the man's pistol was worn on his left front, on the belt.

And that the lower buttons of his white tunic were undone. To facilitate a fast draw.

Buonatempora gazed at his two clients. 'Please believe me, there is no charge for keeping the money on deposit. The request for this transaction is entirely yours.'

Danny poured milk into his coffee, stirred it and sipped. He turned to his partner. 'Pierre?'

Kolosov shrugged. 'How much interest has the money earned since it was transferred here?'

The deputy manager did a rapid sum, using a small electronic calculator. 'One point five seven million,' he said.

Silence.

Then Danny picked up one of the quill pens and dipped it in the ink. 'So how about you keep that, plus one of those bearer bonds for five million . . .?'

Buonatempora gazed at him fondly. 'But that would leave my board one point two eight million short.' He smiled, without parting his lips, as if to say, dear dear, a minor error of arithmetic.

'Then what can you do for us, Herr Buonatempora . . .?' asked Kolosov, his eyes briefly flitting over the Sicilian hood in the white tunic. The way he dismissed the guy, Danny remembered afterwards, left quite a chill in the room.

Buonatempora held Kolosov's icy gaze, but not for long. He shrugged. 'Since you are valued customers, gentlemen, and since you will doubtless be bringing more business this way . . .' his two clients gazed back, expressionless, 'I think my board will accept, in this one instance, let us say . . . a round figure of seven million dollars.'

'Daylight robbery,' replied Davidov, but he scrawled the signature of Bernard Muhler across the bank cheque.

After a long moment, Kolosov did likewise.

'We would like three titanium combination strongboxes.' Danny indicated the bearer bonds, which Kolosov was sorting into two piles of fifteen, and one of just two.

'Of course,' said Buonatempora, and pressed a switch on his desk intercom.

Kolosov slid one five-million-dollar bond and the solitary two-million-dollar bond across the table to Buonatempora.

The bank's seven-million handling charge. In cash.

'And we would wish to rent a secure place for them, in your underground safety deposit vault.'

'We are honoured, Herr Muhler,' beamed the deputy manager. 'How do you wish to dispose of the interest, the one point five million still in your joint account?'

'Leave it on deposit. Take deductions from time to time for the safety deposit rentals.'

'We are flattered by your trust.'

'We assume you are prudent men,' answered Kolosov levelly, his expression leaving no doubt about what would happen to anyone who took liberties with his money. Even here in Palermo, which was not a town that seemed to faze him particularly.

'And now,' said Danny Davidov, without the trace of a blush, 'my colleague and I will require to be satisfied on the question of the security of your vault.'

The deputy manager studied his two clients. Infrequent visitors to Sicily. He knew enough to be aware that their vast deposits were not earned in normal, legitimate commercial dealings. Otherwise they would not be here. But they were willing to trust the bank with 150 million in negotiable bonds. It was probably understandable that such men should be reassured about the bank's impregnability.

Perhaps Signor Buonatempora should have consulted the horoscope for his star sign, which was Leo, that morning, in the Italian daily newspaper, *La Stampa*. 'Be prudent,' it had read, 'do not place your trust in strangers . . .'

Nancy Lucco stooped slightly over the washbasin, brushing her teeth and making circular movements around her gums, the way her mother had taught her when she was a kid. It was a routine from which she had never wavered, and she grinned, getting toothpaste foam on her face, as she remembered the way Eddie used to watch her, counting the seconds on his wristwatch, as she did thirty-six seconds on the upper teeth, and thirty-six seconds on the lower ones. They had been living in a cramped but happy two-room apartment in Queens, New York City. Eddie was a Lieutenant of Detectives in the Homicide Department of NYPD, working out of the 14th Precinct.

And she had been a tough and ambitious defence attorney, sometimes earning more in a week than the big Wop jerk had taken home in a month. The fact that it had been one of the world's great love affairs had never occurred to her. But then, it never does.

She rinsed her mouth and dried her face. No need these days to check which towel was hers. For Nancy Lucco was a widow. A fuckin' widow, she thought. Who'd've dreamt it?

At first, Eddie's disappearance, while it had been taken seriously, had not caused inordinate panic at NYPD. He had been heavily involved in an undercover operation, recruited, unbeknown to his boss at the 14th Precinct, by the DEA's Director and the US Treasury to accept a 4-million-dollar bribe from the Colombian cocaine cartel run by Pablo Escobar. This was before Escobar agreed to go to jail for just a few years, in a deal he had agreed in secret talks with representatives of Colombian President Caesar Gaviria. And way before Escobar had gotten tired of the idea of even token incarceration – he had designed his own prison, in comfortable quarters, overlooking his home town of Envigado in the environs of Medellin, the most dangerous city in Colombia and therefore in South America, which was a very dangerous sub-continent.

Eddie had phoned the duty cop at the 14th, one Sunday, and told him he was flying to Bogota to pursue an investigation he was currently working on.

The days of silence thereafter had become weeks. And when nobody heard from Eddie, Nancy Lucco had gotten in touch with Dan Mather, the Special Agent in Charge of the DEA's New York Field Office, the man who had recruited Eddie, with Washington's approval. For the only two people outside a handful in the DEA and the Treasury who had been admitted into Eddie's secret were Nancy and his partner, Sam Vargos.

Mather had told her that the DEA and other US agencies in Colombia were actively looking for Eddie, but so far there was no indication as to his whereabouts.

Six weeks had passed before the dreadful moment when Nancy heard the phone ring in her office, and her secretary speaking softly before putting the call through. Even with the first ring, she had known. The way an animal would know. That her mate was dead.

The body had lain in a Bogota mortuary since the day after he had arrived there from Miami International Airport. Found in a sewer, robbed and shot. ID and money gone. A John Doe, as unidentified corpses are called in police parlance.

It had been a big funeral, with all the moving panoply of dignified grief that NYPD accords to its own. The DEA had quietly erased all traces of her dead husband's heroism, but had let Nancy know, whatever she needed, in terms of support, she only had to ask.

And here she was, a year and a half later. Working for the Treasury. A sinecure granted by a grateful administration in recognition of Eddie Lucco's contribution to law enforcement. No way. The administration had a colder heart? The job had been offered to Nancy on the recommendation of one Judge Almeda, a New York City judge who had become impressed by the young woman attorney's spirited defence of an innocent junior banker who had been framed by his Ivy League, patrician employer into taking the rap on an insider dealing charge.

The banker had got off. Judge Almeda (who was unaware he had been a hero of this young woman's late husband, on account of how he had worked his way through law school, playing the piano nights at the Algonquin Hotel on West 43rd Street) had heard on the grapevine about Counsellor Lucco's recent bereavement and he had mentioned her cool nerve, wickedly alert intelligence and her obvious complete integrity to a colleague who, over the years, had risen to become head of the US Treasury's Legal Department. The upshot was that Nancy had been invited for an interview with this august senior government official, to discuss a career with the Treasury. Six weeks later, while she had been defending a member of the Gambino clan, one of New York's major-league Mob families, on charges of incitement to murder and extortion, Nancy had received a letter from the Department of the Treasury, offering her an appointment with the grade of Legal Counsellor, to be based in Washington, DC. They proposed a decent (as opposed to handsome) allowance for moving from NYC, and pointed out, coolly, that it was a higher grade than usually offered to applicants, but that her age and experience had been taken into consideration.

Age and experience! At thirty-four Nancy Lucco was reminded that her twenties, her wonderful twenties with that big jerk of a husband, were long gone. She discussed the offer with her mother, with Judge Almeda, whom she had invited to dinner at the Algonquin – as much a gesture to Eddie's memory as anything else – and the venerable former jazz piano-player had told her what the job would entail, how the pay would never be that hot, and how rewarding he thought it would be for Nancy. Then he had sat in with the Lester Wilmington trio and played 'Mood Indigo' and 'Night Train'.

The next day, Nancy Lucco had written back, accepting the job.

Washington, DC was familiar territory, for she had worked on a dozen big court cases there. She found a pleasant apartment on 34th Street, which was west of Wisconsin Avenue, in Georgetown, not far from the University, and buried herself in her work. Learning a whole new job.

For legal work at the Treasury embraced everything from the law on forgery to insider dealing in government stock, to the fiscal procedures for funding government agencies such as the FBI and the Bureau of Alcohol,

Tobacco and Firearms, in addition to the Armed Forces and the CIA.

Security clearance took a few months to process, and it was graded according to several parameters, but in particular, the subject's reliability and fitness to handle secret information, top secret information, and the several classifications beyond those. It was also limited to the subject's need to know.

Nancy Lucco was a known quantity to the legal establishment. Her late husband had been a highly respected detective, and they had both been given (unbeknown to either of them) a comprehensive security check during the last months of Eddie's life, when he had been working undercover for the DEA.

Thus, within seven months of joining the Treasury, Nancy found herself with a high-security status and an assignment to the United States Secret Service, as Legal Counsellor. After a further six months, known as Assimilation, to USSS's Personnel Department, she was sent on the Service's Agents' Course, because Jim Farley, the Director, had liked her attitude and temperament, and saw a serious career ahead of her.

McClay had explained to Nancy that she should take the course, in order to understand the agents she represented in Legal Affairs. But of course he had another motive, and when a fitter and leaner Counsellor Nancy Lucco emerged from Agent School, she was appointed to run the Legal Affairs office's liaison programme with the CIA, FBI, DEA and other Federal agencies. She was also one of three counsellors responsible for liaison with the State Department and foreign law enforcement agencies.

All in all, Nancy felt, as she stepped out from the shower and glanced through the wisps of steam at her slender, firm body in the long mirror on the back of the bathroom door, not a bad career move. She had a fascinating job, which challenged her – let's be frank – considerable intellect and training. There was always something new and unusual. And so far, she hadn't screwed up.

Plus it kept her mind off the big Wop cop, who had come back from Bogota in a beautiful ornate casket, paid for by the Colombian Policía Nacional out of their Sports Club welfare fund.

As she dressed, Nancy Lucco thought about the day ahead. New York Field Office had filed a formal complaint about an undercover operation conducted against them by Internal Investigations. They alleged that the agent concerned, one Elmore Williams, had acted illegally and had put the lives of New York City agents at risk. Not to mention innocent civilians and a gangster called Harry Cardona.

Elmore Williams . . .

Now, why did she know that name?

There is a seven-hour time difference between Washington, DC and Beirut, and round about the time when Nancy Lucco had been thinking about turning in, the night before, say about 10 o'clock, David Jardine was in a deep sleep, between soft, clean linen sheets, in an upstairs bedroom in the villa above Dhouer El-Chouer.

In his dream, he was back in Alisha's apartment, not far from the Rue Georges Picot. It was early evening and the sunset cast a warm, rust-gold glow into the sitting room through the slatted blinds. He was sprawled on the comfortable sofa, a colourful, woven wool Berber rug folded over the back, and Bedouin cushions in the corner. And as he watched the golden-pink sunlight scattered in geometric shafts across the bookcase and the white walls, he stroked Alisha's long silken hair falling over his bare flank and arched his back in pleasure, as her tongue teased his maleness with slow, gossamer-slick arcs.

It was quiet, in the Beirut evening. Outside, occasional sounds of low voices, speaking Arabic, in the alley. And goats. Somewhere there were goats – oh, surely a man could die of such pleasure – the goats were really very close, and nearer, a 50-cc Velocette had rasped untidily into the yard.

What yard? There are no yards near Alisha's apartment.

He gazed lazily around the room. It was darker now. And beyond the bookcase, which seemed in no way illogical, was a gently sloping field, with a herd of goats grazing.

And a man, a boy, it was Hassan, arrived sedately, silently, on a 50-cc Velocette and stopped on the rug beside the couch. And when he turned to smile at Jardine, it was difficult to see his face, for it had changed to that of Salim Jaddeh.

Ahh . . .

A dream.

It was a dream. And David Jardine began to remember events of the day and evening before, vaguely at first, then with more accuracy, for his was a mind trained to such circumstance.

He still had an erection, almost painful, and it still felt alive, as if it had an agenda of its own, and it was with some reluctance that he slowly abjured the embrace of Morpheus and let his brain rejoin the real world.

Jardine lay still, opening his eyes and blinking the drowsiness from them. It was dark, with a roseate glow of first light beginning to creep into the room through the shuttered windows.

The perfect clarity with which he recalled every detail of the previous evening, the previous appalling day, right up to the moment when he had stretched out his arm, glass in hand, for a refill of Lagavullin whisky, coincided with the sound of soft but authoritative voices outside – a man's and a woman's – and the oiled clunk of a key turning in a big lock. The door opened and Alisha Abdul-Fetteh came in. She wore a faded pink cotton shirt, neatly pressed, and brown cord jeans, with worn, comfortable trainers. And she carried a small kidney dish, with fresh dressings and a bottle of pink liquid.

She paused by the door until it had swung gently shut, and the sound of the key in the lock had stopped.

David Jardine watched her coldly, as she walked to the

side of his bed nearest the shuttered window and, taking a thermometer from her shirt pocket, pushed it towards his mouth.

Jardine turned his head away. 'I don't need that.'

Alisha, just recently Pomegranate, shrugged. With a businesslike movement she lifted the sheet covering the Englishman and flicked it back, exposing him. She smiled.

'Some things never change,' she said quietly.

Then, very professionally, she checked the fresh dressing which Jardine discovered was wound around his abdomen.

'How did this happen . . .?' she asked.

'Precisely what I was about to ask you,' he replied, surprisingly urbane considering the circumstances in which he found himself.

He reached down and placed the sheet over his loins, almost primly. She did not seem to notice as she cut through the dressing with a pair of surgical scissors which had appeared as if from nowhere. Jardine was reminded of a conjuring trick.

'We had no idea you were wounded.' She spoke in French.

'It's hardly a wound.'

'Injured, then. Cut.'

Silence.

She peeled away the dressing and gazed at the swollen line of sutures. Jardine instinctively sniffed, and was relieved not to smell the sickly scent of sepsis, just the reassuring, tangy aroma of iodine and some sort of alcohol-based antiseptic.

'If we had known, we would have given you immediate treatment. Reuven trained as a doctor, you know.'

'Then he should be ashamed of himself.' While she bathed and cleaned his wound, Jardine gazed at a framed photograph of a hillside in the Bekaa Valley, bright red flowers making patchwork with the wheat. He knew the flowers were poppies. And that their gum would be refined into heroin, to be sold in London, Rome and Marseilles, to finance the many private armies and fundamentalist terrorist groups who were all waiting, like snakes under stones, to see if the latest attempt to restore the tortured Lebanon to sanity and prosperity would fail. Like all the others.

'I never thought you were a hypocrite, David,' murmured Alisha. Misunderstanding what he had meant.

'The man conspired to have your father murdered, do I have to spell it out . . .?'

Alisha stopped. She stared at him. Amazed. 'Who told you such a thing . . .?'

David Jardine turned to gaze into her eyes. Working now. Earning his crust. All personal feeling completely gone.

'It's something we have been aware of. For some time,' he lied. And was immediately aware he had touched a very raw nerve.

'Well, you are wrong. You are wrong and you are extremely stupid to say such a thing. If that's the grade of intelligence you place credence on in SIS, thank God I was not relying on you. To look after my ass.' And she dabbed fiercely at his leaking, sutured gash with the astringent pink antiseptic, forcing him to suck air through his clenched teeth, in reaction.

'Well, David. How are you feeling?' asked Reuven Arieh.

They were sitting at a table on a terrace overlooking the mountain road which they had driven up the previous day, about two hours from Beirut. The Arab woman servant had brought a fresh pot of strong coffee, which she placed on the table, and retreated, taking with her the empty plate, which had been laden with scrambled egg, chick-peas, new-baked pitta bread and small stuffed vine-leaves. All of which Jardine had wolfed down, aware that, whatever his captor's motives, he was going to need the fuel.

It was about an hour since his conversation with Alisha. They had not really got anywhere. It was obvious she did not believe that Reuven Arieh, or Salim Jaddeh, or whatever his real name was, had connived at the murder of her father, presumably as part of an Israeli plan to set two Beirut factions at each other's throats.

It had also been clear that she felt genuinely ashamed of her duplicity in having betrayed Jardine, her SIS recruiter and controller. But his attempts to find out when, why, and how much Pomegranate had damaged SIS by feeding it misleading intelligence had been stonewalled.

He thanked God that he had resisted all attempts by the Middle East Desk to let them run Alisha from Rome or Cyprus. That would inevitably have resulted in her becoming aware of the identities of one or two members of Beirut Station. And with the ability and experienced skill of Mossad behind her (for Jardine no longer had any doubt that Jaddeh was indeed Reuven Arieh), that would have resulted in the network being infiltrated and manipulated – and betrayed, if it happened to suit Mossad's operational convenience – with an inevitability as bleak as it was certain.

Thus, at least, the damage was contained, restricted to Agent Pomegranate.

'I'm fine.' Jardine watched Reuven Arieh pour out two cups of coffee. 'Let's cut the smalltalk, shall we?'

'Sure.' The conversation was being conducted in English, which Arieh spoke with an easy East Coast American accent. He went on, 'The fact is, David, you were lured here. I was the person on the other end of the signals exchanged between Beirut and your Embassy cipher room in Washington. Avvy Eitels had been told to watch you and report on your attitude to your new job. And your state of mind.'

'My state of mind?'

'You were bored shitless. Your very own words, I believe.' Arieh poured himself more coffee. 'So it was really quite predictable that you would grab the opportunity of Pomegranate's signal to fly out here and play spies. Really quite predictable . . .'

Suckered. As David Jardine's American colleagues would say. He poured some freshly squeezed, diluted lime juice from a jug that had a sprig of mint floating in it. There was a hint of honey after the tang of the limes. Jardine was reminded of the intrinsic civilization of the Lebanon, for all its centuries of massacre and internecine conflict. This drink, ancient as time in this land that once linked Egypt to Mesopotamia; the ancient books of Arab poetry in the villa's sitting room or library or whatever it was; the sixteenth-century copy of Nompar de Caumont's field chest. Now converted to a liquor box. That perhaps said it all.

He glanced at Arieh and held the Israeli's gaze. 'What's your angle, Mr Jaddeh? I know your organization doesn't actually adore SIS. But we are supposed to have one or two aims in common. I can't see this little episode helping cooperation between us.'

Reuven Arieh shook his head, incredulous. 'Cooperation? What cooperation are you talking about? Your goddam Foreign Office – you really think it feels like cooperating with the Jews? Lawrence of Arabia, Glubb Pasha, Gordon of Khartoum, gimme a break, your foreign policy would happily have accepted the destruction of Israel a dozen times since we kicked you out of Palestine, and you know it.'

'We kept Sadaam Hussein from raining Scuds on you . . .' Jardine's eyes narrowed. For the first time in months he felt angry. Very bloody angry. Who did this Red Sea secret agent think he was dealing with?

'We would've stopped Sadaam in his tracks and you know it.' Reuven Arieh touched the toe of his black slip-on shoe, on the foot of his right leg, which he had crossed, to show how relaxed he was, over his left knee.

Then he turned his head to meet Jardine's eye. 'You do know we were ready to nuke Baghdad . . .?'

'We kept our part of the bargain. British and American Special Forces stopped his Scud launching capability dead in its tracks.'

'Sure you did.' A bead of perspiration trickled down Arieh's handsome nose. He really did look more Arab than Jew. 'To keep the inconvenient Jews out of the war. To keep your Saudi pals sweet, don't make me sick. Don't, please don't, tell me the UK did that to actually protect Israel or one single Israeli, listen, we know better . . .'

Finally the urbane master of his emotions – how many times a day must he have had to suppress them, in his persona as Salim Jaddeh? – had lost his cool. He took a deep breath.

'Forgive me. That is bad . . . hospitality.'

Jardine relaxed. It had not taken long to turn his captor into a human being. The one persona he felt, instinctively, the Israeli spy felt least comfortable with.

Having thus redrawn the ground for this particular small battle, the Englishman felt more comfortable. Happier to proceed. 'Tell me what this bullshit is all about, Reuven.'

'Ah, so finally we can talk.'

'We're both grownups. Get on with it, I have a plane to catch.'

Reuven Arieh glanced at Jardine with something approaching respect, for, being a prisoner, the man was hardly in a position to stroll out and call a taxi.

'Okay. Your future with SIS is uncertain. Believe me when I tell you, Sir Steven McCrae does not want you on board. I think, we think, at the Institute, maybe it's personal. I mean, it's almost as if you were both fucking the same woman . . .'

Jardine remained expressionless. But in his mind he had an instant recollection of a certain bathroom cabinet above a certain young woman's – a certain ambitious young woman's – washbasin. And there, inside, on the top shelf, almost too high for anyone but a man of David Jardine's six feet and three inches to reach, was a man's razor, shaving foam, some poncy cologne from the utterly chic Diptyque shop in the Boulevard Saint-Germain in the fifth arrondissement, in Paris. And a pair of men's cufflinks.

Blue jade and gold, which Jardine knew, because McCrae had made sure every one of his colleagues knew, that the Chief, 'C' in the Office's parlance, or Charlie, had had specially made for him when he was Head of Station in Hong Kong. By King Antiques, of Swire House, Kowloon-Side.

Yes, they had – very briefly – shared the same girl.

'Whatever,' went on Arieh, 'by promoting you, McCrae in effect kicked you upstairs, out of operations and in the general direction of oblivion.'

Jardine gazed down over the valley, past Dhouer El-Chouer towards the Bekaa Valley, where the murderous and fanatical Hezbollah still held sway. He had known Bill Buckley, the Company Station Chief they had captured and skinned alive, recording his screams on video and sending it to Langley, where one of the young analysts whose duty it was to study such horrors had killed himself by driving off the turnpike and into a flyover support, at ninety-seven miles per hour.

There had been no trace of alcohol, narcotics or stimulants in his autopsied cadaver.

'Make your point,' he said.

'You were so bored you dropped everything to fly out here on the merest hint that Pomegranate was in trouble. Within hours of arriving you get stabbed by a street urchin and almost arrested by the Beirut Deuxième Bureau. Jesus, Jardine, you fit the profile. A senior intelligence executive, passed over, past his prime, bored and – privately, I don't expect you to agree with us – feeling hard done by and unappreciated by the hierarchy in your Firm.'

In his heart, David Jardine knew that the Mossad appreciation was correct. Spot bloody on. But if they thought that was going to make him a potential recruit to betray his country, then they clearly knew fuck-all about David Arbuthnot Jardine.

In the road down to the valley, two Range Rover four-wheel-drives meandered upwards, followed by a white station-wagon of uncertain make.

Please God it was not an attempt by Beirut Station to rescue him. That would be the last bloody straw.

'Okay,' said Reuven Arieh, 'this is my pitch. I make it in respect, sir. And I make it with the full authority of the Mamounieh.'

Jardine smiled grimly. The current Mamounieh, the Director of Mossad, and he had crossed swords in the past. For David Weissman had run an illegal Israeli operation in the UK, when Jardine had been a mere stripling of a lad, say about thirty-two, and his job at that time was what the Office's desk officers called streetfighter, with London Station. London Station was an operational unit of SIS, with both grey (whose identities were known to other agencies but not to the general hoi polloi) and black (which is to say clandestine and deniable) operators. Which gave the lie to the old saw that the Foreign Intelligence Service did not operate inside the UK.

Weissman's operation had been sweetly simple. Its task had been to discourage agents of Yasser Arafat's Al-Fatah, George Habbash's Popular Front for the Liberation of Palestine (General Command) and Abu Nidal's Moscow-trained murder gang from setting up supply and political cells within the UK.

And most effective Weissman had been.

David Jardine's job had been to keep tabs on Weissman, to make sure he did not get too arrogant in his trespassing on British soil, and to liaise with, and advise, the Security Service (MI5) and the Metropolitan Police Special Branch, whose every (and legal and proper) instinct was to try their damnedest to arrest Weissman and his team and, at the very least, to expel them from England as personae non gratae.

Reuven Arieh's feeling that there had always been elements in the British administration who were pro-Arab and less than warm towards Israel was substantially correct, then as now, and Jardine had been instructed one May afternoon by the then Chief – a round, owlish, medieval scholar with personal experience of Middle East shenanigans and no lover of terrorists – to do his best, dear boy, to keep this dreadful man Weissman and his outrageously illegal business out of the ken of the Arabists in the Firm and within the Foreign and Commonwealth Office.

In other words the young David Jardine had been tasked, on the personal word of his Head of Service, to let the Mossad agent get on with it, but to keep him in check, don't for God's sake, my dear, let him think he's anything but a hunted man. And at the merest hint of a wheel coming off, hand the whole bunch over to the Box, as the Security Service was known, and have them bundled back to Jerusalem or wherever they came from.

The end-result was that Weissman had been allowed to 'discourage' some extremist Arab terrorist cells from setting up shop in the UK and, when a young David Jardine had decided, on his own judgement, that things might just get out of hand, the Mossad teams – two groups of six – had been arrested in the Europa Hotel in London's Mayfair, and at the Odeon Cinema in Manchester, where the northern team had been watching *Kelly's Heroes*.

Within ten hours, they had been handed over to an official of the Israeli Embassy, on the tarmac at Heathrow Airport, and put, still handcuffed, on board an El Al flight to Tel Aviv.

Jardine could remember as if it were yesterday the moment when the short, wiry David Weissman had paused at the foot of the steps to the aircraft, last man to board, and had gazed keenly into his eyes.

'One day, my boy,' he had said to Jardine, 'one day you will find the boot is on the other foot.'

David Jardine smiled grimly and listened to the rasp of a 50-cc Velocette, which puttered out of the yard at the side of the villa and wound its way down the narrow road towards Douer El-Chouer. Everything, he mused, comes to him who waits. Now it might just be Weissman's turn.

Reuven Arieh was gazing further down the valley, watching the small convoy, which continued to climb inexorably upward. 'We don't want to compromise you in any way,' he said. 'My Director made it clear to me that you should know that.'

Yes, and monkeys might fly out of my butt, thought Jardine. It was a catchphrase from the movie *Wayne's World* and was much used by his son and daughter. He sipped his lime juice, with its hint of honey and mint. 'Get to the point.'

Arieh took a deep breath. 'We have a real problem on our hands. And we think that, by providing you with some information that can help you re-establish yourself in your service, you can help us. By helping yourself.'

Reuven Arieh sat back. He had really become quite tense. A vein on his temple was pulsing.

So it was that important.

David Jardine smiled.

'I have to confess,' he said, 'I'm intrigued.'

A small procession of homeless people was being manoeuvred towards Pennsylvania Avenue by three cops on horseback and six cops from patrol cars on routine duty not far from the Headquarters of the United States Secret Service.

It was snowing lightly, turning the sidewalks and gutters to mush. A couple of weeks earlier, it had lain eight or ten inches deep, and Elmore Williams had bought a pair of rubber overshoes to keep his brown brogues from getting stained by snow and salt.

But although the sky had taken on that yellowing, dull look and the temperature had surely dropped below freezing, Williams assured himself that the snow wouldn't lie. After all, wasn't spring just around the goddam corner?

You foolish optimist, Elmore, he told himself. As a matter of fact, the word purblind came to mind. He was not 100 per cent sure what purblind meant, but it seemed to fit the bill. And purblind optimist sure fitted a good description of him, he thought. For on that leaden-skied morning, stepping past the rag-tag of dispossessed souls in their woollen caps and tattered fedoras, stained with God knew what, and leather winter army hats with the ear-flaps flopping down, as if they did not care any more, and layers of threadbare coats tied around with twine, Elmore Williams had nothing to feel too good about.

He had kissed his wife on the cheek, hugged his daughter Melanie and walked to his '92 Chevvy as if he had not a care in the world. He had driven to the Willard Hotel underground garage, out of habit. For although Elmore was suspended from duty, pending the outcome of an inquiry by NYPD Homicide into his adding 2.2 ounces of lead and copper jacket to the head of Samuel J. Hubbard, and could have parked in the Secret Service garage, Elmore Williams was essentially an undercover man and old habits died hard.

And now, walking past the Sharper Image, whose sybaritic goodies for the space-age family seemed to clash with the motley group of crusading vagrants, Williams shook his head at his natural optimism and started to figure out just what he was going to say to this legal eagle, Legal Counsellor to the Service, in a few minutes' time. For Elmore Williams, in addition to being an optimist and among the slowest draws on the East Coast, had a kind of prescience, a sixth sense, that had saved his ass more than a few times over the last thirteen years. And he just had a hunch that this meeting with Counsellor Lucco was not going to be a simple rubber stamp on the elimination of one more lowlife.

'Agent Williams,' said the slim, dark-haired broad who had turned out to be Counsellor Lucco, 'SAIC New York City has filed a one five four against you. You know what a one five four is?'

'Yes, ma'am,' replied Williams, 'I sure do . . .'

A one five four was a formal complaint of gravc profcssional misconduct, bringing the Service into disrepute. It could only be brought by a Special Agent in Charge, and it had to be ratified and confirmed by Headquarters, who would then suspend the accused officer, pending investigation and a disciplinary hearing. The result could be a finding of not proved, or a fine of some kind, like deduction of pay, or a demotion, or a term of suspension, or dismissal. In cases where illegal stuff was involved, it could also lead to an arraignment before a Grand Jury.

Shit.

'Do you have anything to say at this stage? Bearing in mind you have all the usual citizen's rights, including you are not required to say anything etcetera and like that.' She spoke with a definite New York accent. Her eyes were intelligent and like two benign ice-picks. A tough and handsome woman.

'Yes, ma'am. Are you perchance related to one Sergeant Eddie Lucco, who used to work outa the 14th, in Manhattan?'

'As a matter of fact I married him.'

'No kidding. How is the man . . .?'

'He made Lieutenant.'

'Boy oh boy. There ain't no justice.' Williams grinned, showing pink gums and white teeth. He was pleased for Eddie.

Nancy Lucco gazed at him. She knew then where she had heard the name before. Elmore Williams had been a cop in the 14th Precinct, she remembered Eddie used to talk about him, with some respect. The two of them had worked on an undercover narcotics detail, a couple of years before she and Lucco had met. Mambo Hat, he had called Williams, because that was part of Elmore's dress code in those days.

It was obvious the Secret Service agent did not know that Eddie was dead. People lost touch. That figured. And they always assumed they could pick up the threads. Just with a phone call.

She touched the files on her desk. Elmore Williams' personal dossier, the reports on the 43rd Street counterfeit bust that had ended in a gunfight, Joe Pearce's cold and thoughtfully worded formal complaint against Williams, and various notes from the agent's boss, which did not quite state, did not state categorically, that Williams had infiltrated the counterfeit operation and failed to inform New York of his presence there, on direct orders from his superiors.

Her gaze travelled to the framed photo of a laughing couple at a table in Barolo, an Italian restaurant in downtown Manhattan, with tables out back in a sunken garden, surrounded by brownstone. There were trees, with lanterns in the lower branches. Lucco had gotten Bolognese sauce on his necktie which was, as always, worn loose, with his shirt collar undone.

She realized neither of them had spoken for a couple of moments. The suspended agent was watching her intently.

'This is a pretty shitty time to tell you,' Nancy said, quietly, her eyes meeting his. 'Eddie's dead.' She raised her elegant shoulders.

Elmore Williams stared at her. She gazed back, then glanced at her telephone, as if, he thought later, she half expected it to ring and for the big Wop detective to be on the other end of the line.

'Aw, fuck, pardon me, aw, shit . . .' and to his embarrassment, a couple of tears rolled from his lazy brown eyes. The hard-assed, take-no-crap Secret Serviceman pushed a big paw across his face and sniffed.

He took a deep breath and started to say something but the words got kinda choked up.

He started again. 'We were buddies. Eddie and me were partners. Worked outa Midtown South. Narco Squad . . . Ten years back but it seems like yesterday.'

A big clock on the wall clicked on one more minute of their lives.

'I know . . .' said Nancy quietly. She patted the pile of files on her desk.

'When . . .?' asked Williams. 'How . . .?'

'Two years back. He was murdered, in Bogota. That's Colombia. Took them six weeks to make an ID.'

Elmore Williams nodded. Eddie Lucco was the best. The guy was a real fuckin' hero. Twice a week, sometimes. He could remember how terrifying it had been to work with him. The man had no fear.

'Just don't imagine', said Counsellor Nancy Lucco, 'this changes a goddam thing . . .'

And her eyes met his. And she sure meant it.

'Yeah.' Williams nodded. Wiped his nose with the index knuckle of his left hand. 'Well, he wouldn't want it any different.'

There was a moment's pause. Then Elmore Williams announced, gravely, 'Fuck him, for getting wasted . . .'

Nancy Lucco glanced at her fingernails, the way women sometimes do. A kind of displacement activity.

'Yeah,' she said. 'Dumb Wop . . .'

Then she opened the first file and proceeded to give Elmore Williams the most comprehensive and merciless grilling of his entire career.

7

Not So Nice

DAVID JARDINE SAT in the front passenger seat of a bilious-green Mercedes 500SEL sedan, driven by the older of Reuven Arieh's two Mossad hoods. The younger one, with a wisp of black beard, sat in the back, a silenced Skorpion 7.65-mm machine-pistol resting on his lap, with the safety off and the firing mechanism switched to single rounds.

They were approaching the Furn El-Chebbak district of East Beirut, after a journey from Arieh's mountain villa.

Behind them, a Dodge four-wheel-drive with three back-up men provided not so much protection as a clear signal to the several disparate marauding groups that continued to be part of Beirut's lethal ambience – all heavily armed and used to casual violence – that here was a small, tight convoy representing someone with influence and access to the only two things that made a difference there: money and force.

It was not a watertight way of avoiding trouble but it discouraged the bands of young armed troublemakers from acts of random machismo.

As the Mercedes turned left off Avenue Pierre Gemayel into Avenue Sami El Solh, Jardine tapped a pack of Winston cigarettes Alisha had slipped into his jacket pocket and watched the ruined Place Omar Beyhum draw steadily closer, its once splendid buildings and centrepiece long wrecked by exploding shells and anti-tank rockets, and pockmarked with bullet-holes from the heavy .50, rapid-fire turret cannons of Israeli tanks and visiting Syrian peacemakers.

This square sat astride the Green Line dividing East and West Beirut, and at one time crossing it would have been perilous, even for the tight and heavily armed mini-convoys of men with political and financial clout. But times had changed and there was a fair chance that the Lebanon's latest Prime Minister, himself a multi-billionaire who was investing seriously in the city's reconstruction and future, might just be bringing some sanity and (comparative) tranquillity back to the country's once magnificent capital. For he was supported by Syria, whose strong military presence – military 'assistance' – in Beirut had succeeded in keeping the murderous rival factions in check.

His Israeli captor had promised Jardine a safe escort to the airport and he had not argued. How else was he going to get down from the Metn Hills? However, he had no intention of allowing himself to be driven into such a closely observed environment by this bunch of thugs, believed by every agency, domestic and foreign, to belong to the mysterious group of Salim Jaddeh, who enjoyed such close relations with Abu Nidal and Sadaam Hussein.

So as they drove through the war-ruined Place Omar Beyhum, under the eyes of the crew of an armed jeep of the Lebanese Army, backed up by a T-62 battle tank of the Syrian Army's 8th Tank Brigade, David Jardine had two things on his mind. The most immediate, but by far the least weighty, was getting out of the hideous green car and slipping away. The other was fairly thought-provoking, and that was the essence of an astonishing item of secret information with which Reuven Arieh had furnished him, together with, and very possibly indivisible from, a request the Mossad man had made. A request, when it boiled down to it, and even though it had been presented with more than a whiff of blackmail, for Jardine's assistance, using his clout (what remained of it) with the British Intelligence Service.

The information and the request would take some chewing over before he could properly evaluate them. But Arieh and his boss the Mamounieh must think the game was worth the candle. By kidnapping a senior SIS official, by revealing that Jardine's agent Pomegranate was an Israeli spy, and that 'Salim Jaddeh' was a deep-cover Mossad illegal, they had really taken a monumental risk. Pieces of theatre, in the espionage game, to convince Jardine that, even when vulnerable, he was a trusted man.

But why had they chosen him? Because he fitted the profile of a susceptible, disenchanted operator? Because he was neither pro- nor anti-Mossad? Because he still had some mileage in him? Would that prove to be well judged . . .?

Or was he a pawn in some bigger game? Was he being set up for some Israeli gambit against the Firm? Against British interests overseas?

And if so, where did that leave Jardine?

Would he be astute enough, subtle and . . . devious enough to swallow his injured pride and use Reuven Arieh's 'pitch' to further his own career? No, let's face it, David, he mused, to *rescue* his own career from an unsuspected, and one-way, excursion to the doldrums.

He could still hear Steven McCrae's cultured voice: 'I can't really see much future for David, in the new structure . . .'

Heavy stakes and just think, only seventy-two hours before, he had been bored to distraction in Washington, DC, listening to the interminable and essentially worthless deliberations of J-WISC.

It was still a funny old world. Thank God.

And what about the pack of Winston cigarettes? He still couldn't figure out why Alisha had slipped it into the pocket of his old linen jacket, whose worn cuffs and faint, irredeemable, much-laundered stains from wine and gun oil and Ambre Solaire from that girl in Valparaiso, and more recent events, could not hide the exquisite cut, which would doubtless earn his tailor a place in Heaven.

Along with the cigarettes she had put the battered brass Zippo lighter he had given her about seven years before.

Maybe it had been some quixotic impulse, to lessen the betrayal. Or maybe she had done it on the orders of her Cell Commander, Reuven Arieh, a.k.a. Salim Jaddeh.

There was something about the gesture that did not sit well with all that had transpired up there in Arieh's villa.

What was it they said to you at airport security these days? Did you pack your bags yourself, sir? For it was not beyond his hosts to have decided to blow him up in mid-air. Or even here, in this car, on his way to the airport. Maybe his two escorts were surplus to requirements.

Jardine lifted the cigarette pack from his pocket and opened it gingerly. Inside, still in their cellophane wrapper, were twenty Winstons. They seemed harmless enough.

He eased the Zippo out and, with a 'here goes' attitude, flicked the flint. A neat flame bloomed instantly.

So much for paranoia.

The driver tapped a plastic notice, in Arabic, stuck to the bilious-green dashboard. Translated, it read, 'We thank you for not smoking.'

David Jardine made an uncharitable reply, which suggested the man embark upon a physically unrealistic endeavour, and started to unpeel the cellophane wrapper. The driver glanced in his rear-view mirror, checking out two overtaking trail-bikes, each with two men on them. Young Wispy Beard had turned to his left to observe them, his Skorpion held just that bit more firmly.

Now would be a good opportunity, to shoulder open the door and roll sideways out of the car. That's what the SAS noncom, Spike Hoe, had taught them many years ago, when SIS still had its own Direct Action teams and training was shared between the Firm's own experienced instructors and a number of hard-eyed, dauntingly fit young men from 22nd SAS Regiment's Hereford barracks. It had proved to be the thin end of the wedge, for the SAS

Directorate, with its offices in Whitehall, had used its political leverage to acquire a Direct Action role of its own, 'in support of Government Foreign Policy', and until quite recently, when the Secret Intelligence Service had a requirement for clandestine-trained thuggery, the personnel more often than not were seconded from Hereford.

However, rolling out from a car travelling at thirty or forty miles per hour, on to the safety of a Welsh country lane, or an airfield tarmac, was not quite the same as attempting the exercise in a Beirut boulevard, with war-shattered buildings either side and groups of Syrian and Lebanese soldiers with fingers on the triggers of cocked and loaded weapons.

Plus there was the stitched wound on his side. That would probably rip apart once again.

The two trail-bikes snarled past and pulled away, banking first right, then left as they wove round the Rond-Point Chatilla, heading south-west towards the airport. The Mercedes entered the Chatilla roundabout and instead of following the motorbikes, made a right into the Avenue du 22 Novembre, which went north through the El Horj quarter and led quite quickly into access roads leading to the Hezbollah no-go areas of Sanayeh and Al Zarif.

'This is not the way to the airport,' Jardine said, wondering if he could start some sort of diversion with the Zippo and the cigarette pack.

The driver smiled, gratified it seemed by the English spy's discomfiture, and spun the wheel left, directly across the path of a huge truck rig with, of all things, 'Henry Heald & Company S.A.L.' in huge letters on the side. The truck's horn sounded as loud as any ship's foghorn and the Mercedes rocked in its wake as it slowed and cruised to a stop in the Rue El Fidayeh, where bulldozers and tar machines were busy restoring the surface of a street that had all but ceased to exist under the rubble of thirteen years of civil war.

At the kerb, on the far side of the street – just another sample of surreal Beirut – was the ubiquitous knife-grinder and his rickety wooden cart that Hassan had pointed out to Jardine when they had been getting away from Alisha's apartment. Was that really just the day before? Jesus.

And in a neat row, just across the road, was a taxi rank. Mercedes, Peugeot and Fiat sedans. Five of them. The drivers hunched on the sidewalk, what was going to be the sidewalk in the new Beirut, gossiping in the desultory, uncommitted way that cab-drivers have the world over. They reminded David Jardine of jazz musicians engaged in casual conversation before returning to their next break, without missing a beat.

Behind them, the big Dodge four-wheel loomed up and stopped, really close. It was very much in Jardine's mind that those could be his last moments on earth. He had served in this town. He had seen the crumpled, untidy cadavers, left-overs from this or that piece of score-settling in the jewel of the Lebanon, as the Tourist Board, unbelievably, had continued to describe Beirut throughout the madness.

The driver beside him switched off the engine and sat, relaxed, slightly smug, it seemed.

A metallic rattle came from the back seat. Doubtless Wispy Beard's Skorpion. In the side-mirror, doors from the Dodge opened and three young and fit-looking men dropped out, two carrying AKS assault rifles, the paratrooper's versions, without shoulder stocks, the third, a .45 Colt pistol, chrome-plated, with pearl handle. They checked all around, and moved towards the Mercedes, grimly purposeful.

Jardine was annoyed with himself. Sorry he had been such a shit to Dorothy, whom he loved more than himself and that was saying something. Sorry he was not to receive absolution but then, in his heart, this Catholic convert did not really believe he deserved it. He watched them as they moved in on his door. Jardine's heart was thudding and he stared into the eyes of each in turn. Would they drag him from the car? Which one would fire first? Nice enough young men, he found himself thinking, with their cold, serious expressions and long, untidy haircuts.

And surprised, even though his heart was pounding so, to feel no dread, no real fear.

The one with the pistol leaned down and peered at him. Scrutinizing Jardine's features. Doubtless to make sure he was slotting the right man.

The driver unlocked the car's central locking system. The whoosh of hot Beirut air turned the air-conditioned cool interior to damp humidity.

'*Monsieur Ramseyer*,' said the man with the pistol, '*je ne pense pas que vous veuilliez déboucher à l'aéroport avec des voyous commes nous. Voilà un taxi. C'est pas dangereux . . .*'

Jardine nodded, as if this was just what he was expecting to hear. I don't think you would like to be seen at the airport with a bunch of hoods like us, was what the young man with the gun had just said. Grab a taxi, it's not dangerous.

David Jardine nodded, and climbed out from the Mercedes. One of the men with an AKS opened the rear door and took Jardine's battered Bogota leather grip from Wispy Beard.

The Mercedes had moved off before he got halfway to the row of taxis. And by the time he reached the bleached blue Peugeot station-wagon at the front of the queue, the Dodge's engine growled and it too moved away.

Suddenly Jardine felt very alone, in a half-repaired street in the middle of downtown Beirut, on what continued to be the wrong side of the Green Line.

'*'fendi . . .*' said one of the drivers, a man of between forty and sixty, revealing blackened spaces where some important teeth should have been.

'Airport, let it be the will of God,' said Jardine in Arabic.

The driver nodded and opened the back door of his Peugeot, scratching his head without removing the flat cap that perched precariously on his grey hair.

'Let it be his will,' he replied automatically, and that is how David Arbuthnot Jardine left Beirut after a not uneventful forty-eight hours, pausing only to make two phone calls from the airport.

*

In Palermo, it was 7 o'clock in the morning. The two officer cleaners, women in their forties, one clearly of peasant descent, the other a native of Sciacca, on the south-west coast, part-Moorish, part-Sicilian, had just finished vacuuming the carpet on the stairs from the ground floor to the basement of the Banco di Calabria's securely guarded and expensively furbished mercantile branch.

The one from Sciacca was coiling up the electric cable from the vacuum-cleaner. Her friend, Bella, had opened the door to the closet that contained buckets and mops for wiping the white, blue and yellow ceramic tiles on the basement floor. They were engaged in a desultory conversation about the relative value for money of two brands of infant food, as advertised on Italian television, when the deputy manager, Signor Alfredo Buonatempora, came down from the securely protected administrative area, looking slightly flustered. He wore a grey pullover, sports coat and dark trousers, the first things that had come to hand.

For Buonatempora had been in the bed of his twenty-seven-year-old mistress, wife of a bank employee whom he had sent to Licata, on the Mediterranean, on a three-day audit, when his mobile phone had rung and he received a report from the local Polizia, that two men, both in their forties, had been seen leaving the bank by a rear entrance at 4.10 that morning. Why it had taken the Polizia so long to communicate that information had annoyed him considerably. Because, in addition to having eight armed guards on the premises at all times, and a comprehensive alarm and passive surveillance system covering every room, corridor, door, closet and elevator, the Banca di Calabria paid the local police around 60,000 US dollars a year for special cooperation in the protection of Sicily's most impregnable safety deposit vaults.

The guards on duty, however, had assured Buonatempora that no alarms had gone off and that video surveillance of every part of the bank's premises had been monitored throughout the night. So the report was probably wrong. It was easy at four in the morning to mistake one rear door in a Palermo alley for another.

Soon after the deputy manager started to check the electronically locked doors to the sub-basement and the vaults, he heard agitated voices from the stairs to the floor above, the ground floor, and one of the guards descended, stepping past a bucket laid out by Lucita.

'*Signore*, there are two clients upstairs. Demanding to see you immediately.'

Two clients? At five after seven in the morning?

'Who are they?' asked the deputy manager.

'One is called Muhler, and one with a French name. Jacques something . . .'

Jacques-Stiguer. And Bernard Muhler. *Porca madonna*, thought Buonatempora. Just great! Two big customers, who only yesterday had deposited 150 million dollars, in bearer bonds, in titanium safety deposit boxes stored in the vault. Who had been shown just a few of the bank's elaborate measures, from sophisticated electronic surveillance and detection devices and alarm systems to the five special vaults, beneath seven decoy vaults in the sub-basement, whose walls and floors were enclosed in boxes of a ceramic plastic four times more blast-, heat-, cold laser- and diamond-head-proof than titanium, one of the hardest metals known to man.

Muhler and his taciturn companion had seemed reassured by the security arrangements, which included an invisible, paralysing, smell-free gas and devices to lock the entire building down, trapping any intruders who were foolhardy enough to tamper with the combination of electronic and regular locking devices which protected the twelve vaults.

And here they were, two strangers in Palermo. What did they want at this time in the morning, if it was not to check out rumours of intruders just three hours before?

'Herr Muhler,' beamed Buonatempora, as he emerged into the ground-floor lobby with its smoked-glass and antique-mirrored walls, marble floor and granite columns, heavy leather seats and polished chrome. '*Buon giorno. Guten Morgen*. What can I do for you? Some coffee perhaps?'

'No.' Jacques-Stiguer spoke in English, with little trace of an accent. 'We are sorry to disturb you, *signore*, but our time in Palermo is limited, and we wish to have access to our safety deposit boxes in your secure vaults . . .'

Had Buonatempora imagined it, or had the man hesitated, before using the word 'secure'?

'Pardon me, gentlemen,' Buonatempora switched from German to English as smoothly as befitted a cosmopolitan executive of a cosmopolitan bank, 'that is not possible. I explained to you yesterday, our vaults are electronically locked, with a time-clock.' He spread his arms. 'Also, there are procedures for security. Which must be followed. Please come back at, say, 9 o'clock. I will escort you personally. You are, of course . . . special and valued customers.'

Herr Bernard Muhler – Danny Davidov – met Buonatempora's frank and yet unhelpful expression. He had been standing dwarfed beneath a huge oil painting of Garibaldi, revolutionary Italian hero. The massive frame of gold leaf seemed out of place, yet not unexpected, in the chrome and mirrored marble hall. Then Danny nodded, turned, hands thrust deep in trouser pockets, and ambled without a word to the armoured glass door which looked out on the Via Maqueda and the world of gaiety and poverty and violent death that was Palermo.

In the silence that ensued, the lack of response finally unnerved the usually urbane deputy manager. He crossed to join the man he knew as Muhler.

'*Signore . . .?*'

When Danny Davidov spoke, his voice was quiet but confidently lethal. 'I imagine, at this particular time of the day,' he checked his wristwatch, 'seven twenty-three, I imagine not many people, not many of the bank's clients, have heard that your impregnable . . . that is the word you used yesterday, that two prowlers were seen leaving your impregnable bank at four ten this morning . . . That is my information. We are serious men, *signor*. And well informed. Believe me.'

The faint drone of the vacuum-cleaner moaned, like a Greek chorus, from the basement.

Alfredo Buonatempora spread his hands, without moving his elbows. 'Rumours. I have just been down to the vaults. Believe me. There have been no intruders down there.'

Please God I am right, he prayed. But right now the bank's reputation was more important than the truth.

'Now, I'm sure,' went on Danny Davidov, 'I am sure that our 150 million dollars are safe. And just as soon as my colleague and I have confirmed that is so, we shall leave you in peace.'

They were joined by the taller man, the one with the fake French name and the wolf's gaze.

'If, on the other hand, we leave here without inspecting our strongboxes,' Kolosov murmured, peering at his slightly distorted reflection in the pale gold and pink antique glass wall, 'the whole of Sicily will know that the mercantile branch is vulnerable.' He glanced at his friend.

Danny nodded. 'How would the Minister for Agriculture feel about that?' he asked, glancing at his watch.

Danny and Kolosov knew that the Minister for Agriculture had around 600 million in cash and cocaine stashed in the *banca*'s vaults. In fact, they had spent eight months and 1.4 million in bribes to acquire full details of many of the bank's anonymous clients.

'Or Don Giovanni . . .?' added Danny helpfully, meaning the *capo di tutti capi*, the Prince of the Mafia himself. Giovanni Favorito Noto.

Alfredo Buonatempora felt suddenly light-headed as the blood thumped through his veins. The *stranieri*, the two wealthy foreigners, had called him out. Either he could stand his ground and risk a stupid scandal – for in his bones he felt sure there had been no break-in – or he could give in gracefully and let these urbane and dangerous men check out their bearer bonds, locked down in the vaults, and then get the hell out of what was turning into quite an upsetting day.

Buonatempora forced a polite smile on to his unwilling face. 'Please excuse me for one minute,' he said, and left them by the armoured glass door.

Inside his office, Alfredo Buonatempora found the sanctuary of his polished hide swivel-chair and sank into the soft leather even as he lifted the green telephone and punched out a number he knew by heart, but very seldom had occasion to use. The line was the private one of Dr Dante Giuliano Corso, President of the Banca di Calabria.

Buonatempora had never been to the legendary equestrian stud in the remote south-eastern hinterland of Italy, where the President, Il Dottore, bred polo ponies and kept his exquisite collection of European Old Masters and T'ang pottery, along with Bugattis and antique airplanes. But he had seen the video of the bank's 100th jubilee, when his boss had been one of fifty senior officials who had attended a three-day gala celebration, along with their families. The place looked like something out of a Hollywood movie.

He could imagine, as the ringing tone commenced, Il Dottore taking English tea on the terrace of his splendid villa overlooking several thousand well-kept acres of grazing land and sandy forest, leading in undulating tiers to Lake Cecita and the picturesque twelfth-century villages of La Mula and Giardino di Neto. There would be white-jacketed servants and lithe *contadini*, girl servants, to screw when the fancy took him.

'*Si,*' answered the voice of an educated man, a voice used to power, as was obvious to Buonatempora from the utterance of just that one word.

'*Padrone,*' started the deputy manager, sitting more upright in his comfortable leather swivel-chair, 'this is Alfreddo Buonatempora, deputy manager of the mercantile branch, in Palermo.'

'It better be good,' replied Dante Giuliano Corso, 'to phone this early in the morning.'

'*Dottore Presidente,*' commenced Buonatempora, and he explained, in a level-headed and businesslike way, his dilemma. About the reported possible intruders, of which a close search had revealed no trace. And about the two awkward clients, demanding to be let in, out of hours, to count their money, which was in bearer bonds totalling 150 million US dollars.

When he had finished, giving his account in the no-nonsense, matter-of-fact style every senior executive had been warned was the only way to make one's mark with the boss, Il Dottore, there was silence down the telephone line. A silence so deep that Buonatempora, in his imagination, almost had time to picture the cable from his ear to the President's, some 300 miles away to the north-east.

'How much did you say those gentlemen have on deposit . . .?' asked Corso, with a softness which was deceptive.

'One fifty-seven million US, in bearer bonds, *signor*.'

'And they have been customers how long . . .?'

'Just over nineteen months. They say they are French and Swiss. They started with 700,000, and it has grown with sizeable deposits. At the beginning of the year, they transferred forty-one million to a Cayman Islands merchant bank, which left just 100,000 with us. Then, three weeks later, about a month ago, 157 million was electronically transferred from a bank in Japan. Tokyo. Into their joint account.'

'Has any outside . . . agency been making inquiries about them?'

'No, *dottore*.'

'And references . . .?'

'Impeccable. Including one from Sheikh Fadlallah.' Sheikh Fadlallah was an Iranian cleric and politician who had been systematically transferring hundreds of millions of his country's cash assets into banks like the Banco di Calabria – banks which asked no questions – all around the world.

'Alfredo,' said a voice that indicated, I am tired of this

nonsense, 'Let the men into the vault. It is their goddam money.'

'Of course, *Presidente*. I just thought it was prudent to check . . . Even if –'

'Open the vault, Signor Buonatempora. Thanks for your call.'

And the line went dead.

Buonatempora felt a bit of an *ottuso*, a dumbfuck. A goddam fool. Open the vault had said the boss, to whom personal calls should be rationed, employees were abjured, so that they could avoid appearing indecisive. And let the gentlemen count their own money.

The deputy manager replaced the receiver and sighed. He shrugged and strolled out, lighter of foot. For the decision was no longer his to make. It was the decision of Il Presidente, the big boss, in his big damn rancho deluxe, far away from where the real work was done.

Che magnifico . . .! How very goddam fantastic.

Muhler and Jacques-Stiguer, still in the lobby, rose from their seats in the waiting area. 'Gentlemen, please forgive me. I have decided to arrange for the time-clocks to be overridden.'

'Wow, you can do that?' exclaimed the shorter of the two men. Herr Muhler.

'This is not a backwater, sir.' Alfredo Buonatempora smiled thinly. 'Please follow me . . .'

Seventeen minutes later, Danny Davidov and Nikolai Kolosov were standing inside Deep Vault Number Three, below the sub-basement with its five decoy vaults, which housed the treasures of mere millionaires.

Buonatempora had initiated an emergency code which overrode the time locks, and had summoned two trusted under-managers, who had turned up early because they had heard something was happening at the bank, the way news travels in Palermo. It required the three of them to supply the electronic codes and the manual keys, to gain access to the sub-basements and the vault which housed the two men's 150 million.

Three armed guards stood outside the vault, backs to one wall. A heavy door slid open and Buonatempora ushered in the two customers.

Inside, an armoured glass screen, with an armoured glass and titanium steel door, separated them from the ranks of strongboxes that formed the greater parts of the other three walls.

'As I explained to you yesterday, gentlemen,' said Buonatempora, with commendable courtesy considering the ruthless way in which he had been forced to give his two customers access outside normal banking hours (but then, such things were not exactly unheard of in Palermo), 'the guards are for your protection and will remain outside while you are using your strongboxes. The door to the vault will be sealed. To leave, merely press those two buttons located on the left of the door. They must be pressed simultaneously. I trust that is clear?'

Kolosov nodded. '*All ist verstoden. Dankeschon, Herr Buonatompora . . .*'

Danny Davidov said, '*Ja. Grossedanke.*'

Buonatempora gazed at Davidov. 'I'll be upstairs.' He glanced around the walls, which consisted of slate-grey safety deposit box front sections, of many sizes, with a mixture of relief and pride. 'As you can see, there has been no break-in.'

'I cannot tell you how comforting that is to my colleague and me, *signore*.' The taller of the two smiled, relaxed and patient now that he had got his own way.

And at about the same time as Buonatempora was getting into the elevator taking him up two levels to the ground floor of the mercantile branch of the Banca di Calabria, one Salvatore E. Betancourt, a voice-over artist from Cinecitta in Rome, who could mimic almost any Southern Italian male voice to such perfection it could fool a voice-print monitor (which in the technology of law enforcement and espionage was considered to be as good and as unique as a fingerprint), was helping a former Yugoslavian Technical

Security agent to pack up his illegal telephone intercept from an access tunnel not even a block from the bank.

'That was impressive, and I've worked with a few artists,' remarked the Technical boffin.

'Well, the pay's good and the hours are short,' replied Betancourt. And the voice he used was the one Alfreddo Buonatempora had heard on the other end of his phone conversation.

In fact, Buonatempora was to swear on oath that it had been the voice of Dr Dante Giuliano Corso. And sadly, that would be the cause of his untimely death from what was known in Palermo forensic circles as lead poisoning.

But you can't, as Danny Davidov observed to Nikolai Kolosov, make an omelette without breaking eggs.

Ronnie Szabodo was waiting at Terminal 2 as the first-class passengers emerged off the Swissair Flight from Geneva. Jardine caught his eye and noted that the squat Hungarian – former Hungarian – had actually put in his denture plate. One of Szabodo's front teeth had been knocked out in a brawl with an American sailor in Saigon, many years before, but the denture felt uncomfortable and he only slipped it from the pocket of his tweed jacket into his mouth on special occasions. Like being summoned to the Clandestine Accounts Office, to explain his expenditure of government money, or making an assignation with some lady he had taken a shine to. At that time, the lady in question was the wife of the barman at his local British Legion club. A waiflike forty-year-old, with hair that crackled from excessive dyeing. But love is blind and she thought Ronnie was wonderful, which is always a good start. And in his own way, thought Jardine, as they strolled through the terminal and approached the old Jaguar XJ-6 illegally parked on two yellow lines by the arrivals exit doors, he *was* rather wonderful.

Szabodo cast a grin of immense charm at a female traffic warden he seemed to have recruited to make sure his car was not towed away, and she actually blushed as he opened the back door to let Jardine put his battered Colombian leather grip inside.

They did not speak until the Jaguar had nosed sedately out of the airport and was gathering speed on the road connecting Heathrow to the M4 motorway.

David Jardine searched the glove compartment for cigarettes. 'Ronnie, I don't know if it's a good idea to go straight to the Office.'

Ronnie nodded. 'Why do you think I brought my own car?'

Jardine glanced at his watch. A fake Rolex Oyster he had bought for 65 dollars in Singapore. 'We need to talk.'

'Sure.' Ronnie Szabodo slid the car off the motorway at Junction 3, and twenty minutes later, after using a series of back routes that would have done credit to a taxi-driver, they were strolling along the towpath at Barnes. Two crews were rowing on the Thames. Fours. And a small wooden boat with an outboard motor moved fussily between them, a trainer using a megaphone to deliver advice and instructions to the rowers.

Jardine had told Szabodo everything from his arrival in Beirut, the stabbing, his conversation in Le Camel café with Hassan, his kidnapping by Salim Jaddeh, who had turned out to be the legendary Mossad black operator Reuven Arieh, the fact that Pomegranate had been doubling for the Israelis for some years, maybe all along, the tape of Steven McCrae and the firm's Director of Personnel discussing Jardine, right up to the moment on the terrace, gazing down on Dhouer El-Chouer, when Reuven Arieh had said he had a proposition.

Szabodo nodded, as if he heard such bizarre stories every day. Well, maybe not every day, but certainly once in a while. He stuck his hands deep in his pockets and gazed, shoulders hunched, at the rowing skiffs and the busy motorboat, faint exhortations drifting over the lazy Thames with its sludge-coloured water, driftwood and the occasional dead dog. 'What is it, David? His proposition . . .?'

And David Jardine told him.

And as he told him, he was back there, the whiff of orange trees and cedar smoke, the somehow melancholy hint of honey in the fresh-made lime juice with its sprig of mint, the memories of such piquant smells and tastes which could only be the Lebanon.

Reuven Arieh had told Jardine about an international figure, a multi-millionaire called Robert Maxwell, a man who had died in mysterious circumstances, falling off the stern of his luxury yacht near the Canary Islands. How the Czech publisher and newspaper magnate had approached Mossad twenty years before, and had started to pass on information, when it came his way, that might be of use to the Israeli nation. It had been generally low-grade economic and political intelligence, and the man had been more humoured than respected. But it had been the Institute's prognosis that Maxwell was on his way to power and enormous wealth and they had kept him sweet, even providing him with a case officer from Mossad's Political Assets department.

Robert Maxwell's codename had been 'William', so prosaic as to verge on the banal. The small staff of the Political Assets department had nicknamed him Malvolio, after the character in Shakespeare's *Twelfth Night*, who was so puffed up with self-importance that when he fell for a lady, he was persuaded to strut about in ridiculous yellow cross-garters, assured that would grab her attention and arouse her passion.

But Maxwell the joke-figure did indeed rise in wealth and international importance. And even as his real stature increased, he continued to nurture his somewhat absurd delusion, his secret – that he was really an agent of Mossad.

David Jardine and Ronnie Szabodo understood this pathetic story, because the reality of the espionage world was virtually unknown to the rest of humanity, to which the Hungarian drily referred as 'Wonderland'. The only glimpses that others had of the covert firmament was in the occasional grand fuck-ups, memoirs of disenfranchised former officers, pulp fiction and movies, or newspaper 'exposés' by reporters who, for some strange reason, never seemed to understand how the business of espionage worked. Even those among them who had trailed their coats and, in the process, allowed their journalistic integrity to be compromised, did not seem to be able to catch the true whiff of the cold-blooded, highly dedicated, imaginative and ruthlessly searching professionalism that was the essential stuff of clandestine work.

Notwithstanding their necessary ignorance, outsiders continued to be fascinated by hints, intimations of a sort of . . . what? Magic? Freemasonry? A remit to behave illegally, outrageously, in the patriotic service of the nation? Whatever their perceptions, to many ordinary, otherwise sensible, down-to-earth people, secret intelligence work seemed sexy and dangerous, and they imagined it conferred some kind of aura upon those admitted to its cabal.

What bullshit, thought David Jardine. And he continued with his story.

Since 1987, according to Arich, 'William' had been handled by Mossad's Deputy Director Operations (West), a former team coordinator in Operation 'Wrath of God', in which members of the Institute's Action Service and Unit 101 had conducted an illegal and murderous war against Palestinian terrorist groups in the Middle East and Europe. The Deputy Director was a former IDF paratroop officer called Danny Davidov.

'I remember him,' said Ronnie Szabodo. 'Short, slim fellow. Used to smoke cheroots. He was in Cyprus in '86. Op Parsifal. He was the Israeli man. Hissing Sid was the Yank.'

Jardine smiled. Ronnie used words like Yank and gosh without a blush. With sublime unawareness, he massacred with his Magyar consonants a form of speech which he fondly imagined to be the laconic drawl of the public school and Oxbridge men who had still formed the backbone of SIS when he was recruited, fresh from the Hungarian uprising in 1956. Szabodo had been a Budapest teenager, in the last year of high school, and he had fought fiercely in the desperate and doomed street-by-street battles against an entire Soviet tank army and divisions of Mongol and Tartar infantry, sent in on the advice of Ambassador Yuri Andropov because of their propensity to rape and loot and kill without conscience. For Terror was the name of the Soviet game.

Ronnie had saved the life of a young British journalist working for Reuters, who had been an officer of the Firm. And SIS had been quick to respond when the sixteen-year-old Hungarian had presented himself one night, about 11 o'clock, at the British Embassy in, of all places, Warsaw, Poland.

He had been fed and rested and brought to London on a diplomatic passport. After evaluation, he had been sent straight back behind the Iron Curtain, to work as an agent, with no guarantees and no comebacks if he was caught or compromised.

Two years later, Ronnie Szabodo had been exfiltrated and once more brought back to England. Not yet twenty, his exploits had earned him the respect of that band of sublimely educated pirates who ran things in those happy, innocent days. The shadow of Burgess and Maclean had not really shaken the outfit, Harold Adrian Russell Philby was still considered to be reliable and was working under journalistic cover in Beirut, and the Secret Intelligence Service continued to have a flavour of the Elizabethan Court, with a whiff of the Hellfire Club.

Young Szabodo had been coached in A-levels and sent to St Antony's College, Oxford, where he worked assiduously, aware of the great opportunity he had been given, and having burnt the midnight oil for three years, he just scraped through with a poor Second in Slavonic History.

The Firm, however, embraced him, and while Ronnie Szabodo was never going to attain great things, he soon gained a reputation as an able and reliable operations man. And over the years he had become a permanent fixture, never working in Broadway Buildings or, later, Century

House, the appalling glass box at St George's Circus, but always a streetfighter, attached now to London Station, working out of Brompton Road, now to Direct Action (UK OPS), an outfit that did not exist, even to the Firm's Clandestine Accounts Section, and sometimes just working out of a couple of nondescript vehicles and a converted railway arch at the back of Brixton Station.

It had actually been Ronnie Szabodo who had recruited Jardine, a million light years ago, had been his mentor, when David Jardine was a real secret agent, working in a variety of Denied Areas from Saigon to Afghanistan, and who had assiduously watched his back and kicked his arse when need be, all the way through Jardine's steady rise through the foothills of secret power. No wonder they called him Renfield, to Jardine's Count Dracula.

'Anyway,' went on Jardine, 'the fact is, Maxwell turned up one day at the home of Mossad's Clandestine Ops chief, who was based at that time in Paris, as you will recall, Ronnie.

'Robert Maxwell was by then in control of the vast Pergamon Press empire, which was virtually his own to do with as he chose. "I know," said Maxwell, agent 'William', "what every secret service needs more than anything else."

'"What is that?" asked Nathan Zamir. You remember him . . .?' Szabodo nodded. He remembered Zamir.

'"Money," replied Maxwell. He knew, you see. He understood that the Achilles heel of a truly secret intelligence service is that it has to account for its funding to its political masters.'

'Who come and go,' observed the Magyar, 'and might want to meddle.'

Jardine went on, 'Now, any service worth its salt has overbudgeted for many years. And because many of its most effective areas of expenditure are acknowledged to be too sensitive for detailed balance sheets, it's possible to acquire very considerable unaccountable funds.'

'Difficult for the Israelis.' Ronnie Szabodo fumbled in

the pocket of his immaculately cut tweed jacket. 'Their service has been busy since day one and before. It's a small outfit in a small nation, hard to salt too much away. For a raining day.'

The jacket looked too new. And the Tattersall check shirt, in the sort of thick Viyella that shrinks and irritates one's neck, suggested just a bit too much of the shires for a London suburban towpath.

Jardine went on with his story. '"I can provide you with millions," Maxwell offered. "Directly from me to offshore funds, or in cash, choose your currency." And he made it very clear he meant the money was for Mossad and no one else. To help them create a secret fund.

'Nathan Zamir took advice. They put together one or two tests, one or two charades, the way we sometimes do, Ronnie, and established that whatever else he might be, and they really did not like the man one bit, Robert Maxwell was 100 per cent discreet and 110 per cent pro-Mossad.'

'As opposed to pro-Israel,' observed Szabodo, producing a Peterson briar pipe from his jacket pocket and holding it to stare at, as if he did not remember putting it there in the first place.

'Pro-Mossad. He believed he *was* Mossad. The man was obsessed with the idea that he was one of them. A fully paid-up operator.'

'Who just happened', Ronnie understood at once, 'to have struck it lucky and become a zillionaire publisher. And confrère of Royalty and presidents . . .'

Jardine thought Ronnie meant confidant but he touched a stone on the path with the toe of his shoe and agreed. 'That's exactly it. And for about twelve years, Robert Maxwell became a principal source of funding for any operations the Tel Aviv Institute did not want to tell their political masters too much about.'

'Like, anything at all . . .?'

'Just like that,' replied Jardine. It was suddenly very quiet. The outboard motor on the small wooden boat had stuttered to a stop and he had not realized how much background buzz the thing had been making till it ceased.

Two seagulls cried, wheeling overhead.

'It's going to rain, do you think?' Jardine asked nobody in particular.

'What makes you say that?' inquired Szabodo.

'Seagulls. They don't often come this far inland . . .'

'And that means it's going to rain?'

They watched the birds, who seemed to hover and dip aimlessly.

'To tell you the truth,' replied Jardine, 'I've absolutely no idea.' And he grinned.

Ronnie Szabodo gave him a long look. 'Don't try to snow me, David. Something's shaken you to the core.'

'Anyway,' David Jardine ignored Szabodo's prescient remark, 'Danny Davidov was Maxwell's case officer.'

'And he put his hands in the till drawer . . .' Ronnie nodded. It was an old story.

'They were very cross. Trusted him, you see. He had been chosen by Marty Effriam himself.'

'How much . . .?'

'Well, Maxwell, "William", fell off that bloody boat and they buried him on the Mount of Olives. He had certainly paid for it. With tens of millions to the Israeli Government in addition to his secret slush fund to Mossad. According to Arieh, Tel Aviv Accounts Section did a routine audit. They were worried because while, before, they had not bothered where the money had originated, murmurs were gathering of a staggering theft from newspaper pension funds. They had assumed Maxwell was just stinking rich.'

Ronnie Szabodo tamped fresh tobacco into the bowl of his pipe, eyes narrowed as he affected to understand what the rowing crews were about. 'So how much?'

'Maxwell arranged secretly, for Mossad, or to be more precise, if my hunch is correct, Ronnie, what he believed to be Mossad, to receive around seventy-three million pounds sterling. That's what the audit revealed. But it was not all accounted for.'

The Hungarian watched Jardine quizzically, as if he already knew what was coming. 'Do you have a light?'

'Sure.' And David Jardine handed over the brass Zippo he had given to Alisha, in a time when he imagined he had a handle on his work.

'This is a nice lighter. It looks as if it has lived a little.' Szabodo sucked and puffed the way pipe-smokers do. His hand cupped over the flame.

'Your tobacco will smell of petrol,' said Jardine.

'I like the smell.'

Jardine thought of the sixteen-year-old Hungarian lobbing Molotov cocktails down the barrels of Russian T-54 tank guns.

'Davidov had put about seven million sterling in his back pocket,' he said. 'Exchange rate at the time worked out about eleven million dollars.'

They strolled on, bored with the shouts and ineptitude of the men trying to start the outboard motor, ignoring their polite, almost diffident calls for assistance.

'Which made Danny Davidov less than flavour of the month,' observed Szabodo, trying out one of the modern, but essentially English, expressions he liked to record in his spidery copperplate, in a little green diary.

'His masters were in a bind. Reuven Arieh's version of events is that not many people in Mossad knew about their financial arrangements with "William". It was a closely guarded in-house secret, he says. What courses were open to them?' Jardine glanced at his colleague.

'They could hardly try him in a regular, or even an in-camera, court,' Ronnie Szabodo meant a secret court where justice might be seen to be done but the facts were never heard, 'if what they had done was in itself unconstitutional and illegal. I suppose they could have bumped him off . . .' This was the option most of the democracies' secret services never talked about. But it would be fanciful to imagine it did not exist.

'Difficult,' said Jardine, 'in a small nation like Israel. People would eventually get to hear. Bad advertisement.

Mothers would not want their sons to join an outfit that murdered its own. Wives . . . sisters.'

'Fire him and swear him to silence . . .?'

'Very feeble, Ronnie. If it had been me I'd've sent him on an assignment to Bosnia, or South America. And made sure he became a casualty of war.'

Ronnie Szabodo looked at the tall man beside him. He knew Jardine was not joking. 'So how did they resolve it?'

David Jardine explained how Davidov had been hauled across Tel Aviv to that safe house where traitors to the State and terrorist leaders were interrogated. How he had not been let out of the sight of his jailers until he had made electronic contact with a number of offshore accounts and had returned just over five million dollars, claiming he had invested the balance in bad currency deals and providing the paperwork to prove it.

'They formally stripped him of his Israeli nationality and provided him with new identity,' he said.

'South African or Belgian?' inquired Szabodo, who was no child in the maze of new, as opposed to false, identities.

'South African. But he soon ditched it.'

'You look like shit, David. Why are you limping?'

'Never mind that. The deal was, Danny had to disappear like a good little wandering Jew and keep his head down. He had to swear on the Torah to that effect.'

'Here's a bench. Let's take some weight from our shoes.'

Jardine settled on the bench. He did indeed feel exhausted. But nothing like the night before, when he had fainted clean away. He instinctively touched the left side of his abdomen with his right hand. Aw, hell. Damp again. And was it his imagination or did it not smell too good?

'But he did not', Szabodo went on, 'keep his head down . . .'

'Far from it. At first he seemed to fall off the edge of the planet. Then, again according to Arieh, they got a couple of sightings, in Delhi and in Sydney, Australia.'

'I do know where Sydney is, David.'

'Tel Aviv Interpol always had a Mossad man popping in

for a cup of whatever these people drink.' Jardine shrugged.

'Eventually they linked certain international financial crimes to Danny's modus. His reputation had been built up on deception and disinformation operations. Some of them verged on the brilliant. It was apparently no surprise when the documents proving he had squandered nearly 6 million dollars turned out to be forgeries. It's not that Davidov himself had the skills. But he had, on computer, people all around the world he knew he could buy, who were masters of their crafts. Counterfeiting. Electronic accessing. Special papers. Voice artists. The lot.'

The two skiffs scythed smoothly through the water, oarsmen in perfect harmony. The motorboat drifted into sight, about 200 yards away, turning aimlessly, carried by the tide, mocked by three wheeling seagulls.

Jardine went on, 'The signature crimes, as Reuven Arieh put it, grew more ambitious and more daring. And the amounts of money now involved were becoming distinctly unfunny. One fifty-seven million out of Tokyo via St Petersburg. And just today, Ronnie. Even as I left Arieh's place, if he is to be believed, something in excess of 2000 million, from the vaults of a bank in Palermo. Now that takes balls.'

'I thought a bank would keep that to itself,' remarked Szabodo.

'They think they have. The Israelis got wind of it, someone in the Italian Ministry of Agriculture.'

Ronnie Szabodo puffed at the dregs of his pipe, making a disgusting sucking sound. At some juncture on the stroll along the towpath, he had pocketed the denture.

'I don't want to intrude into your fascinating story, David. But you have gotten nowhere near telling me why you do not completely believe Reuven Arieh's story. Or indeed the nature of his proposition, or how he has compromised you.'

In the silence that followed, David Jardine would gladly have traded places with those turkeys stranded out there on the Thames, trying fruitlessly to start their flooded outboard motor.

'So what happened? Do you want medical attention for that cut in your side first?' Nothing escaped Ronnie Szabodo.

Jardine took a cigarette from its pack and put it in his mouth. He flicked the Zippo.

'Where did you get the Winstons?'

'Alisha. Pomegranate.' And before Jardine could touch the cigarette with the flickering flame, Szabodo plucked it from his mouth.

'Maybe you should try another brand. I'd like to run this lot through the labs . . .'

'Isn't that a trifle dramatic?'

'Just very occasionally, David, very rarely, this job can get a bit dramatic.'

'Really,' Jardine replied drily.

'So how did he get to you?' pursued the Hungarian. 'How has it changed you? For just after this one hour, David, I can assure you it has . . .'

Jardine sighed. It always boiled down to his need for a certain type of woman. Good looks, long legs, intellect, a certain unattainable quality and, of course, that latent streak of something close to depravity which transmitted only to those few on the same wave-length.

Ronnie concentrated on wrapping the cigarette packet in a blue silk hankie he had probably bought in some posh Jermyn Street shop, to bolster his self-image as an English gentleman, waiting for his superior to reply.

'By revealing,' said Jardine, 'by demonstrating quite dramatically, that for some years now, Alisha has been a jewel not, as I fondly imagined, in my crown but in Mossad's. Arieh put me in a position where, without saying it, without being so vulgar, it was tacitly suggested that nobody need know. That if I take up their offer of access to Mossad intelligence on Danny Davidov, in order to help them stop him before he becomes too great an embarrassment, then no one in Century need know.'

'And Pomegranate could continue to seem to be run by you, as your prize asset inside the Lebanese Government . . .'

Jardine nodded. He wondered what was in the pack of Winstons. A message that she was still loyal to SIS? A message of love? Details of Davidov and his crimes? Signposts to future moves by the Israeli renegade? Cyanide? Or was it just a pack of cigarettes? That still got his first vote.

'Either way, Ronnie, I was suckered into running off to Beirut because I am no longer the switched-on operator I once was.'

'Bullshit.'

'Nice of you to say so. I got myself stabbed by a teenage kid because I was not even switched on when I was back at work.'

'Could have happened to anyone.'

'And by leaving it up to me, what I disclose in my debrief, they know if I leave anything out, I will be their creature for ever. Because we've done that. You and I have done that to people. It's how we run our bloody business, isn't it?'

'And have you left anything out?' The Hungarian passed the bowl of his pipe under his nose, sniffing it, as if he was not really interested.

'Not a single thing.' Jardine had even declared, in his early Pomegranate reports, the day, seven years before, when he and the agent had become lovers.

'And yet you feel compromised. David, I don't understand.'

David Jardine arched his aching back. His wound felt dull and sore. He was thirsty. He wondered if he had subconsciously allowed Ronnie to bring him here to interrogate him. To test his account, before taking it to the Office.

'You understand perfectly well.'

Szabodo half-closed his eyes. Considered for a moment. Then he nodded. 'They chose, for this . . . unusual approach, someone who fits a certain profile. Somebody who can use all the resources of a service other than their own, to get the result they want. Someone who feels he is not appreciated by his own people. Who is ungruntled.'

'Disgruntled.'

'Somebody they could make feel stupid somehow, then pick up, treat with respect and show a way to regain his reputation, by doing what? Stopping Danny Davidov stealing a few billion dollars?' Szabodo frowned. 'Come on, old boy, you're far too grownup to fall for that.'

'They ran the case past a team of psychologists and shrinks,' Jardine replied, 'with access to Danny's operational history. This produced a prediction which I tend to agree with. Given that Davidov is possessed of a devious, quite brilliant, criminal mind.'

'Isn't that an asset in this business of ours, David?'

Jardine ignored the comment. It was maybe too close to the mark. 'They believe his ultimate target is coming up fast. Time, they allege, is not on their side. Actually, he said, "our" side.'

'So what's the prodigal spy going to do? That's got them wetting themselves?'

'One of his areas of expertise – he lectured on it for years inside Mossad – is destabilizing currency markets. By disinformation, deception and counterfeiting. It would not be fanciful to predict that he plans to rock to its foundations a major international currency. The yen, the pound, the dollar.'

'With a view to what?' asked his old mentor. Unsurprised, as ever.

'Extortion. They think he plans to shake the tree, leave it standing in return for a pay-off of several thousand millions, as in billions, Ronnie, in sterling or dollars.' Jardine shrugged. 'Maybe Deutschmarks. I dunno. The forecast also is that Danny Davidov will leave a trail that points to Tel Aviv.'

'That must have them worried . . .'

'I did sense a certain desperation behind that bastard's icy demeanour. He's so personally uptight I was ... intrigued. Star operator like Reuven.'

Ronnie Szabodo seemed to be fingering the denture nestling in his jacket pocket. 'Let's suppose that Reuven Arieh is running the op to find and stop Danny Davidov. Okay so far?'

'Sure.'

'So put yourself in his place and it's a nightmare. Davidov will probably slip up and get himself caught. Nations and big banks don't let this kind of thing happen, David. And let Mossad try to explain its hands are clean? No way, Pedro. And nobody is going to forgive Israel for letting it happen. But why tell you? Why tell *us*?'

'Maybe they're telling a few people. So that they can turn round and say, Don't look at us. We tried to warn you all.'

The Hungarian kicked at a stone on the towpath. As if trying out the mannerism he had seen the really English Jardine enact a few moments before. He sometimes reminded Jardine of a rather lethal version of Winnie the Pooh.

'If you ask me,' Szabodo said, 'this is not Mossad. The whole ... panoply of the Israeli Government's Intelligence Service surely has the capability to reach out and slap Danny's hand before it got this far. Also, David, they would, of course they would, have passed on discreet warnings. To friendly services.' Ronnie chose his words carefully. 'This has to be a piece of private enterprise that's gone wrong.'

And there it was.

Trust Ronnie, who knew better than most that one of the multitude of risks attending clandestine services is that other, more clandestine organisms can grow from within. And take quiet root, undetected by their hosts.

Jardine watched the motorboat drift away from the welcoming safety of a ramshackle jetty, one man in the bow reaching out in vain with a brass-tipped boathook.

'So, this rogue element, David. Inside the Tel Aviv Service. Who? Who, precisely?'

'Reuven Arieh, of course. And his Middle East outfit. Danny Davidov . . . Avvie Eitels, who approached me in Washington.'

'Nathan Zamir,' added Szabodo, 'the man Robert Maxwell approached in the first place. Head of Operations, at that time. Quite a high-powered bunch.'

'And they did not use the money for themselves.' Jardine felt the merest blip of optimism. Maybe, just perhaps, events were not completely outside his control. 'For there was no graft, or they would not have been so outraged when Davidov put his hand in the till . . .'

Szabodo thought about this. 'A secret element, secretive. Used to dissembling. Who never bothered to ask the men running their service if it was permissible to take Maxwell's vast . . . funding.'

'All those men, Ronnie,' Jardine's mind raced over what he had learned about them, what the Firm knew about them, over the years, 'all those men are hawks. They have all worked on black operations to destroy the terrorist threat to their small, endangered nation. Look at it their way. Maxwell's millions were a gift to them. To get on, unfettered, with their own hidden agenda.'

He passed over the Zippo lighter. Szabodo was having about as much luck with his pipe as the three men in the boat were with the theory of internal combustion.

'Thank you, David.' Ronnie sucked and puffed. 'But what they did to you was . . . outrageous.'

Tell me about it, thought Jardine. But the answer was obvious and Arieh had clearly thought it through. 'Only if I complain,' he said.

'Yes . . .' Szabodo understood. 'Which would leave you looking like a prize pilchard.'

David Jardine stood up, in mild pain, stiff-muscled, neck hurting, thirsty and needing a pee. He knew Szabodo meant pillock, but he felt no inclination to correct him.

'Precisely,' he replied.

'And you have figured out a way to turn this to your advantage?'

Jardine smiled. His eyes met Szabodo's. 'That's what I love about you. You have more faith than Mother Theresa.'

Alisha moved from room to room in her small apartment, stepping over the detritus of Jardine's thorough and professional search. Drawers hauled out from bedside tables and the contents strewn on the floor. Very personal contents. Clothes scattered from the big old wardrobe she had bought in the souk behind the Rue Georges Picot and even from her laundry basket. Cotton blouses she had carefully ironed creased and crumpled on the Berber rugs she had brought back from the conference at Fez, six years ago.

Alisha Abdul-Fetteh was a battle-hardened survivor of the worst moments of Beirut's years of mayhem. She had seen sights and experienced horrors soldiers with chestfuls of medal ribbons could not match. She had endured the tension and dangers of working as a spy for not one but three different ruthless agencies. But she was first and foremost a woman, and tears brimmed in her eyes at the thoughtless chaos of her ransacked place. Her home.

Only her father's books, she noted, had been treated with anything approaching respect by the British spymaster.

As she gazed at the cat, who was perched on the dresser, watching her balefully, the stocky and idly sympathetic uniformed police captain, who had arrived within twenty minutes of her return from the Metn Hills, appeared in the doorway from the tiny hall.

'There is blood in the kitchen,' he said.

She nodded, as coldly empty as she would have been as the result of a completely unexpected break-in.

'And in the bathroom.'

'I know.' She picked up a discarded drawer from the bedside table and gently slid it back into its grooves. Who on earth had alerted the police? Certainly not Reuven. Bloody Daniel. Getting his own back.

'I'm sorry to ask, but it wasn't there before?'

'What?'

'I mean, you did not have an accident before you went away for the day? Or a friend? A servant?'

Alisha realized what he was trying to establish. She shook her head. 'Absolutely not.'

'Do you think there was a fight?' He was one of life's short people. Nice enough. With a little black moustache that bristled sufficiently to intimate its owner could probably do the same.

Alisha glanced around the debris, looking for a pack of cigarettes. Jardine, had he been present, could have saved her the time.

David Jardine. This was a side of him she had never experienced. There was a cold exactness, a clear method in his ransacking of her apartment which was becoming apparent to her, as a fellow professional.

'I really don't know,' she said. 'You're the policeman.'

In Washington, DC, it was four in the afternoon. Nancy Lucco was dictating letters and memos to her secretary, Toni, an attractive twenty-four-year-old from Tucson, Arizona, who studied nights, with a view to getting a place at Georgetown University.

'I'll get these done presently.' Toni closed her shorthand pad and stood up. Then she said, 'Oh.'

'Oh what . . .?' Nancy glanced at her watch. She had a meeting with Justice at five. 'Anything urgent?'

'Inspector Williams. Today's the date for a decision. You want the file?'

'No.' Nancy frowned. It had been dumb of Elmore Williams to stick with Sammy the Nose and Harry Cardona, after it had become clear that his back-up was not going to make it to the 43rd Street rendezvous. Elmore's case was that he would have blown the NY Field Office's sting by bugging out.

These guys – Elmore's words – were plenty jumpy already. Plus, he had made that essential, going by the book, phone call the night before, telling the Duty Officer in Office of Inspections what was going down and formally requesting a team from DC, a team of unfamiliar faces, to get on up there and watch his ass.

It had not been his fault, Williams asserted, that the guys from Inspections got caught in a goddam traffic jam.

The rules could not have been clearer. Apart from the Service's insistence that no counterfeit investigation was worth one agent's life, and that no undercover man had authority to act without at the very least a partner, any investigation of suspect Special Agents required the formal nod of the Assistant Director, Inspections, plus a comprehensive support element to ensure that the investigator remained free from just the kind of complaint Joe Pearce had levelled against Inspector Williams. The substance of which was that Elmore was negligent and undisciplined to remotely imagine that a phone call that late could possibly have given his unauthorized, self-assigned, one-man investigation any legal credence.

But Nancy had given Williams the third degree and she believed Elmore when he insisted that one, he had acted with reasonable cause and two, time and circumstance had conspired against him.

Joe Pearce was absolutely within his rights to have filed a formal complaint of unprofessional conduct against Williams. But Nancy Lucco reckoned that while Joe was one of the most solid, nicest guys she had met in the Service, wounded pride, bruised ego . . . outrage at a blot on his precious Field Office's spotless reputation, had figured in the SAIC's outraged reaction.

Even after Elmore Williams had shot Sammy the Nose and saved the lives of two Special Agents.

'Toni, let's recommend to the Director that we beach Agent Williams pending a formal audit of New York and the interviewing of SAIC Pearce here in Washington.'

Toni pushed her hair off her face. She reminded Nancy of that actress from *Silence of the Lambs*, what was her name? 'You figure by inconveniencing Joe Pearce, he might drop the complaint?'

'Joe is Irish, Toni. Nothing will stop him from seeing it through. But next time he feels like setting those wheels in motion, he'll think twice.'

Toni smiled and left the room.

Nancy touched the framed photo of her dead husband and patted it gently. Don't worry, Eddie, she thought. I'll cover your partner's ass for you . . .

'Allah-ha, Akbar . . .' The call of the muezzin echoed over the rooftops of North Beirut, relayed from minaret to minaret, or from structures high enough to stand in for mosque minarets until they rose again from the shattered, shell- and bullet-blasted city.

God is great, they were calling, and there is no God but Allah.

Alisha wondered how many Christians knew that Jesus was considered to be a prophet, in her religion.

She stood near the open window, ironing her cotton shirts and silk blouses, the gentle rumble of the washing-machine from her small kitchen the only other sound. Apart from the purring of her cat, who was evidently pleased to see things being restored to normal.

The idly sympathetic, potentially bristling police captain had departed and, in company with burglarized householders the world over, she doubted that she would ever hear from him again.

The kitchen and bathroom still had to be cleaned up, although she had washed the blood from the freezer door and from the kitchen and bathroom sinks. He had taken a shower and – and this was unlike David – had not bothered to clean the bath. And traces of his blood would forever be on the terracotta tiles of her kitchen floor. Like stigmata.

But none of that was of much importance to Alisha Abdul-Fetteh, for as the personal affront to her sensibilities, and the shock of her vandalized apartment wore off, she could not rid herself of the total recall of his words to her. As she had bathed the ugly wound in his side.

'. . . the man conspired to have your father murdered,' he had said.

And, '. . . it's something we have been aware of, for quite a while.' Something like that.

She had stopped ironing, resting the steam-iron upright to avoid scorching a mint-green shirt.

'Allah-ha Akbarr . . .' the muezzins called.

The man – he meant Reuven – *conspired to have your father murdered. We have known for quite a while . . . no, for some time*. That was what he had said. His exact words. And Alisha felt that was a lie. That had been a lie. We have known this thing. It was definitely a lie. For this was a man she had lain with. A man whose tenderness and imaginative . . . hunger had excited her so much that even years later he still made her aware of herself in ways that made her secretly blush.

She supposed that, since he had been the first man ever to reach her like that, it would be honest – embarrassing, slightly annoying, but honest – to admit he was the first man she had ever loved.

And just as she knew David Jardine had been lying when he had said this was something the British Service had known for a while, so she felt instinctively, even though it could not possibly be true – the idea was nonsensical – that he really believed Reuven had somehow been involved in her father's murder.

She did not think he had said it, made it up, just to sow dissent in the Institute's most potent Middle Eastern cell. Although that was what her training and experience suggested to her. Why on earth had he believed such nonsense? And if it was not true that they had known for some time, then he must have learned it recently. How recently? Since he arrived in the Lebanon? Or while preparing for his fleeting visit?

Troubled, Alisha returned to her ironing. Watched over by Buster, her oversized alley-cat whom she had rescued from the rubble of the US Embassy, after a suicide bomber had driven a truckload of Iranian RDX high explosive past the US Marine Guards and into the building. Buster was the double of that cat in the Tweety Pie cartoon movies, Sylvester. But his worn leather collar had the name 'Buster' on a tarnished brass disc and Buster he had remained.

It did not bear thinking about, what David Jardine had so calmly alleged. It occurred to Alisha, as she replayed over and over again the few words that were to alter the entire course of her life, that he had been . . . thrown to realize she didn't already know this damning item of information.

And he had let it drop. That was like David. Ruthless, a total bastard, yes. Sure. But deep down, vestiges of decency, of kindness even. It had been those things she had detected and which had turned her need for him into wanting, into a yearning for his friendship. For his love.

She knew he had known that. And, David being David, he had used her emotions to recruit her into the not so tender network of British espionage in the Middle East.

Reuven too. She supposed, in a way she had never before thought of, she had fallen into the arms of Mossad on the rebound, annoyed with Jardine for failing to understand it had been him she was ready to die for, not the bloody SIS.

Then her father had been murdered. Her clan had decimated the family of the killers. And it had been Reuven who had come to her rescue, who had spent many hours quietly comforting and counselling her. Reading to her out loud some of the most compelling passages her father had written in his newspaper. For he had toiled until his last hours to stop the madness that was to tear Beirut and the Lebanon apart.

And it had been Reuven Arieh who had persuaded Alisha to join with him, to work clandestinely for a new, free and civilized nation that could rise from the ashes and once again become the jewel at the crossroads of East and West.

Her blood chilled. Suddenly. The mint-green blouse hissed under the steam-iron. What was she thinking about? It had not been Reuven Arieh to whom she had committed herself. Not in those days. Then, he had still been Salem Jaddeh . . .

The worst part of the Banca di Calabria job had been hanging around in Palermo until that afternoon, for the lawyer of Giovanni Favorito Noto, the man who called himself Franco Cagliaro, had arranged a meeting there, to provide the services of two Vietnamese forgers.

Sometimes Kolosov wondered if his diminutive Israeli partner was not suffering from a mild dose of hubris, for his own instinct had been to leave Palermo, leave Italy in fact, the moment the job was done. There had been a morning flight from Palermo to Pisa and from there to London.

But Danny had explained his rationale. The stuff they had lifted from the most secure vault of the bank had been handed over to their trusted back-up team of three – Danny of course referred to them as his 'cell', using intelligence parlance – who had left the Old Port in Palermo on board a Carabinieri launch, the police noncom skipper of which had been paid 20,000 dollars, with a further 20,000 to come, and were at that time on their way to rendezvous with the tramp-steamer *Elsinore*, sister ship to *Sumaru*, sixty-five miles west-sou'-west of Gozo island, which was part of the Maltese island group.

If Danny and his partner had left at once, a check might be made of the vault's contents, thereby allowing a chance that the corrupt Carabinieri skipper of the fast police boat might become aware of just how much his three passengers were worth.

So it was more prudent, if more nerve-racking, to act naturally.

Trust the Jew, thought Kolosov. You have to hand it to him.

There is a bar and restaurant in the Old Quarter, not far from the Piazzo di Quattro Canti, called the Café Rosita. Danny Davidov and Nikolai Kolosov had sat there with Cagliaro, discussing the Mafia's fee for the deal, whereby they would retain for a number of weeks the services of the Vietnamese, the grandfather and grandson Nghi.

Cagliaro had just suggested ten million US dollars.

'That's outrageous,' said Danny. 'If you had suggested such a figure in Antigua, the negotiation would have stopped right there.'

Cagliaro raised his shoulders, as if to say, Look at me, I'm crying. '*Signore*, that's the price. These are two very valuable *oumini*.'

'From what I hear, your *padrino* Don Giovanni is no longer called Don, even by his fellow Calabrians.' Kolosov raised a hand to a nearby waiter and pointed at his empty glass of mineral water. Everyone knew that Giovanni Favorito Noto had his back to the wall.

Every day brought more arrests of Sicilian and mainland *mafiosi*. The big boys were being flown to Rome and from there to an impenetrable jail on a heavily guarded island off the north coast, due west of Genoa. Despite two massive landmine explosions which had murdered two successive senior government investigators, despite devastating bombs which had destroyed priceless parts of the nation's heritage, in Florence, Milan and Rome, the net was closing in and Noto's virtual declaration of war on the Italian Parliament was generally reckoned to be an act of immense folly. For the criminal Cosa Nostra was not the only *mafia* in a country whose roots included the Medicis and Julius Caesar and the pagan empires.

A group of businessmen, bankers and rival leaders of the Mafia had put a contract out on Noto's life. Bookmakers were laying odds that he would be dead or on that fortress island by the end of the year. But, like a cobra, Giovanni Favorito Noto was never to be considered harmless until his head was burning in the grate.

'My . . . employer continues to be held in the highest esteem by Sicilians and by millions of others in Italy, *signore*. It would be most imprudent for you to forget that.' Cagliaro glanced at the waiter who was waiting for his okay, about Kolosov's request for mineral water. He nodded. The waiter moved to comply.

'Okay, seven million and that's it. Final and ultimate. Like that.' This from Danny. He guessed even Favorito Noto would be glad of four million as he became increasingly fenced in.

Franco Cagliaro stroked his chin. 'If you lose them, the Viets, there is a big forfeit.'

'What is it?' inquired Nikolai Kolosov, his grey eyes casually probing into Cagliaro's brain. For once, without effect, because this *consigliere* of the most murderous *capo* in Italy, feared even by the five families in New York City, was accustomed, to the point of ennui, to such death stares.

'Your lives, gentlemen.'

'Fuck you, pal. My offer has just gone down to four million.' Danny Davidov did not like being threatened. It had happened more than seldom in his various careers, and he was still around.

'Ten is the figure, it's not negotiable. But you do understand, gentlemen, your lives are my guarantee of getting our assets back, undamaged.'

'You'll get them back,' said Kolosov.

'Four, don't push us around, Signor Cagliaro.' Davidov's eyes had narrowed.

'Or the fuckin' deal's off,' added Kolosov with true Russian aggression. Thanks a lot, pal, thought Danny. We really need those Viets. Plus I wouldn't mind leaving Palermo with my pecker in the right place and not stuffed in my mouth along with those *cojones* that survived even a marriage to the lovely, insatiable Rita. For that was the local way of indicating disapproval.

Cagliaro gazed at the waiter as he replaced Kolosov's glass with a fresh one. '*Grazie,*' he said with quiet authority. The waiter moved away among the red-and-white-checked tablecloths, each one decorated with a flower in a wine bottle.

'Don Giovanni', he said, 'will accept eight million dollars. Money upfront.'

'Bullshit,' replied Davidov. 'Four now. Four in one month and two when we hand the Viets back.'

The long silence was punctuated by discordant strains of music, as a *paesano* band set up their instruments for the evening's entertainment. The ex-KGB man thought he could discern fleeting chords from the tune they played at Sonny's wedding in the movie, *The Godfather*. The music was certainly possessed of a certain jaunty menace.

Cagliaro finally inclined his head. 'Cash . . .'

Danny Davidov said, 'Bearer bonds. As good as cash. In many respects, probably safer.'

'Not so much bulk,' volunteered Kolosov.

'Drafts drawn on what bank?' asked Cagliaro.

'First National Bank of Boston,' said Kolosov, expressionless. Aware that some day very soon the deputy manager would have his ass in a sling, when it was discovered that 2000 million dollars' worth of bearer bonds, exquisite, rare uncut emeralds and diamonds, and priceless documents, letters and photographs relating to the science of blackmail, had all been secreted in corsets under their loose-fitting clothes by Herrs Muhler and Jacques-Stiguer, only this morning, to be replaced with excellent forgeries.

But not too excellent, otherwise the bank might be able to hide just how immaculately it had been done over, and Danny did intend the world to know, in his good time, the very magnificence of his caper.

Even the Russian's heart began to beat faster. After all, the millions they were haggling about were themselves forgeries. For the two grand shafters had even replaced their own 150 million with perfectly counterfeited First National Bank of Boston bearer bonds. It was the culmination of an operation that had started months before.

Cagliaro nodded. Clearly his intelligence network, as effective and as well funded as many minor nations', had informed him about Davidov's and Kolosov's transaction the previous afternoon, so he knew they were good for the money.

'My own fee for arranging this is three million.'

'Jesus Christ,' said Danny.
'One,' said Kolosov.
'Two,' said Cagliaro.
'Done,' said Danny Davidov, and they all shook hands.

8

The Man Who Dreamed of Seagulls

KATE HOWARD CROSSED her legs and fixed the tortoiseshell glasses, which were slightly askew. She sat in the old scuffed leather wing armchair on one side of the flickering, mock-log gas fire. David Jardine was slouched in the facing armchair, a big, comfortable one acquired from Tulleys in the Fulham Road about twenty years before. It had been re-covered once, but the dun-coloured fabric had seen better days.

Jardine had changed into old corduroy trousers and a navy polo shirt. Ronnie Szabodo had cleaned and dressed the knife wound, which had been expertly resutured by Alisha, and, while mildly inflamed, it was not infected and apart from leaving an untidy scar, would heal nicely.

The squat Hungarian sat on an upright kitchen chair at the table which Jardine used as a desk. It was cluttered with reference books, an old Remington typewriter, a small compact disc-player and two small but powerful speakers, a rack of various bottles of wine, mugs with pens and pencils and a general accumulation of mail and journals.

'Go on,' said Kate, touching the half-empty glass of Berry Brothers' Good Ordinary Claret on the table beside her. Next to a photograph of Dorothy Jardine and David, in morning-coat and looking quite slender beside his generously proportioned consort, standing in front of

Buckingham Palace displaying his order – Companion of St Michael and St George – which had just been conferred on him by the Queen.

CMG was a sign of going places, in the Office. Call Me God, was the joke. Next one up was a knighthood, KCMG. Kindly Call Me God.

Poor David was not going to get his K, mused Kate. Not as far as this sorry tale of being, at the very least, embarrassed by the Israelis was concerned. Not if Mossad's tape of Steven McCrae's view of Jardine's future was genuine.

'Well, that's just about it, really.' Jardine nursed a cut-crystal tumbler of Jack Daniels sour-mash bourbon. He had gone off his lifelong favourite, Lagavullin, since Reuven Arieh had played games with it back there in the Metn Hills, in the Lebanon. 'Arieh had me driven back into Beirut and they dropped me off at a taxi rank. I phoned from the airport to put a red flag on Pomegranate. And here we are.'

He glanced at Szabodo, who scribbled on the A4 pad in front of him, then looked up and nodded.

'That's exactly what you told me,' he said to Jardine but for Kate's benefit.

Kate Howard reached for her wine and sipped it, more to avoid having to look at Jardine than for enjoyment. She knew that Steven had never been a terrific fan of the big man. Kate had graduated in behavioural psychology from Oxford, and she had been recruited, originally, to the firm's Personnel Directorate, where she had earned a formidable reputation. Her quite ruthless ambition had been well hidden, as befitted a girl from Cheltenham Ladies' College and Somerville. A young lady whose father was a career diplomat. But the ambition was there, nevertheless, and Kate had set her sights on getting transferred to operational duties, which in SIS was exceptionally difficult for a female. Unless, as the wags said, you happened to be sleeping with someone who could make the necessary arrangements.

Well, Kate had achieved her ambition, the first part of it,

and had spent two years with London Station on a more or less operational assignment. Safe houses and defectors.

Then the Director of Security had suffered a major coronary on the squash court during a game with a manic fitness freak from the CIA, and Steven had offered her the job. She remembered the moment with cold clarity. It was a Thursday evening and she had been sitting astride him on her bed in her small flat overlooking Battersea Park. He had been grinding away gently, rock-hard and slippery as usual, and she had been rotating her pelvis the way he liked, when out of the blue he had said, 'Katherine' – he always called her Katherine, Steven McCrae was the only person she knew who became more formal the better he knew someone – 'you know dear old Bunter's gone down with a dicky ticker . . .?'

Yes, she had murmured, rotating away, she knew that.

'I've had a word with Tim' – Tim Lewin was Director of Personnel – 'and we both feel the Office could, to its advantage, skip a generation and slot someone younger, more lateral-thinking, into the job.'

Kate had stared down at him. It was like fucking a man with two heads. How on earth could he keep doing what he was doing and carry on a conversation about personnel policy?

'Oh, really . . .?' she had heard herself whisper.

'And we are probably going to offer the job to you.'

Kate had underestimated Sir Steven as an experienced lover. For her unquenchable ambition was like a G-spot, that erotic nodal point which varies in each of us, and as the news sank in, she arched her back and had a series of multiple orgasms that would have stunned the ex-wife of Danny Davidov.

So she got the job as Director of Security and, having a proper sense of propriety, that had been the last time she ever agreed to go to bed with the boss.

And as Kate sipped the wine and relaxed, toying with her wine glass, she studied David Jardine, sitting across the room. On the other side of the hearth-rug where once, a hundred years ago, he had kissed her with more passion, more erotic sensitivity, more promise, than Steven bloody McCrae had ever dreamed of.

Jealous.

'Steven's always been jealous of you, David,' she said, and her eyes met his. Ronnie Szabodo, who never missed a trick, averted his gaze and slowly shook his head.

'He's jealous that you actually have been out there and mixed it with hoods from the KGB, the IRA and the Colombians.' She continued to gaze at him.

Jardine knew what else Kate Howard meant that little shit McCrae was jealous of. He smiled tiredly and inclined his head, thankful for the small compliment.

'However,' she went on, 'there is no doubt that Reuven Arieh – you are convinced it *was* him . . .?'

'Absolutely.'

'There's no doubt he chose you very carefully indeed. Probably took months. Which does, sort of, generate a tiny worry. I mean, it's something I had certainly never seen in you, but he's right. You do fit, the way you have sketched it yourself, just now. You do actually fit the profile. The sort of intelligence officer who is actually vulnerable. To an approach.'

'I say!' protested the loyal Renfield.

'Ronnie, she's right.' Jardine raised a tired hand and the Hungarian lapsed into silence.

'Now I know, and you know,' she went on, 'and so does Ronnie here, that you would die before compromising the Firm, David.'

'Well, thanks a bundle.'

'But.' Kate laid down her glass and gazed deliberately, like the behavioural science graduate she was, at the photo of Jardine and Dorothy. 'Of course I appreciate that this conversation is off the record, you both stated the ground-rules before we started. However . . . maybe it would be a good idea, just to protect all of us, if you don't mind, David. Just jot down on a couple of pages everything you have told me tonight. And sign it. You have my word it will go straight into my private safe and no one will ever see it.'

Provided, Jardine knew she meant, that whatever the Israelis are trying to do, it doesn't blow up in your face.

Plus, of course, it was something she would have over him until the end of time.

'Of course,' he replied, as casually as anything, 'you will have it on your desk tomorrow.'

Kate smiled sweetly and smoothed her Jaeger skirt over her knee. God, she was still incredibly – stop that, Jardine told himself.

'Tell you what,' she said softly, 'let's just put it on paper right now. While it's still fresh in your mind . . .'

It was ten minutes before two in the morning when David Jardine closed the door on Ronnie Szabodo and Kate. Beyond the solid oak, he could hear the sound of a taxi's diesel engine ticking as it passed in the moonlit street, pausing at the Europa food shop on the corner. Even the stoic Pakistani workforce would have closed up by this late hour.

Kate had been a good choice, he mused, slightly caught out by her cold-blooded efficiency, for Director of Security.

He wondered if the job had gone to a woman out of slavish adherence to the awful atmosphere of political rectitude that had spread out in wraiths, like ectoplasm, from under the door of the acrobat's son at Number 10 Downing Street. Or if it had been an honest choice.

Small-mindedness, meanness of spirit, were not among Jardine's many faults, and he did not imagine for a second that personal commitments had influenced the boss in deciding to promote Kate Howard a good three rungs up the ladder. He knew perfectly well that Steven McCrae, Sir Steven, the Chief, Kindly Call Him God, had been enjoying a liaison with her over a period of two or three years. He knew that fact from personal experience and observation, for he had seen Steven's cufflinks and shaving things in her bathroom cabinet when he had stood there naked and far too pleased with himself, about two years ago. The one and only time he and Kate had let their unspoken mutual attraction get as far as her delicious bed.

He still suspected, and was not unimpressed by her tactics, that she had left the cufflinks there deliberately, or at least had not taken the trouble to hide them. A subtle message to say, now wasn't that nice but this is the way the cookie crumbles.

And that had been that.

Jardine sighed. Women. It was surprising his weakness for them had not been his downfall. He smiled wryly. Perhaps, in fact, it had . . .

With hardly the energy to shove his back from the door, he climbed wearily up the stairs and flopped on to the bed, still wearing his shirt, and as he pulled a blanket over himself, his mind was filled with vivid memories of the past. Of, to be more precise, Alisha. So slender, so trusting. Her intelligent, amused, green-brown eyes. He remembered the way his heart used to beat faster as he made his way along the Rue Bliss, on his way to that little apartment. Just eight years before. The anticipation of her body almost equal to the longer-term prospect of planting an agent deep inside the Lebanese political . . . mess. One could hardly call it an establishment.

And he had got it absolutely wrong. Alisha had proved not to be the totally trusting, trustworthy acolyte he had so lazily, effortlessly recruited. He had looked upon the sexual involvement as fucking for the Firm. At least, that was how he had reconciled it, in his reports.

Fancy Alisha turning the tables. Tired as he was, Jardine felt his face flush as the thought occurred to him – just how many other times had he made the same mistake . . .?

And as he drifted off, in those drowsy moments before sleep, he wondered if perhaps Alisha was an inevitable element in the unpredictable skein of things that were to be his fate. His *moira*, he remembered from far-off days at lazy tutorials, was what the Greeks called it. Only those kings chosen by the gods were permitted to know in advance their *moira*, their fate, essentially, the manner of their death, and David Jardine finally managed a faint smile, as sleep wafted over him. He had certainly not been chosen by the gods to be king, or to understand his fate. As a matter of fact, he believed the whole notion was nonsense.

Which was probably just as well.

In Washington, DC there is a bar in Georgetown called Nathan's. It is a long, wood-floored place, with a bar running down the left-hand side, windows to the street and a connecting passage to a small restaurant next door, with red-and-white-checked table-covers and candles in wine bottles. The joint is always jumping and it is a good place to drink if you are serious about beer and rock music and conversation with whoever is standing next to you. The barmen are mostly football players or Georgetown University athletes working nights. Which is probably completely wrong but it had always seemed thus to Elmore Williams. He nodded to Fletch, a big young Irish-looking guy who came in about six and touched his glass.

'One draught Mick coming right up.' Fletch lifted a clean mug from the rack.

'So how'd it go . . .?' Williams heard his wife's soft voice behind him.

'Creepin' up on you again, Joe,' the bartender wisecracked. For Elmore Williams had worked undercover in DC for five years and everybody who thought they knew him believed him to be Joe Marcus.

'Oh, so-so.' He wished he had better news, as he put a big paw on Martha's shoulder and pecked her on the cheek. Somebody at that moment had turned on the jukebox, which usually started about 6.30. It was a Percy Sledge number, 'Stand By Me'. And it was loud enough so they could talk.

'I stay on the beach. Pending further investigation . . .'

Martha Williams gazed at her husband. His lean, leathery

face had aged since that shooting in New York and all the bad stuff that had gone down since then.

Elmore's de facto suspension was affecting him more than he would admit. But Personnel had assigned him to Training, where he was running a refresher course in VIP Protection, spending every hour of the working day practising immediate reaction to every conceivable permutation of armed attack on the President, and that was at least using up a lot of his frustrated adrenalin.

'What'll it be, Mrs Marcus?' Fletch asked.

'Gimme a glass of red wine. Zinfandel, you got that?'

'Comin' right up . . .'

As Fletch disappeared in search of the wine, Elmore Williams let his eyes widen the way he did, like some stage actor. 'Whatcha lookin' at me like that for?'

Martha laughed. 'You crazy person. Are you not afraid for your job?'

'Listen, they put me outa this job I'll find a proper one with sane working hours, just you wait and see.' His eyes got serious and he lifted his mug of beer. He gazed into it and his wife's heart melted. She knew the Secret Service was the best thing that had ever happened to him. In the fall of 1983, he had met a Secret Service man during some drugs investigation involving a US Government attorney at the United Nations in Manhattan.

The agent had been impressed by Williams and three weeks later Elmore had received an invitation to visit the Secret Service office in Washington, DC. He had gone, thinking it was just a kind of social occasion, like for the guys who had worked on the UN bust, but on arrival, he had been taken to the Director of Personnel, a tall, intelligent man with patient eyes, who still managed to convey he was not a man to mess around with. And he had sat Williams down and given him a cup of coffee and talked and let him talk, and at the end of forty minutes, the Director of Personnel had offered the New York detective a place with the Service. After training, he was to work on undercover assignments in places other than New York City.

Elmore Williams had felt privileged to be part of the 14th Precinct and it took a lot of thought before he made the jump. It had in fact been his Captain, Joe Bell the Third, a huge Irishman with a Polish wife, who had given him the best piece of advice he had ever had.

'Elmore, my boy,' Joe Bell had said, 'you get to travel all over the USA with the Secret Service. You get to be a Federal Agent without having to descend to joining the FBI. You get to travel to foreign places and they treat each other like brothers, just like us. So listen to fate's siren song,' Joe Bell always talked like that, being Irish, although he always managed to put in a coupla hours' duty the day after St Patrick's, 'and seize the moment with both your honest free man's hands . . . Take the opportunity as God's gift and good luck to you, they already asked us all about you and I said you were not half bad. For a man from the mainland.'

Joe referred to any American not born on Manhattan island as being from the mainland. Elmore had taken his advice, and on the day he won his Special Agent's badge, from SATS, the Special Agent Training School in Washington, at 3.14 that afternoon, while the band was playing 'Camptown Races', Captain Joe Bell died instantly from being hit in the face and upper body by four .357 slugs from a Colt revolver fired by a small-time crack-dealer called Alvin Lightfoot, who claimed to be part-American Indian but that was a lie. He was from Sligo.

Elmore Williams sipped at his beer, never a man to drink to excess, and smiled coldly.

'It'll be okay. You wait and see . . .'

Take the Paon Rouge, for instance, thought Alisha. Once the only place to be seen. Nadia Gamal used to dance there, the most talented and attractive belly-dancer in the Lebanon. Will that ever come back?

She was back in the Mossad safe house, the villa at

Dhouer El-Chouer, sitting on the couch that David Jardine had toppled off when he had collapsed about five days earlier. A programme on CNN was blithely relating some news-filler about how a reconstructed Beirut was rising from the ashes. The insultingly reassuring tone of the American narrator relentlessly – mindlessly, it seemed to Alisha – conveyed the impression that here was a place that, in just a few weeks, you could happily bring Mamie and the kids to for a vacation that would be as safe as . . . where, she wondered: Sarajevo? Mogadishu?

And the Narieh Souk, would that ever recover from the killings, by the Druze, by the PLO, by the Israelis? Even if they restore the narrow streets and wash them clean of the blood, will it ever be the same? With its books, its wicker baskets, its very ordinary plates and spoons.

She remembered David's merriment when she had read out to him, eight years before, a line from an earlier US Embassy booklet on the city, composed just before the madness: 'Bargains can be made, but there is jostling!'

And while she was reading that aloud, she had had to shout, because right outside in the alley, a Phalange Ford pick-up truck, with twin ASU-23 anti-aircraft cannon welded to its platform, was belting rounds point-blank between the neat, once sought-after (now mostly roofless) apartment buildings, and occasional clanging blasts from wildly aimed RPG-7, hand-held anti-tank rocket launchers shook the room so that the piano strings twanged excitedly and books on the shelves tumbled over on their sides, literary casualties.

She was still smiling when Reuven Arieh came into the room. He seemed preoccupied and after glancing at the television screen, he went to the counterfeit Crusader's chest and poured himself a beer.

'Do you think he'll buy it?' Arieh said in Arabic, too offhand, as he flopped down on a big Egyptian cotton-covered armchair.

'Who'll buy what?' Alisha knew he meant Jardine.

'Your Englishman.'

'He's not my Englishman, Reuven.' She turned her brown eyes on him. Hazel, with flecks of green.

'Tell me what you think he will do now.'

Alisha pointed the electronic wand at the television and muted the remorselessly asinine commentary. But she continued to watch shots of the rebirth of 'war-torn Beirut'. It might yet be stillborn, she thought to herself.

'He'll have made a full report. Have no doubt.'

'Omitting what . . .?'

Omitting that I once loved him, I hope.

'Omitting nothing. He's not stupid.'

'Boy, did you see his face?'

'Of course I saw it, how would I not see his face?'

'You know what I mean.'

'Reuven, I very seldom know what you mean . . .'

Arieh halted the tumbler on its way to his lips. 'Meaning . . .?'

'Why did you have my father killed?' She had switched her gaze in a cold instant from the television set to stare hard into his eyes, and past them, it seemed, to the back of his skull.

And that was when she knew. Alisha Abdul-Fatteh was a survivor from way back. And Reuven Arieh was maybe the jewel in Mossad's crown, their prima donna of black operations, but the lie was, just for a millisecond, there, oh, for the merest fraction of a tenth of a millisecond. But few men can completely hide a lie from the women they have lain with, although in many cases, those same women have an almost lemming-like capacity to ignore that gift, that instinct. The alternative being sometimes too final to contemplate.

'I wondered when that would rear its head.' The Israeli looked really quite sad. He had answered in Hebrew, which was the language he kept for intimate briefings or for making love to her.

'Reuven, no bullshit, please.' It was rare for her to use his real name. If, indeed, Reuven Arieh was his real name.

Arieh studied her over the top of his glass. There was

certainly no defensiveness there, nor hostility. He laid the beer aside, a gesture of grace, acknowledging her right to receive his committed attention. Alisha found herself noting it was a gesture more Arab than Israeli. And therefore, possibly, whatever he said next would be in the persona of his Arab identity. His false one.

'There was a rumour at the time that your father's murder was orchestrated by outside forces, to set the Druze and the Phalangists at each other's throats.'

'I am aware of that.'

Reuven spread out his hands, palms up. 'Well. One rumour is that the Tel Aviv Institute was behind it. And since I was running Mossad's Middle East networks at the time . . .' He shrugged. 'Some . . . uninformed foreign agencies attached my name to the rumours. I'm surprised it took this long to get to you.'

You're very good, Reuven, she thought. In the few seconds since I hit you with this, you have understood completely who planted the seed – David – and you are keeping your options open till you can find out just exactly what I have heard.

'Just tell me why. Please tell me why that was considered necessary. Killing one of the few men who might have brought stability back to the Lebanon.'

'Well, of course that would have been a factor which would have – um – made his killing a practical proposition for us. In a strategic sense. A stable Beirut was not at that time in our interest.'

That statement would have shocked, even outraged, most people. But Alisha Abdul-Fetteh had been embroiled in Levantine politics since she could listen. And Levantine politics made the Courts of the Borgias look like Sunday School.

She nodded, her eyes never leaving his. When Salim Jaddeh, as he had been then, had finally revealed to her that she was not in fact working for an Iraqi terror group – the irony being that David Jardine had actively encouraged her to get recruited – but had become, unwittingly, a key member of an Israeli intelligence cell, he had provided Alisha with convincing evidence, surveillance photographs, tape-recordings and letters in her father's unmistakable hand. These proved, beyond reasonable doubt, that her beloved, murdered papa had worked with (not for, Arieh was always sensitive to what would and what would not be acceptable to his recruits) Mossad for over sixteen years. The letters and recordings demonstrated that he believed that only when the Lebanon could get rid of the Palestinian parasites and the gangsters of rabid Fundamentalism, could the golden archway between Europe and the Middle East be restored to its former peaceful contentment and liberty.

Well, Alisha knew her father held those political convictions. And he had written many thousands of words in his newspaper along those lines, at the same time urging Israel to make territory available to the PLO, to make their peace and so on. It was just inconceivable, though, that he could have withheld the fact of being close to Mossad from her. They even used to think the same thoughts, communicate without speaking. The way those with great love in their hearts can sometimes do.

But Reuven had asked her gently, lying beside her in that small bed in her apartment, both of them slippery with perspiration, had she ever told her father she was spying for the British? And she said no, she had not.

There. He had said it. And being bereaved, and feeling abandoned by her tall English lover with the broken nose and the intimate understanding of a woman's needs, Alisha had abandoned herself to the Israeli with the cruel mouth and the rock-hard body.

Even learning Hebrew. Jesus Christ, what a fool she had made of herself.

'Don't insult me,' she said.

'Anyway, I was not in the country at the time. I was in jail in France. They thought I was Abu Daoud.' Abu Daoud was the PLO terrorist chief responsible for the Munich Olympics massacre, claimed by Black September, which had been Arafat's brainchild.

'I can find out,' said Alisha who, in addition to her many talents, had the boss of Syrian Foreign Intelligence eating out of her hand.

Reuven Arieh smiled. 'Please do.'

He rose like a man without a care in the world. 'I'm so sorry you have been worried with this nonsense. I don't blame Jardine for trying to set the fox among the pigeons.' This he said in English which, because Alisha was the more fluent, made him sound less than infallible. As if reading her thoughts, he switched back to Arabic. 'Now I'm going to play tennis with Abdul, then we should talk about finding an asset in the Hezbollah clergy. Nasser Latif was found this afternoon on the steps from his minaret. Throat cut. Eyes stuffed up his anus. Don't forget you're dining with General Oufkir, Morocco's leading collector of small boys and hashish.'

And he was gone, leaving the beer untouched, as if he had suspected it of being poisoned.

Alisha stared at the amber glass. Oh, no, nothing so quick for you, Reuven.

About a week had passed since David Jardine got back from Beirut, and the cut on his side was healing nicely. He had gone to bed early for a few nights and had walked to work each day from Tite Street in Chelsea, along the Embankment, over Chelsea Bridge, past Battersea Dogs' Home to the south side of Vauxhall Bridge, where the ghastly sand and dark green Batman's Tower (which was what people in the Office were beginning to call the new SIS building) brooded on the banks of the Thames, through the back streets near Lambeth Walk to the Imperial War Museum and on to St George's Circus and the Great Glass Box that was Century House, home of the British Foreign Office's most secret department.

Someone had written someplace that Century House reeked of stale boiled cabbage and other smells reminiscent of second-rate boarding schools. Jardine sniffed as he emerged from the elevator on to the seventh-floor landing and slipped his plastic security card from his wallet. There was not a hint of cabbage. The aroma of the place was one of polished rubber tiles, wood and people who felt comfortable in one another's company.

After all the years he had moaned about this fifties monstrosity, with its mirrored glass windows which had eventually been replaced with dull, bomb-proof, see-through armoured plastic, David Jardine realized how attached he had become to it.

Only now, with a move imminent to that vaguely ridiculous edifice on the Thames Embankment, did he feel an irrational fondness for the Great Glass Box. He shoved the security plastic into the requisite slot and prodded some buttons in a certain order. There was a click and he pushed a wooden door open, stepping into a small closet with a metal grilled door at the far side. Beyond, a corridor and various offices off it, some with their doors open.

Jardine touched the necessary open-sesame switches and, with a more solid clunk, the metal grille unlocked.

'Good morning, sir. Minutes from J-WISC have arrived, the Agency sent them over from Grosvenor Square.' Heather, his Scottish secretary, pushed her fair hair off her forehead and smiled as he peeked in from the corridor.

'My cup is full and runneth over,' Jardine replied, deadpan. Heather grinned. She loved the whole business of working in the secret world and harboured, probably irrationally, the dream that one day she would be admitted to the business of clandestine operations and offensive intelligence work, abroad. In the field.

Recruited at the age of eighteen straight from Mar College in Troon, Scotland, Heather had little chance of becoming an executive grade, because she did not have a university degree. Which meant, ruminated Jardine, that in about fifteen years, Heather would probably know more about what was really going on in SIS than the Chief, whoever that would be, and please God that did not mean Kate bloody Howard.

The office they had moved him to, upon his 'elevation' from Sphere Controller to Director Grade 1, was on a corner of the building, with views across the rooftops of South Lambeth towards Tower Bridge and the dome of St Paul's.

There was a big kilim from Afghanistan on top of the government-green wall-to-wall carpet tiles, his black teak desk he had had brought up from his West 8 office, two leather armchairs, a plastic mock-leather sofa and a set of Property Services Agency glass-fronted bookshelves, which were apparently to indicate he had arrived. Controllers were only allocated open-fronted bookshelves, of that dreadful crushed wood fibre that doesn't burn.

On a small set of Jacobean shelves behind his desk, under one window, sat a Georgian carriage-clock, a present to Jardine from his wife, Dorothy, on the occasion of their first wedding anniversary. David Jardine's grandfather on his mother's side had been a clockmaker, and out of a fondness for the old man, he had developed an encyclopaedic knowledge of antique clocks.

Dorothy's gift was a genuine classic hybrid, with mechanism by Thomas Mudge and the case by Christopher Pinchbeck. He had known Dorothy could not afford the £200 it had cost, and that made him love her all the more. And wherever he worked, the Thomas Mudge clock always had pride of place.

As David Jardine sat in his green leather chair and frowned at the pile of pink folders on the desk, Heather entered quietly and put a mug of coffee in front of him, along with a plate with a croissant and a small pat of butter.

'What's this?' he asked.

'Try it.' She stepped back and watched, apprehensive.

'Make it yourself?' Jardine touched the croissant. It was pleasantly warm. He parted a small piece from it and sniffed, put it into his mouth. Chewed it. 'Mmm . . . delicious.' He lifted the knife and spread some butter on another piece.

'Really? Is it really okay?'

'It's smashing. Really.'

Heather looked pleased as Punch.

'Did you make it yourself?'

'No, of course not. There's a new pâtisserie at Waterloo Station. Not bad. If you like them I can bring in a few each morning.'

Jardine patted his stomach. 'You're a bad influence.'

She smiled, as unafraid of Jardine as his Labrador dog, down at the house in Wiltshire.

'Mrs Jardine phoned. She's due back from Zagreb tonight, plane lands 8 o'clock. Will I send a car?' Heather meant a hire car, the office did not supply transport for spouses. Dorothy produced current affairs programmes for the BBC.

'No, I'll go. Drive us both down to the country.'

'What an attentive husband.'

'Oh, yes,' said Jardine.

'I hope I end up with one as good as you.'

'Me too.' David Jardine smiled gently at the babbling fool. 'The croissant's delicious.'

'More?'

'No.'

'I've got more truckloads of stuff from the news library.'

'Good girl.'

'And a Bill Childless phoned. From Scotland Yard.'

'Get him, would you?'

'Of course.' And Heather left, a slight spring in her step. Jardine envied her youth, her faith in the future and her innocence.

The 'truckloads' were two wire trolleys with newspaper and magazine cuttings, video and sound tapes of news items from around the world, charting the history since 1991 of major scams involving counterfeiting of some kind, of electronic expertise and of massive amounts of money from targets which could conceivably have been ruined by the crimes, but were always simply relieved of enough to make an individual exceedingly rich.

Jardine, as had been his routine all week, scanned those

reports, weeding out the ones that particularly interested him, writing up a chronology, poring over a large map of the world in a wood frame on one wall. Marking it with coloured pins and ribbons, linking some to others.

The office, Jardine's inner office, protected by Heather like the Egyptian tomb dog-god, was now out of bounds to all but a few of the Director, Forward Plans's colleagues.

And in this particular week, David Jardine, whose powers of concentration – when it suited him – were legendary, had made use of the vague nature of his perceived responsibilities to devote his every waking moment, in the office and back in Tite Street, to building up a picture of Danny Davidov's series of master-crimes.

He had used the plethora of stuff he was culling from every possible source – Scotland Yard, the Serious Fraud Office, Interpol, the Bank of England Intelligence Unit, various contacts in the newspaper business – to allow it to become leaked that he was interested in the subject. And by creating such a smoke screen, he quietly, and always with the knowledge of Kate Howard and Ronnie Szabodo, obtained answers to every informed question he needed to have answered about Davidov's 'footstep' crimes, each one bigger than the one before, and where and how the evidence pointed to a major Western currency being the eventual target.

David Jardine had also become aware that someone was taking a close interest in his personal movements, during the course of that first week back. And although Kate had sworn she had kept his secret, as promised, for the time being, he knew it could only be his own service, or at any rate a British service, the Red Sea pedestrians or . . . who?

He mentioned this feeling of being watched to Ronnie Szabodo, who put his team of pavement artists to work and, while they were not able to uncover anything specific, their very presence, professionally discreet though it was, seemed to do the trick.

At least, thought Jardine, life was continuing to be interesting, and he knew as each day passed, as each particular in the picture he was building up helped to reveal the Israeli Danny Davidov's plans and operational methods, that circumstances had just possibly presented him with a way to turn, as the loyal Ronnie had suggested, his embarrassing predicament to his advantage.

'David. How's it going?' Bill Childless was a young and ambitious detective chief superintendent from Scotland Yard's National Criminal Intelligence Unit. He specialized in computer crime, international theft by electronic means and entry to computer systems by counterfeiting computer security access locks.

They were in an office rented by Scotland Yard in the City of London. Childless was running an undercover operation against a group of Japanese entrepreneurs, the details of which he had been vague about. Always cheery, always smiling sincerely behind each bland half-truth and evasion, the detective was unaware that Jardine had him marked for possible recruitment to SIS, for he had the aptitude, and he spoke fluent Japanese and Mandarin Chinese. Which had probably helped him to such high rank at the age of thirty-four. That and his skill with computers and things electronic.

'What do you have for me?' asked Jardine.

Childless swivelled his grey plastic chair and reached to the white Dexion metal shelves behind him. He lifted a battered cardboard shoebox and put it on the desk in front of him. It held about twenty 3.5-inch floppy discs. He sorted through them, and selected three. He slotted one into his IBM desktop computer and slid the other two across the desk to Jardine.

'I'll give you this one in a minute. It's all there, though. There've been a definite eight, that this little baby tells me have been committed by the same man. One little, um, hiccup. But we'll come back to that. How's things in South Lambeth?'

'We're kept busy,' Jardine replied.

'Cagey . . .' Childless smiled, as if his computers could

tell him anything he really wanted to know. Jardine prayed he was wrong, but the Firm's review of computer security the year before had revealed some terrifying holes in the supposedly watertight system. Which was one reason why he was using the separate and self-contained set-up run so efficiently by this young policeman.

'Okay.' Childless's fingers had sped over the keyboard with a rapidity that David Jardine had only seen matched by his son Andrew, who had been a wizard on the things since the age of five. 'Drag a chair over here.'

Jardine lugged his ungainly chair behind the desk, so that he could sit and look over the detective's shoulder.

Childless had accessed a file he had called PRO♯1.

'This is your classic footsteps crimes,' he said. David Jardine noted the computer expert's grammar was not up to the standard of his other skills. 'He started in 1990, with a simple credit card operation, beautiful in its simplicity. Did you know some airlines pay for aviation fuel by plastic?'

'No . . .' replied Jardine.

'Well, they do. Just imagine how much a 747's tanks hold.'

'And they pay by credit card?'

'Some places. It's by arrangement, of course. Well, chummy managed to con several million gallons of fuel on immaculate forgeries of Cathay Pacific's plastic, over a period of six days, which was stretching things to the limit. Eight point two million dollars' worth.'

'Which he then sold on, presumably at a discount?' asked Jardine, and the policeman glanced at him with something close to pity.

'David, no actual stuff, no actual aviation fuel, ever changed hands. It was all on the basis of corrupting a few airport clerks, untraceable of course . . .' He jabbed his fingers over a dozen keys. The VDU screen threw up some unintelligible graph. Bright green on black.

'You see how he did it . . .?' Childless was delighted with the beauty of a scam which might have been portrayed in Kanji as far as David Jardine was concerned.

'Fascinating,' he said.

'And very special. Requiring a very special insight into satellite communications, and into human nature. That's what gave me the clue. Once I knew what to look for, the others shouted at me, the other footsteps. This is very professional work, committed by some very experienced and professional operator.' Childless removed his steel-rimmed spectacles and turned to look Jardine in the eye. 'This isn't one of your people turned funny, is it?'

Jardine laughed quietly. 'I wish we had one or two like him . . .'

But Childless did not share his amusement. He flicked through several graphs, all meaningless to the intelligence man. 'They get bigger. Look. Brunei. This one cost the Sultan nineteen million, sterling. He had written it off as a rip off by some very heavy Islam Fundamentalists who have muscled in on his tiny kingdom, but it was in fact a minor functionary in his Treasury who uncovered it.'

'How was that done?' asked Jardine, sloughing off any pretence at understanding the VDU screen.

'Nobody is quite sure. Perfectly counterfeited letters of credit. Plus accessing the Minister of Finance's secure communications network.'

'Satellite?' Jardine was catching on.

'Yep.' To Childless the question was hardly worth answering. 'He, they, and this gets back to the hiccup I mentioned, was able to read the Sultan's several unbreakable cipher programmes.'

Provided, mused David Jardine, by GCHQ, as part of HMG's ongoing and increasingly fruitless wooing of the small, oil-rich kingdom in the South China Sea.

'Are you sure it's not someone from you people? Some spook on a get-very-rich-quite-quickly piece of private enterprise?'

Not bad for a thirty-four-year-old cop, even one with Japanese and Mandarin, thought Jardine.

'I don't actually know, Bill,' he lied. 'But my instinct is no. We know the few of our people who could do that sort of thing. And they could not physically have done it, they've been kept too busy with other things . . .'

Childless let it go. He knew doing business with SIS was a one-way traffic. He exited the programme and popped the floppy disc out, sliding it across to Jardine.

'Cup of something? I could use a coffee.'

'Tell me about the hiccup.'

'Well . . .' Childless stretched back in his chair and clasped his hands behind his head. David Jardine lugged his own chair back to the side of the desk.

'David, my own brain, my own personal computer', he tapped his head, 'tells me, for I do have a certain nose for this sort of activity . . .' He meant it was his job. 'It seems to me there must be more than one guy doing this.'

'Well, of course,' replied Jardine. 'All the various elements of expertise, the forgers, where to get the plastic, communications wizardry and so on. Our man has enough money, we know that, to pay for expert help.'

Childless frowned. He tugged open a drawer and pulled out a pack of Marlboro. David Jardine made a mental note to chase up the labs on their examination of Alisha's pack of Winstons and the Zippo lighter.

'It's more than that. Of course, scams like these need hired help. Natch.' He lit the cigarette and exhaled luxuriously. 'But . . . and this is not just my own feeling for I programmed an analysis, without letting this dumb instrument here', he tapped the computer affectionately, 'know what answer I wanted, and it came up with the same response. You see, in any criminal or indeed any calculated and imaginative enterprise, a guiding sensibility can always be identified and, to a certain extent, quantified. That's how we identify the buggers. That's how SO 12' – he meant the Special Branch of the Metropolitan Police – 'can identify IRA planners and controllers, even though it might not stand up in a court of law, for it's not yet become an infallible science.'

'And your dumb computer came up with more than one

guiding intelligence . . .' Maybe Jardine knew little about computers but he was quick on the uptake.

Childless nodded, letting smoke curl out from his nostrils. If David Jardine had hated boffins he might have strangled the detective at that point, but in fact he had something of a soft spot for anyone who was really expert at their job.

Eventually Bill Childless spoke. 'Two.'

'Any hints?'

'I don't know anything about your business, David, but I can suggest you look for two very different individuals. One is shrewd and calculating, secretive and with . . . I suppose a breadth of vision in his own perverted line, his own criminal mind, that is, um, let's say, global, strategic, as opposed to limited or parochial.'

'And the other?'

'I think the other is probably a chess-player. I think the other has a thick black book crammed with the necessary access to all the kinds of people they need to . . . assist them. Lists like that are fairly personal and acquired over a number of years, so he or she is probably slightly older than the mastermind . . .'

Jardine gazed at Childless. There was little doubt in his mind they would have to poach this young man away from Scotland Yard before too long. It had been like a visit to some gypsy fortune-teller.

'Anything else . . .?'

'Sure,' Childless flicked ash into his trashcan, 'and this is just a wild guess on my part. But it's not because the material came from you, I'm not that subjective. It seems to me, David, they are, or were, both in the same line of business as yourself.'

Jardine did not reply. Bill Childless smiled, and like all good policemen he let the silence multiply upon itself. Outside, a police loudhailer could be heard, warning of what was probably a bomb scare. But there was little sound of activity within the building. Londoners were easily bored and the edge had gone off bomb scares, or even bombs themselves. The poor old IRA were probably the only terrorist group in the world who were being ignored into extinction.

Finally the detective nodded at the VDU. 'We have a programme for identifying national characteristics, you need that in the City. We have thirty-eight nationalities working with billions of billions, in this Square Mile.'

'And?'

'According to Bo-Peep – that's the program – your mastermind could be Jewish. Hebraic learned intellect.'

'And the chess-player?'

Childless smiled. 'This dumb IBM says Polish. An inherited Polish thought process. Listen, it's only a computer. You're probably looking for an Icelandic ice-skating queen and an Australian bookie.'

David Jardine smiled and stood up. 'Bill, you're wasted here.'

'Don't you believe it,' replied the cop. 'The pay's good and nobody understands what the hell it is I do . . .' He reached out his hand, without rising, his body language saying, Don't come the big spy with me, pal, for if you could have worked this out on your own you wouldn't have come.

Peace in Beirut was a fragile flower, and many deadly weeds threatened to return the garden to its previous savage state. Thus murder was not yet a rare enough occurrence to warrant particularly intensive police investigation, unless the facts were clear-cut and did not involve the more powerful political groups who were quietly settling old scores, an inevitable hangover, perhaps, from two decades of brutal insanity.

The most obvious sign of a return to civilized norms was that the streets and souk alleys were no longer littered with bloated corpses. That at least was something. With the coming of each dawn, details from the militia and Citroën and Mercedes ambulances from the city morgues would tour the usual dumping grounds and tidy away any evidence that might embarrass those negotiating the investment of millions from foreign bankers and businessmen towards the phoenix of restoration struggling to rise from the wrecked metropolis.

Thus it was some weeks before the corpse of a young Arab male was identified. It had been found in the trunk of a BMW 730 sedan, hands bound behind its back, dispatched with two 7.65 slugs fired approximately four inches from the right ear. There was not much left of the left side of the head, but the face was intact. The morgue attendant noted that the deceased had been injured some days prior to death. For there was bruising and discoloration to the left eye, cheekbone and brow.

There was also evidence of torture on the soles of the feet and in the genital area, where burn-marks, possibly from the attachment of electrodes, were visible.

The stocky police captain with the bristling moustache, who had turned up at Alisha's apartment, was not quite so casual a fellow as she had considered him to be. His name was Teufik Rassi and he took his business seriously. He also had a most excellent memory for faces and for the kind of detail most people would think inconsequential.

He had attended Mam'selle Abdul-Fetteh's ransacked apartment in person, not just because she was a respected functionary of the Government, political adviser to the Foreign Minister, and protocol suggested it, but because you never knew when such a contact, however impersonal, might bring some advantage – perhaps, for instance, access in the future to someone in power. And once he was there, his remarkable memory had worked instinctively, storing away all manner of things.

Thus, when he was in the morgue on unconnected business, looking for the body of a detective who had been missing for eight days, the face of the murdered Arab youth rang a bell.

Rassi did not find his missing detective that day, but the bruised face of the boy nagged at his memory. It was not until he was driving home, along the Rue Hamra, that he remembered where he had seen the victim before. The woman Abdul-Fetteh's apartment.

When Teufik Rassi had been, apparently languidly, mooning around the apartment, two things had been clear. The place had been most professionally searched. And there had been a short but brutal fight. The spray of blood along the kitchen wall, facing the fridge, indicated to his experienced eye that a knife had been used. Possibly slashing at an adversary whose pulse-rate was understandably high. The discarded bandages, sewing needle and alcohol-soaked tea-towels meant someone had applied immediate first aid, verging on battlefield surgery.

And among some photographs, in a printed Kodak wallet with the Mdina chemist's stamp across it, had been one of Alisha and a bright-eyed, grinning kid, sitting in a café, Le Camel it could have been, drinking Coca-Cola ice-cream floats. He smiled as he remembered the boy had had ice-cream on the tip of his nose.

Yep. That was the same kid.

Teufik Rassi glanced at his wristwatch, a gold Rolex he had accepted from a mullah in return for allowing the man to leave a house of ill-repute without a stain on his reputation. He glanced in his mirror and spun the wheel, cutting across outraged traffic and heading for the Ministry of Foreign Affairs. Mam'selle Abdul-Fetteh would still be at work. He remembered a colleague saying she and the Minister worked till eight most Tuesdays.

Alisha shivered in the chill of the mortuary room, knowing, before the attendant lifted the green sheet, what she was about to see.

Even so. Even after all the deaths, all the cadavers, as common to someone who had lived through the years of insanity as dead leaves in autumn. Even then, it was just dreadful to see the face, empty in death, of Hassan Abdul-Ratif Rashdan.

The exit wound had been dressed with a gauze pad. Swollen bruising half-closed the left eye.

She nodded, and reaching out, touched the boy's lank hair, dry now. She had taken him to Le Camel for his eighteenth birthday, just two months before.

Captain Teufik Rassi was grave and sympathetic. It seemed to be his trademark. 'Well, mam'selle . . .?'

'This is – was – Hassan Rashdan.' Alisha seemed reluctant to quit the scene. As if her presence might somehow rewind the remorseless clock and restore the boy to his bouncing vitality.

Rassi watched, interested. Everyone in Beirut knew the Rashdani clan had murdered Alisha Abdul-Fetteh's father. And that her own family had slaughtered his killers and their kin.

'Mam'selle . . .' he murmured gently, and held open the door from the room of death.

But Alisha continued to gaze at Hassan's lifeless face. So, she thought. This is how it ended for you.

'God bless him,' she said quietly, and turning, walked out and, ignoring the policeman and the mortuary clerk, went through the doors to a green and cream tiled corridor and out into the sunlit parking lot.

Inside her nondescript grey Fiat – the most prudent form of personal transport in Beirut – Alisha pushed the key in the lock and started the engine. She must have been sitting there for some minutes, lost in feelings of helplessness at the mess which was her country, at the ease with which her fellow Lebanese seemed able to kill each other, when there was a quiet tap at the car window, and there was Teufik Rassi.

Alisha lowered the window. 'Can we perhaps complete your formalities some other time? Hassan was a friend of mine.'

Rassi nodded. Maybe he was not such a bad guy, for the expression in his eyes was one of compassion. He rested an arm on the car roof and leaned down, sliding an envelope from his tunic and letting it drop into her lap.

'It is a very serious thing to withhold evidence. Particularly where murder is concerned. I want you to know,' he said, his eyes checking they were not being watched, 'that I have no intentions of pursuing the informations contained in this letter. Let us agree I have never seen it.'

Alisha frowned, always suspicious of being set up. 'What is it?'

'Your father was a good man. Many of us looked to him and those like him to save us from our enemies. From ourselves. I am truly sorry about the boy. Please do not anticipate too strenuous an investigation. Let us say, he is another casualty of our, um, normalization process. The will of Allah.' And he stood up, tugged his tunic straight and strolled away.

She stopped the car on the Corniche road, between some piles of rubble that had once been a row of boutiques, overlooking the Mediterranean. As seagulls cried high overhead, Alisha opened the envelope. Inside was a note, once crumpled small, now straightened out. God knows where Hassan had hidden it.

And in his neat, schoolboy penmanship was set out the precise story he had told Jardine. How Salim Jaddeh was, beyond any doubt, the man who had visited his father and brothers, and had persuaded them so eloquently to murder Youssef Abdul-Fetteh, in the name of the Druze militia.

She did not need to read it over and over again. Once was enough. And quickly. Now there was no lingering suggestion of innocence. Salim Jaddeh, her master in espionage and in bed, real name possibly Reuven Arieh of Mossad's Direct Action Service, had all the time been the instrument of that grief she lived with from day to day. The bastard had even comforted her when she had sobbed for her lost daddy, naked, in bed, in the arms of his assassin.

As she gazed, not really seeing, at a motor-yacht crossing the bay, Alisha's clouded anger gave way to something clear and infinitely more profound. She had absolutely no doubt what her next move would be.

*

The older of the Vietnamese forgers sat at a table set up for him on the afterdeck of the tramp-steamer *Sumaru*, oblivious to the gentle Atlantic swell, as the sturdy little ship made a steady ten knots on a course that would take her to the isthmus between Morocco and Spain, the keyhole to the Mediterranean.

He was gazing with complete attention at a photograph of a letter, on a print ten inches by eight, which had been written nearly 200 years before. The old man was called Huynh Tan Nghi. He had those features peculiar to scholars of the Hue region, where during the American war, the Vietcong's Tet offensive of 1969 had delivered a bloody message – you can't win.

The Nghi family had been forgers for generations and their mastery of the art dated back to the eighth century in the Vietnamese calendar. The CIA had recruited five of them and housed them in a safe place in Saigon, where they spent the entire period of the war falsifying with heroic skill North Vietnamese, Chinese and Russian passes, documents and, in particular, currency, for that is the quickest way to subvert a nation's economy – by flooding it with worthless money.

At the end of the war, certain members of the Nghi clan slipped quietly back to Hanoi, where they received decorations from the Government of North Vietnam for their work as secret agents. Others threw in their lot with the big pink men and fled to the USA, where their particular talents ensured they were never short of cash.

The boss of all the Colombian cocaine cartel bosses at that time had been the addicted hoodlum, Pablo Escobar Gaviria. Escobar was making two million dollars a year from cocaine and he was able to run his affairs like a small state, with political, economic, security and scientific advisers of the highest calibre. Word had reached him of the existence of the Nghis, and he had acquired two of them to do more or less precisely what they had done for the CIA.

In the early nineties, the Colombian Government and

those cocaine barons less hooked on violent confrontation conspired to destroy Escobar and his ruthless *grupo*.

Giovanni Favorito Noto, whose tentacles reached out from Palermo to touch places as far apart as Saigon and Bogota, then sent Franco Cagliaro to the jungles of Antioquia in Colombia, to the equivalent of Escobar's fire sale. There Cagliaro had acquired, among other items, the Nghis, payment being made in solid gold bars flown into a Colombian clearing on board a chartered C-130 Hercules air transport.

Huynh Tan Nghi was the grandfather of the younger man who sat on a cushion nearby, resting his back on the ship's rail, and studying an identical photograph. He too wore pebble-thick glasses but he lacked the straggling goatee of the old man. He was called Lee Xuan Nghi, and he was probably the best forger of Western calligraphy in the world. For if that had not been so, Don Pablo would surely have hired the man who was.

Danny Davidov emerged from a door beneath the wheelhouse and gazed at his two acquisitions. He leaned on the bulkhead near the older Viet.

'Okay, I may as well tell you now,' he said. 'I did not really hire you from Don Giovanni just to forge dollar bills . . .'

After a long time, maybe two minutes, Huynh Tan looked up at him, unblinking.

'Of course you didn't,' he replied.

Two thousand, one hundred and eight miles to the north-east, David and Dorothy Jardine strolled in the late afternoon sunlight, the breeze tugging at his hair, ruffling her skirt, towards a small country churchyard on a slope above their farmhouse.

Fotheringham Manor sat in about four acres of south Wiltshire meadow and woodland, on the edge of a sprawling sporting estate. It was surrounded by birch woods to the north and east, and its parklike lawn, after about ninety yards, became meadow, dotted with apple and cherry trees, descending gently to the orchard in the west. Jardine liked the remoteness of the place and the privacy he cherished, when not in town. He and Dorothy had scraped up just enough to buy it in 1973, from the sale of their three-bedroomed flat in Highgate and the proceeds of David's father's will, following the old man's untimely death as the result of a collision with a CND bus while riding his bicycle the wrong way round Trafalgar Square.

The house had been built in 1638 for the local squire, a baronet called Sir Richard Fotheringham. Six years later, his nineteen-year-old son, Guy, lost a leg to a Parliament cannon-ball on Clay Hill during the Battle of Newbury. The boy was brought home by the family retainers, and on a bright but blustery spring morning a few days later, Fotheringham died from the cuts of eight cavalry hangers of German steel, on the farm's cobbled courtyard, basket-hilted broadsword in hand, defying a troop of Scottish Horse searching for his wounded boy, who lay hidden in the barn attic.

The house was then ransacked and put to the torch by Cromwell's troopers, and young Fotheringham, Sir Guy for those last few seconds, was butchered in the barn. But only after accounting for three of his attackers – two with his percussion pistols and one with a horse axe hurled across the barn.

Father and son lay buried in the estate's ancient and cramped churchyard, and every spring, on the anniversary of that day in 1644 when Sir Richard and Guy Fotheringham had died so gallantly, the Jardines placed flowers on their graves, and David Jardine, to his family's intense embarrassment, would say a prayer commending them to God, and seeking the strength to find similar courage, should the need arise.

David and Dorothy reached the wicket-gate and stepped into the old churchyard. They paused by the graves, each marked with a long tombstone and a shared headstone, with the inscription, barely legible, 'Here lie Sir Richard Fotheringham and his heir, Sir Guy. Died for the King. April 19 1644. Requiescant In Pace.'

Withered remnants of the bunches of flowers Jardine and the family had placed there just five weeks before were still on the long, crumbling, weather-beaten slabs.

Dorothy glanced at her husband as he gazed down at the bits of daffodil, and lily-of-the-valley, and forget-me-not.

A complicated man? Not to her. She had always known, from the moment she had realized that she was doomed to love him, that if life was to be really and truly lucky, it would come to this. A deep and profound, loving friendship, bound by a fierce and unshakeable loyalty.

When they had met, and made love, all those many years ago, in his rooms behind the cricket pavilion on the banks of the Isis, it had not seemed so important that she knew, with a wisdom beyond her years, that their love would become . . . platonic? But looking back now, she could tick off the signposts along that route. Two clever and ambitious people, she with her rise through the world of television journalism, he with his spies and need for danger, on whom the years had taken their toll. God knows, she had put him through enough: two ridiculous affairs within a couple of years of their marriage. When she was still a slender beauty and driving men crazy. Then the workaholic phase, then the drinking. The dear old boy had had reason a few times over to call it a day. And yet . . . here they were.

He squeezed her hand as he contemplated the gravestones. As if he sensed her thoughts. And that of course was what made him thrive in his job, she guessed. Because he was quite good at sensing other people's thoughts.

And here he was, a lump in his daft throat as he gazed at the dry graves of another man's tragedy, in another time.

He was only at home here, she knew that. Probably more than she was. For everyone knew that Dorothy Jardine was as tough and practical as . . . well, her nickname at the BBC was the Iron Woman, while David was essentially a romantic.

But she knew she was part and parcel of his home. Of

David Jardine's emotional hidy-hole. And she liked it like that. It was comfortable.

Dorothy had come to terms with his innate stubbornness, his apparent arrogance which masked a natural compassion, for it had been David who without condemnation had helped her through the profound hopelessness of near-alcoholism, who had understood, and never bullied, who had cajoled and listened and sat with her through the terrors of drying out, insisting that she 'beat this fucking thing', and nursing her out of the dark and back to normal life, which now included the occasional glass of wine, 'For otherwise you would be an appalling companion to have in one's later years, old sport.'

And she had heard, from others in his most reticent profession, that Jardine was held in great esteem, that he was a brave man, brave and without fear.

She smiled when they said that. They had not lain beside him at dead of night and felt him wrestle with demons, heart pounding, perspiration soaking him. No one was without fear. But the big mutt managed to keep it at bay, most of the time. And that took a hell of a lot more courage than being a stranger to fear and self-doubt.

A stillness, a silence had fallen. It was that cusp between late afternoon and dusk. Then came with the breeze the sound of sheep calling for their lambs, and the small, innocent cries of the lambs replying.

'So,' said Jardine, 'what's for supper?'

'I've invited a few people round,' Dorothy replied. 'The Samsons from Tisbury. And that new young couple from the village. You'll love them – he's in corporate finance and a candidate in the next by-election.'

David Jardine looked stricken. 'Jesus Christ, you're kidding . . .'

'Of course I am. It's macaroni and cheese. With soggy tomatoes out of a tin.'

'May God and his angels guard your sacred throne . . .'

And they held hands like teenagers as they strolled back down from the churchyard to the house.

*

At 2 o'clock that morning, Dorothy awoke to find her husband gone from bed. The slight dent in the mattress, where he slept, was cold. Puzzled, she waited for a few moments, then got out of bed, threw her dressing-gown over her shoulders and stepped quietly into the hall.

The stairs creaked as she tiptoed down to the stone-flagged hall and crossed to the library, where a warm golden glow framed the closed door.

Inside, Jardine was sitting at the big refectory table, on which were files and documents and a mug of coffee. He looked up as the door gently opened, and smiled.

'What's the matter . . .?' she said, softly.

'Trying to solve a conundrum.' He rested his head on her midriff, as she stood beside him and stroked his hair.

'Is that your tummy rumbling?' he asked mischievously.

'Does that mean you're hungry?'

'Wouldn't mind a sandwich.'

'David, it's three in the bloody morning.'

'You did ask . . .'

'Cold ham and pickle?'

'Perfect.'

In the silence, the old house creaked, and the quiet, steady ticking of old, good clocks sounded comforting.

'Is everything all right? At the office . . .?'

'Why?'

Dorothy shrugged, watching him working. 'I think something's worrying you.'

'Nothing special. I promise.' He sat back and arched his aching back, pressing his spine against the hard back of his chair.

Over supper they had talked about Dorothy's ten days in Zagreb. She had broadcast a live report from there, as part of her current affairs series, with interviews with some of the major players in the nightmare that was being acted out in the former Yugoslavia. Jardine had got hold of a video tape, at Century House, and had managed to scan through it, to get the gist of what it had been about.

'I'm sorry Zagreb was such a bastard,' he said, beginning to think about the ham and pickle sandwich.

'They're hell-bent on catastrophe. Thoroughly nasty people, some of them. Mustard?'

'Yes, please . . .' and David Jardine smiled as his wife padded out, heading for the kitchen. He prodded at Jugs, the black Labrador dog asleep at his feet. Dorothy was something else. Thoroughly nasty people? Well, that summed up the Balkan horror story pretty succinctly.

Amused, he returned his attention to the notes and jottings in front of him, where he had been trying to make some sense out of Bill Childless's analysis of Danny Davidov's ever-larger footprints of crime.

Bo-Peep, the detective's computer program, had suggested a second guiding intelligence. A partner in crime. It had even suggested a nationality – Polish. And so much else of the Bo-Peep stuff was accurate, when compared with Reuven Arieh's information and other research material, that the computer was worth taking seriously. But everything the Office had been able to throw up on the Polish Intelligence Service seemed to be leading Jardine further and further away from that sudden blip of adrenalin he had felt a couple of days before, in Bill Childless's City office.

Then, it – something, whatever it was – had seemed just within his grasp. Because if there were two men behind those crimes, which Mossad was genuinely alarmed might threaten some major Western currency, either Arieh knew that and had not passed on the knowledge, or he and Mossad did not know. Which meant, if Bo-Beep was right, that David Jardine might just be able to pull something from the ashes of his career and his pride.

But Polish . . .?

That was proving to be a wild goose chase.

He sighed and closed his notebook. He could hear Dorothy in the kitchen.

Home sweet home. He closed his eyes and tried to picture Danny Davidov's home. Where the former agent was, right now. But try as he might, he could not get a feel for it. Maybe he was losing his touch.

When Dorothy came back with the ham and pickle sandwich, David Jardine was fast asleep, sitting in his chair. She touched him gently and he awoke, blinked and smiled.

'What were you dreaming about?' she asked.

Jardine frowned.

'Seagulls . . .' he said.

9

The Moscow Mafia

GEORGETOWN WAS HOT. It was strange how one day it could still have that chill from a really tough winter, even though the sun was shining, and next day, quite early in the morning, it had suddenly become spring. And spring was late, Easter had passed in sullen rain, but here it came. Temperature, said the local radio station, in the low eighties. That was better.

Nancy Lucco had a tiny headache. She grimaced as she reached for the glass of water by her bedside, wondering if she should take some aspirin, but that always left her feeling lousy, kind of liverish, for the rest of the day.

Her clothes lay on the rug beside the bed. Even the Pierre Cardin skirt. Along with a discarded book by Robert Persig. *Lila*, it was called, *an investigation into morals*.

Well, an investigation into the morals of Nancy Lucco would reveal . . . what? A tall, good-looking broad in her early thirties, holding down a good job, self-contained – a cop's widow. But the move to Washington, DC from New York City had saved her from becoming Eddie Lucco's Widow.

And what would Eddie, the big Wop, have thought of his widow Nancy's morals?

For while no libertine, no pushover, a girl had to live her life, and Nancy was not ready to marry again, or even settle down with one guy. The reason was that big Wop cop, with his tenderness and his ballsiness and his downright, dead-straight attitude to his job in Homicide, his marriage and his hard-won place as a cop who was going places in NYC. He had spoiled it for any other guy who came along. 'There will never be another you', went the song and that was it, as far as Nancy Lucco and serious relationships was concerned.

She pushed herself up and sipped the water, and sipped again until the tumbler was empty. Beside her, the quiet young Assistant DA from Tony Faccioponti's office, in downtown Manhattan, was sleeping peacefully, his face unlined and . . . not innocent, for sure, but somehow, untroubled.

She shook her head ruefully. This was a real rare occurrence, and she had no intention of blaming the Southern Comfort, although it was not a liquor she normally touched.

He was not even snoring. Lucco used to snore. Lucco had to be turned on to his side, that was a job and a half.

But this . . . boy, he was the same age as Nancy, they had established that, but he seemed five years younger, this young guy just lay there, fast asleep, breathing peacefully.

Some kind of decongestant might be the answer. Lift the fumes of Southern Comfort from her sinuses.

Delicately holding the bridge of her nose, between her eyes, Nancy Lucco eased the duvet aside, gently swung her legs over the side of the bed and sat up, slowly.

'Oh, boy . . .' she muttered. Sorry the glass of water was empty.

It had been a pleasant night. Couple of drinks at Smith's jazz bar, a stroll up Wisconsin, dinner at Paolo's, back to Smith's Riverside jazz club. That had been the mistake. Like a good attorney, she soon zeroed in on the fatal moments. And Jed Berenson had been so attentive and such an easy companion, maybe it had been the combination of a good night out, the Spike Henry Quartet's mellow sounds, the coming of spring . . .?

Gimme a break, Nancy, she said to herself, it was the goddam Grand Old Drink of the South and his well-maintained young bod. And the fact that you are a woman and you ain't breaking no laws.

And now for a pint of water followed by a pint of orange juice followed by some flapjacks and maple syrup, fresh coffee . . . but first, a pee and then the pint of water, then a shower, a wonderful, luxurious shower, and . . .

The boy had wakened up. He had reached out and touched her back. ''Morning . . .'

'Hi. You want some orange juice? Cup of coffee . . .?'

'Are you kidding . . .?' Jed Berenson grinned and gently tugged her hand, pulling her back towards him.

'I need a drink of water, honest,' she said, as he somehow rolled her to lie on top of him. 'And my breath must smell like shit.'

He wrapped his arms round her, gently. It felt nice. Comforting. When his eyes met hers, he wasn't that young. Not at eight in the morning. Thank God. She had somehow got it into her head she had raped a minor.

'Do I detect regrets, Counsellor?'

She lay there. Relaxed. His warm body felt firm and . . . like it felt like an honest and regular thing to be doing.

She gazed down at him, her heartbeat increasing. 'How's my breath? Should I take a Lifesaver?'

'Your breath's fine,' he said, softly. And they kissed.

The tramp-steamer, the SS *Sumaru*, had just crossed the 30th parallel at its junction with Longitude Line 30, which put her about 600 miles due south of the Azores and 710 miles west of the Canary Islands. Nearer, in other words, the African/European side of the Atlantic than the American coast.

After Danny Davidov and Nikolai Kolosov had told them what they had really been hired to counterfeit, the Nghi pair had hardly moved from their chosen spots on the afterdeck, except to retire to their tiny cabins to sleep.

They had sat there ignoring the movement of the small,

fat ship, and the cries of a half-dozen seagulls which had deserted the stern of a passing frigate of the Russian navy, hoping to catch a few scraps from the *Sumaru* as it drew ever closer to land.

Danny Davidov leaned on the flying bridge, beside the wheelhouse, watching the two forgers. All they seemed to do was sit studying the seven examples of handwriting, two letters, two diary pages, two pages from a draft manuscript and one perfectly focused, perfectly printed colour photograph of a number of examples of the same signature.

All the samples were sealed inside laminated plastic envelopes.

Davidov had asked the Viets to study those sealed documents carefully, the first day out from Antigua, where he and Kolosov had flown them, by chartered aircraft, from Bogota. He had not anticipated they would take so long.

He heard the routine thud, thud, thud of the Russian's feet as he ran round and round the deck, up and down ladders and companionways on a ceaseless mission to maintain his indecently high level of physical fitness.

Finally he could contain his curiosity no more. Davidov climbed down from the bridge and crossed over to the grandfather Nghi who, with his straggly white goatee beard, looked uncannily like Ho Chi Minh.

'How's it going?' he asked.

The old man thought for a long time. Then he tapped one of the sealed documents against his small table. It was an old, faded letter, written by somebody with really old-fashioned penmanship. And the writing paper had a bald eagle embossed on the top.

'How . . . serious are you? About a perfect . . . facsimile?' he asked. Danny had noticed that, just as spies just about never use words like spy or intelligence or secret, so these two men never used the words forge or counterfeit.

'Pal, we have paid millions for your services. You are the best there is. Your charming employer has reminded us that our skins will be lifted off our living bodies if we lose you. We are truly serious. Believe me.'

Huynh Tan Nghi nodded, thinking slowly. Or carefully. Probably both. He pushed the bunch of sealed samples into the centre of the table, finished with them.

'If my grandson and me are to do what you ask,' he said, his pale grey, emotionless eyes baleful behind the pebble-glasses, 'we will have to see real documents. Original examples. Written by this man. We are serious professional men, Monsieur Muhler. To reproduce such a man's hand, the pressures, the pauses, in the midst of words, the flow. It will be necessary. Oh, yes.'

'Are you saying you want to take them out of the plastic wrappers? Go on. It's okay. Go right ahead . . .'

Nghi raised his shoulders, as if to say, throw me overboard and sacrifice your skin, but this is how it is.

'These are excellent . . . facsimiles.'

'These are the genuine article, pal. They come from . . . I don't mind telling you this, just to reassure you. These are original letters, authenticated by archivists at the Jesse Bradbury Museum and the Smithsonian Institution, of Washington, DC.'

Huynh Tan Nghi spread out the seven plastic-sealed examples of handwriting, examining each one. He shook his head.

'My family have done this work for over eight hundred years. These are very, very good. But when you really study them, which is my . . . work, the cross on the letter "t", that is too regular. The differences in the letters "r" and "b". The sameness of pressure, how the pen leaves the page. These have been made by the same hand. Hand of . . . forger.'

'But the age of the paper. The chemical analysis of the ink . . . The dates have been authenticated. Two hundred years old.'

'Maybe they were done two hundred years ago.' Nghi glanced up, shrewdly. 'Is this a test? Did I pass?'

'It's not a goddam test.'

The old Vietnamese sighed.

'Lee Xuan agrees.' He indicated his grandson, who was

listening, resting his shoulder against the ship's rail. Lee Xuan nodded. 'With these . . . we could only make perfect reproduction of . . . fakes.' Nghi tapped the discarded letters and shook his head. 'You would not get the result you are paying so much for.'

Danny Davidov stared at them. He was of necessity a good judge, had a nose for when he was being snowed. He believed they were telling the truth. Giving their expert opinion. And with their reputation, they had to be right.

This annoyed him, for the information about the Nghis had come from Nikolai Kolosov, and the contact with Cagliaro had been arranged through some criminal contacts of Kolosov's back in the former USSR. It had been Kolosov who had provided the letters, obtained from a Ukrainian antiquarian books dealer, based in New York.

What a waste of goddam time. Here they were, stuck with two men for whose services they had parted with millions, and they lacked the basic tools for the job.

'We know this is important for you, sir,' said Nghi with grave courtesy. 'That's why we have taken so long to reach our conclusion.'

Terrific. *Mazel tov*.

But Danny Davidov had not survived Mossad undercover jobs in Europe and the Middle East without acquiring stunning flexibility of purpose. He nodded. 'Fine . . . fine. And with access to the real, original stuff, you can do the work?'

'Of course.'

Davidov scratched his head. 'Sure. Okay. It's not the end of the world. Say you can see it but not touch . . .?'

Nghi glanced at his grandson. Lee Xuan nodded.

'That would be possible,' Nghi replied.

'Okay. We'll fix it.'

And at that moment Nikolai Kolosov padded round a bulkhead, sweat on his face and shoulders, a towel round his neck and tucked into his tracksuit top. He sported that self-righteous glow of the disgustingly fit.

'What's happening?' he asked Davidov, in Russian.

'Oh, nothing special. Tell the captain to turn right round, would you, Nikolai? We're going back to the USA.'

Kolosov stared at him. At the discarded letters. 'Anyplace special?'

'The Potomac River, Washington, DC.'

'What legend?' asked Kolosov, beginning to understand. 'What do we tell the Port Authorities? The Coastguard?'

'Just turn the boat around. I'll figure something out.'

And Danny Davidov stared at Nghi. 'I knew you would be trouble. Goddam prima donnas.'

And Grandfather and Grandson Nghi gazed back at him. Inscrutably.

It was as if she had never challenged him about those rumours and allegations regarding his involvement in her father's death. Reuven Arieh behaved as if the matter had been aired, discussed and forgotten. Maybe he believed that she was so easily duped. But Alisha Abdul-Fetteh came from a mixture of Berber and Druze stock, and the all-singing, all-dancing star in Tel Aviv's firmament might have been wiser to have remembered that. For the Druze never let up until they have arrived at the truth of a suspected wrong, and the Berbers, like their cousins of Moorish descent in Sicily, never permit a wrong to go unrevenged.

It had been Alisha's intention to kill him that very night, on the day Captain Teufik Rassi had given her Hassan's letter, a letter which was so accurate in every detail that there was no room left for doubt in her mind. Reuven Arieh, alias Salim Jaddeh, had organized the killing as just another facet of his work at the time. Setting Druze and Phalange at each other's throats.

So that night, she had resolved to cut his throat as he slept.

He had been pleased when she phoned him, phoned Salim Jaddeh, that is, and invited herself to his apartment in Beirut's Raouche district, above the new Chez Paul bakery and tearoom. They had drunk some arak and eaten a modest supper of felafel – chick-pea patties – hummus and babaghanouj. Conversation had been desultory and discreet. It was sensible to assume the apartment was occasionally bugged, since Jaddeh was known to be in contact with Abu Nidal and Hezbollah's Iranian illegals, working out of the Fundamentalist stronghold in West Beirut.

Later, after making love in one of the ways Reuven found arousing, they had begun to fall asleep on his couch. Alisha's heartbeat had started to subside, and she reached down lazily, touching her purse, which was already open, and letting her fingers rest on the ivory hilt of the open razor which was to be the instrument of her father's murderer's death.

He had never wept before, and at first Alisha did not understand it was tears that had dropped from his eyes on to her breast and shoulder, where his head rested. She left the razor to brush the warm wetness away, and he turned to gaze at her. Tears running uncontrollably from his eyes, his mouth like an inconsolable child's.

Well, maternal instinct surfaces at the most inconvenient moments. Dear, dear, she found herself saying, and stroking the tears away, wrapping her arms around the sobbing master of espionage. There, there . . .

It transpired that Reuven Arieh had learned just before she had arrived that evening that his youngest brother, a reservist paratrooper serving on the Lebanon border, had been captured the previous week and his body had been found in a ruined gas station, hands and feet hacked off, just eighteen hours before.

Maybe it was the Druze or the Berber in her, or that same part of Alisha that had saved Hassan from being killed ten years before, but she had comforted Arieh and stayed the night with him and, when he fell into a fitful slumber, closed her purse and postponed vengeance until a later date.

And now, three weeks later, his every breathing moment

was an affront to her father's memory. Such are the paradoxes in the business of revenge.

'I don't understand why we can't all eat together,' said David Jardine. 'As we do at the moment. In Century.'

'Officers and other ranks, David. High time we acknowledged the difference.' Steven McCrae picked his way over a long, plastic-wrapped roll of electrical cables, in the bowels of the post-Modernist architectural monstrosity which the Firm was gearing up to move into.

The din of constant drilling and hammering sounded from all around, above and below. It was like this in Sarajevo in the early days, thought Jardine, who been sent there to make a political appreciation and had not been thanked for his report – that the only politics which could possibly stop that particular horror were those delivered by Cruise missiles and, since he knew the non-existent Pax Europa did not have the will or the ethical motivation to intercede on those terms, the Balkans would continue to fester until Greece and Russia and Turkey went at each other's throats.

'We have no other ranks, Steven,' he said. 'This is a small service with in theory only educated people in it.'

'Seniors and juniors, then. Don't be pedantic, dear boy, you know what I mean.'

They reached a wide-open elevator doorway, sans elevator. A rather terrifying moan of wind echoed from the dark hole.

'And I haven't seen a bloody window for ages. Who designed this place? Bella Lugosi?'

'Fish tanks,' replied McCrae brightly.

Jardine stared at the other members of the New Building Committee present. Tim Lewin, Director of Personnel, Gerry Blake, Director of Plans, and Marietta Delice, pronounced 'delichi'. Marietta was the Firm's version of Dorothy. Square-built, about fifty, chain-smoking, hard-drinking, hard-working and very, very shrewd. She had run most of the tasty things, Soviet Ops, Counter-Terror,

Political Action (about which nobody spoke) and Eastern Hemisphere.

In fact Marietta had been first choice for J-WISC but she had turned it down. She would have made a good job of it, thought Jardine, she was still as interested in everything to do with the business as she had been twenty years before, when they had both behaved extremely badly (meaning illegally), on behalf of the British taxpayer, on clandestine operations in Berlin and Cyprus.

She had picked up on his stare of disbelief. 'Fish tanks, Steven?' she asked, pretending to ignore Jardine, in that sort of way that meant if she looked at him she knew they would both become helpless with laughter.

'Fish tanks,' replied McCrae primly. 'It was Polly's idea.' Polly was his new wife, the twenty-seven-year-old daughter of a merchant banker. Jardine began to wonder why he disliked McCrae so much. Maybe it was sexual jealousy. Then he remembered that bloody tape in Reuven Arieh's villa, in the hills above Beirut.

'I can't really see a place for David. In the new organization . . .' That was what the smarmy bastard had said. In very much the same self-possessed tone of voice in which he had just uttered the words 'fish tanks'.

'Fish tanks in lieu of windows . . .?' asked David Jardine gravely.

'It's popular in Japan. Many psychological studies recommend it. Them. Recommend fish tanks.'

'Jolly good.' Jardine detached himself from the others and set off over the rubble, past what he had assumed was going to be an enormous underground car park, before being told this was the canteen for lower grades.

'Who did design this, anyway?' he asked Marietta, who had left the committee to join him.

'Someone called Farrell. Terry Farrell. Plus a committee. At one time it was going to be a shopping mall and courtyards of apartments, looking on to squares, or across the river. With some offices.'

'So how did we get it?'

They reached an elevator, grimy with grey concrete dust, which worked.

'Discreet, I suppose,' said Marietta, expressionless, and stepped inside. Jardine followed.

The journey to the top floor was so fast it almost occasioned a nose-bleed. Jardine and Marietta stepped out, giggling and slightly stunned. To their surprise, Kate Howard and her Security Section were making some kind of group inspection. It reminded Jardine of those bunches of tourists who can be seen wandering around Westminster, led by some fruitcake holding an umbrella aloft as a point of reference.

Jardine started to smile a greeting but Kate chose to convey, with her black belt in body language, I am far too busy with my school prefects here to exchange bourgeois pleasantries.

After Kate's group had moved on, David Jardine and Marietta went to one of the very tall, post-Modernist windows, set in a protruding semi-circle, and gazed down at the Thames and across to the Tate Gallery and some rows of tiny old terrace houses which had somehow escaped the dead hand of progress.

'I hear you were asking about Poles in the Russian Service,' said Marietta.

'Yep,' said Jardine.

'But you must know, a grownup like you, the Russian Service' – she meant the KGB – 'would never allow a Pole into their midst. Iron Felix was probably the last.'

'Iron' Felix Dzerzhinsky was the founder of the first post-revolutionary security apparat in Bolshevik Russia. He had been born a Pole and had studied as a seminarist, before embracing a life of terror, on a broad canvas.

'Still . . .' said Jardine.

They watched a tugboat lug some barges up-river, little toy boats far below.

'Couple of years back, I had my eye on a very ambitious guy. Rumoured to be Service A. Then he just dropped out of sight.' She shrugged.

'And he was Polish?'

'It was only a rumour.' Marietta hunched her shoulders and took a pack of Winstons from her pocket. She offered one to Jardine.

'Where did you get these?' he asked.

'In a shop. Churchill Hotel lobby. Why?'

He took one. Marietta lit his and hers.

'They're hard to find.' He had received a report from Ronnie Szabodo, who had passed the pack of Winstons and the Zippo lighter to Technical Department, working near Century House in an ugly red-brick building off the Borough Road. The cigarettes had been taken apart and tested for everything from microdots to bubonic plague. Back had come the answer, they were just cigarettes.

And the Zippo? Just a faint trace of a particular brand of Italian cologne, which was Alisha's favourite.

'Um.' Jardine's eyes met Marietta's. 'Is there a name?'

'Just a high-flier in Service A. That's the one that does counterfeiting of documents. Forgery. That sort of thing.'

'And he was Polish?' Jardine found that hard to believe.

'Talk to Sergei. He knows more than he let on. I got that feeling when I asked him.' She smiled, smoke wafting from her mouth like a dragon. 'But he likes you. You believed in him . . .'

It was like hearing the echoes of a long-forgotten waltz, an echo from the days when David Jardine was an all-singing, all-dancing star in offensive intelligence operations, respected in the Service and reluctantly admired by his country's rivals and enemies.

He had been an agent-runner second to none. And when Sergei Rodionovsky had finally come in, after thirteen appallingly dangerous years working as a senior KGB operator in their First Chief Directorate, it had been Jardine who had stood up to the Jeremiahs and the opportunists in the Office, men and women who had never got their own bloody feet wet.

It had been David Jardine who had staked his career on

Rodionovsky being the genuine article. He had been right. And Steven McCrae had never forgiven him.

'I'll do that,' he said. And dropping his cigarette on the floor, he stood on it, the lethargy and self-doubt vanishing as quickly as a dose of the cold, on that fine day when it has suddenly gone, symptoms away, bag and baggage.

This was what he had been waiting for. Only pessimists never notice when they are offered a lifebelt.

The garden in a suburban house not far from Tring, in Hertfordshire, was Sergei's pride and joy. As David Jardine watched him clip just the correct snippets from his budding tea roses, it was hard to contemplate this shy teddy bear of a man, in scruffy grey cardigan and old trousers from a discarded suit, running illegal KGB operatives in the USA, Europe and the United Kingdom so fluently, with such attention to detail and ruthless watching of their backs, that it would have been impossible to have ever detected them, if Sergei had not been, by the grace of God, at the same time doubling for the Great Glass Box, having been recruited by the Firm in Denmark, years earlier.

The young Sergei Rodionovsky had been spotted as a potential defector in place some two years before the approach had been orchestrated in an elaborate minuet, masterminded by a shrewd Scot (the same officer who had recruited Kate Howard years later, at a dinner in Magdalen College, Oxford) who was even then a senior SIS operations pro, aged forty-five at that time, working in the SovBloc Directorate and later, nearer the moment of make-or-break contact, in close consultation with the local Head of Station and the Chief of the Danish Service.

When the approach had come, the way these things sometimes happen, it had been Sergei who had made the first move, to everyone's consternation, for they wondered if that meant he had gotten wind of their careful schemes and was playing the game back against them.

But the quality and quantity and the regular delivery of

his product, and the absolute damage it did to the Soviet empire and its most secret plans for war against the West – which were well in hand and most seriously intended – stunned even the most sceptical, and Major, later Colonel, Sergei Rodionovsky became one of the jewels in the SIS crown, for thirteen years, until finally the gamekeepers of Department S, of the First Chief Directorate, and the security janissaries of S Directorate, the illegals directorate, zeroed in on him, and Sergey, codename Blackbird, was lifted out from Moscow one rainy June day, and spirited back to the United Kingdom, under the noses of his would-be inquisitors.

Jardine knew that Sergei had refused financial reward in those early days, and when asked what he wanted in return for secret KGB intelligence that effectively wrecked Soviet plans to *blitzkrieg* Europe and nuke the USA, had replied, in his special cipher, 'I want, one day, to be a citizen of a free and democratic country. That is all.' For Sergei was not, strictly speaking, a defector, he was a committed Russian patriot. And he had chosen to work to destroy the Communist system that had enslaved his people.

David Jardine had been present at the small ceremony in Buckingham Palace, after the Blackbird's four years of debriefing, when Her Majesty the Queen had invited Sergei to tea and, in the way that she has, with a twinkle in her eye, just as the small group was taking their leave, had said, 'Oh, Mr Rodionovsky, I understand you have always wanted to be a citizen of a democratic nation . . .'

Sergei had blushed, being a shy man, and had said that was so. And the Queen, tiny beside him, had lifted a buff envelope from a silver tray on a small side-table by the door, and handed it to him.

'It's your British passport,' was all she said, then, 'Thank you.' And the way she gripped his hand, she meant it.

Jardine had never thought he would see the Russian with tears in his eyes.

'A Pole . . .' Sergei said, stooping over his hydrangeas,

scanning them for backsliders. 'They would never allow a Pole to join KGB.'

This was always the way a Slav would pick up a pertinent question. What he meant, even if he did not realize it, since such a reply was second nature to him, was maybe they would. But Jardine would have to work for it.

'Surely the Centre has employed one or two non-Russians?' said Jardine. 'I mean, Sergei, over the years.'

'Maybe in the thirties. Maybe some officers from satellite countries, yes. Maybe then. But in 1937, Stalin got rid of them.'

'And that's it, is it? No one since?'

Rodionovsky straightened. He gazed at Jardine. 'You remember when I planted these . . .?'

'Hydrangeas?'

'This garden.'

'Yes, I do. I see you did start a vegetable patch.'

David Jardine and Szabodo had worked over three weekends digging and planting, helping Sergei Rodionovsky turn into a home a house that had been bequeathed to the nation by a retired navy lieutenant commander, who had fought at the Dieppe landings, and had escorted convoys to Murmansk, in 1944, when the chances of survival were about 15 per cent.

The Treasury had offered it to MOD, who had no military accommodation requirements in the area, and no wish to be burdened by a small property at the time of a housing slump. So they offered it to the Firm, who were content to acquire, gratis, a free safe house.

That had been about four years ago. Now the prize defector – no, dissident. The prize dissident – had been given the place, with deeds and other title documents in his cover-name, which was Peter Walter Martens.

'You think it's okay?'

'You've done, um, you've worked wonders. Look at those tea roses. You could show them.'

'The moment your Office has finished peeling onion skins off me, I intend to.'

'Not worried about certain people having a go at you?'

Jardine meant the First Chief Directorate of the old KGB which, with a few personality changes in upper and top command structures, had become the Sluzhba Vneshney Razvyedki, which was the Russian for Foreign Intelligence Service. Under Gorbachev, then Boris Yeltsin, it had been separated from the KGB and answered directly to the Russian President and Parliament. Whatever its new, post-Communist name, espionage professionals saw no pressing reason to stop calling it the First Chief Directorate, or FCD.

Within the FCD was a direct action department, Department 8, of S Directorate, which was tasked with carrying out clandestine illegal acts, such as assassination, outside the former USSR. While Islamic Fundamentalists and foreign agitators interfering in states like Georgia and Azerbaijan, who sought to secede from the Federation, were more likely targets these days than Western personalities, the fact was that the facility to kill enemies of the State remained in place.

SIS knew that there was still a death warrant out for the defector, Sergei Rodionovsky, for his betrayed masters had suffered a severe sense-of-humour failure at the time of his escape to the West. The new Russia was consumed by a struggle for power between those who, like Yeltsin, wanted to sweep aside the old ways and embrace capitalism and democracy, and those, particularly within the military–industrial complex, who yearned for a return to the days of Brezhnev and even Stalin. It was illegal KGB killers, and nobody was quite sure who they supported, or how they were funded, that David Jardine meant, when he said 'certain people'.

'I don't think they frequent flower shows,' replied Rodionovsky.

'So, Sergei. What about this Pole?'

The former KGB man frowned. David Jardine knew he was always happier when he knew what answer was wanted. Not so much because Rodionovsky was keen to please, but because he had found, with the limited horizons of many of his debriefers, that it made for an easier life.

'Why are you going on about this?'

'It's just I've heard a rumour about a Polish officer. Who fell out of favour with the Centre.'

Rodionovsky sighed, touching the petals of his hydrangeas, as if they were much easier to deal with. You got no conundrums from hydrangeas.

'They did have some Jews,' he finally eked out the intelligence, 'until about 1973 . . . but Russian Jews.'

Jardine refrained from glancing at his watch. 'So I have been misinformed . . .?'

'We had no Poles.' The Russian moved along to some heather he was cultivating on a small bank which stopped abruptly against his neighbour's fence.

'Unless what . . .?'

Rodionovsky's voice was muffled. He seemed to be conveying his message to the shrubbery. Jardine crossed to stand next to him.

'I didn't hear you.'

'Unless, David, he had lied about his nationality.'

Rodionovsky straightened and peeled off his gardening gloves. He grinned. 'You ask the correct question, you get the correct answer. If a candidate filled in the box, in his Positive Vetting form, Box Five, everyone in KGB knows this number, Box Five, which is Nationality. If, say, he had been technically born Polish. But . . .'

'Adopted?' Hallelujah!

Rodionovsky nodded, as if David Jardine was a terribly backward pupil. 'Yes. Suppose he had been adopted, during the war, towards the very end of the war. By a senior Red Army officer on the drive through Poland, towards Germany, from the Donbass . . . for argument's sake.'

He nodded as Jardine digested this. 'Maybe,' he went on, '*mozhet byt*, he did not even know he was born a Pole. Not when he was a young candidate for the KGB.'

'With a senior Red Army man for a father . . . I can see that,' said Jardine casually, and all the time his impatient brain was demanding, the name, the name, tell me the bloody name, Sergei, you're driving me crazy.

Rodionovsky gazed at Jardine, reading his thoughts, it seemed. 'So,' he demanded, the pedagogue to the end, 'who am I talking about . . .?'

Jardine smiled, letting the small game of chess draw out, 'You are talking about the son of, what? A colonel? A general? Who fought his way up from Stalingrad, or the Donbass, probably in his forties then, and found an infant in the – I don't know, wreckage of some bombed-out village or town. General and wife have tried without success for a child. So the baby is wrapped up and sent back to Russia, fog of war and all that. Sent to privileged schools. University. KGB. Naturally, when he gets to Box 5 of his PV form, he writes, Russian. For he believes, at that time, that he is.'

'Not bad. In fact, extremely close to what I heard. Rumours. When I was with FCD here, in London Embassy.'

'What's his name . . .?' Enough is enough, for God's sake.

'It never got as far as a name.'

'You're kidding.'

'And I was never interested enough to try to find out. Such gossip is everyday in KGB. Like women's hairdressers.'

Well, it shouldn't be too hard, thought Jardine. Provided the rumours had some substance.

'Your Office can identify him from this information,' said Rodionovsky. 'Couple of hours on the computer. Staying for tea?'

David Jardine gazed at him. 'I'd love to. Have you stopped putting bloody jam in it . . .?'

And they both laughed.

'I even hold my little finger like this now.' The Russian demonstrated. 'Lapsang or Lord Grey?'

Lord Grey will be fine, Jardine replied. Knowing Sergei Rodionovsky meant Earl Grey. That most English of teas.

It was rumoured, in the Office, that Sergei had even stopped drinking Stolichnaya, the best vodka in the world, and now favoured a dry sherry before dinner. Jardine devoutly hoped not . . .

A couple of times, as he wandered around the corridors of Century House, David Jardine had noticed Steven McCrae deep in conversation with Tim Lewin, Director of Personnel. And was it his imagination, or each time, had the Chief broken off in mid-sentence, and seemed, well, shifty, at the sight of Jardine?

That's how Reuven bloody Arieh is affecting me, thought Jardine. It was insidious, like having caught some kind of virus. But his instinct was strong now, that if he ran with the ball passed by Arieh and the Mossad – the poisoned chalice of Danny Davidov and the threat he presented to an as yet unidentified Western economy – no matter what their real motives had been, he might just play himself back into the sunshine. Vis-à-vis his place and his future with SIS.

It was noticed that David Jardine did not take lunch in the Great Glass Box's all-ranks canteen, and Heather mothered him with Marks and Spencer sandwiches and baguettes from the new pâtisserie at Waterloo Station. He was working late in the evenings, in his corner office on the seventh floor. And the light in his Tite Street apartment was observed glowing into the small hours.

To her credit, Kate Howard kept her word, and the signed report by Jardine, of his kidnapping and what could be interpreted as his having been compromised by Mossad, remained in a sealed envelope, in the combination-safe behind her desk, in her office. She liked David, and she knew he had already been the subject of a searching and uncompromising security investigation by her predecessor, following the loss of a contract officer, Harry Ford, in Colombia and the voluntary admission by Jardine that he had been having an affair with the agent's wife.

She suspected that Steven McCrae, although he had earnestly professed that he wanted nothing more than for

David to emerge with a cast-iron clearance, would have been less than heartbroken should the security investigation have denied Jardine Positive Vetting status. For there was no place in the Firm for anyone without it. It would not have been in the National Interest. Even a former Chief, Sir Maurice Oldfield, had been fired on the same day he had his PV clearance withdrawn, after a lifetime of selfless and sterling service. Because giving baths to waiters and masturbating choirboys was not compatible with the job.

Well, David was strictly heterosexual and not, actually, all that promiscuous. It was just, as Kate knew only too well, and the memories continued to give her a delicious private pleasure, that when David Jardine decided he wanted something, he did not hesitate, like more moral (more timid? Less attractive?) men. He went for it, in his own quiet but determined way.

She had been interviewed by the Nasty People, as Ronnie Szabodo called the Security Section's investigators, and had innocently assured them that the then Controller West 8 had always been a courteous and perfect gentleman, in his dealings with her. No, he had never made an improper suggestion. And Kate felt she could have taken a lie detector on that one, because when David Jardine had taken her to bed, he had been perfect. And gentle.

And he had not made an improper suggestion to get there, for that had been her idea.

The security investigation took months, and all the time Jardine had patiently and without complaint soldiered on, running West 8 and infiltrating Pablo Escobar's *grupo* for a second time, using a young contract officer he had recruited from the Crown Prosecution Service. Half-Argentinian, of Scots descent, the agent had even gone to prison with Escobar and at that moment, as far as Kate Howard knew, was still with him, on the run now and very much at bay, the hunters' net closing in. Thanks, in large part, to the continuing success of Jardine's painstaking recruiting and placing of his operator, whose name was Malcolm Strong.

The inquisitors reported no scintilla of evidence that David Jardine was anything other than a loyal and able senior officer, and they noted the esteem he was held in by every professional they talked to, even those who did not particularly like him. When it came to the business of agent-running and offensive intelligence-gathering, Jardine was almost without equal.

Which left the more mundane areas of security investigation.

Apart from a disdain approaching hostility towards most politicians of whatever persuasion, Jardine had no strong political leanings. His religion was Roman Catholic, converted from atheist in 1979. He had a good credit rating and a small private income from investments inherited from his father. No debts. He did not gamble and held his drink. He was monumentally discreet, without being overly secretive, which the Firm had finally decided was a distinct disadvantage.

Anyway, all of his boxes had been ticked Positive and Jardine had survived and retained his security clearance, which gave him access to the most sensitive intelligence material, way beyond the classification Top Secret.

But the business of his affair with the stunning Elizabeth Ford, which unfortunately coincided, it seemed, with the death of her husband, did militate against him. Not, however, as devastatingly as it might have done, for only David Jardine himself had been there, in that graveyard on a hillside above Bogota, on that appalling afternoon, and the secret of how Harry Ford had met his death he would take with him to his Maker.

Steven McCrae, in his wisdom, promoted Jardine out of West 8 and gave him the Forward Plans Directorate, which had the smallest staff and office accommodation of any SIS Directorate, with a broad remit to liaise with foreign intelligence agencies, and, of course, a seat on J-WISC and direct access to the Chief.

Kate persuaded herself that Jardine's potentially damaging Beirut/Pomegranate report need go no further than her private safe, precisely because of the job description for Director (Forward Plans): 'To liaise, both formally and informally, with all foreign intelligence services, excepting absolutely those with whom the nation is in a state of war, hostility or confrontation'.

Well, the UK was not at war with or in confrontation with Israel. Therefore, it could be said, if push came to shove, that the Beirut débâcle had been 'informal liaison'.

Thus luck can help us even when we least deserve it, maybe especially then. And David Jardine was indeed fortunate to have a friend in Kate Howard, to keep his secrets and discreetly watch his back.

Being suspended, even on full pay, is just what it says. Out of work, away from everyday stuff with colleagues, in a kind of a limbo. Like Purgatory, neither Heaven nor Hell. Not guilty, and yet not innocent either. Just left hanging on a decision that probably has been consigned to somebody's pending tray. Out of sight and out of mind.

It is one hell of a sentence and a hard one to serve, because of the waiting, and the uncertainty.

If Elmore Williams thought any of these things, and God knows he did, he sure as hell did not let it show, even to Martha and the kids. But Martha knew.

'Elmore, summer's on the way,' she started, and Williams smiled that slow smile of his.

'No kidding.'

'So I thought . . .'

'Uh-huh . . .?'

'Well, maybe you could mend the lawn-sprinkler.'

Elmore Williams turned from the kitchen counter, where he was soldering the handle back on to an enamel coffee jug that his wife had bought in New Orleans, when they had first gotten married.

'The lawn-sprinkler?'

'It's getting real dry out there.'

Elmore Williams laid the soldering iron down carefully

and stepped across to his wife, who was putting the lunch things into her dishwasher.

'You ain't trying to keep my mind off things, are you?'

'You get back to your side of the kitchen, Elmore Williams, I know that look . . .'

'I can think of ways to keep my mind occupied.'

'Be serious, Elmore, it's broad daylight. The kids might come back.'

'The kids are at school.'

'The bedroom . . .'

'Don't mess with me, woman.'

Fortunately, the soldering iron automatically switched itself off after a few minutes. And preoccupied as they had become, neither Martha nor Elmore Williams noticed the rasp of a Suzuki trail-bike, as it cruised past the front of the small, detached house, with its neat lawn and unsprinkled grass.

And if they had, if Elmore had, would he have thought twice about it? Maybe, for he normally had a sixth sense for such things.

After eleven days of comprehensive research into every detail the Firm had on the KGB's First Chief Directorate's officers and operators, David Jardine finally found a snippet, a hint, of an identity for the rumoured war orphan who had perhaps unwittingly withheld his Polishness from the KGB, when filling in Box Five of his first Positive Vetting form, which required an answer to the simple query-Nationality?

The man had been a colonel in the First Chief Directorate, now the Russian Intelligence Service. According to an SIS report from an agent, a cleaner at the Yasenevo complex on the southern outskirts of Moscow which was the home of the KGB's Moscow Centre, jealousy among his fellow Deputy Directors in Service A had resulted in a denunciation that led to his suspension and dismissal.

Three days later, having zeroed in on this one KGB,

former KGB, officer, Jardine lifted one of three black telephones on his desk and made a direct call, on a secure line, to Ronnie Szabodo, who worked out of an undercover office which fronted as a car stereo import agency and repair shop, off Brixton High Street.

'Ronnie, let's get together for a quiet drink somewhere,' was all he said.

'How about the Phene?' replied Szabodo.

The Phene was a pub in Chelsea, with a garden. Ideal for discreet conversations, particularly in inclement weather.

'See you there. Six o'clock?'

Ronnie Szabodo said that would be fine. He went on, 'Pity about Avvie?'

'Avvie who?'

'Avriam Eitels. Tel Aviv's man on J-WISC.'

'What about him?'

'Paris. Mugged at École Militaire.'

École Militaire was a station on the Métro.

'Is he okay?'

'They buried him this morning. Blow to the neck. Adam's apple.'

Jardine shrugged. 'Poor old Avvie. I do wish they would stop teaching karate to hoodlums.'

'Does that leave you out? Think about it.'

Jardine smiled as he hung up. What a bloody way to go. He remembered Eitels' droll conversations and the way the Mossad man had always reminded him of Woody Allen.

Later that May day, in the garden of the Phene pub in Chelsea, which was cold and blustery, the two men sat with large Kentucky bourbons in their hands, coat collars turned up, and David Jardine explained precisely what he required the squat Hungarian to do.

Just as well, he mused, on the walk back to his flat in Tite Street, that we don't (we, being the Firm, SIS, the Great Glass Box) have to worry about the readies when it comes to financing illegal operations in denied areas. For he had just set in motion a completely unauthorized information-gathering operation in Moscow, using people Century House did not even know existed. Tapping wires, intercepting mail, a little bit of burglary, the lot.

It took Szabodo about a week to set the thing up and results were flowing back to Jardine within the fortnight.

The day after his drink with Ronnie Szabodo, David Jardine had consulted with Sir Steven McCrae and Kate Howard, Director of Security, without revealing his hand, and secured their agreement for him to take up a long-standing invitation to make a liaison visit to the Sluzhba Vneshney Razvyedki, the Russian Intelligence Service.

He then signalled the Office's Moscow Station, working out of the Embassy, in semi-covert, or grey, status, requesting certain facilities, and twenty-nine days later he boarded British Airways flight BA 872 to Moscow, as a VIP guest of the SVR, which was based at a complex of buildings designed by a Finnish architect and completed in 1972, at Yasenevo, on the Outer Orbital Road, South, about sixteen kilometres south-west of the Kremlin, which was at the heart of Moscow, in more ways than one.

A black Mercedes 500SEL coupé swept across the tarmac and stopped by the steps being set against the rear port exit of the British Airways 747 from London Heathrow.

'Jesus Christ. David Jardine. I never thought I would see the day when we two, you and me, would be working together as comrades. This is a special day. Boy oh boy.'

David Jardine smiled politely and shook hands with the enthusiastic Russian who had leapt from the back of the car and waited impatiently at the foot of the steps for the only passenger to disembark. The others had all been directed to a set of steps at the front of the aircraft. Jardine felt vaguely insulted that the SVR had sent a callow youth of about thirty-seven, until he heard his name.

'Forgive me.' The SVR officer's English was pure John Belushi. 'I am Anatoly Andreyevich Dzerzhinsky. I thought we might avoid the VIP lounge, where my service usually greets guests of the *kontora*.' The *kontora* was how Russian spies referred to their service. It meant 'the office', although the origin of the word is uncertain. It is certainly not Russian.

Jardine knew all about this Anatoly Andreyevich; great-nephew of one of the most feared Bolsheviks in history – Felix Dzerzhinsky. Founder of the Cheka. Architect of the Great Terror. Iron Felix. And this descendant of his was known to SIS as a leading member of the Russian Mafia, who had reached the rank of KGB Colonel in the time of Gorbachev, when he was only twenty-eight.

As the Mercedes sped south on the Leningradskoye Highway towards Moscow and the FCD Complex on the other side of the city, the two men relaxed and exchanged pleasantries about how wonderful it was that Communism was extinct, that democracy was in Russia to stay, and that finally two former Cold War enemies were able to work together on certain projects.

Jardine had brought himself right up to date on the subjects of international drug smuggling, the terrorist threat vis-à-vis the vast nuclear arsenal which remained as a hangover from the Cold War, and which was not always guarded as securely as one might expect, and the threat to Europe and world order from the inexorable rise of Islamic Fundamentalism spreading from Iran to the southern states of the Russian Federation. For these were the subjects he was ostensibly in Moscow to discuss.

'Now, David, we have arranged a villa for you in the Yazenevo grounds. You will have a pass admitting you to our Heads of Service restaurant, in the company of a conducting officer. The Deputy Director of the Sluzhba is there this week. Also the Head of Planning and several deputy heads of our various departments.'

'Thank you,' said Jardine, 'I'm sure I will be very comfortable.' This was a first, for both intelligence services. No SIS officer had ever been invited (or permitted) to stay in the Centre, as a guest of the Foreign Intelligence Service, formerly known as the First Chief Directorate, prior to its separation from the KGB.

How times had changed. Jardine had intended to stay at the British Embassy, which was normal, but the Firm's Director, Russian Federation/Former Soviet Bloc, had urged him to take up the offer. For with the collapse of the Cold War, SIS had slashed SovBloc's intelligence budget, and any intelligence David Jardine could glean from such an opportunity would be more than welcome.

'I'm surprised you didn't bring an aide,' Dzerzhinsky remarked casually, as the Mercedes joined the Leningrad Highway and began the twenty-mile drive south through Moscow to the periphery of the city's south-western outskirts at Yasenevo, not far from Yugozapadnaya Metro Station.

'The Embassy is supplying me with two,' replied Jardine, 'an interpreter and the Deputy Head of Station, Jimmy Melrose. They said they would be at the Centre when I get there.'

'Ah. Then they're probably there.'

Jardine smiled to himself. Of course they were there. Unless they wanted to be on the next plane back to England.

'You know, David – or would you prefer me to call you General . . .?'

'Why on earth would you do that?'

'You're an SIS Director grade. Head of a department. In KGB, which we're now to call the Ministry of Security, that's equivalent to Lieutenant-General rank.'

'No, really, please, David is fine.' Mister Jardine to you, you sleek twerp, thought David Jardine. But he relaxed and nodded comfortingly.

'The KGB is now tearing itself apart over who is pro-Yeltsin and who still hankers for the bad old days,' announced Dzerzhinsky, unprompted. It was like getting a message in a séance. 'The only foreign postings are within the former Soviet Union and very occasional Embassy security jobs. No, David, the Foreign Intelligence Service is where it's all happening, believe me.'

'I'm absolutely fascinated to see how things have changed within the two services,' Jardine replied, truthfully.

'Or,' continued Dzerzhinsky, 'I have a wonderful apartment off Prospekt Michurinsky in the Southern Port.'

'Very sought-after, I hear. Near the Olympic Village, is it?' The former Olympic Village, built for the 1980 Olympics, was a choice place for up-and-coming Muscovites to live, having been created to impress foreign visitors to Russia, with little expense spared.

'Couple of blocks from it. You are welcome to stay there, as the guest of my wife and me.'

Jardine smiled. No wonder the guy was big in the Mafia. He had the chutzpah of a Brooklyn numbers man.

'Thank you, Anatoly,' he said, 'but the villa will be fine. I can't tell you what a thrill it will be to stay there. And to eat in the Mess? My colleagues are green with envy.'

In the easy silence that followed, Jardine gazed at the drab, high-rise blocks and the sporadic queues of down-at-heel citizens of the new Russia, outside dull-looking stores and food shops. He wondered, heretically, if they had not been better off under the iron heel of Soviet realism.

'Green with envy, eh?' Dzerzhinsky smiled cynically. He had observed Jardine watching his capital city's grey streets and melancholy population. 'Anyway, I hope we can lure you away from the Centre for at least one night out on the town. Sample the delights of freedom, for the few Muscovites with a dollar or two.'

You really just don't care, do you, Anatoly? David Jardine thought to himself.

'I wouldn't miss it for the world,' he replied, and meant every word of it.

Now, the way things go, the way events unfold, as history's footnotes occur, unnoticed at the time, other agencies had become aware of the increasing boldness of a mystery criminal enterprise which had established an ever-growing pattern of brilliant and outrageous crime, always involving counterfeiting of one kind or another, now in the Far East, now in Europe, then South America, and so on.

Over the last couple of months, Nancy Lucco had noticed

among the endless classified updates she and other US Secret Service officials found moving across their desks, at first isolated, brief, one-paragraph reports among Treasury and State Department intelligence updates, noting that such and such a foreign law enforcement agency was investigating the crimes, without success, and trying, with even less success, to identify the perpetrators.

'When', some FBI analyst had noted in neat handwriting in the margin of the most recent update, which concerned the St Petersburg computer robbery, 'are these jokers going to hit the USA?'

Good question, thought Nancy. And after reading a copy of the US Credit Express local manager's report, she was struck by the ingenuity and the awesome amount of planning that must have gone into the crime.

Just thirty-four seconds to get in and out, without the Intertel 9 Security Failsafe program shutting down the entire Credex computer system worldwide. And it had taken three weeks to link that with the loss of 157 million dollars from the Credex Tokyo office.

Brilliant.

But why had they not struck in the US?

Not yet, was the obvious answer. And since the gang's target was reputed by analysts to be an eventual coup of several billions, maybe it would be a good idea if one small team was given the task of monitoring this group of so-called master-criminals and blocking them by second-guessing them.

So Nancy Lucco pressed a switch on her intercom.

'Yes, Miz Lucco?'

'Toni, come in, would you?'

Toni came in and sat facing Nancy.

'This is for Andy Hernandez, Office of Investigations . . .' and Nancy dictated a memo, suggesting the Secret Service open a file on these guys and try to keep one step ahead of them.

'Just so', she said to Toni, 'when the shit hits the fan, nobody can point the finger at us, at the Service.'

Toni nodded. The remark was probably lost on her, busy as she was with night classes. 'Copy to the Bureau?'

'I don't think so. Let's not seem alarmist.'

But as Toni left, and Nancy Lucco settled down to more pressing work, she kept thinking about those audacious crimes. They were bound to be heading this way.

The Director, who had had his reasons for sending Nancy through the Special Agent's induction and advanced training courses, would have been proud. For she had been taught how to think like a law enforcer, like an investigator and not just as a lawyer.

And that was what the Director wanted in his Secret Service. In all departments and at all levels. Very much on the same principle that in the infantry you might be a cook or a clerk but, when the bullets start to fly, you gotta know the basic job – fight the enemy.

And it was thanks to Nancy's memo that the system would have a name to turn to, when the subject arose, as it surely was going to. For a scruffy tramp-steamer, the SS *Sumaru*, registered in Glasgow, Scotland, was at that very moment requesting, by radio, permission to berth at the commercial shipping port, on the Potomac River, about twenty-nine miles, as the crow flies, from the Legal Department offices of the United States Secret Service in Washington, DC.

As the *Sumaru* was making its unremarkable request to the Potomac Regional Port Authority, 4870 miles to the north-east, the black Mercedes 500SL slowed, on the Orbital Road, the Moskovskaya Koltsevaya Avtomobilnaya Doroga, and entered a slip-road near the suburb of Yasenevo.

David Jardine watched, quietly aware that even five years earlier his emotion would undoubtedly have been very different, if he had been sitting in the back of a car with the great-nephew of Felix Dzerzhinsky, approaching the unobtrusive grey pebble-dash blockhouse and high grimy, once cream-painted wire gates that were the west entrance to the sprawling concrete complex which had been the headquarters of the First Chief Directorate of the KGB. Now coyly renamed the Sluzhba Vneshney Razvyedki, or Foreign Intelligence Service.

The guards on the gate were like security guards anywhere. They did not smile as they examined the driver's pass, even though his face was well known to them, and they checked Dzerzhinsky's carefully, before saluting and waving the car on.

The complex occupied about seventy acres of Moscow's outskirts, and the car motored on past groups of men strolling, deep in conversation, hurrying secretaries and messengers on scuffed black bicycles. There was a fresh breeze blowing and the secretaries laughed as their hair blew and their skirts caught in the wind.

Jardine had a feeling that he was in truly alien territory. Like Luke Skywalker in the *Star Wars* movies.

And yet, there was a chilling normality to the place.

'What do you think of the Centre?' asked Anatoly Dzerzhinsky.

'Great curving ships. Of glass and concrete,' Jardine said, in Russian. Quoting a poem he had read years ago. He thought it was Yevtushenko, but he could not be sure. 'Going nowhere on a sea of grass, and asphalt . . .'

'Very poetic. Some say it's like Langley.' The SVR man refused to relinquish his use of English. It occurred to Jardine that Dzerzhinsky even looked like Elwood, in the Blues Brothers. He wondered if a pair of sunglasses would perfect the resemblance.

'What do you think . . .?'

'I'm sorry?'

'Langley. Virginia. You think it's like Langley?'

Jardine considered, gazing around. He remembered the coolness of the CIA headquarters, the same busy secretaries, the groups of men rapt in conversation as they strolled the vast expanses of asphalt and grass. The vast, long buildings of concrete and glass, in slight ellipses, just like here.

'No,' he replied, 'it's not in the least like Langley.'

Maybe, he thought, he hoped, maybe one day, if everything works out for your country's precarious grip on democracy. Perhaps. *Mozhet byt.*

'Ah.' Dzerzhinsky seemed slightly crestfallen.

But his spirits had recovered from that minor put-down by the time the Mercedes stopped at the side-entrance to Zdaniye Vosiem, Building Eight.

If this is the side-door, thought David Jardine, the main entrance must be straight out of Metro Goldwyn Meyer, for it had pink granite steps and an impressive steel and glass doorway.

Inside the lobby a polite girl was waiting, with excellent legs and a slender figure, not completely spoiled by a print dress and cardigan. She smiled and stepped forward as Dzerzhinsky ushered Jardine inside.

'David, this is Elena Constantinovna,' he said, speaking Russian for the first time since they had met. 'Elena Constantinovna, please welcome Mr David Jardine, of the English Service.'

'This is indeed a pleasure, sir.' Elena Constantinovna extended her hand briefly. It was cool and . . . friendly.

Jardine smiled to himself. Even you, David, he thought, are not that dumb. And, amused, he avoided the eye-contact game which Elena Constantinovna had initiated as she stepped aside and ushered them into the elevator.

'Isn't she beautiful, David? Like a little, perfectly formed ballerina.' Dzerzhinsky made a face at the young lady, who stuck her tongue out at him. 'For a tiny theatre.' Dzerzhinsky's Russian was more cultured than his English. Clearly he had been educated at one of the *nomenklatura* schools in Moscow, reserved for the rulers of the Soviet Union, as it then was, and their children's children.

'*Gadkiy,*' muttered Elena Constantinovna, under her breath. 'Disgusting, nasty . . .'

Anatoly Andreyevich looked away, ignoring her.

'*Gad'yuka,*' he breathed, gazing at a notice abjuring smoking in the elevator cabin. The word, literally viper, was extremely insulting when applied to a lady.

Times were indeed changing. Jardine remembered the year he had spent with a White Russian family in Paris, twenty-four years ago.

'Gadkiy! Gadosti! Gadalyuka!' These words had been hissed around the playroom of the big house with its own courtyard, off the Rue Napoléon in Saint-Germain, by six-year-old Count Nikki and his sister, Princess Katerina, aged eight.

Happy memories. But for two SVR (which was not all that removed from the KGB) intelligence officers to indulge in such . . . pretensions.

How interesting.

'Mr Jardine, welcome.' Major-General Yuri Zemskov extended a firm hand and waved Jardine to a chair.

Dzerzhinsky and Elena Constantinovna entered circumspectly, much more grownup now, and Anatoly Andreyevich closed the door quietly.

'You have met Anatoly Andreyevich and Major Elena Constantinovna Ratanskaya . . .'

'Indeed.' Jardine liked this man. Yuri Serafimovich Zemskov had survived every shake-up in the old KGB. He had been expelled from Britain, in the mass-expulsion of 105 Soviet spies in 1971, when he was only twenty-seven and working under diplomatic cover as Press Attaché at the Russian Embassy in Kensington Park Gardens.

He had made a big success of running four separate FCD illegals networks in the USA and Canada, and had survived three years as Rezident in Kabul, during the Soviet war in Afghanistan where he headed the KGB Office.

Back in the USSR, Zemskov had seen the way things were going and had been one of the first to hitch his wagon to Gorbachev's star. It is a little-known fact that Gorbachev was first set on his route to the top of Soviet politics, and therefore power, by Yuri Andropov, boss of the KGB before succeeding Brezhnev as ruler of the USSR.

And Andropov had recommended Yuri Serafimovich Zemskov to be promoted to Deputy Director/Security in

Gorbachev's KGB personal guard, the Protection Service, formerly known as 9th Directorate.

Only the most trusted KGB officers were permitted to guard the lives and security of the country's rulers, and Zemskov made sure that his men, and his agents, permeated the everyday lives and peregrinations of Mikhail Gorbachev and all the former Politburo bosses.

No student of Machiavelli would be surprised, therefore, to learn that it was Yuri Serafimovich Zemskov himself who had tipped off Boris Yeltsin about the abortive coup, which informed rumour suggested the Gorbachevs had connived at, to break the power of the new Russia's reformist government and seize the entire Parliament, who were holding an emergency session in the White House, as their building was called.

Paratroop General Pavel Grachev, commander of the Kremlin garrison, had listened to Zemskov, who was in close touch with Yeltsin's group during the night of the coup attempt, and it was largely thanks to Zemskov's arguments that Grachev refused to obey orders from the conspirators against freedom, to storm the White House and arrest the entire elected Russian Parliament.

A grateful President Boris Yeltsin had rewarded Yuri Serafimovich with a Directorate of the First Chief Directorate, which within days was removed from control of the KGB and created an independent service.

'It is indeed fine to meet under these circumstances, don't you think?' said the Major-General.

Jardine glanced at a portrait hanging on the wall behind Zemskov's desk. It was of Felix Dzerzhinsky, in leather coat and worker's cap, his head framed by a heroically fluttering red flag, with a suggestion of flames in the background.

'Oh, yes,' said Jardine politely. 'It's wonderful that so much has changed . . .'

And while David Jardine was sitting in the office of a Russian Service general in the secure area at Moscow

Centre, it was ten after eight in the morning, 4718 miles to the south-west, in a Virginian suburb of Washington, where Elmore Williams was carefully slicing the top off an egg that his daughter Melanie had boiled.

'It's okay, I boiled it just like you like.'

'I'm taking my time, girl, because last time you boiled me an egg, it ran all down the eggcup on to my plate and it had gotten cold by the time I mopped it up.'

'That ain't true.'

'Sure as hell is.'

'Is not.'

'Is, is, is times two hundred and four.'

'You just wanna tell any boyfriend I bring here that Melanie can't boil an egg.'

'Boyfriend? Whatta you mean boyfriend, you're ten years old, goddammit.'

'Don't swear at your daughter, Elmore, it isn't nice.' Martha came into the kitchen, carrying the morning's mail and the Washington daily paper.

'He's a cop, Mom. Cops swear all the time.'

Williams laughed. Martha, checking through the envelopes for something other than a bill or a mailshot, said, 'You see . . .?' the way wives do.

'So what's in the mail?' he asked, dipping a spoon into the beheaded egg.

'Letter from the Bells, when are we going to visit them in Wyoming?'

'Answer?' Williams munched his spoonful of boiled egg, aware that Melanie was watching intently.

'Not *this* century . . .' Martha grinned, and sat down, reaching for the coffee pot.

'Mom, you want an egg?'

Martha met Elmore's eye. Infinitesimally, he shook his head.

'I'll pass right now, honey.'

Elmore Williams was laughing quietly as he backed his Pontiac Firebird coupé out of the car port at the side of his small, four-bedroomed house in Alexandria, Virginia. It was a quiet neighbourhood and while folks by and large kept themselves to themselves, there was always a 'Hi there' or a cheery 'How's it going?' which made it a pleasant enough community.

The Firebird was Williams' pride and joy. It was a 1979 model and he had lovingly restored it, between undercover assignments. And now, since the Service had taken his Chevvy back, pending the outcome of his suspension, Elmore Williams was using the Pontiac as his regular automobile.

With his neck twisted round, reversing the car, he just glimpsed Martha and Melanie emerging from the house, on to the front steps. The first bullet hit the child on the lower left shinbone. For a fraction of a second, Elmore Williams thought she had tripped, for she just stumbled, nothing dramatic. Then Martha juddered, as if she had walked into an invisible wall, and Williams knew precisely that this was a hit and he stood on the gas pedal and spun the back wheels, and as the car lurched backwards, accelerating, he spun the wheel left and blipped the handbrake, making the best J-turn from a standing start possible, and braking hard to position the car between the gunfire and his wife and daughter, and even as he thanked God it was the Firebird with its six-litre engine and that he had warmed the motor, the big cop had shouldered open the driver's door and rolled on to the small sloping lawn, his 9-mm Glock automatic in his right hand, and looking every which way for the source of the bullets which was no trouble for there were two Suzuki motorcycles stopped on the road, each with a black-helmeted rider and guy on the back and the guys on the back were firing MAC-10 Ingrams and there was no sound because they were using silenced weapons and the dry grass around him was kicking up dirt and he was glad he hadn't fixed the sprinkler and Elmore Williams thought fuck this, and as the bullets cracked around him and glass on his Pontiac Firebird shattered and bigger glass from his sitting-room window dropped out, he covered the left-hand target and squeezed off two rounds, BLAM-BLAM! real noisy without ear defenders, then swivelled, with minimum movement, in the space of a fifth of a second, covered target number two, fired two, biker number two, fired two, biker one, fired two, all bikers good hits and crumpling off their Suzuki trail-bikes and Williams was up, on his knees and firing just-make-sure rounds into each of the targets, then he was up and walking towards the four men on the ground, the engine of one bike racing with a dead hand on the throttle and the Secret Service man was swinging his pistol, two-handed and checking for back-up attackers, *wanting* them, *looking* for them, but there were none although he was aware of a big motor revving and a slight squeal of tyres from further up the once quiet avenue.

The attackers on the first bike, with its shrieking 250 cc engine, were motionless. The two on the other Suzuki were moving slightly, and Williams shot each one right through their black helmets, still holding his Glock two-handed, looser now, almost casual. He would testify later that in his judgement as a law enforcement officer they continued to present a clear danger.

And none of his neighbours in that neighbourly avenue even considered contradicting him.

Then he did the same to the two on the first bike, the two who were not moving, switched off the howling engine and breathing hard, his heart pumping all the stuff his system had made such good use of just seconds before, he turned every which way, looking for more targets.

Silence.

Then, so clear, the sound of a woman sobbing, hurt bad.

Martha.

Elmore Williams ran, terrified, towards his bullet-riddled automobile, dreading what he would find behind it on his front doorstep. He dodged around the car and there they were, the kid was bleeding bad and Martha was half-sitting, half-lying against the shattered glass door, crimson jelly-like streaks where she had slid sideways. Her face was streaked with tears and there were four small blue puncture marks in a line from her right shoulder to above her left breast.

Melanie lay trembling, in shock. Her leg was probably broken but it was loss of blood that Williams attacked first, ripping off his belt and making a tourniquet just below the left knee, all the time saying, 'There, there, baby, there there . . .'

He was checking Martha for lung punctures, looking for that tell-tale frothy blood on her lips, when the howl of two police squad car sirens and a paramedic truck approached, getting louder and then winding down, as help arrived.

It had been eleven minutes since the first shots and the screaming and the noise of crashing glass had alerted the Williams' neighbours to the attack.

Events in the former USSR had shifted faster than sand dunes in the Gobi Desert, leaving political analysts more confused than, being professional wiseguys, they cared to admit.

Russia had moved towards friendly normalization of its relationship with the West and, in particular, with Europe, which the younger, more cosmopolitan of its citizens wanted as an eventual trading and diplomatic partner. There had been a few false starts, the worst being the 1991 counter-revolutionary coup some alleged had been brokered by Raisa Gorbachev. US President Clinton's initial lack of foreign policy experience, when he found himself faced with the murderous civil war in Bosnia, had provided a diplomatic advantage to Moscow, which had lost no time in forming a closer, if mutually reserved and suspicious, relationship with Britain and France, to present a common front on the whole Balkan can of worms.

So during the preceding year, Jardine's job had brought him into contact with a number of senior people in Moscow's Foreign Intelligence Service. In particular, the

Heads of Departments responsible for Counter-Terrorism, Nuclear Proliferation and Narcotics, along with SVR Station Chiefs (*rezidentiy*) in London, Washington, Paris, Bogota and Cyprus. He had also had clandestine dealings with Russian Service networks in the former Yugoslavia, Iraq and Iran.

David Jardine knew how fragile the seeming reforms and democratic outlook were, for there was a formidable, restless, only just restrained monster lurking below the surface of Russia's new freedom. The old Communist Party had refused to lie down and die, and a powerful series of seditious alliances had been forged between the dispossessed apparatchiks, the industrial barons who had lost their Party status and privileges, the Red Army officers who had been thrown on the scrapheap along with their tanks and missiles, and the die-hard committed Communists of the former KGB.

Some of the most obvious Party loyalists had been dismissed from the Intelligence and Security Services and the Army, but most of the rank-and-file remained in the new organizations. Clearly there was an element of disaffected officers, who were keeping silent, keeping their powder dry, and keeping in close touch with President Boris Yeltsin's former ally and current chief rival for power, Alexander Rutskoi and his henchmen in Russia's Parliament of unelected deputies, a hangover from the Communist era which continued, hand in glove with elements of the military-industrial complex, to prepare for a return to the days of Brezhnev, if not of Stalin himself.

Even though he was aware of all this, Jardine found himself taken by surprise at the interest and flow of real intelligence his presence at Moscow Centre was generating.

Senior SVR officers, including Major-General Zemskov and Dzerzhinsky, whose appointment was never made clear, began from Day One to communicate all kinds of valuable information, from the results of Russian covert operations in Baghdad, Belgrade and South America, to suggestions for further joint ventures, following their fruitful joint penetration of all sides in the Bosnian civil war, with its potential threat to European and Russian stability.

They spelled out, with detailed frankness, that the 'Red/Brown' alliance of dispossessed Communists and extreme nationalists was manipulating the gullible and easily flattered Rutskoi towards a second coup, to overthrow Yeltsin by armed rebellion and reverse the democratic process. The White House, Moscow's resplendent Parliament building, was becoming an armed camp and informal, even clandestine, base for those plotters.

There seemed to be a hunger in the SVR to swing into gear with Europe and the West, and to make plans to deal with perceived threats from Islam, the Balkans and – for the future – the People's Republic of China.

Jardine noted a certain naivety in the broad forecasts they tended to make about the future of world events, and mutual threats requiring joint action, but his business was the acquisition of all intelligence emanating from the Centre, so he absorbed the line they were pushing and every evening he was driven through the Moscow traffic to the British Embassy on the former Morisa Toresa Embankment, now renamed Sofiyskaya Naberezhnaya.

There, Jardine worked with Jimmy Melrose, Deputy Head of Station, on a nightly digest which they sent back to Century House in secure form, from the cipher room.

In fact his Moscow visit was producing product so valuable to the Firm, and for the appraisal of future British foreign policy, that David Jardine found himself with little time to pursue his hidden agenda – research into the KGB officer of Polish descent who had been forced to quit, and whose identity he firmly intended to keep to himself, for the moment.

Dzerzhinsky had not, after three days, followed up on his offer of a night on the town, and Jardine was beginning to wonder how he might find an excuse to slip away from the Centre and from his colleagues in the Embassy, without arousing their interest or curiosity.

The Heads of Service dining room is on the ground floor of the Yasnigov complex's main building. You enter by the impressive glass and steel main entrance and turn right, passing the general commissary on a spur to the right and the medical and sports centres on the left. Straight ahead is the door to the exclusive Senior Officers' Mess.

David Jardine took breakfast there and he was amused to observe the confused reactions of certain senior Sluzhba officers to the presence in their midst of the first SIS man many of them had seen.

Sometimes conversation was stilted and formal, and sometimes he was ignored by former enemies who clearly were more conservative than Zemskov or the young, well-placed Mafia smoothy, Dzerzhinsky.

Other times, the more adventurous, or simply more friendly, officers would deliberately sit opposite him, or next to him, and engage him in conversation in either Russian or fluent English on a broad range of topics, from English soccer to American movies, to tentative, slightly daring jokes about President Clinton and her husband Bill.

All in all, it was an historic experience Jardine knew he would never forget. But, being an old Cold War warrior, he just could not bring himself to shake off the anger and enmity that stemmed from twenty-three years fighting these bastards in Cold War back-alleys from Berlin to Saigon. He knew what they had done to entire villages in Afghanistan, and he was not impressed by the refrain that at the end of the day, 'We are all in the same line of business.'

Now, David Jardine knew he was inclined to let his hormones rule his common sense, when it came to the fair sex, and there had been professional occasions when he had behaved with appalling ruthlessness, but, flawed as he realized he undoubtedly was, at least he endeavoured, at least he tried, to conduct his work along an ethical and broadly moral path.

When push came to shove.

With the exception of Bogota and all that led up to that . . . horror.

'You bastard . . .!' had cried the man he had betrayed.

So, with that exception.

But he had not, ever, contemplated engaging his service or his agents in the kind of things these people had done as a matter of policy. As a matter of course.

Leaving the Mess dining room, on the fourth morning, Jardine went to the men's room and relieved himself. He splashed water on his face and, as he dried it, he became aware that Anatoly Andreyevich had entered.

'*Zdravstvuy*, David,' he grinned. 'Good morning. Free morning today?'

'No.' Jardine dried his face on a neatly folded, freshly laundered towel, placed ready at the side of the washbasin. It reminded him of the men's room in the exclusive Connaught Hotel, in London's Mayfair district. 'I'm seeing Director Rogachev today. Crack-cocaine in, heroin out, is the topic. We're having lunch at the Narcotics Direction Seventy-two.'

Direction 72 of the SVR's Narcotics Department was the hub of Russia's growing and comprehensive war against the import and export of drugs, something that was getting a terrible grip on some sections of the Federation's workforce.

'Director Rogachev is quite sorry,' Dzerzhinsky used the word quite in the American sense, meaning very, 'we have just bust wide open a big cocaine gang and the Director has flown to Novastopol. He says please wait for him, he will be back tomorrow.'

'I understand, Anatoly Andreyevich. Frankly, I could use a day just to look around Moscow.' Here was the opportunity he had been looking for.

'Of course, you have never been here under your own name before . . .' Dzerzhinsky chuckled.

Jardine remained poker-faced, wryly aware of the irony of his situation. 'Maybe we could have lunch,' he said. 'I'll take you up on your offer to show me the town.'

Dzerzhinsky shrugged. 'Hell, I wish I could, my friend. Today the Sluzhba is making me work for my living. But I could give Elena Constantinovna the day off. She has a car.'

'No, thanks. I'll get the Embassy to pick me up. There's plenty to do down there . . .'

Dzerzhinsky gazed at him. He leaned with his back against the door. Then, looking less sure of himself than David Jardine had seen him, the great-nephew of Iron Felix dipped a hand into his pocket, and the skin on Jardine's back threw up goose-pimples. Adrenalin thudded through the heart muscle.

A millisecond of precognition.

And sure enough, Anatoly Andreyevich Dzerzhinsky produced from his pocket a battered brass Zippo lighter identical to the one Alisha had slipped into Jardine's pocket. Which was the one he had given her when they became lovers.

The silence of the moment was tangible.

Dzerzhinsky's eyes met Jardine's. His open palm displayed the lighter. Then he whispered, in Hebrew, words which meant, Next Year In Jerusalem . . .

And a tear ran down his cheek.

A tear? From Anatoly Andreyevich Dzerzhinsky . . .?

Jardine gazed at the Russian, stone-faced. Reserving judgement on this. Performance, or a genuine moment of emotion? 'Or I can just take the day off and go sightseeing with Elena Constantinovna,' he said.

Dzerzhinsky nodded. That would be fine, he replied. And he composed himself, and splashed his face.

David Jardine handed him a clean towel, and they left the Head of Directorates' washroom, in the heart of Russia's Foreign Intelligence Service, on the outskirts of Moscow.

10

Storm Petrels

IT HAD BEEN three weeks since the SS *Sumaru* had docked at Pier Eight, in the dock basin at Washington Harbour, about five miles, as the crow flies, from Capitol Hill and the US Treasury.

Danny Davidov sat in a bar on 6th, just south of the divided highway that split E and G Streets, not far from the tidal basin. It was 5.05 and the place was quiet. Two middle-aged workers, whose conversation indicated, bizarrely enough, that they worked at the Bureau of Engraving and Printing on 14th Street, a few blocks away, sat in a corner, under a faded framed photo of the boxer Gene Tunney. The Bureau of Engraving and Printing was where they made the US dollar bills, in all their various denominations, and the conversation of the two blue-collar employees was laced with words like Jeffersons, Abe Lincolns, blue glue and electrolyte, which, while gibberish to most people, were the currency of many discussions and research notes of Davidov's over the last two years.

For all of the former Israeli's efforts, from the very first exercise in robbery by counterfeiting, with a leavening of corruption, had been towards one goal. The psychologists and shrinks of Mossad had been right.

Danny Davidov was aiming to shake the tree of the almighty dollar. It is strange how fine minds can become obsessive, but the fact is well documented. And the US dollar was the Israeli's – former Israeli's – goal in life. His total obsession. And he had proved in spades, with his meticulous attention to detail, that he had it in his power to do it.

That first operation, involving the fictitious credit card purchase of 8.2 million dollars' worth of aviation fuel, and the subsequent unprotesting payment, by a major world airline, had been the shot in the arm he and his recruited partner, Nikolai Kolosov, had needed. It had gone like clockwork and Danny had been a much-relieved man. He knew that he could not have retained the commitment and loyalty of his ex-KGB associate if the entire heist had not proceeded without a hitch.

Davidov glanced at his wristwatch and raised a finger when he caught the bartender's eye.

'Same again, Buddy?'

Danny nodded. This was one of those small downtown bars where the barman goes, 'Hi, I'm Jerry,' and you feel obliged to say who you are, so Danny Davidov had said he was called Morry, a very Jewish name in the USA, being short for Morris.

The bartender, Jerry, had turned out to be on the aurally inconvenienced side, and he had said, 'Hi, Buddy, how's it going' and like that, and it had been Buddy ever since.

And 'ever since' had been going on for almost four weeks. For those crazy Vietnamese forgers had spent all that time visiting every museum and preserved house, from the birthplace of the man whose handwriting they were charged with reproducing just exactly like the original, to the Smithsonian Institute, where many of the great man's letters and diaries were kept for prosperity, under glass cases, securely protected.

And each evening, Huynh Tan Nghi and his grandson, Lee Xuan, painstakingly wrote, from memory, in exactly the hand, the precise penmanship, of the long-dead, greatest-ever American, Abraham Lincoln.

And the next day they would return to gaze for hours at

the letters and diaries, using the 800 years of counterfeiting which were in their blood, which made them among the finest forgers in the world, to compare the work they had done with the genuine article, and to remember each indentation, whorl, comma, and pressure when touching and when leaving the paper.

That was all they had been doing for almost four weeks.

Davidov and Nikolai Kolosov had taken turns accompanying their rented forgers. And when they had retired to the seedy hotel they had booked into, in downtown Washington, Danny Davidov and the Russian had eaten frugally, which was beginning to drive him, a zillionaire, crazy with the irony of it, and had quietly prepared their other, possibly more vital, plans for their ultimate coup, the Really Big One.

For the Abe Lincoln letter was in fact merely a test – the elder Nghi had been right, intuitively – to ensure that their real work of forgery, more mundane perhaps but a hundred times more authentic, would beat the experts, or at least so confound them that they would make the one fatal slip Danny needed, just the one, to let him penetrate the United States financial structure's most secret defences.

Danny glanced at his watch as the bartender, Jerry, placed a glass of draught Michelob in front of him.

'There y'go, Buddy.'

'Thanks, Jeffrey,' replied Danny, and the door opened and in came Kolosov. Who had told the barman his name was Harry Kolvik.

'Hi, Barry . . .' Jerry sang out cheerily.

Kolosov and Danny Davidov exchanged glances. All in all, it was a perfect place to hang out.

'Club soda?' asked Jerry. Kolosov seldom drank liquor before about eight at night.

'Vodka,' said Kolosov. And he shook his head as he sat on a stool at the bar. 'These goddam guys . . . all they ever do is stand and stare. Stand and stare. All goddam day. Wherever we go. Sometimes they sit. They never speak, they never go to the john . . .'

'They're the best.' Davidov gazed morosely into his beer.

'They're driving me crazy,' replied Kolosov and drained his vodka the moment Jerry the bartender put it in front of him.

One of the government employees from the Bureau of Engraving and Printing glanced across and smiled. Danny and Kolosov had become regular visitors to the bar. 'Tough day?' he said. His name was James Fenwick.

'Yeah. Bitch,' replied Danny. 'Buy you guys a beer?'

'Why not? Mine's a draught Mich. My buddy here's Corona, Spanish stuff, right?'

'Coming right up,' called the obliging Jerry.

So Danny and Nikolai Kolosov crossed the bar and sat in a quiet corner with the two other men, under the photograph of Gene Tunney, who had been a boxing champ.

Jerry the obliging bartender would have been surprised, disbelieving even, if he had learned that seven months earlier, both Bureau of Engraving and Printing workers had been recruited by a former FBI Special Agent, who had retired ahead of time to become Washington Circuit Manager of something called Operation Medusa – which he honestly believed was a top secret US Government activity.

In fact, Operation Medusa was the brainchild of Danny Davidov, and he and Kolosov had invested many millions of dollars setting it up and tweaking it until it ran like a beautiful, but secret, Swiss watch.

'Medusa' was composed of a total of forty-six unsuspecting recruits, each believing he or she was doing something deeply secret for their country, or their political cause, like that. But each group, each 'cell' of never more than four agents (for that is what they had, unwittingly, become), was unaware of the existence of any of the others.

And Medusa was international in its scope. Some of the agents were bank employees, others minor functionaries in government departments, newspaper financial journalists,

Stock Exchange personnel and dissatisfied security and intelligence officials.

When Kolosov had joined Davidov, he had brought with him thousands of files on 3.5-inch computer discs plus his comprehensive, and incomparable, lists of contacts; previous agents of the KGB's First Chief Directorate, Service A, of S Directorate which was the KGB department responsible for the illegal insertion of operators abroad (sometimes whole families), clandestine acts of disinformation including the forging of correspondence between target Heads of State or senior political or administration figures.

It was from the FCD's register that Kolosov had produced the names of various counterfeiters, telephone-tappers, computer scientists and impersonators who had been so valuable for operations like the St Petersburg raid on Credex International and the Banco di Calabria in Sicily.

Davidov had made substantial and imaginative contributions of his own, and together the two scoundrels had built up six overlapping clandestine circuits of six cells each, all unaware of each other.

So, far from being confronted by a couple of confident and lucky, thus far, ex-spooks carving their way to a stupendous fortune, assisted perhaps by a few pavement artists and con-men, what the US Treasury was soon to find itself up against was a small but professionally organized and directed intelligence network, with a budget that many national agencies would have coveted.

The six Circuit Managers were redundant former Cold War warriors, discarded or merely demoted officers of a number of clandestine services. It is a matter of some simplicity to convince someone who needs to feel loved and wanted once again that his or her Secret Service or Internal Security Service has chosen them, earmarked them, for a confidential role in serving their national or political cause.

In a way, Danny Davidov sometimes thought, rather wistfully, wouldn't it be nice if his own outfit, the Tel Aviv Institute, Mossad, were to tap him on the shoulder and make him feel loved and wanted, with something to contribute to his nation's security? Tell him all was forgiven and maybe they had judged him too harshly. He would have dropped everything and run back to Israel on the next plane.

So he understood, being both humane and professional, that the stuff of codewords, brush contacts, recognition disciplines, surveillance avoidance and personal security measures was meat and drink to those poor abandoned former spies, and so well chosen had they been by Davidov that not one of them had breathed a whisper of their clandestine activity to lovers, families or confessors.

Also, they were being handsomely paid.

Then, between the Circuit Managers and the two Medusa bosses, Davidov and Kolosov, were interposed two tiers of cut-outs: Network Controllers, two in number, and two Operations Directors. The job of each Network Controller was to ensure the security and efficiency of three circuits – split into two global regions – to pass on orders, to report on the Circuit Managers' reliability and to guard against penetration by inquisitive agencies.

The Operations Directors scrutinized each circuit and tested its security and reliability.

Finally, there was a Chief Operations Director, whose job was to oversee and report on the other Directors and Controllers.

Only this man had access to Danny Davidov and only he was aware of the immense scope of the worldwide criminal enterprise. It was perhaps not a position with a great future, had he paused to think about it.

Anyway, here they were in a bar in downtown Washington, Danny and the Russian. And among the several beers they drank, and the general conversation about the World Series, rumours about a film star and a gerbil that got stuck up his back passage, and bad-mouthing the President, which had become a national pastime, Danny and Kolosov contrived to pass to the two men, their agents in place, within the US Treasury apparat, instructions for an enterprise in the near future which would allow the two criminals entry to the secure area within the Treasury archives, where records of Treasury transactions during the Civil War were held.

By the time the two men strolled back to their cheap rooms, Kolosov was in high good humour.

'Hey, Nikki babe, don't tell me your Russian soul's found a little happy, down there in the tundra . . .' Danny spoke like this after a few beers.

Kolosov grinned like a Siberian tiger. '*Malinko,*' he said, meaning little guy, 'you know, I think we might just do this thing.' He breathed in expansively, waved his arms around. 'Hey, look out, Washington. Here we come . . .!'

And they turned away from the street that would have taken them directly to their run-down hotel and took a taxi to a bar in Georgetown called Nathan's. Where, in one of those little moments in life which Jung calls synchronicity and the rest of us call coincidence, a good-looking woman was having a drink with two New York detectives who had been in town for a trial and who had been buddies of her late husband, Eddie.

Nancy Lucco, Danny Davidov and Nikolai Kolosov remained unaware of each other's presence, or the effect they were to have on each other's lives.

Elena Constantinovna's car was a dusty Moskvitch four-door, that looked about five years old. It had dents on the fenders and the red and orange plastic on the left back-light assembly was broken.

The seats had been re-covered in Scottish plaid material. And there was a fluffy Moscow Olympics teddy bear stuck on the facia top, which had slipped to a slightly irregular angle.

David Jardine had changed into informal casual clothes. A pair of old faded jeans, with shoes, shirt and imported light brown Italian wool jacket he had bought in the special store inside the complex where the SVR had allocated him a comfortable villa, with its own mini-bar and daily maid service. It made him look quite Russian, or at any rate not British, but the quality of the clothes subtly indicated that here was a man with the right Moscow connections. With a degree of *Vliyaniye*, of influence.

He wore no necktie and with the jeans had a faded leather belt of the pattern issued to *Spetznaz*, special forces, during the Soviet Union's Afghan campaign.

They had driven from the SVR complex into Moscow, approaching the city on the Prospekt Vernadskogo. Elena Constantinovna had been quiet, and slightly thoughtful.

Jardine was content to let matters take their course. After serious reflection, he had no doubt that Dzerzhinsky was a Mossad agent – Moscow Station files had noted that his mother was born Jewish but had renounced her faith when she married Aleksandr Grigorevich, nephew of Iron Felix. That had been in 1957, which was just about the time the Israeli Service had begun to get into its stride, with a quite superb team working closely with Prime Minister David Ben-Gurion to sow the seeds of a network of deep-cover sleepers in the USSR and through Europe and America.

He did not believe that there was any other explanation for the Zippo lighter, identical to the last dent and scuff-mark. That was why Alisha had slipped it into his pocket. It was a recognition symbol, which needed no words or absurd signals of behaviour to verify. Only Jardine and Alisha Abdul-Fetteh knew about that lighter.

And if someone produced a facsimile, a perfect replica, then he was identifying himself as a creature of Mossad. And, if Jardine's theory was correct, as a secret accomplice in an unauthorized operational group which, unknown to its masters in Tel Aviv, had illegally accepted the tycoon Robert Maxwell's millions for its own hidden agenda.

Jardine felt distinctly uncomfortable at the number of delicate, sensitive details this renegade Israeli outfit was revealing to an officer of a rival, and not always trusted, outfit. And a goy to boot. It made him feel like a man without a future, after he had done their dirty work for them.

And because he was a professional, the ruthless single-mindedness of their planning was beginning to impress him.

As they headed towards the Luznikovsky Bridge, in south-west Moscow, passing on their right the Metro station, Leninsky Gory, a militia man stopped the traffic to let two Zil limousines race across an intersection. Jardine thought he recognized one of the faces, a minor official in the former KGB. He said, without looking at her, 'Elena Constantinovna, there is one thing I utterly insist on . . .'

The girl glanced at him with an expression of uncertainty. The enormity of colluding with a member of the British SIS seemed to be weighing her down.

'What is that . . .?'

Jardine paused, then said, 'No museums, no theatre workshops, no art galleries, no Lenin's tomb and above and beyond the foregoing, no bloody Gorky Park and no stultifying bloody Zoo.'

She drove on in silence. Then a big smile took over, transforming her solemn face.

'What is stultifying?'

'Boring. Forgive me, but I'm a rotten tourist. Do you know, I've never been in the Tower of London?'

Elena Constantinovna shrugged. 'So where do we go?' There was something about the way she said it, something about the way she moved her legs as she used the brake and accelerator pedals, leaving Komsomolski Prospekt and entering Zubovski Bul'var, part of the broad Garden Ring around inner Moscow. She wore a print dress that clung to her body above the hips, then flared out in pleats. Jardine glanced away, studying the passing streets.

A few soldiers strolled along the sidewalks, with that lost look of soldiers in uniform out on their own. He realized he had become aware of her scent, which was of some fresh soap. Leave it alone, David, he mused. You must be out of your tiny mind.

'Let's hit a café,' he said, in Russian. 'A small one, without tourists.'

So they drove into Moscow and went to a half-deserted café a couple of blocks from the Stanislavsky and Nemirovich-Danchenko Theatre, where the other patrons were young people with a certain energy and earnestness, which Jardine was glad to see. Moscow so far, this trip, had not been a barrel of laughs.

'This is okay?' asked Elena Constantinovna.

'This is perfect.' David Jardine gazed around. The café was low-ceilinged, with a bar counter and marble-topped tables on ornate metal legs. There were scrolled mirrors along one wall. A bird in an antique golden cage. 'It reminds me of a place in Venice.'

'Many interiors of old Moscow were designed by Bove,' she rehearsed, earnestly, 'who planned the restoration after the great fire of 1812. He also designed much of the interiors in Venice, for instance, Florian's, the famous chocolate house.'

'Really?' said Jardine. 'I didn't know that.'

'It's not true,' Elena Constantinovna grinned. 'But it's still in my 1974 guidebook. A little socialist bullshit.'

She held his gaze. 'Like all the rest . . .'

'Do you really believe that?'

'Hmm.' She lapsed into silence. It was still difficult to elicit a real political opinion from a Muscovite. For the wind might yet change direction.

A waitress, aged about nineteen, put a plate of baklava, a sweet and sticky Turkish dessert of thin flakes of brittle pastry, honey and pistachio, on to the table and smiled to Elena Constantinovna. Then, glancing casually at Jardine, she left.

'Courtesy of the house?' asked Jardine, surprised at such largesse in a city of shortages.

'I used to come here when I was a ballet student. That waitress was a kid then. Helped her sister to clean up at the weekends.' Elena Constantinovna ducked her head. 'She knows I have a sweet tooth. Baklava's my favourite.'

There were two forks on the plate. She turned the handle of one towards Jardine. He lifted it and hewed out a piece of the sticky pastry.

'So you really were a ballerina . . .?' He chewed a delicious mouthful.

Elena Constantinovna nodded. 'Until I was sixteen.'

'And then what?'

She looked as if a cloud had cast a shadow over her. Just for a moment. She shrugged. 'Duty called . . .'

She avoided his gaze.

Jardine thought he understood. Beautiful, if petite, ballerinas who failed to grow to the minimum height required by the Bolshoi had sometimes been recruited into the KGB as low-level contract agents and trained in the arts of seduction. Generally of foreign diplomats, or important businessmen, or journalists. Sometimes blackmail was the objective, sometimes it was merely a method of keeping tabs on the target.

Lastochki was the Russian name for these girls. Swallows.

But he had never heard of one of them ever becoming a cadre officer, one of the KGB elite. And although Jardine felt life had few surprises left, he could not reconcile this waiflike young woman's past with her present powerful rank.

'And here you are, a major.' He wondered what that meant. Head of all the Swallows? Or just a flight or two? It certainly explained her guarded sexuality.

'Major is usual in your service? For women of my age?'

Jardine smiled. 'What age is that?'

'Guess.'

'Oh, dear. Um, about twenty-nine,' said the gallant spymaster. His honest guess was about thirty-two.

'Close enough. I'll be twenty-nine on Sunday . . .'

She had come back into the sunlight. Her smile revealed just a hint of real laughter.

'Well,' said Jardine gravely, 'that's on the young side in my country, for a major. Although we don't use military ranks in, um, in my service.' Perhaps she was with a military unit of Internal Security, like Border Guards, attached to SVR for some sort of liaison function.

A couple of times, at the Centre, he had inquired casually what Lieutenant-Colonel Dzerzhinsky did there. But each time, the question had been most politely ignored.

Elena Constantinovna seemed satisfied with his answer. She munched a mouthful of baklava thoughtfully. Then she pointed her fork at him accusingly.

'You think I am *lastochka*. Don't you?'

'Good Lord, no.'

Her smile became a grin. Sometimes she looked younger than twenty-nine. 'I was, for about three years. Then I moved into the Ninth Directorate. Bodyguard to Mikhail Ragozhkin.'

That explained her rank. Ninth Directorate had been a military arm of the KGB. Ragozhkin was Head of the FCD until the abortive coup. Only recently, his trial for treason had been postponed indefinitely. But it still did not explain how this educated, *gamine*, self-admitted former seductress had achieved the impossible – a commission in State Security. Unless, Jardine contemplated ungallantly, she had fucked her way into it.

'I understand there were three attempts on his life.' Jardine had read the reports filed from Moscow Station.

'I was shot, here.' She touched her right ribs with her left hand, just beside her small breast. 'That was attempt number five. An Afghan war veteran whose mother had been imprisoned by the KGB for taking part in a protest meeting in Volgorod.'

'Protesting about what?'

'Pensions for veterans of the Afghan war.'

Jardine nodded. The FCD had nothing to do with internal security and Ragozhkin must simply have been a target of opportunity. Probably the first KGB boss the would-be killer happened upon.

'What happened?'

'Ragozhkin liked jazz and he also liked to move around

the city without being recognized.' She shrugged. 'One night he decided to go to Sinyaya Ptitsa.'

'What's that?'

'It's a jazz club on Ulitsa Medvedeva. Anyway, we sent three agents in ahead. Two men and a girl. At the inquiry, it turned out that one of them was friendly with one of the waitresses. Director Ragozhkin and four companions, plus three more agents, including me, turned up about 9.10 in the evening. A few drinks. I stuck to ginseng tea.'

'Yuck,' said Jardine, in English.

'It was a phase I was going through. Ragozhkin went to the men's room. Alex, one of my team, accompanied him. Next thing I see is medium-height, wiry, no, thin man. Long hair, bald on top, moving like he means it, towards the men's room. He's carrying a coat kind of wrapped round his left hand.'

She looked around. Jardine knew that look. He fished in his pocket and brought out a pack of Winstons.

'Cigarette?'

Elena Constantinovna smiled. 'I don't smoke. You go ahead.'

Jardine tugged a cigarette from the pack. 'So what happened?'

'I tried to speak to Alex, but our personal radios are crap.'

'So are ours. Specially in a jazz club . . .' He flicked on his brass Zippo and held the flame to the Winston cigarette. No reaction of any kind.

'Specially. By the time I get to the men's room door, the suspect has gone inside, so I follow. There he is facing Ragozhkin, who is standing taking a leak, back to us both.

'Alex is combing his hair, sees me just enter, understands, reaches for his pistol. Suspect fires, through the coat wrapped round his left arm, hits Alex. I already have my pistol ready and fire three shots, the first one through my purse. That's where I kept the gun.'

'You missed.' This was a statement. Jardine knew that firing a handgun in such heightened circumstances was very different from training. The first few shots tended to go high and to your left, if you were right-handed.

'I hit him once. Right shoulder. It made him spin round. He fired twice and I fired four rapid, to tell you the truth by that time it was me I was protecting not damn Mikhail Sergeyevich Ragozhkin.'

Jardine could just picture it. Elena Constantinovna was not as young as Hassan, who, as far as Jardine in his ignorance knew, was still lurking around the Beirut offices of Salim Jaddeh, earning the few hundred dollars Jardine had paid him. But she had the same quality of streetwise innocence that made her seem both a born survivor and, at the same time, vulnerable.

'And this time you hit him.'

She looked fierce as she remembered the moment. 'You bet.'

'And he hit you.'

She touched her rib again, bending her neck to gaze at it. There was a zip, hidden by a pleat, running down the print dress, close to the spot. 'Just here,' she said. 'The bullet went through two ribs and damaged the lung.' She shrugged in the way of the immortal young. 'I'm fine – that was four years ago.'

The waitress appeared with two glass mugs, a pot of tea, a saucer with slices of lemon and a tub of raspberry jam. David Jardine thought of Sergei and his Lord Grey.

They drank their tea in silence. Jardine smoked his cigarette.

'What do you think of Moscow?' she asked.

'I think it's strange now. When I used to come here before, to Moscow, somehow it seemed less . . . foreign than now.'

'That's because nobody knows if it's real,' she said. 'People are too astonished, with their freedom. It sits on them like the Ancient Mariner.'

'Albatross.'

'I beg your pardon?'

Jardine glanced at a couple of militia men who had just

come in. They sauntered to the counter, near the backstore, with the look of the type of cop you find worldwide, who is on the take. 'The Ancient Mariner was an old sea captain and the albatross was the cause of all his troubles. It was strung round his neck and he couldn't get rid of it.' He glanced, pointedly, at the two cops.

Elena Constantinovna nodded, she knew what he meant.

'It was written by a Russian,' she said with grave authority.

'Nonsense, it was written by Samuel Taylor Coleridge. Who was an opium addict.'

'Was written by Sergei Vorontsov. Plagiarized by Coleridge. Every Russian is taught this in school.'

Jardine stared at her. 'You're kidding . . .'

Elena Constantinovna smiled, a prim little smile. Pleased with herself. 'Of course,' she replied.

After lemon tea in the café near the Stanislavsky Theatre, they walked back towards her small car. Jardine stopped to tie his shoelace. Then he remembered he had forgotten to take his copy of the *Izvestia* newspaper from the café. Then he took the wrong turning on the way back, and by the time he finally rejoined Elena Constantinovna, David Jardine was reasonably sure they had no interested observers, no tail. So far.

Elena Constantinovna started the engine as he got in and pulled the door shut. She turned to him. 'Where now? I know, I know, no Zoo.'

'It's your town, Major.'

'Listen, you choose.' Elena released the handbrake and joined the traffic from a side-street of old buildings and an ornate little church with pink and burnished copper glinting in the sunlight. 'That way you can be sure I'm not arranging events.'

She meant, not leading him into a surveillance trap. Although, thus far, the entire KGB could have been watching them and they had done nothing remotely suspicious.

'Fine, take a left and head for Pushkinskaya Ploshchad.'

Elena Constantinovna looked at him, shrugged and said

no problem, and headed the beat-up little car towards Pushkin Square.

The George Washington Memorial Hospital is some fourteen miles from Elmore Williams' home in Alexandria. Set in park-like grounds, it has cared for some illustrious patients, but none more important to the Secret Service agent than his wife and daughter, who were in a private room on the second floor, protected at all times by two armed agents from the USSS Protection Division.

Melanie had sustained a broken left tibia, with lacerations from the bullet and slivers of bone. She had lost about three pints of blood before her father applied the tourniquet and the paramedics had arrived and put her on to intravenous plasma. The blood loss and the shock would probably have killed her if immediate first aid had not been so expertly given.

Martha Williams had taken four 9-mm copper-jacket slugs in the upper torso, from right shoulder to just above the left breast. Two had passed clean through, tearing muscle and making puncture-breaks of the right shoulder-blade. One had grazed her trachea, causing bruising of the organ and severe discomfort when swallowing. The fourth bullet had broken left lateral ribs two and three and lodged against her left shoulder-socket. There was internal muscle and ligament damage, causing bleeding and haemotoma thrombosis. The patient was also suffering trauma from impact and systematic shock.

And yet, when the young Jewish surgeon who had removed the two bullets from her body and cleaned and sutured and dressed her wounds expressed relief that they had, by the grace of God, missed all her vital organs, Elmore Williams had wept with relief and thanked God that his wife had only been whacked with four copper-jacket slugs that had been moving too fast to spin or wobble when they struck. For that would have proved fatal.

Now here she was, four days later, sitting up in bed,

sipping orange juice through a plastic straw and watching *Divorce Court* on television.

'Trying to tell me something?' asked Elmore Williams as he looked in the door, with a bunch of flowers to add to the many bunches all around the room, and a Japanese portable video game gismo for Melanie.

'Hi, babe. How'd it go?'

'Just fine. The cops have taken all the statements they need for now. My Sac and the FBI have started a joint investigation and I've been downtown all day these last three days, when I weren't sitting here just watching you get well again. Hi, smartypants.' He kissed Melanie and put the box with the video game on her bed.

Melanie's leg was in plaster and in traction. But she had gotten that kid's bloom back on her complexion and her eyes lit up at the gift.

'Gee, Dad, you ain't so bad after all.'

'Don't say ain't, honey,' whispered Martha, 'say are not.'

'Sure, sure, Mom. You is not so bad, Dad . . .' And daughter and father grinned.

Williams had no intention of telling either of them about what had emerged from the inquiry into the attack. And he was real glad that they had not seen, because of their injured condition and the position of the shot-up Pontiac Firebird, their beloved and gentle father and husband shoot four men through the head, without pity or remorse. Or that Counsellor Nancy Lucco, who was turning out to be quite a woman, had had two yelling matches with the DA's office over an inclination on the District Attorney's part to charge Williams with unjustifiable homicide.

And later that afternoon, Special Agent Elmore Williams drove his rented dark green Mustang back to DC and parked in the Secret Service office's underground car park.

The Director himself had come into Special Agent in Charge Sid Longstreet's office for the internal conference on the Alexandria shootings. Also present in the room, furnished with a grey-green metal desk, filing cabinets, wall maps, a few spartan chairs and framed photographs of Longstreet with Presidents Bush and Reagan, Margaret Thatcher and crime writer Ed McBain, were De-Sac Tom Roberts, the agent in charge of the Secret Service end of the investigation, Washington Police Department Homicide Inspector Dennis MacDowell, Legal Counsellor Nancy Lucco, and Sid Longstreet.

They were all sitting in various chairs around the room and they turned as the door opened and Elmore looked in.

'Elmore, come on in.' Longstreet was leaning back in his chair, hands clasped behind his head.

Sensitive to atmosphere, Williams detected no hostility. The very opposite, it seemed.

'How are the patients?' asked the Director, Jim Farley.

'Improving. Martha's able to take fluids by mouth. Melanie's getting lippy again.'

The others laughed. Williams found himself a seat.

'Dennis, tell Elmore,' said Longstreet.

Williams glanced at McDowell. 'Tell me what?'

Dennis McDowell indicated a blackboard that had been set up with pathologist's mugshot photographs of the four dead attackers. The faces were macabre. The wounds made by Elmore Williams' coup-de-grâce bullets had been repaired, to provide an indication as to what the men would have looked like before the exchange of gunfire.

'One Hispanic, one black, one Caucasian, one European type. Italian dental work. We have an ID on three. This guy . . .' McDowell, lean and about five feet nine, got to his feet and tapped one of the faces. Even in death it looked mean and evil. Menacing, with high Tartar cheekbones, narrow eyes and a drooping black moustache. The nose had been rebuilt with wax, but was probably quite accurate. 'Andreas Torres Osorio. Alias Miguel Sanchez. Age thirty-three. Illegal immigrant, country of origin, Colombia. Pro mechanic for the Ramirez Country Club.' The Ramirez Country Club was the name of one of the most ruthless and well-organized crack-cocaine gangs in Washington, DC.

'This guy . . . Andrew Maxwell. Age forty-two. Hell's Angel enforcer for the Wichita Wiseguys. Eight years in Marion for assault with a deadly weapon, paroled and ran, 1989. DEA have a trace of him working as a bounty hunter in Dade County, Florida. Fingered by five different informants as contract killer, mostly for Miami Cubans but also for the Sicilian Mafia.'

'What do you mean, Sicilian?' asked Williams.

Everybody knew the Mafia was an Italian–American confederation of organized crime syndicates with roots in the old country, principally the island of Sicily.

'I mean the Palermo-based Cosa Nostra, Elmore, run by Giovanni Favorito Noto.'

Elmore nodded. *Time* magazine had run a piece on the guy, about two years before. 'The Prince of Death' had been the somewhat dramatic title of the piece.

'Nice people,' he said.

'And this one . . .' McDowell touched thc photo of a black guy with shaven head and long rat's-tails falling from a top-knot. Two tribal scars on each cheek. One of his eye sockets was stopped up with cotton. 'Abdulla Patrice. New York crack-dealer, only surviving member of the Patrice family – the other two died at the hands of some Colombian mob that went through NYC like Serbs at a Sunday School picnic.'

'When was this?' asked Nancy Lucco.

'Year before last, April, May. Abdulla, being a wise man, disappeared back to Jamaica for a while and this is the first he's been seen back in the USA. The John Doe has Italian dental work.'

Longstreet stretched his legs under his desk and linked his fingers, making a cracking sound. 'Intel says here Favorito Noto took on a whole bunch of enforcers and quote unquote skilled labour, from Pablo Escobar in Colombia, when that jerk's operation started to go down the tubes.'

'Who drove the bikes and who fired?' asked Nancy.

'Abdulla and Mr No-name did the shooting,' replied Elmore Williams, and nobody contradicted him, for even though their faces had been hidden by helmets, you don't forget who was trying to kill you and your family.

'Study that face.' Director Farley pointed at the mugshot of the unidentified hitman. If anything, the dead face was even more menacing than the others.

'I wired a mugshot to the Embassy in Rome, with copies to the Carabinieri and the Anti-Mafia Commission in Palermo,' said Tom Roberts.

Elmore Williams' boss, Sid Longstreet, gazed at him. 'So who have you pissed off that's with the Old Country Mafia?'

'You haven't been moonlighting for the DEA, Elmore?' asked the Director, making a joke.

'This guy, I tell you, don't put it past him,' said Longstreet, without smiling.

Williams scratched his cheek, up near his right eye. 'Man, I have pissed off just about everybody . . .'

He said it so matter-of-factly that the others smiled.

'Think hard,' said the Director. 'Some investigation concerning dope? Maybe peripherally?'

Directors use words like that.

'Sir, I'm on the beach. I ain't, am not, investigating Jack shit. Respectfully.'

That little fishing expedition met with blank expressions.

These guys were not born yesterday. But it must've had some effect, for Jim Farley, the Director, said to Homicide Inspector Dennis McDowell, 'Thanks, Dennis. Thanks for coming over. And thanks for sweetening the DA.'

'No problem,' said McDowell, and being able to take a hint as well as the next man, he picked up his jacket and briefcase and left, saying take it easy and see you later and like that.

In the ensuing moment's silence, everyone studied the mugshots pinned to the blackboard.

'Elmore,' said Nancy.

'Yes, ma'am.' Williams met her gaze and smiled. He liked Nancy Lucco.

'Think Sicily. You know we have a dozen cases involving Mafia counterfeiters.'

'Yeah, I know, but I was stuck on the New York case, and . . .'

'There was no New York case, Elmore.' Longstreet speaking. 'Which is why you are kicking your heels on full pay. Remember?'

Williams flashed his snow-white shark's teeth. 'How could I forget?'

'Hold the phone,' said Nancy, 'this New York case. You went into NY under cover because you felt that NY Field Office might be . . . refresh my memory.'

She meant tell the others. Like, this room with all these people might be a good time to air this.

'Sure. This jerk-off Cardona and Sammy the Nose got involved in conversations with a New Orleans informant of mine . . .'

'Who?' asked Longstreet.

'It's a solid source and the party has my word on discretion.'

'Don't fuck us about, Elmore. Who?'

'I can't say.' Williams scratched his neck. Maybe he had been bitten by something.

'This is just the kinda thing gets you in the kinda shit you keep getting into, Elmore.' Tom Roberts was scratching too. Maybe there were fleas in the boss's office.

'Yeah, well it did, know what I mean?' bit back Williams.

The Director touched his nose, hiding the grin he could not suppress.

'And this information,' went on Roberts, 'which came from a proven good source, led you to believe . . . what? Exactly?'

'That Cardona and the Nose were going to sell some funny money and they had a line into NY Field Office they claimed gave them protection from any sting. Any interference. It was bullshit, as we know now.'

'So you came on to Cardona and Sammy, where? Whose jurisdiction?' asked Roberts.

'Atlantic City,' mumbled Elmore Williams. The others sighed. Atlantic City was New York's territory.

'And you failed to register your one-man operation with your own superiors in Office of Inspections.' Longstreet shook his head, as if the lynch noose was already dangling and there was nothing he could do about it.

'I phoned this office. I requested back-up and approval. I was told back-up would be on the site. And if approval was not forthcoming, I would get a signal and abort the investigation.'

'You spoke to a secretary, for Christ's sake.'

'Time was passing. We're talking hours here. I swear I did not know I was walking into a sting.' Williams shrugged. 'Neither did the two bums I was with . . .'

'Yeah, well, if that's the best you can do I don't hold out much hope,' replied Longstreet.

Nancy stared at her fingernails. This was not the direction she had intended the conversation to take. She gazed at Jim Farley, the man who had had the foresight to make her go through agent's training. He met her eye for a moment, then seemed to come to a decision. He cleared his throat and stuck his hands deep in his pockets, then gazed at each of them in turn.

'Suppose,' he said quietly, 'Agent Williams had informed me.'

The silence was tangible. Elmore Williams was stunned. But he tried to look as if, oh yes, this was so sensitive I could only tell the Director himself. Sure. He willed himself to believe it.

'Would that', asked Farley, quietly, 'make a difference?'

Longstreet looked embarrassed. 'What are we saying here? That I'm not to be trusted?'

'I'm saying if an agent knows he's going out on a limb, risking causing grave offence, which he did, to a dead-straight SAIC and NY Field Office, and he did not want to risk souring relations with Office of Inspections here in DC, by making it formal. Say till he had made his own judgement. Maybe, *if* that's what Elmore Williams had done, and *if* I had let him risk his job to do his job. Would that change matters . . .?'

This man is a star, thought Williams, as he watched Longstreet relax and nod thoughtfully. If Sid Longstreet and Nancy Lucco bought this, it let everybody off the hook. Jeez, no wonder Farley had made Director. *Capo di tutti capi*.

After a long silence, during which Longstreet gazed thoughtfully at Williams, with occasional glances at Nancy Lucco, he nodded. 'Sure. That would change the whole thing. From Office of Inspections point of view, and this is formal; that explanation answers the case against Special Agent Williams and clears him entirely. Sure thing . . .' He pushed some folders around on his desk and said, 'I'll speak with Nancy and we can issue a result, um,' he glanced inquiringly at Nancy, 'before the end of the day?'

Nancy Lucco nodded gravely. 'Sure,' she replied.

'Okay . . .' Longstreet opened his desk drawer and produced Elmore Williams' leather wallet with his badge and ID. 'There you go.' He studied the mugshots of the four dead men. 'Something tells me you still have your personal weapon.'

He glanced around, and finally the others began to relax.

'I guess we need to assign somebody to investigate this Sicilian angle,' said Tom Roberts. He gazed pointedly at Elmore. 'My first choice would be Elmore Williams, but you're the guy they want to kill so that would put you at unnecessary risk.'

'What more risk could I be in? Let's get down to it.'

'Sid . . .?' asked the Director.

Longstreet frowned. He gazed at Elmore. 'Listen, man, think this thing through. We can look after your family but out there you'll be at risk.'

'Hey, I'll be at risk whatever. If you think I'm the guy for the job, that gives me no problems.'

Longstreet rubbed his neck. 'Well, okay. Sure thing. Elmore, get your ass into gear and get back to work.'

Hallelujah. And moments later, after a few formalities, Elmore Williams, Nancy Lucco and the Director, Jim Farley, quietly left the room, not daring to exchange the merest glance.

Moscow is like a spider's web of streets radiating outwards through four rings. Two of these rings contain the hub of the city, which is north of the great loop the River Moskva makes, joining the south side by five bridges.

The first ring is in reality a semi-circle, formed by a number of streets and avenues around the north part of the Kremlin Palace. The second is another semi circle, the Boulevard Ring, about 1500 metres from the Kremlin and mostly divided highway, with Moscow's thinnest public park – twenty metres by eight kilometres – sandwiched in the middle.

Jardine's directions eventually took them to Tverskaya, an old district less spoilt by the years of socialist heroic/drab modernism than most. The Boulevard Ring passes through there, and they parked the car on a dirt space, where an enterprising gypsy stallholder dispensed ice-cream, a common sight, but his other delicacy on offer was advertised as SHRMAK, which was Russian for 'Big Mac'.

Trees created a leafy avenue, speckled with sunlight and somehow remote from the traffic on either side. Whole families of 'bench people' seemed to live there, but with more organization and resourcefulness than New York's bag ladies or London street dossers. A tall man in a long black coat played a viola, and excited children ran around, chasing an enormous mongrel hound.

There was a smell of cherrywood smoke in the air, along with some kind of meat. It could be lamb, but Jardine remembered, perhaps cynically, that dog, properly cooked, could smell very similar.

They locked the car and strolled away, relaxed and seemingly at ease in each other's company.

'How old do you think my car is?' asked Elena. And as she did so, her eyes took in every detail of the environment around them.

Jardine watched her casually, feeling he would sense if she observed a colleague. A tail, or surveillance team, sent on ahead by Dzerzhinsky or whoever this girl really worked for. After all, that business about you choose where we go, where we stop, could have been a version of the five-card trick – and whatever destination he had chosen, they would have ended up under surveillance.

For he had done the same thing himself.

'I reckon about, what? Five years?'

'Excellent,' she replied. 'It is four months only. Not second-hand. New. A new car. Three thousand miles on the clock. Three thousand two hundred and thirty-one. You did not look.'

'I didn't look, Elena Constantinovna.' He glanced back at the car, using the moment to check for too disinterested strangers. Nothing.

'New cars, you see. People get jealous. They hit it with iron bars. Break windshield. Slash tyres. Or steal it. Black market pays good money for new car.'

'So you trashed it yourself.'

'Exactly.' And she looked really pleased with herself. Satisfied at having beaten the criminals at their own game. Then she stopped and gazed at the children chasing around with the mongrel hound, through the trees.

'Did Anatoly Andreyevich mention Jerusalem this morning . . .?'

Here we go.

'He mentioned it.'

'And he offered you a light? With a lighter like yours?'

'It was a Zippo. Like mine.'

She hunched her shoulders, hands in the pockets of the shapeless green cardigan she had thrown over her cotton dress.

'And he said you should spend today with me.'

Jardine rubbed his chin, he had shaved about seven and it was beginning to feel rough. 'That's it. Just like that.'

The noise of the children's laughter could be heard, and the rumble of traffic on either side of the Boulevard Ring. Only a very old woman, wrapped in layers of black, with a black headscarf, sitting on a bench, legs along the seat, was observing them. She was out of earshot and Elena Constantinovna had her back to her.

'David, I am to find out what really brings you to Moscow.'

'For whom?'

'For the Israelis . . .' She kicked at a stone with her shoe, and Jardine could remember doing just that on a towpath beside the Thames.

'Anatoly Andreyevich has been one of them, since he was nineteen.'

One of *them* . . .

'I see.'

'His mother was Jewish, did you know that?'

'Yes.' Jardine often found the truth was simpler. 'Lying should not be second nature to a good operator. It can get you killed.' Alice Hanson, the Farm, 1969.

'Anyway,' went on Elena Constantinovna, 'somebody like Dzerzhinsky always needs someone to betray.'

Yes. Jardine could see that.

'So he chose Russia,' she said.

Ah-ha. And you did not, Elena Constantinovna?

'Tell me about it.'

'Well, KGB wanted to investigate him.' She avoided his gaze. 'You can understand how that was done.'

By you going to bed with him, Elena the *lastochka*, the little swallow.

'Of course.' Jardine wondered if he had sounded . . . prim.

'He was very good. We screwed like pipistrelle bats for four months. Not a hint, not a trace of anything out of place. I reported back. The heat was off him.'

'What caused them to be suspicious?' Such an operation was not routine. And pipistrelle bats? He had always thought of them as rather circumspect little creatures.

'They never told me. Anyway, after the investigation was terminated, and he was in the clear, we were still friends. Anatoly Andreyevich has attractive qualities.'

It was possibly his Mafia chums who wanted him investigated, Jardine considered. Or someone for once on the level, investigating Dzerzhinsky's Mafia contacts. And one of his attractive qualities has clearly been to rise inexorably, always one step ahead of the sheriff.

'Oh, come on, he must've known, he must've guessed about you.'

'Sure,' she said. 'I think he knew from the start.'

'And you remained friends . . .?'

'He understood where I stand. Which is one hundred per cent behind Boris Yeltsin.'

This was the thing about Russia. Politics could not stay out of anything, from the kitchen to the bedroom.

'When did he recruit you?' David Jardine meant, for Mossad.

'At first he recruited me for a group, a secret group, with assets inside and outside the Sluzhba' – the KGB – 'which was dedicated to fighting the military–industrial complex. And they mean to put the clock back fifty years.'

It was an old story. You recruited an agent by telling them what they wanted to hear. In this case, that you were on the very team she had probably been hoping would approach her, for she had aspirations to help in the fight for democracy and freedom in the new Russia.

'When did you realize it was Mossad?'

She seemed to be listening for something. The children and the big dog had moved away. Then suddenly, in a burst of laughter and barking, they exploded through the line of trees, yelling in coarse Russian, half-hoarse with excitement.

'When it was too late.'

Poor little *korova*, poor cow. Trapped by her patriotism into betraying her country.

'Elena Constantinovna, listen to me.' He glanced at the tears streaming down her cheeks, this twenty-nine-year-old KGB major, hero of a gunfight in a Moscow jazz club comfort station, promoted beyond her ability by a ruthless member of the Russian Mafia and agent of Tel Aviv. What a terrific business to be in. 'It's never too late.'

She wiped her nose on her cardigan and sniffed. The old babushka in black watched balefully. Men are all bastards, you could catch the vibes.

'I too believe so.' Elena Constantinovna nodded, suddenly many years older than twenty-nine, and suddenly very Russian. She composed herself and tossed her head, as if shrugging these problems away. 'Okay. I am to find out what you are doing here. If it is to do with somebody or something called Danny. And if so, how they can help.'

David Jardine felt, almost, what his children would call a buzz, for there were few things more deeply satisfying in a spy's life than that moment when something of real substance appears from the shadows. Particularly when you discover you are dealing with a black asset of another service.

For spies are, essentially, very nosy.

A Mossad cell, right inside the new SVR, and the Russian Mafia. If nothing else came of it, this made his trip worthwhile.

'Danny? I'm not quite with you. Tell Dzerzhinsky I have no idea what he's talking about.' Which message meant, negative, no thanks, *mazel tov*, get lost.

They continued their stroll. Elena Constantinovna seemed more than usually thoughtful. 'Anatoly Andreyevich is convinced you are here researching something called Danny. Otherwise he would not have initiated this contact.'

'I'm sorry to disappoint him.' Which was two lies in one.

'I'll tell him. Also, I will tell him I believe you. They seemed to think I am a judge of character.' She slipped an arm unselfconsciously under his elbow. Pressed close to him. Acting the girlfriend, for the benefit of passers-by. Her fresh aroma, some brand of carnation-scented soap, was appealing.

Jardine glanced down at her, the top of her head reached his shoulder. 'What is it?'

'Do you think we are under observation?'

'I think we're okay. For the moment.'

'How long will you need?'

David Jardine frowned. 'For what?'

'Nobody expects us back till about six. Later, if I drop you off at the British Embassy.'

'I have actually no idea what you're talking about.'

She stopped and gazed back down the avenue of trees. There was no one in the slightest bit interested in them, or even near.

'I would provide you with a alibi.' She shrugged. 'It's all I can . . . contribute.' And she gazed at him. 'If you mean it. If you mean it's never too late.'

Wow, was Jardine's immediate reaction. If ever he had heard a set-up, this was it.

'Why would I need an alibi?' he asked.

'I've been with you for four hours now. You have something on your mind. Listen, maybe it's no big deal. Maybe, *mozhet byt*, you want a woman. Maybe some old friend, or some . . . *dyelo*. Some business. So let me cover for you. You go. I stay here. Genuine offer. Believe me.'

'Why should I?' He glanced around, half-expecting to see microphones and zoom-lenses in every shadow.

'I was suckered into working with Mossad.' She looked angry. 'Because I am committed to helping democracy flourish here. You are British. Like the American, whatever else your faults are, you believe in freedom. If you can swear to me that you are not harming what you know I am fighting for, then you can trust me with your life.'

Jardine remembered the words of Sergei Rodionovsky. 'I just want to be a citizen in a free country . . .'

'And where will you be?' he asked.

'I will find a quiet shade. And sleep.' She stuck her hands into the pockets of her big cardigan. Gazing at him. 'I know how to make myself scarce.'

Everything about Mossad's game, up to this moment, everything about Moscow, screamed at him this was a trick.

But as the redoubtable Alice would say, there are times out there, in the firing-line, when you have to take action which, in the cold light of day, would definitely seem altogether unwise. Imprudent. And at such times, my dears, the decision will be yours. If you remain 100 per cent prudent, throughout your work out there, in the field . . . your recruiters and trainers will have made a complete bollocks of the job.

Dear Alice Hanson. Dead with edelweiss in your hand and a smile on your lips. He nodded. 'I'll meet you here at . . .' he checked his wristwatch, 'seven ten. This evening.'

Elena Constantinovna nodded. Then she said, 'David, this is not the Moscow you remember from the cold war.'

He knew, because he felt it, with every step he took in those once-familiar streets, that she meant it was far, far more dangerous now.

'Before, nobody could be killed without a direct order from KGB.' She smiled, nervous. 'And you know what bureaucracy is like.'

'Indeed I do.' Why did he feel so . . . protective, towards this urchin of the espionage playground?

'Now, apart from all the graft, all the violence,' – she said 'wiolence' – 'the struggle for capital, which is another kind of power, as corrupt as bureaucracy power, there is a . . . second nation forming. It calls itself,' she glanced around, casually. No one was near enough to hear, '*Staraya Zemlya*, Old Earth, and it hides, like crocodile below smooth surface of muddy water, within a new political alliance of the most formerly powerful men in Russia, the Party Tsars, the Industrial and Politburo controllers, the Red Army and the KGB power-brokers. This political alliance calls itself *Nasha Rodina*, Our Native

Land, and it boasts it has no need to take part in elections because democracy will soon be a thing of the past.'

'Do you mean Rutskoi, and the likelihood of an armed coup?' Jardine remembered his conversations at Moscow Centre.

She shook her head, dismissive, 'Rutskoi is a buffoon. Of course he will attempt a coup. Of course it will result in bloodshed. And of course, David, it will be put down, but only if the West has the courage to back Yeltsin and let our army commanders know that. But *Nasha rodina*, *Staraya Zemlya* . . . ? They will remain aloof. Their plans are long-term and deep.' She raised her shoulders, as if the burden was great, 'Slave labour camps, suppression of democracy, control of our nuclear arsenal . . . that's their agenda. And they mean business, believe me.'

In the mellow warmth of that Moscow afternoon, David Jardine felt his blood chill. Where had he heard this before? Every extremist political body in the twentieth century had feared and hated democracy, and every one had its secret, clandestine, party within a party – which mutated, once power was wrested, into a secret state within a state. Look at the Nazis and their Gestapo, the Soviets and their KGB, the South American dictators with their secret police, the self-evident truth that history had a genetic fault in that it remorselessly repeated itself was small consolation.

'Our Land', 'Old Earth'. The slogans of fascism, to which bitter and still powerful discarded communists were clinging with grim anticipation of better days to come. And blood, of course, would be squandered.

This was the true Europe, after two world wars and half a century of nuclear Mexican stand-off, nations like the USA and Britain, countries whose men and women had through centuries fought and suffered for freedom, were now reduced to pampered nations of media-opinionated, politically correct, well-meaning ostriches, heads firmly in the sands, able but not willing to understand all the grim intimations of still-avoidable horrors to come. And the Four Horsemen of the Apocalypse leered out from Bosnia and the former Soviet Satellite nations, mouthing the obscene message; 'We're coming your way, real soon.'

'You have not heard of this, David? Those names are not in your files? At Century?'

Jardine gazed at her. He smiled and shook his head, 'Maybe some analysts, maybe the Embassy here. But it certainly is news to me.'

Once again she glanced around.

'In your jacket pocket,' she said, 'is a book of matches.'

She must have dropped it in during the car ride. 'Behind the cardboard is a tiny square of microfilm. All details we have . . .'

'You and Dzerzhinsky?'

She shook her head, dismissing the suggestion. 'I belong to a small group, inside SVR, trying to help the future . . .'

The major suddenly blushed, at her pride, perhaps, in her confession of faith.

Jardine held her gaze, 'You finally got there.'

She nodded.

He touched his pocket and, sure enough, a book of matches was there.

'All details,' she went on, 'about *Staraya Zemlya*.' She leaned up to embrace him, her mouth brushing his cheek, her breath calm and sweet, and whispered, 'The leader is Oleg Kouzmine. Oleg Kouzmine faction is dangerous and for some reason they are interested in you. Be most careful.'

And then, doubtless for the benefit of any casual watcher, she kissed him, without reserve, on the mouth. It was so spontaneous, so lingering, he found himself responding and held her close to him, feeling her heart beating against his body.

When they parted, they gazed at each other. Perhaps in a different light.

'That was a nice surprise,' he said, softly.

'Go now, David Jardine. When you come back, maybe we can talk about the future.'

He presumed she meant some form of clandestine link to the Firm. No way, Jose, he thought to himself, but he was not going to have another chance to grab a few hours to duck out of sight.

'See you,' he said. And he turned and strolled away among the trees.

Elena Constantinovna watched him go. And although the sun was warm, she shivered.

The address which David Jardine had guarded so jealously was not, in fact, far from the Yasenevo complex where he had spent the last few days with the Russian Foreign Intelligence Service.

He had left Elena Constantinovna Ratanskaya at ten minutes before noon, and had walked for about twenty minutes through a series of back-streets to the Sadovaya theatre district, all the time checking for surveillance. At the junction of Sadovaya Boulevard and Tverskaya Street, he went into the Mayakovskaya Metro station, which Jardine noticed was less clean and well-kept than in the bad old days of totalitarian rule and the State's unsporting insistence that everybody had a job, even if it paid peanuts.

He paid his ten roubles and took a train to the Gorkovsko line, one stop, to Belorusskaya. There David Jardine changed to the Circle line, heading in an arc for Prospekt Mira station, where he changed to the Kaluzhko–Rizhkaya line for three stops, getting off at Ploshchad Nogina, and it was like that for a series of random changes of subway train and route, sometimes waiting until the doors were just about to close before getting off.

A couple of times he would get out as soon as the train pulled in, hang around, and squeeze back on board nimbly, for such a big chap, just to lose or spot anyone trying to follow.

Thus Jardine found himself, at 12.46 p.m., leaving Taganskaya Metro station, caught up suddenly and alarmingly in an angry exchange between a bunch of black-market thugs, overweight and wearing shapeless cheap suits over old paratroopers' blue-and-white-striped sweatshirts, and some punters they had shortchanged. He was squeezing past them, along with a half-dozen other passengers, when about seven militia men came bundling in from Skalova Street, grim-faced and backed up by two real paratroopers, carrying AKS assault rifles.

Amused at the idea of what the reaction would have been in, say, Piccadilly underground station, London, or Queens subway, NYC, if the army was to appear in support of the local cops, the Englishman emerged into the street where bright sunlight heralded the coming of summer. Suddenly unreasonably cheerful, he stepped on to a bus that was heading back the way he had come.

Two bus rides later, David Jardine paid another ten roubles for a Metro ticket, and thirty-four minutes later, his peregrinations finally deposited him outside the University Metro station on Prospekt Vernadskovo, on the south-western outskirts of the city.

He purchased a hot dog from a street trader, along with a bottle of beer, and while he consumed these, checked yet again for a tail. No sign. No bad vibes.

After about ten minutes a minibus public taxi stopped to let two fat old women out, followed by two young students, one with a beat-up guitar case.

Jardine climbed in and, when the minibus got close to the junction with Kostoyanka Street and Yudalkova, in the vicinity of Olympic Village, he grunted to the soldier sitting between himself and the door, '*Vyxhoditye?*', which means 'Getting off?' but which really means, if you're not, I would like to, and moments later, he was within 600 yards of his destination. The reason why he had come to Russia . . .

Somehow, although he had never been near the area of Prospekt Michurinsky and the pleasant apartments near the Samorodinka Lake and the river, around which the village and modern facilities for the 1980 Olympics had been built, David Jardine felt a sense of recognition when he got there. For this was the culmination of weeks of painstaking investigation, using top secret files on the hierarchy and gossip of the KGB's First Chief Directorate.

Jardine did not place complete reliance on those forms of computer science which had largely taken the place of the art of deduction and the application of experienced hunches, upon which so much skilled espionage had been based down the centuries. He knew that much of the intuition he was credited with, even by his enemies, was more likely to be learned instinct, stored in his subconscious from a lifetime in the business.

So when one name, from different reports, filed by a variety of SIS departments and at different times, over a period of several years, had begun to bob to the surface of his deliberations, David Jardine had allowed himself to pursue that line, rearranging and evaluating and digging ever deeper, until suddenly, like upon the lifting of a dawn mist, things became clear, and he had felt sure he had found his quarry: a rising star in KGB disinformation, with access to all its panoply of counterfeit and deception, and the essential skilled people, often criminals, who would be necessary to back up an operation like Danny Davidov's.

The subject was a senior officer in Service A (Disinformation) of the First Chief Directorate, who had quite suddenly disappeared from the sights of the Kremlin watchers in the SIS's SovBloc Directorate. His father had been a major-general in Vladimir Chuikov's 62nd Army, which in 1941 had broken out from the German army's siege of Stalingrad and fought all the way to Berlin and victory, *through Poland*.

Major-General Ivan Nikolaiovich Kolosov had died in 1986 and had been buried with full military honours, as befitted a hero of the Great Patriotic War. In 1990, his only son, Nikolai Ivanovich, at that time a Head of Section in Service A, had been promoted to full Colonel and made one of three Deputy Heads of the Service. A note on the file suggested that Nikolai Ivanovich was being considered to succeed the First Deputy Head, which would have put him on the first rung of the privileged classes, of the *nomenklatura*, with their plots of land in the country where they could build a summer home, and special schools for their children, teaching English, German or French from an early age, shopping facilities in exclusive stores and access to Communist Party- and KGB-owned dachas in pleasant rural areas miles outside Moscow.

In short, everything a sensible KGB or Party apparatchik worked his ass off for, and schemed and toed the line for.

One intercepted letter from the man to his wife, during a visit to Hong Kong – reason unknown – in 1989, had suggested that his marriage was in less than good shape, and he was offering the carrot of future promotion to keep it going, 'for the sake of Irenya', who a margin note – and Jardine agreed with it – suggested was the daughter, age unknown.

But within six weeks of his subsequent promotion, the late Major-General's high-flying son had been suspended from duty during a review of his Positive Vetting status.

Why?

The subject's codename had been Hedgehog – his two fellow Heads of Service were Groundhog and Warthog. On 4 September 1991, someone had scribbled in the margin of the latest intelligence summary, 'Where is Hedgehog?' and a wag had scribbled the reply, 'Maybe he tried to cross a busy highway.'

More likely, Jardine reckoned, Colonel Nikolai Ivanovich Kolosov had by this time failed his security review and been forced to resign or seek other work with the KGB 'old boy' network.

And without security clearance, there would be few people who would want to take him on.

David Jardine smiled at the recollection of Elena Constantinovna's Ancient Mariner allusion. For dear old Hedgehog would certainly have proved to be an albatross round the neck of anyone tempted to use Kolosov's particular expertise.

Not within the strict parameters of an establishment like the KGB.

A perfect profile, therefore, for the slightly daft, if not

stark, staring mad, Danny Davidov, to recruit as a partner in crime. The question remained, why on earth would a sane intelligence professional hitch his wagon to Davidov's crazy star?

A couple of discreet signals to Moscow Station, made not by David Jardine but by Ronnie Szabodo from his car stereo import and repair shop off Brixton High Street, had elicited the intelligence that a Madame Natalya Kolosova had secured a divorce from Colonel Nikolai Kolosov on 3 March 1992, and that by mutual agreement she had remained in residence at their three-roomed apartment on the fifth floor of the 'Yuri Gagarin' block near Prospekt Michurinsky, at Olympic Village.

Delicate, light surveillance had been tasked by Szabodo, using his personal (and illegal, in every sense) team of Moscow watchers, a team whose existence was unknown to anyone who fondly imagined they were controlling SIS operations from the comforting, secret, glass-enveloped fastness of Century House. Any form of electronic eavesdropping was out of the question, because so near the Intelligence Service at Yasenevo one had to anticipate regular counter-surveillance sweeps. Even so, by mail intercepts and physical telephone wiretaps, it had been established that Natalya Kolosov had a part-time job with a Moscow publishing house, and was generally at home between two and five, on weekdays. And that with some frequency she received male visitors, getting rid of them before her daughter, Irenya, returned from the exclusive Makarova special school where she was studying English and the history of ballet.

As Jardine strolled past a tree-lined park, with the Samorodinka Lake just visible, he wondered for a moment if that was where Olympic rowing and sailing events had taken place in 1980. Then, as he realized the lake was too small for that, he saw for the first time, and with a frisson of excitement, the three apartment blocks. He wondered if she would be in.

I mean, David, he said to himself, all this bloody way

and maybe she's gone to visit her mother in Minsk or Omsk or some bloody place.

He had reached a battered Gaz van, with the name of a van rental outfit, 'Yuri Joint Venture – Vans for Rent', on the side, and as he passed, a squat, broad-shouldered Hungarian looked up from where he was changing a wheel, and smiled his gap-toothed Magyar grin.

'Nice day for it,' he said in Russian. 'The customer is there and alone. She saw two together yesterday. Do you think they're making porn videos?'

Magyar one-track mind, thought Jardine. There were a dozen reasons for her male visitors, from political conspiracy to the black market. Transcripts of her phone conversations had revealed no clue. They had merely arranged dates and times. Some visitors were more frequent than others.

'I don't know,' said Jardine in a loud voice, 'I'm a stranger here myself.'

'Glad you finally turned up,' muttered Szabodo, and thrust a sheaf of printed bills at him, advertising Yuri's Car Rental. 'Here, you never know when you might want to rent a van . . .'

As David Jardine bent slightly to read the proffered bills, his left hand steadied the sheaf for a second, and when he straightened up and walked on, saying no thanks, *tavarishch*, it was back in his trouser pocket. He had palmed two slim cardboard folders, one of which was the ID card of an art restorer from St Petersburg, the other that of an Inspector of the Moscow Militia, Vice and Narcotics Division.

The lobby of the 'Yuri Gagarin' apartment block was clean and pleasant. Mirrors on two walls, four elevators to the left of the entrance, and a mural of Colonel Yuri Gagarin's Earth-orbiting spacecraft behind the concierge's desk.

The concierge was a small woman, with the pigeon-like, sparkling eyes of a heroin addict, although Jardine put that down to the cigarette she kept jammed in her lips.

'Zdravstvuy,' said Jardine, and flashed his Militia ID card.

The concierge nodded, as if she had seen it all before. Russia was a nation used to inquirers and officials and knocks at four in the morning. Such memories did not vanish with the arrival of Boris Yeltsin and democracy, whatever that was.

'You have an apartment vacant on the sixth floor. Number four . . .'

She watched him with her bleary, smoke-filled eyes.

'My boss would like me to take a look. He's getting promoted and he's sent me to look at a few places.'

'A cop?'

'Sure. A senior one. What's the matter?'

She raised her shoulders to meet her ears. 'This is for, hmm, cultured folk.'

'How would you like a fire safety inspection? And a round-the-clock militia patrol in case of burglars? Maybe a narcotics raid . . .?'

The woman reached behind her and fumbled around a board with dozens of keys on separate hooks, without looking round, like a blind person.

'Up a bit. To your right.' It was like being on a game show.

Eventually, she lifted a key from the rack and put it on the table. Her eyes held his. 'There are people in this building could have you out of your job and shovelling salt by breakfast-time tomorrow. But you have a job to do.'

David Jardine gazed at her. And took a US ten-dollar bill from his pocket. He folded the note and laid it on the counter. 'Thanks a lot. Narcotics investigators make a ton of dollars. Don't ask me why . . .'

He gave her a knowing smile.

'I've already forgotten I saw you,' she said, and palmed the money.

Jardine lifted the key and crossed to the elevator, his heart beating faster than normal.

The elevator stopped at the sixth floor and he went

down the fire stairs to the floor below. He pushed a heavy swing door and found himself in a carpeted corridor.

Number three was a pale green door with a square, wood-framed piece of thick coloured glass at about face-height.

David Jardine gazed at the door and listened to the sounds. The carpeting muffled most, but he could just about hear a television set from number four, across the hall. Wind sighed down the elevator shaft. He wondered if even now a police squad was on the way, following a phone call from a suspicious concierge.

He pressed the doorbell buzzer, thinking, Listen, God, I know you and I are not on terrific terms. Mainly because you must, being omnipresent, know just what a shit I am. But help me here. It's almost a blasphemy for you know what I'm intending. But if ever I needed fortune to smile, this is the time . . .

Across the hall, muted sound of laughter from some TV game show.

The door opened.

She was slender, aged about thirty-six, good deportment, with intelligent eyes and an amused mouth. She wore a pleated plaid skirt, in subdued greens and reds, a cashmere jumper and expensive Italian shoes. Height without shoes, about five six.

'Please . . .?' Meaning, what do you want?

'Madame Kolosova?'

'That's me.'

'I'm Mikhail Sergeyevich Olenyev.' Jardine smiled shyly. 'I don't know if Arkady Romanovich has mentioned me . . .'

He contrived to blush and gazed earnestly at her.

Natalya Kolosova gazed back. She leaned past him, smelling of a hair shampoo and conditioner that reminded him of some lover from his past. One of those long-legged and lithe young bodies that were doubtless contributing to many aeons in Purgatory.

She glanced briefly up and down the corridor. Then smiled and gently pushed him inside, closing the door. The hall was floored in small parquet squares, not unlike the polished wood floors at Yasenevo, just a mile or so away.

'How is Arkady Romanovich?' she asked and led the way into the sitting room, which was longer than it was wide, but had a big picture window overlooking some trees and beyond them the lake, giving a feeling of space. The sky was a dusty blue colour and the apartment was pleasantly warm.

'He's busy these days,' replied Jardine, basing his response on a digest of intercepted mail, from Tbilisi, in Georgia, hundreds of miles to the south.

'Still, better Rostov than here.'

'He's in Tbilisi, I think.'

Natalya Kolosova turned, her skirt spinning slightly, and, opening a cedar cigarette case inlaid with ivory, she offered him one. 'They're Marlboros . . .'

'Thanks,' said Jardine. If she now produces a brass Zippo lighter, he thought, I'll just jump out of the bloody window . . .

But she lifted a model Sputnik space satellite and a slim gas flame appeared. He wondered if it had been a complimentary gift, when they moved into the 'Yuri Gagarin' apartment block.

Jardine leaned down and lit his cigarette. They both exhaled slowly and she looked at him, as she moved to a corner of the window. 'And you have a message from Arkady?'

'Um, not really. He just spoke very warmly of you. And said I should call, if I was in the area . . .'

She paused, gazing out at the park. 'And what brings you to the area?'

He knew she meant, are you at Yasenevo, with the *kontora*, with the Office, my ex-husband's old Office?

'The University. I'm from Petrograd. I, um, restore paintings. Icons. Stuff like that.'

Natalya considered this. She looked back into the room at him.

This was make-or-break time. Say, the blindingly obvious suggestion occurred to him, when her husband got chucked out, this slender and attractive Natalya

Katerinovna stayed with the SVR, or the KGB, or whatever they called themselves these days.

Wonderful, David. Are we looking forward to, at the very least, a diplomatic outrage?

'Did he mention a price?' she said, meeting his gaze coolly.

Jardine smiled his slightly lopsided smile. 'I think, um, he was too much of a gentleman . . .'

She laughed wryly. 'Are we talking about the same Arkady?'

Silence.

Had the concierge phoned the militia, to check him out? Or her local KGB? At least they didn't know what apartment he had gone to. And what the hell am I doing in this very upmarket, self-possessed, attractive woman's home?

In some other apartment, above them, a small child was having a tantrum. It was only just audible. More a distant high-pitched whisper.

'Four hundred American.'

'Okay . . .' He nodded. We're getting warm. Is it dope? How much cocaine did you get in Moscow for 400 dollars?

Or does she tell your fortune? And do I really want to know?

English or German lessons? Could be. She had been educated at the exclusive Maurice Thorez Institute, being the daughter of a senior Party official who was now disgraced, having sided with the group that tried to overthrow democracy.

'I don't wish to be indelicate, Mikhail, but do you have that much money available?'

'Yeah. Sure. Of course.' Jardine was aware that, while his Russian was that of a native, educated yet colloquial, he did not have the assured, cosmopolitan speech patterns of Natalya, who was just not fitting into the mental image he had of a slightly bitter divorcee.

He took his wallet from his jacket pocket.

'Did you get that jacket at Yasenevo?' she asked.

'No,' he lied, his heart stopping.

'My husband was a colonel in the First Chief Directorate,' she said.

'I'm sorry. Is he dead?'

'We divorced. The senior officers' store there has Italian clothes just like it.'

Jardine contrived to look pleased with the compliment.

'Ah,' he said. And counted out 400 US dollars, in twenties and tens.

Natalya tugged at a cord, and pulled a net curtain across the picture window.

'No one can see us now,' she said softly.

'Good.' Jardine glanced around and sat in a comfortable armchair, trying to look relaxed, as if this, whatever it was, was the kind of thing he was comfortable with.

She watched him, slightly amused. 'Would you like a drink? Some real champagne . . .?'

'I'm fine. Really.'

Natalya moved slightly, framed against the pale net drapes. She held his gaze and moistened her lips with her tongue.

'Would you like me to take off my skirt . . .?'

God bless you, Ronnie Szabodo. Right again.

'Why not . . .?' Jardine said. Suddenly, surprisingly, embarrassed. He cleared his throat.

'Or perhaps, if I sat here, like this, you could look up it, like a naughty boy. Would you like that . . .?'

She was not wearing underwear.

Jardine smiled. 'That's nice,' he said, and rising, shrugged off his Italian jacket, with a dreadful feeling that even the bold Alice Hanson would not have advised such a course of action, for there was a fair to passing chance that David Arbuthnot Jardine CMG might just be the star of the KGB's 9 o'clock follies.

But he was not. And afterwards, over a glass of real Coca-Cola, naked but for his shirt, with one arm round her shoulder, he and Natalya Katerinovna Kolosova had a most interesting conversation about divorce, and how she was pissed off with her ex-husband, Nikolai, because some months after his fall from grace, he had suddenly become a favoured son once more, of the KGB.

You mean the Sluzhba Vnezhniy Razvyedky, Jardine had murmured, the new Foreign Intelligence outfit. No, she had replied, stroking his moist abdomen, the bastard Nikolai had been picked up by a dyed-in-the-wool bunch of old KGB hardliners, anti-Yeltsin, anti-democratic. Not that she had anything against revisionism, you understand. It was just that, now that he was back in favour, with some new job, he had laughed at her suggestion they should get back together.

And it had been many months since he had even bothered to take their fourteen-year-old daughter out. What a bastard.

What a bastard indeed, replied Jardine, and Natalya had told him he'd better have a shower and go, before the child came home. She asked him most gently to please not mention this little transaction to anyone, or she might lose the apartment.

Of course he would not, swore Jardine. Not a soul in the whole of Russia. She had his oath on that.

'You must think I'm a real slut,' said Natalya, as she unlocked the front door.

He kissed her gently, on the forehead. 'A girl has to survive,' he said. 'I think you're very nice.'

'Nice? Come off it.' But she seemed pleased.

'My dear Natalya. You have made me very happy, in the short time we have known each other,' Jardine whispered, meaning every word.

And as he left, by a back way, and stepped out into the sunlight, he began to whistle.

You see, Alice? He sent the thought heavenwards. That wasn't prudent. But look at the bloody result.

A rumble of thunder sounded in the distance. And great spots of rain, like may-bugs, landed on the shoulders of his Italian jacket.

The old van was nowhere to be seen, and by the time Jardine had found a bus stop, it was pouring, and the skies were dark.

11

Bridge of Sighs

JUST ABOUT THE same time that David Jardine was so intimately engaged with the ex-wife of a KGB colonel, Harry Cardona was leaving his cell on Number Three Landing of B Wing of the New York State Penitentiary, where he was remanded, awaiting trial on counterfeit charges relating to the 43rd Street shootout when Elmore Williams blew away Sammy the Nose and got himself in real bad with Joe Pearce, Sac of the New York Field Office.

There is a steel staircase leading from Landing 3 to the communal latrines and ablutions facility. The six landings run round a central well, about a hundred feet by eighty feet. There are high rails and mesh between the tops of the rails and the next floor up, to stop anyone taking an easy route out of society's garbage can.

There is also wire mesh stretched across the well, at Landings 2 and 4, so all in all, B Wing of NY State Pen is a difficult place to fall to your death from.

Except, it would seem, for the six-inch drop from the washbasin area to the white-tiled floor of the ablutions facility.

Cause of death was neck fracture and severing of the spinal cord. Cardona had been dead before his head struck the white marble and split open like a watermelon. Although the pathologist never identified a murder weapon, the fatal blow was in fact delivered by a piece of rubber insulating tube, filled with five-centimetre steel bearings, both of which had been returned to the machine workshop and put back in their boxes before the screw who found the body could press the alarm code that would close the place down.

And this was the morning Elmore Williams, who had flown to NYC, officially this time, planned to interview Harry, to try to find out who the deceased Sammy the Nose's Mister Big might be.

'You'll never know now,' said Sid Longstreet, when Elmore phoned Washington with the news.

Yeah, thought Williams, I guess that was the general idea. But it seemed to confirm that whoever had sent the grease-gun bikers after him was probably linked to Cardona and that New York disaster.

Rain had soaked David Jardine's Italian wool jacket and was running down his neck from his hair, as he walked along the tree-lined, narrow park that was the Boulevard Ring, past the gypsy stallholder towards the bench that the old babushka in black had been sitting on.

The relentless rhythm of blue and red flashing lights, and the white and sodium-tinted glare from police and militia squad cars and an ambulance, gave the place a carnival atmosphere. The tall man in the long black coat was still there, having sheltered from the rain under one of the leafy plane trees, but his violin hung silent from his right hand. The big grey mongrel lay at his feet.

Jardine pushed his way through the rubbernecking bench-people and evening strollers, to the white and blue tape that now cordoned off the very spot where he had promised Elena Constantinovna he would meet her in, he glanced at his wristwatch, nineteen minutes' time.

Afterwards, he wondered if he really had not guessed, if he had truly imagined that the paraphernalia of police vehicles and the ambulance's open rear doors, revealing a black PVC body-bag, unzipped, lying open like some man-eating plant, on a stretcher trolley, waiting for its prey, was for some other player in one of life's myriad tragedies. If he had not known, from the moment he set foot on Tverskaya Bul'var, for whom this particular, grim circus had come to town. Because in retrospect, it seemed, somehow, to have been a murder that might have been foreseen. And therefore, perhaps, avoided.

The flash of a Forensics Squad camera briefly illuminated her face, eyes not yet dull. She seemed about to say something for her mouth was slightly open, her expression one of . . . mild surprise. Only the small blue hole about one inch above her staring left eye gave an indication that Major Elena Constantinovna Ratanskaya was no longer with us.

Two uniformed militia officers stood talking quietly, along with a stocky man in a crumpled suit, who looked like any homicide detective in any city in the world. And a taller man, wearing a good topcoat with an astrakhan collar, even though summer was making its presence felt.

Just as Jardine was deciding if he should beat a hasty retreat to the British Embassy, the tall man turned sharply, as if, with all the noise of passing traffic on either side of the narrow boulevard park, and the muttering of onlookers, he had heard a twig snap.

And he looked directly into David Jardine's eyes.

It was Anatoly Andreyevich Dzerzhinsky.

So now we'll know, thought Jardine. Now we'll really know.

But Dzerzhinsky let his gaze slide off Jardine and travel around the onlookers, before he ignored them all and turned back to speak with the detective.

At which moment, Euan Liddell, a thirty-four-year-old Scots officer with Moscow Station, carrying diplomatic cover as First Secretary with the Commercial Section, appeared at David Jardine's side. Liddell was the SIS man tasked by the Embassy with Jardine's safety while in Moscow, when the senior officer was not in the care of the Russian Intelligence Service.

Jardine wondered how Liddell had got himself to the murder scene so quickly. For the girl had not been dead more than three hours, judging by her complexion and the rigidity of her limbs. And by Foreign Service standards, that was pretty quick.

He knew that the Station's Technical Section received constant updates on radio and telephone transmissions in and out of SVR and KGB locations in and around Moscow, which might have some relevance to SIS local operations.

These updates came in secure cipher burst via satellite, from the USA's National Security Agency and its little cousin, Britain's Government Communications Headquarters, based at Cheltenham, in Gloucestershire.

Clearly the volume of routine traffic is too great for every conversation to be recorded and itemized. So certain key words are fed into those computers tasked with identifying conversations that might be of interest.

Words like terrorist, pistol, secret, and KGB would be too wide a net to cast and therefore self-defeating. But the names, especially nicknames, of, say, the Russian Service's Director of Counter-Espionage; the leading conspirators in a plot to smuggle nuclear warheads to Iran; known secret codewords and so on, will be fed in, and when they are mentioned in radio or telephone conversation, the NSA and GCHQ tapes will automatically start to run.

If Liddell had been canny enough to feed the names of those SVR officers charged with Jardine's security into the system, then news of Elena Constantinovna's murder, just a few blocks away, would have been on his desk within – in real life? reflected Jardine – let's get real; anything from five days to two weeks. So he must have heard from a paid informant either in the Militia Ops Room, or with the SVR Security Direction on the South Orbital Highway.

Preferably both.

'What brings you here?' Liddell inquired not unpleasantly. 'Or is this just a coincidence . . .?'

'I was with her until round about lunchtime.'

'So how do we play it?' asked Liddell, gazing around seemingly casually.

David Jardine considered. It was clear Dzerzhinsky did not want him involved.

'Diplomatic retreat, I think.'

'Fine.' Liddell was a reliable and experienced operator. 'We leave together. Car's across the street but they won't pick us up till we get clear of this little drama.'

He touched Jardine's elbow gently but firmly, and they both sauntered on, round the periphery of the incident, pushing past the rubbernecks. Jardine expected at any moment to hear a shout and for a team of SVR heavies, or just militia men, to start after him and haul them back for questioning.

One of the people he noticed giving a statement to two detectives was the old babushka, wraithed in funereal black, as if she had known all along how this was going to turn out. She was probably telling them how she had watched the murdered girl sobbing, in the company of a tall man in a fawn woollen jacket, with a scar on his right cheekbone.

'This little drama'. Poor kid. Trying to help Mother Russia. And some bastards had put paid to that.

The Office Volkswagen Passat, with diplomatic plates, pulled up on the far side of Tverskaya Boulevard, near the junction with Malaya Bronaya Street. During their four-minute stroll, Jardine felt the hairs on his neck lift. He had a feeling bordering on certainty that someone was discreetly shadowing them.

And when they crossed the Boulevard, where the traffic was light, towards the Volkswagen, two slender girls were waiting at the kerb. One wore a trenchcoat, the other a fur-trimmed green jacket. Jardine would remember that the slightly too-heavy rouge did not diminish a certain aristocratic bone structure.

'Hi, guys,' said the fair-haired one, 'where would you like to go?'

'Bugger off,' grunted Liddell.

'I can see, Euan,' remarked Jardine, as the car moved

off, driven by a British driver, with a silent and fit young man seated beside him, 'you were always cut out to be a diplomat.'

'Bloody hookers,' replied Liddell. 'The place is crawling with them.'

'I'm not sure if you're a hundred per cent correct,' Jardine replied. 'I don't actually think they were hookers.'

Liddell grunted sceptically. 'So what were they, David? Band of Hope, perchance?'

'It's my guess, just a feeling of mine, Euan, that these two kids are part of a seriously good surveillance team.'

'You're joking.'

'Some kind of tail's been with us since we left the scene of the crime.'

'Bit bloody elaborate for an early murder investigation. Believe me, neither the Militia nor the KGB could rustle up something so sophisticated, at such short notice.'

Jardine leaned to stare into the side-mirror. 'Oh, I don't think this is in response to the killing of that poor girl. Although it might be a continuation of the same operation. Of the same game.'

The driver and his companion had heard all this and they were using their eyes now, not saying a word but, like good bodyguards, paying close attention to everything that might keep their charges and themselves alive.

Liddell scratched his nose. 'David, just what have you been up to? Jesus Christ, a simple liaison visit and already we have a body count.'

Jardine smiled and stretched out, composing in his mind arguments and counter-arguments as to whether his visit to Natalya Kolosova could have any bearing or correlation to Elena Constantinovna's murder. Maybe she had just fallen victim to Moscow's rising crime rate.

Yeah, he thought. And maybe not.

'I don't know what you've got to smile about,' grumbled Liddell, who could see all his painstaking Moscow contacts going down the drain if this turned into something which the Foreign Office would undoubtedly class as 'unhelpful'.

'And neither will you . . . Oh, the joys of our chosen profession, as the song goes. Or is that a song about tarts? And indeed, where's the difference?'

'Wonderful. The boss said you'd be nothing but trouble wrapped in an enigma . . . sir.'

'Did he say that? Good Lord. Well, a little bit of trouble keeps a Station on its toes. Going soft, you New Russia peaceniks.' And David Jardine rested his chin on his chest. Knowing he was in safe hands.

By the time they got to Bolshoi Kammeny Bridge, Jardine seemed to be almost asleep. The driver was paying great attention to his mirrors, as was the quiet young man in the passenger seat.

After a muttered word with the passenger, the driver announced, 'They seem to have cut away, Euan.'

'Yes, well, they've figured out we're going back to the Embassy. That's probably all they wanted to know,' said Liddell, urbanely, which wasn't bad for a man who had started by pooh-poohing the entire notion of a tail.

Jardine telephoned General Zemskov from the SIS secure section in the British Embassy. He said he had seen the incident in the Tverskaya Boulevard and had been greatly shaken to recognize the victim as Major Elena Constantinovna Ratanskaya.

Yes, he had been with colleagues from the Embassy. Yes, since about lunchtime. Why, only this morning the poor girl had been a delight, plying Jardine with baklava and taking him strolling around the city. If only he had stayed with her. He blamed himself. No, no, you mustn't, said the gallant General. Damned black market and Chechen Mafia were everywhere. Poor Elena Constantinovna was probably just in the wrong place at the wrong time. Being in the Service does not give you any protection from the hazards of Moscow's soaring crime rate.

And when Jardine suggested that he might possibly curtail his liaison visit, which had only one day left to run, as Director Rogachev was still in Novastopol on the cocaine investigation, Zemskov had said of course. He would be spending tomorrow with the murdered girl's father, an old comrade from the Washington Embassy days. What a loss. The child was all he lived for.

So a Second Secretary from Chancery was sent out to Yasenevo for David Jardine's things, his battered leather grip from the folk-art shop in Bogota, his fawn Prince of Wales check, double-breasted suit from Huntsman in Savile Row, his shaving things and stuff like that.

Jardine also sent a personal note to Dzerzhinsky, saying he was devastated by the murder and extending his deep sympathy for the loss of a fine colleague and true patriot. Again expressing his honest regret at having left her on her own.

He enclosed a card, with David A. Jardine in engraved copperplate, and telephone and fax numbers which were serviced night and day by the Firm.

Those immediate chores done, Jardine signed for his personal top secret (Crypto) computer disc from the Secure Room safe and after receiving a counter-signature from the Duty Clerk, Sergeant Busby, seconded to SIS from the Intelligence Corps, drew it from its sealed buff envelope and retreated to a corner, where he spent the next hour completing his report to Century on the day's dramatic events.

That report was then enciphered, personally, by Jardine, using his Crypto disc, and transmitted securely by Sergeant Busby to the senior Night Duty Officer at St George's Circus, in South London.

It did not, however, mention his visit to Natalya Kolosova, or what had happened behind her curtains, pleasant though it had been, or the vital intelligence gleaned from the transaction, that her husband had somehow been reinstated in the KGB.

And because David Jardine did, from time to time, justify both his considerable pay and his legendary reputation, tiny bells had started to ring in the recesses of his mind. Noises off, almost, suggesting perhaps that Act Three was about to begin.

For although he had also not mentioned the murdered Elena Constantinovna's secret gift of a book of matches with microfilm between the covers, he finally felt, for the first time since leaving Washington on that mad impulse to Service Agent 1109 – Pomegranate – that frisson, that thrilling surge which made his life truly worthwhile.

Jardine's intuition suggested to him that Nikolai Kolosov was indeed, let's say very probably, the partner of the cast-out Israeli Danny Davidov. And if his estranged wife was to be believed – and why would she have lied? – Colonel Kolosov's return to the KGB fold would coincide with him allowing himself to be recruited by Davidov for the purpose of collaborating in, perhaps even making possible, the former Mossad man's increasingly successful series of international financial crimes.

And – and this was what David Jardine found tantalizing – what if Elena's precious gift of real intelligence on Staraya Zemlya, the Oleg Kouzmine Second Nation, dedicated to the overthrow of Russian democracy and a return to the worst days of Stalin, was somehow connected?

Let's just imagine, David, he thought to himself, let's take a wild guess and assume that this powerful Oleg Kouzmine faction, doubtless with its tentacles in the old guard still with the KGB, is where Colonel Nikolai Kolosov is drawing his pay, and his restored pride, from.

And the ultimate goal, Danny Davidov's ultimate goal, is to attack a major Western currency? So that it could be destroyed, but he plans just to 'shake the tree'?

Well, David old sport, just suppose Oleg Kouzmine's man is right there with Danny, that cool master criminal. Will *he* be content with just 'shaking the tree'? Or will he take a chainsaw and fell the whole bloody orchard, bringing dollars and pounds and yen crashing all the way down?

Take a wild guess.

Now *there* would be an assignment to put David

Arbuthnot Jardine back at the top table and indeed, as Steven would put it, 'above the salt'.

Wishful thinking? We'll see, thought Jardine. He would kick it around with Ronnie Szabodo. Ronnie was good at making him use his brain.

And it was just as David Jardine had started to rough out a signal to Szabodo (copy to Kate? No, not just yet) ordering a complete dossier on Oleg Kouzmine and his political background, that Sergeant Busby appeared at the desk, ostentatiously 'not looking' at either the VDU screen or Jardine's scribbled notes, although any Duty Clerk worth his salt could read upside-down and back to front.

'Yes, Bert?' Jardine had heard Busby's wife call him Bert at a party he had found himself attending in one of those spacious council flats overlooking the Thames at World's End, in Chelsea. His office driver had invited Jardine for a drink with his daughter, who had just announced her engagement to a postman who went to France every year to ride in that bicycle race they have there.

Anyway, there was Sergeant Busby and a woman of about thirty, wearing her hair in the sort of beehive, lacquered style teenage shop assistants favoured in the sixties. And she had called him Bert. Well, she ought to know, and Jardine had taken pleasure in calling Sergeant Busby Bert ever since.

'This is from Fanfare, Major Jardine, sir.'

Jardine smiled thinly. Busby knew perfectly well that he had left the Parachute Regiment 110 years ago, with the rank of Captain. And no gentleman ever used his old military handle in civilian life.

'What the hell's Fanfare?'

'It's this month's codeword for the London office.'

Jardine shook his head. 'Bloody hell . . .'

He accepted the faxed signal, marked Priority – urgent, and as he read it, he felt his heart thump.

The bits of code and number ciphers told him the signal had come by transmitted burst from Beirut. The signal had been made in a particular way and at a particular time that confirmed the sender was a recognized agent of the Firm and that the signal had not been sent under duress.

However, the codename was unknown to SIS Traffic Control at Century and they had passed it on to Moscow Station for Jardine's immediate attention, with a crusty note from Miss Budgen reminding him to keep his list of assets' codenames up to date.

Bert Busby continued to hover. 'Will there be anything, Major?' he inquired.

'No, thanks, Bert. Cup of tea would go down well, can we run to that or are the Treasury cut-backs really biting?'

Busby about-turned and marched to the far end of the room, which was nowhere near a kettle.

The unrecognized codename was 'Mongoose', and the reason it had increased Jardine's pulse-rate was because that had been his nickname, his absurd pet name, for Alisha, all those years ago, when everything had seemed to be much less complicated.

Trying to appear bored with some routine chore of intelligence husbandry, he deciphered the message and this was what it said:

> *Know now you were right, reference SJ a.k.a. RA. What a fool* (*sender*) *has been. You probably do not want to know* (*sender*) *who good* (that was how it deciphered, but she no doubt intended 'could') *blame you? Everything has changed.* (*sender*) *needs communicate much. RA was not telling you real truth. Sorry to be such – I spell – W.I.M.P. but need to meet urgent. Will be Venice in place we went together dates 17, 18, 19. Times will be Beirut minus 5.17 discipline four. This is mad. Do not expect you but* (*sender*) *will be there.*

And it was signed 'Mongoose'.

Well . . . shit. No one but a bloody fool is going to fall for this one, dearie. What the hell do you take me for? thought David Jardine. Then he wondered what Alice

Hanson would have approved of. Then he composed a signal to Ronnie Szabodo, to await the Hungarian's return to London. And this time he did make a copy to Katherine Howard, D (Sy), just to cover his ass.

'Just before you rustle up that cup of tea, Bertie . . .'

'Sir . . .' Sergeant Busby gazed across with undisguised hostility.

'Be so kind as to book me on a flight to Geneva, connecting to Venice.'

'When would you like that, Major?'

And this exchange completed, David Jardine slept soundly in the Ambassador's guest bedroom – His Excellency being in St Petersburg on diplomatic business – and was in something approaching his old form when Euan Liddell collected him at 7.30 next morning and drove him to the airport, informing him that his identity would change at Geneva to that of an English art dealer called Alan Congreve, sleeping partner – Jardine said he would have preferred the term silent – of the flamboyant and delightful Roy Miles, one of England's foremost dealers in Russian paintings.

It is a flight of two hours and forty minutes from Moscow to Geneva, and a further hour from Geneva to Venice, and by the time the clusters of huge, puncture-proof tyres of Swissair's DC-9 were three inches above the runway at Venice, David Jardine had washed and shaved in the cramped but clean toilet and put on the Huntsman suit, a cream Sea Island cotton shirt bought off the peg at Hilditch and Key, and a worn, dark green silk tie with pale blue and sand-coloured stripes, which he had worn throughout his briefings and consultations at the SVR complex in Yasenevo. It was, in fact, the tie which he and some Russian- and Pushtu-speaking colleagues, recruited from the Firm and from Special Forces Directorate, had had made up, following four months on clandestine operations in Afghanistan, when they had successfully posed as 153 Spetznaz Company, of the KGB.

Nobody in Moscow had asked what the tie represented. But Jardine would have been happy to tell them, in the spirit of a new beginning. He was sure Zemskov would have roared with laughter. And he was sure that Dzerzhinsky would not.

He wondered, as he strolled through Customs and Immigration, idly presenting his British passport in the name of Congreve, if he would have behaved so dangerously, indeed irresponsibly, with Natalya in that apartment by the Olympic Village lake, if he had not, maybe subconsciously, been aroused, during the course of that day, by Major Elena Ratanskaya, with her slender waist and her smooth, cool, elegant skin. The way she had moved her legs while driving her beat-up new car, the incredible Slav glances she had shot him, head ducked, eyes sparkling, when he had least expected them.

And that one kiss. It had been a long time since he had been touched by something so vital, so alive and full of promise.

He tried to remember her like that, Elena Constantinovna Ratanskaya, but he kept seeing her face, the last time he ever saw it. At peace in death, but with that slight look of surprise. Or was it regret, at being so utterly alone at the cold instant of departing life?

And just possibly he could have saved her. If he had not left her there alone. It did not bear thinking about.

The airport at Venice has a wonderfully disorganized atmosphere. One is decanted through a green and grey arrivals system which is fairly haphazard, past dramatically military figures in sludge-coloured combat overalls, with mint-green neckerchiefs, black berets worn at rakish angles, and 9-mm Beretta machine-pistols slung from one shoulder. Usually, one of these soldiers has a big, very fluffy German Shepherd dog on a leash. There are constant comings and goings between water-taxi and hotel speedboat drivers and a tall, impressive man, slightly paunchy, in some kind of formal liveried coat, which is worn unbuttoned and rendered slightly casual by a grey cardigan underneath.

The general effect is one of carnival, of *opéra-bouffe*.

David Jardine grinned as a wizened speedboat driver spotted him and barged through a cluster of Americans in Burberry raincoats, who were loudly inquiring after the Cipriani courtesy boat.

'*Signor Jardine. Buon giorno, come sta?*'

'*Grazie, Paolo, molto bene, e lei?*'

'*Mi fa male la gamba,*' Paolo replied. His leg hurt. Also his wife had left him and his dog had fleas. After which résumé of his condition, he wheezed with laughter and reached out to take Jardine's soft leather travelling bag.

So much, thought Jardine, for the Alan Congreve legend. He considered telling Paolo, who had looked after Dorothy and him with great attention and good nature for their several vacations in Venice over the years, that he was with business colleagues and they had organized a boat, but in the end he surrendered the bag and Paolo led him out on to the pier and down some steps on to a jetty, where his immaculate, polished and oiled speedboat in gleaming varnish and navy paint bobbed patiently.

During the journey through the canals, a magical mist wraithed the same crumbling, centuries-old, overhanging facades and arched, medieval footbridges that Canaletto had made so famous. Jardine never failed to be moved by the beauty of the place. And he could not help thinking that, if the Oleg Kouzmines of this world had their way, then this glorious floating city could go the same way as another of Europe's medieval jewels – Dubrovnik, shelled into rubble by the Serbian army.

Paolo chattered on about his family's never-ending saga, which seemed to be straight out of a *commedia dell' arte* libretto, and it was difficult not to wonder if he was making at least some of it up. For such a relentless catalogue of disasters seemed to cause the man great mirth.

The upshot of this chance encounter was that David Jardine told the speedboat driver to let him off at the public transport jetty at St Mark's Square. He managed to give the impression he was probably here to spend some time with a lady friend, and Paolo cheerfully accepted that his fare was not in the mood to answer questions.

It was about an hour after the plane had landed that Jardine arrived in the Square of Santa Maria Zobenigo and checked into the Gritti Palace Hotel, which knew him only as Signor Congreve. For family visits, the Jardines stayed in a tiny hotel on the island of Torcello.

A porter ushered him into a comfortable double room, with a small sitting room, overlooking the Grand Canal.

The light was golden russet, and the dome of Santa Maria della Salute, across the wide canal, glinted copper and faded green. Jardine had opened the double windows and pulled a chair up to sit there, gazing out, taking in the magic of the place, watching a vaporetto ferryboat deposit passengers at the Salute landing, listening to the peace that was Venice.

He reflected on his situation and found himself longing for the relative simplicity of the Cold War. Then, in the spy game, you at least knew where you were. There were the Soviets, and there were their client nations, there were their networks of agents inside Western infrastructures, and there were their sponsored terrorist groups. Give or take the Iranians and the Chinese, nothing could have been simpler to grasp – intricate to fight, of course, but at least everyone knew the name of the game.

But these days, who was the enemy? We have, he considered, a Russian Federation that might or might not be on course for freedom and democracy (and all the liberated criminal elements such freedom brings). And this Second Nation that Elena had provided him with secret intelligence on, led by the mysterious Oleg Kouzmine, was it really so deeply rooted under the surface of Russian society that the Party might once again take over? And next time, no more Mister Nice Guy? And would that necessarily return the world to the worst days of Stalin and nuclear brinkmanship?

Well, we'll see, he mused. He had sent the book of matches with its concealed microfilm in a classified package, via the Diplomatic Bag, to Ronnie Szabodo, His Eyes Only, with an order to produce a printout of the information within, and to show it to no one until Jardine returned to London.

And if the Oleg Kouzmine network within Russia's military–industrial complex was seriously intent on turning the clock back, to establish a Second Communist State, was Danny Davidov really doing such a brilliant job with his series of international financial crimes that their man Kolosov might find himself in a position where he could, having piggy-backed the Israeli so far, simply cut his partner's throat and change gear from simple extortion and theft to damage the West's financial standing so severely that Yeltsin's fragile bid for democracy and individual freedom could no longer be kept alive with the massive infusions of capital it was receiving from the USA and Europe?

He must have dozed off, for the gentle tapping at his door woke him with a start. The copy of the Italian newspaper *Corriere della Sera*, which he had been idly scanning, lay half on his legs, half on the floor.

Jardine removed his reading glasses and padded to the door to the outside corridor.

'*Si?*' he asked, mindful of Elena Constantinovna's warning that Staraya Zemlya was taking an interest in him. And aware that the last time he had flown on a mission to rendezvous with Alisha Abdul-Fetteh, he had been stabbed and still had the fresh scar to prove it.

A soft voice replied in Arabic, 'It's me.'

Jardine opened the door slowly and there she was, looking as good as ever, but he detected dark shadows under her eyes. She was carrying a leather and canvas holdall.

'Come in,' he said, bleakly, and she glided past him like a ghost.

Jardine double-locked the door and looked at her, expressionless.

Alisha glanced down, awkward and embarrassed. 'I did not think you would come,' she said.

'Then you don't know me.' He crossed to the window and gazed out.

'Can we talk here . . .?' she asked softly. Still standing in the middle of the sitting room.

'You tell me, Alisha. You're with the side that plays fucking stupid games.'

'No one knows. No one knows I am here, David.'

'The name's Alan today.' He was talking, it seemed, to the canal. 'What's yours?'

And as the silence grew longer, David Jardine turned to look back into the room. She was sitting on the couch, her face in her hands, sobbing, almost without a sound, her shoulders shaking.

Histrionics, spare me, thought Jardine. He went into the bedroom and took a bottle of Stolichnaya vodka from his Colombian leather bag, collected two tooth glasses from the bathroom and returned. He poured two stiff shots of the clear liquid, took a Rothmans cigarette from a pack on the sideboard and lit it, using one of the Gritti Palace matchbooks.

Alisha continued to sob. It seemed to be genuine, but quite frankly, my dear, Jardine thought to himself, I don't give a monkey's left bollock.

He sighed, as the poor woman continued to weep, for all mankind it seemed, for all the sins and tribulations of the world, from the Massacre of the Innocents to Magic Johnson getting Aids.

Jardine sat down, making himself comfortable in an easy chair covered with pink linen, and sipping his vodka, smoking his cigarette, gazed around the room and across to the window and the dome of the Salute church across the Grand Canal.

It got dark.

He could hear the sounds of an elevator creaking, guests, happy and innocent in Wonderland, leaving nearby rooms and going off to enjoy Venice.

At about 9.20, the room in darkness, gently lit from the moon and its reflection on the water of the canal, she finally let out a long, shuddering sigh, and looked around, probably for a handkerchief, for she was sniffling and her pink nose was running.

Jardine, who could be a total bastard on occasion, for that was what he was paid to be, sat motionless, watching, until the Political Adviser to the Foreign Minister of the Lebanon, and secret agent of Christ knew how many intelligence services, had gone to the bathroom, blown her nose, had a pee, flushed the WC and splashed water over her pale, pinched face with the shadows under her eyes.

She sat down, glanced at the vodka, drained it in two serious gulps, and turned to face him.

'I must be cracking up,' she said.

'Go on,' replied David Jardine, 'pull the other one . . .'

Alisha looked at him, then she shook her head. 'I'm really sorry. I thought I could run to you. It was dumb of me.'

David Jardine watched her, remaining silent for some moments. She caught the pack of Rothmans he threw to her and lit it with, yes, one of the several battered Zippos that were doing the rounds in Mossad circles.

Finally, and with infinite gentleness in his voice, he asked, in Arabic, 'What's the problem . . .?'

And she told him, leaving nothing out, how she had not been able to get out of her mind his remark that Reuven Arieh had contrived her father's murder. How, when challenged, Arieh had failed to refute the accusation. She told him about Hassan's tortured cadaver on the morgue table, and about the bristling but ultimately okay Captain Teufik Rassi and how he had made a gift to her of Hassan's letter, the final nail in Arieh's coffin.

She told David Jardine about the evening when she had intended to kill her Mossad boss, and how she had failed, because of his grief for his dead brother.

And all the time Alisha Abdul-Fetteh, Agent Pomegranate, was telling him these things, unburdening herself as if in the confessional, Jardine was coldly interpreting, trying to separate fact from fiction, and when she had finished, he found that he believed every word.

How can I feel so sorry for her, he wondered, when all she has really told me is that for the last eight years her life has been a total waste – which is precisely what she did to me, during the same period? But compassion chooses awkward moments to strike and Jardine found his basic humanity taking precedence over the spy's mentality, which should have been figuring out how best to turn this to his advantage. To the Firm's advantage.

'Let's take a stroll,' he said. And they left the Gritti and walked over tiny footbridges and along the sides of quiet canals.

As they walked, she took his arm and told him everything she knew about Reuven Arieh, Mossad's Middle Eastern operations, and the business of Danny Davidov, which was driving Arieh crazy.

It became clear that David Jardine's interpretation of events was absolutely correct, if not in every detail, then certainly in substance.

Robert Maxwell's millions had indeed been appropriated by a secret group inside Mossad. The Mamounieh had not ever been consulted, even when the sums became close to fantastic. But no one involved, neither Nathan Zamir, nor Avriam Eitels, nor Reuven Arieh, had ever contemplated using a cent of the funds for their personal use. Until Danny Davidov came along.

So their panic was genuine.

If Davidov succeeded in implicating Israel in his criminal enterprise, some of the Tel Aviv Institute's finest people would fall. That was why Reuven Arieh had attempted to coerce Jardine into helping stop the rogue Mossad man in his tracks. Because he did not dare confess to his own masters just how deep the scandal went.

'But why me?' asked David Jardine, still smarting from the humiliation of that Beirut episode.

'Oh, David.' She laughed quietly. 'You were his hero and his *bête noire* at the same time. He was so thrilled at having recruited me, double-crossing you. Stone Dancer, he used to say . . . nobody has ever gotten one over Stone Dancer before.'

'Who?' asked Jardine.

'Don't you know? Stone Dancer is Mossad's codename for you. They think you are the best there is. In this world of ours.'

And there it was. Reuven Arieh had always been jealous of Jardine. And while he exulted in having turned David Jardine's Agent Pomegranate, even seducing her, just like the SIS man, when he found himself in a tight corner, it was Jardine he had turned to, to help him out. Good old Stone Dancer.

David Jardine grinned. 'What a dreadful codename.'

'They say you are like the elf in some Russian folk story, dancing from stone to stone over the wildest torrents, without ever falling down.'

'I wish,' replied Jardine.

And after supper in a little restaurant called Il Giardinetto, near the Campo Santa Maria di Formosa, where they ate a little risotto con funghi and drank some Brunello di Montalpulcino, the English spymaster and the Lebanese girl who had lost her way strolled back to the Gritti Palace and, taking off their clothes by moonlight, went to bed and slept, eventually.

Madison avenue has to be one of the most impressive thoroughfares of any metropolis in the world, reflected Danny Davidov. Whether window shopping, buying, eating out or doing business, you got the feeling this was the epicentre of developed capital on Planet Earth.

Just across the avenue from an upmarket French bistro called Le Relais, round about 73rd Street, about level with the Central Park Armoury, is an unprepossessing door, and once inside, a gloomy flight of stairs going up to the second floor, where a creaking elevator (Max. 4 Persons) will take you up three more floors to Max Eidelman's antiquarian bookshop and rare manuscript library.

The place reminded Danny Davidov of a forgotten corner of Tel Aviv University Library, as he and Nikolai Kolosov followed a round-shouldered woman of about fifty along dusty lanes of tables and piled books, into a second room, around the walls this time, past first editions of *Paradise Lost* and a complete set of first editions of Hemingway's works, into another room, where you could see from one bookshelf-lined side to the other. There were three wide tables, themselves probably collectors' items merely by dint of the passage of time, back-to-back and forming a T-shape, with more piles of ancient books and dusty files.

Kolosov had noticed a number of early seventies humidifiers in various corners and under a couple of desks, on the walk from the elevator.

Sitting at one table, perched on a Dickensian stool, was a small, birdlike man, wearing a grey wool cardigan with holes in the sleeves, a striped shirt with stiff, detachable collar, and a black knitted silk tie. His dark trousers were cut in an old-fashioned style, the waistband stopping above his slightly protruding belly.

This was Max Eidelman. His greying hair was untidy and wispy. His nose was Semitic and the lines on either side of his mouth, curving up to separate the nose from his sallow cheeks, crinkled as he smiled and lifted a hand to his two visitors.

'So what do you have for me today, Mr Bannerman?'

Danny was Robert Bannerman to Eidelman. Over the last fifteen months, he had carefully established and nursed a legend, on the veracity of which the rare books and manuscripts expert would have passed a polygraph test.

Everything that Danny had brought to him, for valuation and occasionally for sale, had been 100 per cent genuine. Items had included an original manuscript by Henry James, with the author's corrections and deletions, a letter from the poet Byron to his publisher, complaining about the editor's miscorrection of the word 'bark' in one of his poems, which alluded to a little-known but valid description of a wraith of fog – the editor had altered it to 'bank' – and genuine Confederate documents from the Civil War.

Thus Eidelman's perception of Danny Davidov was that of a serious collector, well versed in the business of rare manuscripts and documents but not foolhardy enough to consider himself an expert, and a canny businessman who, on occasion, could come up with a nugget of decent gold.

He had not met Davidov's colleague before, but he had seen the two of them together, at a couple of rare document sales. In fact, he now recalled, Davidov had introduced them once, about six months before. The man collected rare paper. Rare watermarks. That was it. A very specialized business. But sensible, for sometimes the watermarks were worth more than the writing on the old paper.

'You speak a little Polish, do you not, Mr Eidelman?' inquired Danny.

'I am a little Polish . . .' smiled the bookseller.

'I can't remember, have you met my very good friend Mr Casimir Rudnitsky?'

'Yes.' Eidelman offered a hand to Kolosov. 'Watermarks, is it not?'

'Watermarks,' replied Kolosov, in Polish. He gripped the other man's hand warmly. 'I have an extensive collection and I want to enlarge it.'

'It's not a speciality of mine,' said Eidelman, 'but if I can help . . .?'

'Since Casimir became a fellow American, he has concentrated on US paper, going back to the first New Amsterdam papermill.'

'Actually,' the bookseller looked suddenly schoolmasterish, 'the first papermill was on Chesapeake Bay, near Baltimore. But I guess Mr Rudnitsky knows that.'

Kolosov nodded. 'I did.' He seemed suddenly uncertain. As if he wondered if he should have come. It was an attitude that put Eidelman's heart up a few beats. It was a loser's attitude, and the rare documents business made loan-sharking look like a social service.

'Go on, tell him. Can we sit down . . .?' Danny said to Kolosov and Eidelman respectively.

'Please. *Pazhalsta. Sidityе, pazhalsta.*' Please sit down, gentlemen.

Oh, greed is a terrible thing, reflected Davidov.

He gazed at Kolosov, to reassure him, just knowing, without looking, that Max Eidelman was doing the same.

'I've known Max for nearly two years, right, Max?'

Eidelman nodded gravely. 'Maybe just over,' he said, stretching fourteen months and three weeks to the very limit.

'So you can trust him. I've done good business here, believe me,' said Danny.

Kolosov met Eidelman's beaming, confidence-giving smile and nodded.

In the silence, the throaty bellow of a fire engine sounded down below on Madison, and receded as it ploughed its way downtown.

'It's, um, I just bought it for the watermark, Mr Eidelman. I hardly noticed the writing till I got home . . .' said Kolosov, with some diffidence.

This was the kind of remark that either got experts seriously interested, or very, very wary. But Robert Bannerman was a known quantity to Max and an honest client, so serious interest, tinged with the merest smidgen of avarice, was the order of the day. And when Rudnitsky opened his slender, worn leather musician's music case, and extracted a cardboard folder, with tissue paper protecting a very ancient-looking single page of writing paper, maybe twelve inches by eight, Max Eidelman felt merely quiet anticipation.

It was obvious that these two clients believed they had something special. And when Rudnitsky carefully opened the folder and lifted off the tissue paper, the old bookseller understood why. That handwriting, that penmanship, he and many other Americans would recognize it straightaway. It was probably the most forged handwriting in the USA.

Pity the poor immigrant, Bob Dylan's song went. This

Casimir Rudnitsky had purchased at some careless auction, for its watermark, what on the face of it, even to a seasoned collector, appeared to be one page, corrected and scribbled across, of a draft for the Gettysburg Address, written in the unmistakable hand of President Abraham Lincoln himself. But in the cruel light of experience, Max Eidelman had little doubt it would turn out, like most of the others, to be counterfeit.

He glanced up and saw that Bannerman was grinning broadly, pleased to have brought his friend to the right place.

'Whadda you think?' asked Bannerman.

Max Eidelman raised his shoulders, gazed back with pale, watery eyes at the two men. 'Where did you get this?'

'Auction of old letters and effects from a big old house in Vermont,' said Kolosov.

'Executors' sale,' added Davidov.

The room had become so quiet they could just about hear the skinny secretary quietly reading off a ton of serial or index numbers, two rooms away, maybe into a phone, or a tape-recorder. Danny had a sudden picture of the two Viets, back on board the *Sumaru*, under discreet guard by his carefully recruited and well-paid crew.

'Mmm hmm,' said Eidelman and he carefully placed a jeweller's eyepiece in his left eye and proceeded to examine the page and the paper. Then he lifted the page, using plastic tweezers, and held it up to a green glass-shaded desk lamp.

'Mmm hmm,' he uttered. Then turned it back to front and upside-down and finally he laid it back on its folder and removed the eyepiece.

'I would need to carry out some tests, of course . . .'

Of course, naturally, agreed Kolosov and Danny Davidov.

'And I don't want to build up your hopes,' said Eidelman. 'There is, of course, a zillion million to one chance you just might have acquired a previously unknown page from a draft of the Gettysburg. But personally, I don't think so.'

'What about the handwriting?' asked Kolosov, in Polish.

'Oh, Abe Lincoln. You can't mistake that.'

Big smile of pleasure from Kolosov, alias Rudnitsky.

'But such things usually turn out to be forged,' contributed Danny.

'Sure thing,' replied Max Eidelman. 'There are probably more forged letters than President Lincoln ever wrote. There are probably forgeries in the Smithsonian's own, authenticated collection. But you've come to the right place, I guess.'

'Mr Eidelman's the guru on Abe Lincoln forgeries,' Danny told Kolosov proudly.

Eidelman looked suitably modest, but at the same time somehow arrogant. The way gurus do. 'You can't forge the paper, and you can't forge the watermark. The ink? Yes, with a good knowledge of both physics and chemistry. The penmanship? Well, I've never known a forged example to get past the Max Eidelman test.'

He looked up at them, almost unable to resist the urge to touch the paper, to get straight to work on it. Because despite his scepticism, something about it told him he was in touch here with history.

'Max, that's exactly why I brought Casimir to you,' said Davidov. 'Would you please carry out any tests you want on it? All the way to providing authentication if the tests prove it's the real McCoy. Whadda you say?'

Max picked up a pair of oval, wire-rimmed glasses that made him look like Trotsky. He wound the ends round his ears, then blinked and looked straight into Kolosov's eyes.

'It's your letter,' he said, in Polish.

'*Da, pazhalsta,*' replied Kolosov, who was always amused to hear Poles swear that their language was not in the least like Russian. For the two tongues shared a common root and had many words the same, like he had just said yes please, which was precisely the same, in either language.

Eidelman nodded. 'It'll take about three days. Even the

better forgeries sometimes raise a price at auction.' He glanced at them shrewdly. 'Will you be offering it?'

For sale, he meant.

Bannerman and Rudnitsky exchanged glances. 'Not at this stage,' replied Kolosov.

'And I hardly need remind you,' smiled Danny, his eyes friendly, but somehow chilling, 'total discretion.'

'Of course.' Eidelman closed the cardboard folder and slipped the file into a drawer, which he locked, and hung the key round his scrawny neck. 'You want me to work out a fee?'

'Don't worry,' said Kolosov. 'Whatever's fair.'

'Come back on . . . Friday,' Eidelman replied. 'I'll know for sure then.'

Davidov and Kolosov rose and said see you Friday and left, escorted out by the round-shouldered assistant.

Back on Madison, they walked a few blocks, crossing towards Central Park South and Broadway.

'Getting closer,' said Kolosov. Which was a huge speech coming from him. The tall Russian – Polish Russian – had become more and more, not exactly withdrawn, but . . . taciturn, those last few weeks. Sometimes Danny Davidov wondered if his partner in crime was altogether happy.

What the hell, it wasn't a marriage made in heaven, but they sure had pulled off some truly textbook operations.

Danny found himself wondering, more often these days, if his former colleagues in Mossad had gotten the message. If his deliberate footprints, rocking some serious financial boats, had been deciphered, if you can decipher footsteps, as being the work of former Colonel Danny Davidov. And if they would have begun to regret, if the Mamounieh had begun to regret, the day they cast such a brilliant operator out into the Diaspora, out of Israel. Well, *shalom*, pals, you ain't seen nothin' yet.

Kolosov had been saying something.

'What was that?'

'Maybe we should ransom the Vietnamese.'

'Hey, hey. Oi. Don't fuck with the boys from Palermo.' Danny was horrified.

Nikolai Kolosov grinned. The first time Danny had seen him amused in weeks. 'Why not?' he said.

Danny Davidov stopped dead in the street and clapped a hand to his head. He stepped back and stared at the former KGB man, almost knocking Norman, the barman at the Jockey Club, under whose blue and white awning they were standing, into the path of a yellow cab.

'Push away, sure, life is cheap off Broadway,' muttered the bartender and with a glare at the two men went on inside, muttering some imprecation in indecipherable Bronx Yiddish.

'Why *not*?' asked Danny, shaking his head. 'What about our fuckin' skins, Nikita? That guy was not talking metaphors, you know.' The Israeli tugged at his cheeks, at the flesh on his hands. 'We're talking lampshade time, maybe that means less to you than to me, pal. You know? How much, anyway? For how much exactly?'

'If they pass this test, the Max Eidelman test. They have to be worth four million each. I know some Chechen Mafia back in Moscow would pay that much for them.'

Kolosov started to walk on. Danny Davidov hurried to catch up. 'You said ransom. Now you're saying steal them. Sell them to the highest bidder.'

'Why not?'

'What about our skins? Jesus Christ, these guys don't jest. Anyway, we don't *need* eight million, that's cab fares, come on . . .'

Nikolai Kolosov stared down at Danny. 'I never imagined anybody could get to you. You know, Danny, the one reason I'm here is because you never seemed to know the meaning of fear. It's your crazy chutzpah that makes all this fun.' Kolosov shrugged. 'For me.'

Davidov stared up at him. Such a number of consecutive words from this guy was akin to the Gettysburg Address, or Hamlet's soliloquy. And fun was not a word he had associated with the saturnine Muscovite. 'I'll have to think about it,' he said.

They walked on, turning into Broadway.

Danny looked at Kolosov, who was grinning. 'Are you kidding me . . .?'

'Of course.'

They strolled on, checking casually for a tail, out of habit.

'You know, you disturb me,' said the short guy. 'And I thought I knew you.'

You don't know me at all, thought the tall one. But you will. Quite soon now . . . And he smiled, his eyes crinkling in the sunlight, strong in the canyon between New York's skyscrapers.

The morning of that same day, David Jardine had wakened around 6.30, to find Alisha Abdul-Fetteh wrapped around him, fast asleep, their arms and legs entwined. She began to stir and they lay there, the sounds of early morning Venice heralding a new day. And when they made love again, it was as if seven years had never passed.

Around ten minutes after nine, they showered and ordered a huge breakfast, of cereals and fruit, orange juice, eggs and bacon, toast and marmalade and pots of black coffee.

'I really didn't think you would turn up,' she said, chewing through a mouthful of warm toast with butter spread lavishly, so that it dribbled down her chin.

'Business is business,' replied Jardine, deadpan, and held her hurt expression until she saw that, in his eyes, he was smiling.

The Lebanese girl wore Jardine's light blue shirt, from the evening before, sleeves turned up, and unbuttoned. She looked more relaxed, and the dark areas beneath her eyes were beginning to clear up.

'So what do you need, David, to sink this bastard?' she asked.

'Everything you know, everything you can remember.

The Danny Davidov affair, all the men he has dealt with, from the Israeli Service, the Iraqis, Abu Nidal . . . the lot.'

'He did not tell me very much, you know.'

Jardine felt that would be true enough. Reuven Arieh was a professional agent-runner, why should he tell her more than she needed to know? But one of the problems in running a highly intelligent, perceptive, intuitive asset like Alisha was that she was bound to learn much, much more about those running her than they might appreciate.

Over so many years, it was like osmosis.

'I really do mean everything, Alisha. If we are to put the clock back.'

'Wouldn't that be nice? A surgical removal of Time. But let's get real, David. I am here, not for your forgiveness, not to put Time back in Pandora's box. This is dangerous, me being here. So please don't treat me as some dumb chicken, okay?'

David Jardine wiped his hand over his chin and grinned.

'You haven't changed,' he said. 'So why are we here . . .?'

'Are you so civilized,' she asked, 'you British, that you have no concept of . . . revenge? Of the obligation to avenge a crime against your own family?' She jabbed the buttered toast at him. 'Vengeance is an obligation as far as I am concerned. Sure I will tell you everything. I have of course brought notes, names, places, dates, network codes, transmission frequencies, everything you need to destroy that bastard.'

'Will he know you've taken them?' asked Jardine, getting straight to work.

'No. I made copies. By hand. All generations of photocopy are recorded on the special paper they use.'

Good girl.

Jardine took a cigarette from its pack. Put it back again. 'How did you get the Zippo lighter to Anatoly Dzerzhinsky? Who else has one? How does he tie in to Danny Davidov? Where is Davidov? Who are his colleagues? And much more. More like that.'

She frowned. Then nodded, flicking her hair from her

face. 'I can answer. Except, where is Danny? That's what they're going mad trying to find out.'

'And what will they do when they find him?'

She swallowed her toast and sipped at a glass of orange. Finally she dabbed at her mouth with a white linen napkin and nodded, matter-of-fact. 'Oh, they'll kill him . . .'

The rest of that morning, through lunchtime – two plates of smoked salmon sandwiches on brown bread, with a bottle of Italian Chardonnay and a pot of black coffee – was spent in a most comprehensive and exhaustive debriefing of Alisha, formerly Agent Pomegranate. By four in the afternoon, David Jardine knew precisely that his educated guess had been correct. Reuven Arieh was indeed at the heart of a web of deceit which an unauthorized and sworn to secrecy group of Mossad officers had spun around the Maxwell millions. Buried under the smokescreen of a low-level agent-running operation codenamed 'Malvolio', Nathan Zamir, former Director of Illegal Operations, had created a powerful service within a service, accountable to no one and, of course, completely self-financing.

With Danny's breaking his contract, when they had cast him out into the Diaspora, and the ever-growing trail of high-profile financial crimes, Arieh had been tasked with locating Danny Davidov and stopping him 'by whatever means', which was a euphemism used in Direct Action terminology to mean the final sanction. The CIA used the term 'with extreme prejudice'. It meant Davidov was as good as dead.

Reuven Arieh's problem was, as Jardine had presumed, that the Malvolio group, being in itself illegal and unauthorized, was not only unable to bring the considerable power of the whole Mossad into play, they were wetting themselves in case the wise men who ran the Israeli intelligence community got wind of their own crime.

By twenty minutes before five, they were both tired.

Jardine stretched and said, 'Let's take a walk. Shall we have a look at Venice . . .?'

'Is it safe?' she asked.

'We risked it last night.'

'Last night I didn't care.' She lowered her head and glanced at him shyly.

And Jardine told her what Hassan had said. It was never safe in their business. But it might still be nice to see just a bit of Venice.

So Alisha stepped out of his blue cotton shirt, and ran a shower, which they shared. Round about 6.30, they emerged from the Gritti into the Campo Santa Maria Zobenigo, and if Alisha noticed the five watchers – two student types, boy and girl, a Moroccan bead-seller and a squat Middle European type wearing a suede coat with green lapels and a Tyrolean hat – she gave no indication.

She could hardly have missed, several miniature footbridges and narrow canals later, the same squat European, browsing over a stall of second-hand books outside a tiny, grimy bookshop at the entrance to the Campo Manin, a quaint little square on the way to the Rialto. Just as they had passed the bookshop, Jardine said, 'Oh, just a minute.' And he turned back, picking up a dusty book, and glanced cursorily through it.

She did not miss him reaching across the man in the suede coat with a '*Scuse* . . .' to replace the book in a different part of the stall.

And when he rejoined her, she slipped her arm through his, and as they strolled on, she murmured, 'Passed it all on, I see . . .'

David Jardine smiled. 'I didn't want to leave it in our room.'

And by the time they had found a bar, in a narrow street by the Ponte dei Assassini, the Bridge of Assassins, it was 7.25 and Ronnie Szabodo, who took great care of the man who was both his boss and protégé, was sitting in the attic of a damp, dingy, cat-infested building not far from the Rialto Bridge, photocopying the notes of the Pomegranate debrief, her own handwritten copies of Reuven Arieh's most secret diaries, along with her neatly written details of ciphers, sub-agents and operating procedures of Mossad's blackest espionage network in the Middle East.

These he sealed in a Diplomatic Service secure pouch and took, by water-taxi, to the British Consulate, housed in a baroque minor *palazzo* on the Grand Canal. There, he handed the package to the SIS officer in Venice Outstation, a slight, good-looking Scots girl who had been a probationer under David Jardine when he was Deputy Head of Station in Rome, not so many years before. Say about ten. Her name was Kirstie Osborne and there was nothing she would not do to help the man who had nursed her carefully into the business of espionage and had so unselfishly passed on so much of his special tradecraft.

And in answer to very personal inquiries from close friends in the Firm, she had answered, absolutely not, at no time had the big agent-runner with a reputation for naughtiness been anything other than a complete gentleman and easy-going companion.

Thus Kirstie Osborne signed for Szabodo's package and ensured its safe journey to Century House, where it would await collection by David Jardine himself, and no one else, except the sender, Ronnie Szabodo. The clerks in the Dispatch Room at Century held Jardine in great affection, for he never forgot a name or a family problem, and he had that touch of grace which allowed him to get on with anyone, from any Station, without effort. And there would be nobody they would release that secure package to but the man himself.

Round about 10 o'clock, as David Jardine and Alisha strolled hand in hand back towards the Gritti Palace, and she was saying how she felt cleansed, now that she had damaged Arieh's precious secrets, he asked her, 'How did you leave it with Reuven?'

She shrugged, all that was behind her now. 'We did not

see much of each other. This Davidov business meant we had to, because of the need to lure you to Beirut . . .'

'Meaning what?'

'Oh, he'll realize one day I am no longer in town. I think, David, I will go to America. Start a new life, away from all the intrigue of Beirut. All the horror.'

'I thought you revelled in the intrigue. I thought you loved the Lebanon.'

'That was before . . . this. I just want to get away. Not New York. Maybe Santa Barbara. I could work in real estate. Open a chain of beauty parlours. I have some money, you know.'

Surprise me, thought Jardine.

She paused as they entered St Mark's Square. 'Remember we used to go to Florian's? Their hot chocolate, wow . . .'

Jardine never ceased to be amazed at the resilience of the Beirut Lebanese in general, and this lapsed agent of his, there was something about her you just couldn't help liking.

'Would you like one?' he inquired, feeling somehow like some sort of uncle.

'It's too soon. The Institute has agents everywhere. Plus, the delegation will be out on the town.'

Jardine's blood ran cold. 'What delegation?'

'My Foreign Ministry has a cultural delegation here. That's why I chose Venice for our rendezvous. Monsieur Chamman' – Chamman was the Foreign Minister, whom Alisha worked for – 'said I should accompany them, and take a few days off. I had a lot of days off piling up.' She smiled, amused at his discomfiture. 'It would probably not be a good idea for them to see me with you.'

'No,' agreed Jardine, feeling slightly faint.

Later, standing in the window, gazing across the Grand Canal, its lights reflecting on the water, moonlight lending its cold luminance to the darkened room, David Jardine kissed her, and held her head close to his chest, as if he did not want to look into her eyes, as he said, quietly, 'I thought you had an obligation to avenge your father . . .'

You bastard, Jardine, he thought to himself.

'I have given you everything, honestly. You know everything about them that I know.'

She leaned her body against him, her thumbnail making lines on his thigh.

Outside, a gondola slid past, three Japanese tourists sitting on its ornate cushions, taking photos with flashbulbs of the gondolier, while a tinny tape-recorder played 'O Sole Mio'.

'I want you to work for me.' He gently took her hand from his belt. 'I want you to go back there, behave as if nothing has happened.' He held her apart from him and met her gaze. 'Alisha, this is a fucking awful thing to have to ask you. But look how far you've gone, look how you have really started to pay him back. Why not leave Santa Barbara for a while? Get right back in there. Screw the bastard. Not just this Danny Davidov business. The man is vulnerable. So are all of them who took Maxwell's money. Stay inside that group and your feedback to me, to SIS, will ensure your father is avenged every day of every week.' His eyes held hers, unflinching. The only way to win an agent's commitment is to level with them. Tell them why they are so important to you. Well, said Jardine to himself. Second time lucky.

She was thinking, not taking her eyes from his.

'Two hundred thousand pounds. When I come out. Assuming I do.'

So there it is. A price for everything. Even revenge.

Where in God's name was he going to find that sort of money? Aha.

Of course.

The Americans.

And at the same time, up the ante in David Jardine's upward climb to the top table. Above the salt.

'Done,' he replied.

And later, as she got dressed, 'Do you want to stay until morning?'

'No, thank you, David.' Alisha fastened one stocking to her garter belt. 'I will have breakfast with the delegation.

They fly back tomorrow morning.' She slipped into her underwear and smoothed her dress down, glancing at her hair in the mirror. 'They will take our photograph, the cultural group, he'll see it in the Beirut newspapers. So he'll know I was here on government business.'

And she pulled a comb through her hair, kissed him gently on the side of the mouth and picked up her bag as he went to open the door. 'Still Pomegranate?'

Jardine shook his head. 'No. Let's use Mongoose.'

She grinned, and was gone.

Jesus Christ, thought Jardine, I actually think we're back in business. It was only later he noticed two Gritti Palace ashtrays and a hair-dryer were missing.

At an office high up in the World Trade Center, on the twenty-fourth floor, Elmore Williams stood at a window gazing across some rooftops towards the tall office blocks and hotels of Midtown Manhattan.

'Joe, let me make myself clear. This is damned official and I have covered my sweet ass all the way down the line. Are you receiving me . . .?'

Joe Pearce studied his big hands resting on the desk in front of him. 'And all my friends,' he said, 'which thou must make thy friends, have had their stings and teeth but newly taken out . . .'

Williams frowned, watching a helicopter flutter towards the roof of the UN Building, on the East Side.

'Say what?'

Pearce sighed. 'It's Shakespeare, Elmore. That's what.' He reached for a pack of Marlboros, then resisted the temptation. 'Sure I hear you,' he went on, 'Washington's decision has always been final with me. I do what I'm told just like I said I would, when they gave me the badge. So let's get down to business. I am instructed to cooperate. Nobody said I should enjoy it.'

His resentment was almost tangible.

Williams turned back from the window. He stuck his hands in his pockets. 'Joe, can't we just let it go?'

'Hell, Elmore, you have nothing to let go. Breeze into NYC, sucker my office into an expensive operation, that's time *and* money, get a good agent shot. Then tell me, *lie* to me, that it's a goddam official undercover assignment. And make me sweat and then give me that goddam thumbs-up. You know, I have not stopped smoking since?'

Elmore Williams sat down in a green plastic chair, in front of Pearce's desk. He let Joe fix him with one of those real old Paddy-like-the-elephant-never-forgets stares, and tried to talk to the warm man behind the baleful eyes. 'Joe, I apologize. The Director himself gave evidence to the investigating officer, in front of counsel. And the case is closed. Your activity was in question and I investigated it. Thank God the allegations were total bullshit.' He stretched out and tipped the chair on to its back legs, turning his brown eyes on Pearce. 'We do the job, man. That's what we all do.'

Pearce gazed back, like a cussed ram, deciding whether to charge or just chew the cud.

'And', said Elmore Williams, 'we know you would do the same to me, pardner. For you just did shit on me from a *very* great height.'

And as they outstared each other, the two men began to grin.

Joe Pearce slowly shook his head. 'Damn lucky your daddy the Head Man has a strong umbrella . . .'

And they began to laugh. Elmore hauled himself from the chair and offered his hand.

Joe Pearce had the cool, dry grip of a silver-back gorilla (one had once shaken hands with Elmore at the Zoo. It was something you never forgot). 'So how much did that little ruckus cost the taxpayer?'

'Relax, man, they would only have built another goddam road, or a hospital.'

The broad Irishman lifted the pack of Marlboros from his desk and dropped it in the trashcan. 'So how's Martha?'

'Recovering day by day. Melanie's back at school. Some fancy rock star wrote on her plaster, you'd think I done her a goddam favour.'

Pearce nodded, thoughtful. 'All right. I got a theory about who tried to waste you.'

'Same guys who rubbed out Harry Cardona?'

Silence.

'Joe?'

Joe Pearce gazed wistfully at the pack of cigarettes in the trashcan. 'You ever heard of a Sicilian lowlife name of Cagliaro . . .?' he asked.

And 4183 miles to the east, on a small, rocky island in the Tuscan Archipelago which lies between Italy's north-west coast and Corsica, the fruits of the Italian State's vigorous war against the Mafia were held in a prison built from an ancient, fortified monastery and catacombs dug deep into and under the rocks.

Conditions were spartan but comfortable, for most of the prisoners had not yet come to trial, nor would they, for several years. Only their closest family – wife, mother, son, daughter, brother, father – were permitted infrequent visits. And their legal counsels. No one else.

The arrest of Don Giovanni Favorito Noto had been inevitable, and some said he had arranged his capture to avoid the tightening net as Sicily spewed up more informers by the week. And rumour had it that the Carabinieri and the Anti-Mafia Squad would have been less than grief-stricken had he been killed while resisting arrest.

The taking of the Prince of Death had made headlines around the world. Elmore Williams had seen footage on CNN. And on this particular day, just under two weeks since his being remanded by an examining judge to *il buco*, the dump, Don Giovanni was seated on a wooden kitchen chair on the ramparts of the oldest part of the monastery, having his hair cut by the owner of a chain of restaurants in Naples and Manhattan.

He would not have wished to embarrass the man, a

person of some social standing, but no minor hoodlums were incarcerated on the Isola di Cioccioli, Snake Island, and the *capo di tutti capi* was required to keep himself looking respectable.

Two of the guards approached. They were from a Carabinieri paratroop unit, they were armed at all times and never moved around on their own.

'*Scuse, Don Giovanni,*' said the young sergeant, with a lean, earnest, relentless face, '*qui il suo avvocato, Signor Cagliaro . . .*' Here is your lawyer.

And Franco Cagliaro arrived, having climbed the many stone steps without becoming short of breath. He stepped past the guards, ignoring them completely, and without trace of embarrassment bowed to his godfather and kissed the proffered hand, an ancient Sicilian blasphemy which meant the Mafia came even before the Church.

'Don Giovanni, would you like me to finish this another time?' asked the wealthy restaurateur and made (and with the latest crackdown possibly unmade) man.

Noto waved him away, and as combs and sheet and clippers and moist scented towel were hastily gathered up and the man made himself scarce, Don Giovanni rested both his hands on his knees and gazed out across the sea, towards Corsica.

He breathed in deeply, slowly, and exhaled, taking his time.

'I require by law to speak to my client in private,' said Cagliaro to the two soldiers. They nodded, and turning in unison, strode away in step.

Cagliaro waited to be spoken to.

After a few minutes, when he seemed to be listening to the cries of the seagulls, Noto said, 'You look strained, Franco. Maybe a few years of this would calm you down . . .' and he wheezed a kind of laugh. As much, anyway, as you would expect from a Prince of Death.

Cagliaro smiled, which meant, look, I'm amused.

So they talked about this and that, about the government case against Noto, about the thirty-one charges of murder and conspiracy to murder they had filed. And about the day-to-day running of Giovanni Favorito Noto's 1000-million-dollar business, which stretched from Palermo to San Francisco, Argentina and the Philippines.

The everyday chores dealt with, Noto relaxed once more. At no time did he suggest that Cagliaro might take the weight off his feet.

'Tell me, Franco,' said Favorito Noto, to the man who called himself Cagliaro, 'about those Jews who robbed the *banco*. Tell me again . . .'

So Cagliaro, while spreading butter on his toast, inclined his head. 'Of course, *padrone*,' he replied, and for the third time in as many weeks recounted the tale of Danny Davidov and Nikolai Kolosov's coup in getting into the special vault of the Banca di Calabria and substituting real wealth for fake.

Giovanni Favorito Noto listened patiently, occasionally popping a strawberry into his mouth, occasionally toying with the solid platinum .45 bullet which hung from a silver chain around his neck.

And when Cagliaro had finished his tale, Don Giovanni gazed at three of the young paratrooper guards, silhouetted against a wall on the other side of the precipitous bay. Waves tumbled around the rocks far below.

For a full minute there was silence, then he said, 'And tell me about our Vietnamese. Grandfather Nghi and the son of his son.'

So Cagliaro rehearsed once again the nature of the deal he had struck with Davidov and the Russian. And because Il Grupo's intelligence service was very good, he had learned that their real names were not the ones they had given.

But because the two scoundrels' security procedures were impeccable, Cagliaro and Favorito Noto believed them to be called Bannerman and Rudnitsky.

Anyway, when Cagliaro got to the visit of the two to Max Eidelman's rare bookshop, Giovanni Favorito Noto held up a hand. He touched his chin with the platinum bullet. A sure sign he was about to come up with an idea. And some of his ideas were quite original.

Then he smiled.

Cagliario found himself interested.

'Don Giovanni . . .?' he ventured.

'What did you say would happen if they lost the Viets?'

Cagliaro poured some coffee from a big vacuum flask the restaurateur had left. He passed a cup to Favorito Noto. 'I said I would have them skinned.' He put the pot down and reached for the sugar. 'I made it clear that was not a mere figure of speech.'

Favorito Noto's smile grew. He nodded sagely. 'You know, Franco, these guys are far too fuckin' rich. Who do they think they are?'

'My exact sentiments, *padrone*.'

'And they know you mean it? About skinning them?'

'Oh, yes. I would skin them alive.'

It occurred to the Mafia boss that Cagliaro would probably prefer that to having the forgers returned safely.

Giovanni Favorito Noto gazed at the roof of a small chapel about 300 yards from the razor-wired ramparts. Then he glanced at his wristwatch. Cagliaro realized he was checking it for sentries, timing their shifts. Don Giovanni had not survived by accident.

'So they must be so scared they can't shit.'

'I guess . . .' Cagliaro had a vague presentiment of what Don Giovanni was about to suggest.

'Suppose the Viets do disappear . . . How much would it take to persuade you *not* to skin them?'

Cagliaro looked so disappointed that Giovanni Favorito Noto actually patted his hand.

'How much?' he repeated. 'Mmmm?'

'Don Giovanni . . .' Cagliaro shrugged, robbed of some sport. 'I guess all they have, to keep their skins.'

'Yeah, leave them with something. They kind of amuse me.'

'*Si, padrone . . .*' Cagliaro made a quick mental calculation. 'I figure 300 million would leave them with some small change.'

Don Giovanni Favorito Noto's smile became positively beatific. He nodded, and wiped his mouth with a pristine white linen napkin.

'So do that, Franco. Between you and me, maybe we're gonna need that kind of money . . .'

Spring sunlight glinted off the tarnished wall of once so-modern glass that was Century House, in South Lambeth.

Up in the spacious office of 'C', Chief of the Secret Intelligence Service, Steven McCrae sat behind his desk, an impressive antique, which, in the first flush of being given the top job – he had previously been Director (Planning) – some three years before, he had moved in from his William and Mary country house in Northamptonshire. And he had let it be known that the desk was his gift to the Office, for the use of future 'C's. The boss's small attempt at achieving immortality, as David Jardine had described it, in the canteen. And his only hope, he had thought, to himself.

'This new building project is very important to me, David.' McCrae was tamping Dunhills Standard Mixture into an ancient Meerschaum pipe, with the face of somebody one should know, like Wolfgang Amadeus Mozart or Garibaldi, carved on the bowl.

'I didn't know you smoked a pipe, Steven,' said Jardine, as he strolled around the spacious office, examining sporting prints and framed photographs of various events in the Chief's career.

There was Steven with Prince Charles, Steven with the Prime Minister, Steven with other Heads of Service, like the CIA and the Colombian DAS.

That amused Jardine. Steven McCrae had been to Sicily once in his life, for three days, accompanying an official visit by a junior defence minister. There was a clean space where the photo of McCrae with the Head of the French DGSE had been, which meant Steven must have been tipped the man was about to be fired.

Steven Beaming at the Side of Margaret Thatcher came

and went, depending upon who was coming to the boss's office.

One could tell plenty about British secret politics by reading Sir Steven McCrae's walls.

Jardine paused to gaze at a photograph of McCrae's two sons, one in his last year at Marlborough, the younger one at Eton. Then he moved on. McCrae was holding a long match over the bowl of his pipe, puffing manfully. But he had packed in far too much tobacco, too tightly, and the stuff failed to ignite.

'Would you like me to get Ronnie up here to give you a course of instruction?' asked Jardine innocently, and he finally sat down, facing the boss.

McCrae laid his Meerschaum on the desk, waved the match out and dropped it into his wicker wastepaper basket.

'David, I have riffed through your report.'

Riffed. How spiffing of you, thought Jardine. I hope you didn't strain yourself.

'And I'm impressed.'

Sing, choirs of angels.

'That's nice.'

'No, really. You were absolutely right to go.' Meaning, there have been some questions about the wisdom of your trip. 'And I shall be passing on the relevant couple of items to the Secretary, when I breakfast with him tomorrow.'

The relevant *couple* of items. Riffed from nineteen pages. Jardine smiled politely as he wondered if anyone had ever actually attacked the Chief as he sat so smugly behind his eighteenth-century desk of glowing oak and faded green leather.

'We aim to please,' he murmured mildly.

'Now, I've been glancing at your list of subscribers. Is this a draft?'

Subscribers, in SIS parlance, were those departments or individuals, internal and in other areas of government, like the Foreign Office, the Cabinet Office, the Treasury, the Security Service or the Ministry of Defence, who needed to know selected items of secret intelligence, in order to function and to make plans for the future. The more sensitive the information, or the more delicate its source, the more limited the list of subscribers would be – in some cases perhaps just one person. A standard, joke classification was 'Eat Before Reading – Distribution: Nil'.

'No, it's not a draft, Steven.'

'And has it gone out?'

'I thought it would be courteous to run it past you and D-Plans. Since it contains a view from inside the Russian Service which runs contrary to current thought.'

'Did you canvass a broad section of opinion from the toilers at Yasenevo?'

A thin line of smoke had begun to hover just above Steven McCrae's wicker wastepaper bin.

'I did not "canvass" anyone. My Moscow report is based on confidential disclosures, real secret intelligence if you like, by a limited number of senior Russian Intelligence executives.'

'Your distribution list . . .' McCrae sucked at his lifeless pipe. 'Cabinet Office, Foreign Office, Defence Intelligence, GCHQ, for God's sake. I'm mildly surprised you have not included the Prime Minister.'

Jardine watched the smoke begin to seep from other parts of the basket.

'Pencil him in. Good idea.'

McCrae pushed one blue folder open and turned a few of the nineteen pages. Eventually he glanced up and sighed, as if he were a headmaster with a particularly troublesome boy. 'I mean, what this says, quite clearly, is that SIS is making a big mistake, taking resources away from operations inside the former Soviet Union, reducing the budget – I think the word you use is "slashing", mmm? – and taking the view that with the collapse of Communism and the disintegration of the Warsaw Pact, Moscow and its federated countries no longer present a serious threat.'

'That's absolutely right. The pragmatic view their intelligence community is taking is that what they call the Red–

Brown coalition will usurp Yeltsin and the so-called democrats before too long. Certainly within a year.' Jardine ran his index finger along the bridge of his nose, 'Leaving them with all kinds of nuclear goodies, still targeted against America's Eastern Seaboard and, of course, what we laughingly call Great Britain.'

'Be that as it may, David, is it helpful to go around . . . rubbishing the Service like this?' McCrae leaned back in his leather swivel-chair, oblivious to the wraiths of smoke now filling the wicker basket, ominously not rising, but spilling around the edge, like a witch's cauldron. 'I mean, what makes you think you know better than the teams of experts who decide such things?' It was the look of pained constraint on his face that inclined Jardine to let the basket go up in flames, any time now.

'With humble reverence and . . . galactic respect, Steven, I am actually one of those experts. Though I blush even to use the word, it's a fact of life. It's what I'm paid for. My first-hand information from the Russian Service itself is that the old guard, the ousted Communists and Russian nationalists and the Red–Brown coalition are nowhere near to being a spent force. Yeltsin is on a slippery balancing act. There are three things keeping him in power – popular support, his incredible infiltration of his enemies' most secret conspiracies, and the Western Alliance.'

David Jardine felt disloyal, withholding as he was the startling results he had obtained from the developing and deciphering of the murdered Elena Constantinovna's matchbook. There could be little doubt that the 'Red–Brown coalition', which had just crept into intelligence jargon, replacing 'military–industrial complex' as the latest vogue collective expression for pro-Communist dissidents, was merely an inert mass, merely potentially explosive, but that the hitherto unknown Staraya Zemlya militant faction led by the mysterious Oleg Kouzmine was the very detonator it required to blast Russia back a half-century. And the rest of the world with it.

Just a little longer, David, he thought to himself. Keep your powder dry till you muster the Americans behind you. Just a few more days and that place back in the power-house will be thine.

A dreadful way to think? To behave? Of course, but one of David Jardine's saving graces was that he did actually know what a dreadful man he was. God knew, the taxpayer had benefited from just that quality more than a few times over the years.

Steven McCrae sniffed, like a hound dog, his nose up, frowning.

'I think your wastepaper basket is on fire,' said Jardine, mildly and with some reluctance. And the conversation continued as the two men used an Afghan kilim to smother the beginnings of conflagration.

'In my estimation,' said McCrae, 'also the Foreign Minister's . . . and the Cabinet's, David, those three factors will be sufficient. Let us limit our report to that, can we? God, what a mess.' This last sentiment referred not to international affairs, but to the ash and smoke now permeating the room.

'Do you know what General Zemskov said to me?' remarked Jardine. '"*What* Western alliance?" With the dismemberment of Bosnia, the West is indeed a paper tiger. Grim, powerful elements, Steven . . .'

Crouched kneeling on the carpet, holding the kilim wrapped tightly around the basket, Jardine was reminded of the suffocation of the princes in the Tower. Or the witches in *Macbeth*.

'. . . with programmes for the revival of Communist totalitarianism, have been watching. And they have access to nuclear intercontinental delivery. European military power is considered to be a sham. America is in the grip of an administration which, if Philadelphia was nuked – this is Zemskov talking, Steven – would demand an imposition of sanctions on the import of Stolichnaya and Russian dolls . . . And what do we do? Put Russia on the back-burner and cut our intelligence budget more drastically than anyone would believe. I mean, what do they need a KGB for? We've done the bloody job ourselves.'

There, he had as good as told Steven everything but the man's name.

'Dearie me. You old Cold Warriors. Can't you see the future is different from the past? God, the entire room could have gone up, remind me to stop smoking this damn pipe.' Coughing, the room now hazy with burnt wicker and paper smoke, Steven McCrae opened a window and breathed deeply.

'So much for Property Services' smoke alarms,' commented Jardine. 'Steven, I do urge you to take note of this. There could be more. I have some, um, some people researching deeper.' Jardine smiled, and met McCrae's gaze. 'I think, um, watch this space, mmm?'

Now Jardine didn't feel too bad. He could not have done much more. Apart from actually telling the man what he knew, of course.

McCrae pushed a switch on his intercom and spoke briefly to his PA, then sat on the window-ledge and gazed at Jardine in such friendly fashion that for a moment David Jardine wondered if the tape Reuven Arieh had played, back there in the hills of Lebanon, might have been a fake.

'Don't push this favoured son bit, David,' McCrae said mildly. 'Our friends at court are changing. Younger men at the helm. Look, just tone it down, there's a good chap. No point in ruffling too many feathers all at once. Believe me. Maybe one day, you too will appreciate the view from here.'

Jardine watched Steven McCrae with something approaching fascination. It was rumoured the Chief kept a copy of Machiavelli in his desk drawer. To hint to a subordinate whom one had already marked for oblivion that he might succeed the Prince, was that devious or what?

'I will not tone it down,' he said, cautiously, 'but I could redraft it so that the reader will imagine the conclusion has sprung from his own precious intellect.'

The door opened and two PAs and a janitor came in, bristling with fire extinguishers. Sir Steven waved a hand at the mess of Afghan rug, burnt wicker and charred paper.

He and Jardine waited until the detritus had been swiftly and efficiently removed. The door closed. Overhead, the noise of an airliner, scoring its way upwards, departing from London.

David Jardine wished he was on it. To his surprise Steven McCrae flopped down happily in his leather chair, swivelling to meet Jardine's eyes. 'Excellent,' he commented. 'Now, *that*'s what SIS is about, David. We dish up the information. Others can make a balls of the interpretation. It's how we survive.'

I'm really glad to hear, sport, what SIS is all about, thought Jardine. It's been worth waiting twenty-two years for.

'Forgive me, but I feel obliged to put this on record, Steven.' David Jardine affected an expression of gravitas, of concern for the Office and all that it stood for. 'This report indicates clearly that at least one of your senior officers, my very humble self, considers that a wheel might yet come off. In the former Soviet Union. And my advice to you, unsolicited though it might be, is that this service puts very clearly on record that we did, um, indicate the possibility. Even if they do bugger-all about it.'

Steven McCrae nodded. He turned his chair tentatively this way and that, as if it too might erupt in flames.

'An excellent point, David. Thank you for that.' He glanced at an ormolu clock on the corner of his desk. The message being his time was precious. 'Anything else we should talk about?'

'I should perhaps pay a visit to the States. Catch up with Langley.'

Steven McCrae looked visibly relieved. He closed the blue folder and pushed it across the desk to Jardine.

'*Vaya con Dios,*' he said. Which meant, in this particular case, please God, just go away.

'Thank you,' replied David Jardine, and he rose, crossed to the door, smiled politely and left the Chief sitting like Hamlet's ghost, in a fading mist of grey smoke.

And while Jardine prepared the ground for a vital visit, for both the US economy and his own stagnant career, to Washington, DC, Max Eidelman subjected the Abraham Lincoln letter to every conceivable test and it passed all of his professional and scientific criteria. More important, his years of experience in the business of authenticating rare documents amidst a plethora of forgeries told him, gave him a gut feeling, that here was a single page from a draft of the Constitution, in the most illustrious President's own hand.

So when Danny Davidov and Nikolai Kolosov returned to his cluttered Madison Avenue bookshop, on the fifth floor, they expressed excitement and delight. Eidelman valued the document at around two hundred thousand dollars and he was pleased when Rudnitsky, as he believed Kolosov to be called, said he had no wish to sell, but would pay Max, the Abraham Lincoln guru, for a professional authentication.

When they emerged back out into Manhattan, Danny was bubbling over with satisfaction. 'Those goddam Viets, Nikky,' he remarked – he had taken to calling Kolosov 'Nikky' again, ever since the Russian's ninety-eight-word conversation – 'we can do this. We can make this thing work.'

Kolosov nodded, 'I too believe so,' he said. And the thing they had been planning for two years, even during the eight immaculate and very profitable scams, in places as disparate as Tokyo, Rome, Thailand, St Petersburg and Palermo, was finally under way.

And at Rome's Leonardo da Vinci Aeroporto, on Italy's west coast, three men boarded TWA Flight 142, bound for Miami. Travelling first class.

They were Franco Cagliaro and his two bodyguards.

12

Chilli Dogs

ALAN CLAIR WAS one of David Jardine's oldest friends. Together they had operated, Clair on behalf of the CIA, Jardine for the British Service, at the sharp end of the espionage game for more years than either cared to remember. They had first met in the Foreign Correspondents' Club in Hong Kong, the first week of 1968, in the company of the redoubtable *Daily Express* correspondent Donald Wise, who was spending a couple of well-earned days away from the Vietnam war, where he was among those few journalists who actually went up-country to cover the fighting as it was happening, instead of dreaming up stories around some hotel bar.

Jardine was operating under black cover, as a field worker for an international children's charity. Clair was using the name George Clegg and had impeccable credentials from a major US aeronautical engineering corporation.

Twenty-eight days later, they had bumped into each other in Saigon, in the apartment of a freelance journalist on an assignment for the *Reader's Digest*, Peter Anthony, a tall, amiable Bostonian who was renting a spacious pad from a French doctor who had gone to work in a French colony in the South Pacific.

There had been about ten people at the small drinks party. Peter was playing Chopin on the stereo system, which made a change from the ubiquitous Doors and Led Zeppelin numbers playing in many of the bars and cafés in Saigon at that time. It had not taken Jardine, on his first black operation, long to figure out that almost everyone in the apartment had a certain ... individualism, touched by that air of quiet confidence which one operator recognizes in another. He had been invited there by a hoary old war correspondent from a quality London daily paper, who was to be his point of contact with SIS in case of sudden emergency. And just as the twenty-five-year-old David Jardine, calling himself David Crawford, was working out the common factor between everyone, male and female, at Peter Anthony's relaxed drinks party, he realized Alan Clair was watching him with a quiet smile.

Nothing needed to be said. They raised their glasses across the room in a toast to future friendship and pragmatic cooperation.

Later the same evening, at a fairly boozy supper with most of the folk who had been at Anthony's place, at a quiet Vietnamese restaurant called Je Reviens, at Hoc Mon, on the northern outskirts of the city, Alan Clair had given Jardine his card – which small act did not pass unnoticed by his craggy and apparently pissed mentor, holding forth at the far end of the table.

Clair mentioned he had hitched a ride north with a USAF C-130 transport aircraft, to Hue, where he planned to spend Tet, the Lunar New Year festival. He told Jardine where he would be staying – the Tran Phuong Hotel. 'A quiet little place, old French colonial, built round a courtyard. Run by the same family since the Japs left in 1946.'

Jardine had said he could think of no special reason to visit Hue. And Alan Clair had smiled and, after a moment, murmured that the place could probably use a visit from a worker with a children's charity. Who knows, he had said, maybe your Head Office might benefit from such a trip.

The next day, Jardine had taken advice, not on a hunch, from his controller, but from Dan Richards, his for-special-occasions-only gruff old war correspondent.

'I would go. If somebody from the Company offered me the hint,' said Richards.

'So I'll go, then.'

Richards, 'the Bishop', as he was known to his colleagues in the newspaper business, had nodded his great leonine head. 'But I wouldn't ask permission from the drapers' clerks, dear boy. Just turn up.'

Jardine had understood him to mean the desk officers at Century House, via Hong Kong Station, where his controller worked out of HMS *Tamar*, the naval base at Kowloon.

It took him only a minute's thought before he had said, fine. And wondered, should I book in at a different hotel? No, he reckoned. If we're at the same place, people won't think it odd when we have a drink together, and a quiet chat.

In fact, mused David Jardine as he walked with his courteous young CIA escort along a corridor of the D-Ops wing at Langley, Virginia, that decision, twenty-five years ago, when he was still wet behind the ears, was probably the most seminal of his career.

On 30 January 1968, Jardine had checked in at the Tran Phuong Hotel, and there he soon caught up with Alan Clair, who bought him a beer and asked if he would like to meet a Hoi Chanh – a defector from the Viet Cong, under the Chieu Hoi Program.

Jardine had said, why not, if it would be of assistance to Help the Children, and Clair had taken him to a small CaoDai temple, where the defector was being hidden by some priests.

There, the young spy had listened as the Hoi Chanh had talked, giving Clair details of a plan which had been hatched the previous July at the funeral in Hanoi of General Nguyen Chi Thanh, military commander of the Central Office for South Vietnam, who had died of cancer. The highest North

Vietnamese commanders had agreed to launch a military offensive against towns and cities the length and breadth of American-supported South Vietnam. One hundred and sixty thousand Viet Cong and NVA (North Vietnamese Army) had been rehearsing and carrying out recon for months. The attacks would commence at 04.00 on Tet, which was to say, in fourteen hours' time.

When they left the temple and climbed into Clair's four-wheel-drive Peugeot pick-up, Alan Clair had been silent for a while, then he had asked David Jardine what he thought of the reliability of the defector and his story.

'I believe him,' Jardine had replied without hesitation.

'Yeah, me too.' And a thoughtful Alan Clair had dropped Jardine at the hotel and driven off, apologizing for inviting the Englishman all that way and now having to leave him to his own devices. But David Jardine understood the man had plenty to do in a short space of time. He had glanced enviously at the pump-action Remington and the folded-stock Armalite M-16, on racks close to the driver, then he shook hands and they parted, fully expecting to meet up later.

Jardine had gone directly to an SIS contact – the only SIS contact – in Hue, an ex-SAS major, aged about fifty-five, who ran a telex facility for local businessmen, Vietnamese, French and Australian.

There they had swiftly encoded a message, then using a one-time pad, had reduced it to a cipher of five-figure groups and sent it by relatively secure radio link to the British Embassy's SIS Station in Saigon, authenticating it and grading it A-1 reliability.

Jardine assumed Clair would be doing likewise, with the difference that Vietnam was America's war, not Britain's, and while there was no way to avoid the inevitable, the response of the General Staff to the CIA officer's most immediate intelligence might blunt the onslaught and avert catastrophe.

But by 1968, US military commanders in Saigon were inundated with a constant flow of intelligence from the

CIA, and not all of it had proved to be accurate. Whatever the reason, Alan Clair's strenuous efforts over the next fourteen hours were not taken all that seriously by the military and political operational staffs, except that a two-line digest warning of increased Viet Cong activity in urban areas was scheduled for publication in a routine Intel Update, due out at the end of that week.

The rest, as they say, is history. At four the next morning, over 100 South Vietnamese and US urban installations were attacked, catching the defenders off-guard, but, after a week's heavy street and house-to-house fighting, the cost to the NVA and Vietcong was later admitted to have been in excess of 40,000 dead. Its political importance was, however, immense and it was at that point that the American administration realized – in secret – that this was a war they were not going to win.

Hue was hard-hit. The fighting there lasted much longer than down-country and the city was under siege for weeks. The Tranh Phuong Hotel became a principal battleground, being occupied now by Viet Cong, now by US Marines, then by South Vietnamese Ranger commandos, who were dislodged by a company of Viet Cong special troops, the Dac Cong, before, battered and windowless, it was abandoned to its littered rubble of bricks, slates, dead fighters and spent shell-cases. The sickly-sweet smell of death and cordite had permeated even Jardine's jeans and torn, sweat-stained bush-shirt.

On the first day of Tet, he had been led by the owner of the hotel and his wife to the French Consulate, which was as safe a haven as the city had to offer, and from the roof, Jardine, the French diplomats and a few of the bolder Western journalists had watched the panoply of desperate urban warfare all around them.

When the siege was finally lifted, David Jardine had looked around for Alan Clair, but nobody among the US military seemed to have heard of him.

It was not until Jardine arrived in Hanoi, on behalf of Help the Children, that he spotted the American one lunchtime, strolling past the Lao Dong Party headquarters, deep in conversation with a local Party official and the anti-war American actress Jane Fonda.

Doubtless the CIA man was using yet another name and another legend, and Jardine had ignored him.

Two years on, they had been working on illegal operations in Berlin, and the way these things go, had been properly introduced and officially tasked to cooperate. They had worked against a network of Soviet agents who had penetrated the Federal German Security Service in West Berlin. At the end of the job, both men had been promoted.

Now, twenty years on, Clair hadn't changed much. His thick, tousled hair was no longer sandy, his face had a score more lines on it, but the eyes behind the rimless glasses still had that mix of steely toughness, wisdom and, of all things, kindness.

'David, come on in. How you doin'?'

'Ducking and weaving. Situation normal . . .'

They gripped hands. Alan Clair examined his friend's face. He nodded, as if, like some Redskin medicine man, he had read all that had transpired in David Jardine's world to bring him here.

'I hear you were in town a few weeks back. Why didn't you call, you rat?' Clair said, as he handed a can of Budweiser beer to Jardine.

'I was going to.' Jardine sat down on a couch, in a corner of the office, with a window to his left. On one wall was a big map of the world, on another, framed cartoons by various US newspaper and magazine political artists. And on the unpretentious grey metal and plastic desk, a wooden name-piece, with 'Alan T. Clair. Director. Department of Operations', in white letters.

DD-Ops was the top job in the clandestine area of CIA activity. It was also the hot seat, for more Directors of Operations had taken the rap for the Agency, and even for US Presidents, than any other appointment in the intelligence community.

'Yeah, I also hear you left in kind of a hurry. Don't tell me you've been playing in the traffic, at your age.'

'What do you expect? Committees can be a pain in the ass.'

Clair tugged the ring-pull from his beercan. 'So how was Moscow?' he smiled, watching Jardine. 'I will not even ask about Beirut . . .'

David Jardine was not surprised the CIA man knew he had been to Beirut, the Agency had watchers at all Mid-East airports. Whether or not Clair knew about Alisha and the Reuven Arieh gambit depended on how much Mossad had felt like communicating to Langley. Jardine's hunch was, in this instance, zero.

'Moscow was interesting.'

'You figure they're out of the woods? You think maybe the Red Menace is a thing of the past?'

'I think there could be a problem with that.'

Jardine opened his tan leather briefcase, a scuffed and worn item that had been to too many strange places. He extracted a pale pink folder and from it slid a ten-by-eight black and white photograph. It was a surveillance photo of Danny Davidov, taken five years before, in Cyprus.

He placed it on Clair's desk. 'Check it out.'

Alan Clair gazed at the photo, tilting his bifocals to get a better focus. After a while he looked up, and shook his head.

'Can't say that I make the guy.'

'He was Mossad. Daniel Davidov, Grade Four operations man. Mainly Europe and Mediterranean Arab states.'

Clair pushed the photo around and looked at it again.

'So that's Danny Davidov,' he said, nodding.

'What've you heard?'

'The man is buried in Tel Aviv. But he's not. The Institute gave him a new identity and kicked him out of Israel.'

So the US taxpayer was getting something for his money.

'You know why?'

'All they would say was something to do with money.'

That's what I like about the oldest and best friends, thought David Jardine, they never forget if you work for a different government.

'I hear Robert Maxwell.'

Slight pause. Alan Clair reflected. Then he nodded. 'Yep. Me too.'

'And take a look at this. Tell me if it rings a bell.' Jardine handed Clair a file marked 'Secret'. It was a chronology of Danny Davidov's growing pattern of international crimes, each one involving some form of counterfeiting. Each one bigger than the one before. His 'footprints'.

Clair read through the file rapidly. He closed it and laid it on his desk. Jardine put it back in his briefcase. Clair nodded. 'Sure, some legal eagle at Treasury has circulated something very similar. She reckons they are going to hit Stateside, figures it's inevitable.'

Hallelujah, thought Jardine. At least I am not trying to convince sceptics.

'Al, can we take a walk in some park?'

This was what they used to say in Berlin, when they wanted a secure environment in the open air, free from possible eavesdroppers.

'You know when he's coming?' asked Clair.

'Not yet. But I believe I know the target. And it could not be bigger.'

Alan Clair was a very busy man. Even in so-called peacetime, the Central Intelligence Agency had hundreds of covert operations ongoing, and thousands of agents, from black agents to agents of influence, to run. He studiously refused to glance either at his wristwatch or at the clock on the wall behind Jardine.

He pushed his chair back and reached for his jacket.

'Anything,' he said, 'for a pal . . .'

And he opened the door and held out his big paw, ushering the tall Englishman out of the office.

They took Clair's dark blue Oldsmobile out of Langley

and drove to Rock Creek Park, where they strolled and rapped in total privacy.

David Jardine told his friend everything he knew about the illegal, as in unauthorized, Reuven Arieh operation, codenamed 'Malvolio II', to find Danny Davidov and stop him before he wrecked US–Israel relations, not to mention their own careers. He explained about the psychological profile, predicting that Davidov was working towards a final coup, to shake the tree of the US economy by threatening the dollar. And that, if he was true to his earlier crimes, he would not destroy the dollar, but merely illustrate that with his superior skill and cunning he had had its fate in his power, then walk away, very seriously wealthy.

'This guy is crazy,' announced Clair.

'You wish,' replied Jardine. 'Davidov is a born criminal, with the advantage that he's been trained in our trade by one of the best intelligence services in the world.'

'Oh, that's just great.'

'How much would the US Government pay? For he will have calculated that, to the last cent.'

Alan Clair paused, and gazed up at the traffic on the Harrisburg Pike.

'You know some guy got out from his car and opened up with an AK-47 on the traffic queuing up at the Langley turn-off?' he said, thoughtfully.

'About a year ago . . .?'

'Yeah.' Clair scratched his ear. 'Kinda makes you think. This country seems to attract all kinds of lunatics.'

He glanced shrewdly at Jardine. 'What else?'

David Jardine listened to the traffic on the highway passing over the gulley. He shrugged. 'I've been building up a dossier. Maybe we can cooperate on this. You see, we're worried too.'

'Because the dollar is the major world currency.' Sure, Alan Clair could see that.

But Jardine shook his head. 'Maybe Davidov's target is not the dollar. Perhaps it's sterling. That's what worries us . . .'

The CIA man nodded, thoughtful. 'David,' he asked, 'How long have I known you?'

'Far too long to ask that kind of question.' Jardine's met the American's gimlet gaze.

'So I say again . . . what else? You have not come all this way to tell me what I already know.'

In the silence, they could hear a woodpecker drilling away at one of the park's tall redwoods. On the road above them an ambulance, siren whooping, wove its way through the heavy traffic.

David Jardine took a Winston cigarette from its pack and offered one to Clair. Clair shook his head. Jardine put the cigarette in his mouth and lit it, using the brass Zippo, cupping the flame in his hands.

Finally, he exhaled and said, 'We think it's two people. And more sinister forces might be manipulating them.'

Ah . . . Alan Clair seemed to remember the Treasury memo suggesting more than one man was behind the Davidov crimes. A taller man had been seen. But computer ID kits, from St Petersburg to Bogota, had failed to come up with a name.

'Who? What sinister forces? You mean the Islamics?'

Extremist Islam had replaced the Commies in the CIA's lexicon on *bêtes noires*.

'We're not one hundred per cent sure, just yet.'

Alan Clair appreciated his friend's star was no longer in the ascendant, word got around. And if David could find an edge, who would blame him? However, not even good old buddies were going to fuck around with Uncle Sam's precious currency.

'There's somebody we should talk to,' he said. 'Let me make a couple of phone calls.'

Which is how, forty-two minutes later, David Jardine and Alan Clair were sitting in the functional, almost spartan, office of the US Treasury's Legal Counsellor charged with liaison with foreign law enforcement and intelligence agencies – Nancy Lucco.

*

Somebody was practising on the trumpet, the other side of Jackson Heights, the Colombian immigrant district in NYPD's 110th Precinct. The funeral tune that Santana had ordered to be played for the American defenders at the Alamo siege. Over and over again. Night and day.

It was a cold, lonely sound. Elmore Williams had slouched so far down in the passenger seat of the unmarked Ford sedan that the back of his head touched the top of the backrest. His partner was Tony Carmino, whose grandfather had arrived in New York from the island of Ischia, in the bay of Naples, in 1936. Tony had been with the 2nd Battalion/101st Airborne Division, which was one of the units that finally lifted the siege of Hue, after the Tet offensive, in 1968. He had made First Sergeant, and had been wounded in a prolonged fire-fight during Operation Somerset Plain, in the south part of the A Shau Valley, against North Vietnamese Army regulars.

Williams had asked for Tony because they had worked together before on tight assignments; he knew he could rely on him when the bullets were needed; and Tony Carmino was now a New York Field Office man, which Elmore Williams hoped might help to cement further a fresh start with big Joe Pearce's outfit.

They were watching a small street-corner bar called Hato Viejo, which presumably meant something to Colombians.

'He's gonna show . . .' said Carmino, who had slouched to just about the same level as Williams.

'Well, bro, if he don't, I can't figure who else we got.'

The Alamo trumpet dirge stopped, then started all over again, for about the seventh time.

'You want a chilli dog?' Elmore asked his partner.

Carmino moved, to ease his cramped legs, and the plastic seat squeaked. 'Sure. I'll get them.'

'Bullshit. I said it first, man.' And Elmore Williams' eyes roamed around the area before he pushed the door open and climbed out.

At that moment, a silver-blue Porsche growled into the street from an intersection up ahead, closely followed by a brown Oldsmobile sedan with four men inside.

'Shit!' 'Shit!' said Williams and Carmino at the same time, and Elmore Williams slipped back into the car.

The Porsche stopped opposite the bar.

Williams and Tony Carmino watched intently.

'It's him,' murmured Williams.

'That's Dino, okay . . .'

A mahogany-complexioned man of about thirty climbed out, with easy agility, from the low-slung sports car. Above average height, he had the chiselled cheekbones and narrow, dark eyes of the Sicilian mountain people, descended from centuries-old Moorish and Calabrian stock. His jet-black hair was worn long and tied behind in a ponytail. He wore a grey herring-bone tweed jacket and a navy silk shirt, open to the chest. A gold neck-chain glinted in the spring sun.

Three of his bodyguards were already on the sidewalk, unobtrusively covering the area, then one, a broad-shouldered man who padded like a big cat, entered the Hato Viejo ahead of his boss.

The driver remained behind the wheel of the sedan, its engine running.

'You know what?' said Elmore Williams.

'What?'

'I sure hope this connection is a big negative. I hope this guy ain't never heard of Franco Cagliaro . . .'

'Yeah. Know what you mean.'

The stakeout on the Hato Viejo bar was the result of a not inconsequential amount of taxpayers' money being spent by detectives from Washington's Homicide Squad, New York Police Department's Intelligence Division and the US Secret Service's Intelligence Division, working out of NYC.

The Secret Service took the abortive attempt on Elmore Williams and his family just as personally as any of the Five Families of Cosa Nostra would have done. An attack on one was an attack on all, and no stone was being left unturned in the search for the men behind the hit.

A Colombian stoolie, in the pay of 110th Precinct Narcotics Squad, had passed on a whisper that the killing of Harry Cardona had been ordered by Franco Cagliaro, more specifically, by Don Giovanni Favorito Noto's right-hand *consejero* and enforcer, Franco Giuseppe Cagliaro, sometime resident of Palermo, Sicily.

Research into prison records had revealed that one Dino Trafficante, doing time for narcotics trafficking and racketeering, had been the late Sammy the Nose's protector in the slammer. The two had been close on account of Sammy had stepped in and taken the rap for a discipline offence in the prison workshop, and had done twenty-eight days in the sweatbox – solitary confinement with dry biscuit and water – which Trafficante should have done.

Hence Dino Trafficante's offer to the Nose: if he could find a buyer, Trafficante would put up to ten million counterfeit dollars, and pay Sammy a handsome commission.

It interested Elmore Williams that Trafficante was hitherto a known cocaine hoodlum, but had offered funny money instead of dope as a reward for services rendered.

Well, Sammy the Nose's good buddy Harry Cardona had found a buyer – the two Secret Service agents Elmore Williams had steered them towards – and the result was the sting that so nearly had gone wrong, resulting in Williams blowing away Sammy and all that followed.

The question now was, did Trafficante's counterfeit dollars come from Giovanni Favorito Noto's Palermo *famiglia*? And if so, was Cardona's murder and probably the hit on Elmore Williams ordered by Restrepo?

Williams felt sweat run down his back. It was not good to have pissed off the Sicilians.

'So do we do it?' Tony Carmino eased the Glock 9-mm automatic in his shoulder-holster, butt-down, held in place by a steel spring clip.

Williams considered. His plan had been to arrest Trafficante on a traffic violation, and produce a computer printout of a few thousand dollars owing for unpaid tickets. Strangely enough, many a hardened and violent criminal had gone meekly to the local precinct house, knowing he did not owe unpaid fines, and knowing his expensive lawyer would have the mistake ironed out in a few minutes.

This approach obviated dangerous exchanges of gunfire, particularly when the target criminal had armed bodyguards. But now, on the point of making his move, Elmore Williams was having second thoughts.

He figured it like this: Dino Trafficante was no stranger to law enforcement heat. Unless his rights were totally violated, and he was taken to a safe house and threatened with very serious stuff, the Sicilian was not going to say Jack Zero. Suddenly the memory of that terrifying morning with bullets shattering his front window and Martha and his beloved daughter Melanie taking lead from those biker hitmen struck him, almost like a shock wave. That's the way shock sometimes works. Days or weeks, months even, after the event.

And finally post-traumatic stress, as the shrinks called it, had caught up with Special Agent Elmore Williams. It affects different people in different ways. Tears, palpitations, dizziness, depression, anti-social behaviour.

In the case of Elmore, he was gripped by a cold and terrible anger. He was more angry with himself, for going through the motions of this investigation into who had ordered the killing of himself and his family, as if it were just another case. Sheltering, he told himself, behind the very commendable rationale that he was a professional, and personal factors should not be permitted to get in the way.

Well, bullshit . . .

In the silence during which this metamorphosis had taken place – and that is precisely what it was – Elmore Williams had remained motionless, watching the bar through narrowed eyes.

'Chief . . .?' said Tony Carmino. 'It's your call. Jerry's waiting.'

Jerry MacBeth was the 110th Precinct Sergeant of Detectives, attached to the Task Force, and it was he who was going to arrest Trafficante on the parking violation. As a matter of fact, by leaving the Porsche where he had, by the kerb near the street intersection, Dino Trafficante had indeed parked illegally.

'Tell Jerry he can take the rest of the day off,' said Williams, in a voice so quiet that Carmino knew this was going to get very bad.

Nancy Lucco made brief, neat notes as David Jardine outlined his researches into the counterfeit scams which he calculated had netted the perpetrators around 600 million dollars.

Warm sunlight filled parts of her inner office in the Washington Secret Service building. She was glad to be on the twentieth floor. Below the twelfth, it was rare to see direct sunlight because of the heights of the other buildings in that part of town.

She felt a degree of satisfaction that the British SIS had also been taking those 'footprints' crimes seriously. Judging from the lack of response to her memo a few weeks back, warning that it was just a matter of time before those guys struck in the USA, nobody in US law enforcement seemed to be very interested.

And Jardine had a name, Danny Davidov. That was good. A professional with years of training in clandestine espionage operations. Very neat. She wondered why Davidov had been fired from Mossad, for neither David Jardine nor the CIA man Alan Clair had felt it necessary to embarrass their Israeli counterparts by spelling out the Robert Maxwell affair.

'. . . if not already here.' Jardine had just said.

Nancy laid down her pen and gazed at him. There was something about the man that seemed kind of . . . familiar. Although he looked nothing like the big Wop she had thought she was going to spend the rest of her life with, and spoke in that not unattractive, slightly laid-back way of his, not too terribly-terribly English, but with undeniable class, something about him did remind her of Eddie.

Maybe it was the way he smiled, self-deprecatingly, when he had said something he particularly wanted her to take note of.

'One thing puzzles me,' she said.

'What's that?' Jardine met her gaze frankly, as if there was nothing in his box of tricks he was not happy to divulge.

'How do you know so much – unless', here she glanced at Clair, 'other US agencies are holding out on the Secret Service regarding this, um, progressively growing series of international crimes . . .'

'Not guilty,' replied Clair, holding up his clean hands.

'So,' continued Counsellor Lucco, 'how do you know all this stuff and we at the Treasury do not? Mmm?'

Not bad, thought Jardine. Many people in her place would have pretended I was telling them nothing new.

'To tell you the truth' – he was amused to see her eyes narrow – 'this information came to us from another case altogether. Um, political stuff. Not for sharing, I apologize about that.'

'If you say so,' Nancy replied drily. And she recognized what it was about him that reminded her of Eddie. This Limey was dangerous.

'Say you're right,' she continued. 'When? When do you think?'

'If they're not already here, any day now . . .'

'And how serious? In your opinion.'

'Danny's aim is merely to get very rich. I've scribbled some figures and I figure the US Treasury would pay up to twenty billion dollars to get him off your back.'

'Billion?' exclaimed Alan Clair.

'Sure.' Nancy nodded. 'We spend that in a night sometimes, buying dollars to keep the market up. But then, David, we would come after him, believe me, we could not permit him to try it twice.'

'David thinks he has a partner, and the simple crime

Danny Davidov is planning might be taken over by others, to wreck the dollar overnight.'

'Who?'

Jardine shrugged. 'I'm working on it, but my resources are limited, I'm afraid. SIS does not have the budget these days . . .'

'Well, we sure as hell have.' Nancy Lucco stared hard at Jardine, trying to work out what he was holding back. She had worked too many New York court rooms not to get the vibes. Which was what he had intended.

'If you're right, this Davidov business could really fuck us.'

David Jardine met her gaze and replied, equally gravely, 'Sideways and upside-down, ma'am.'

Inside the Hato Viejo, Dino Trafficante was standing at the bar, sipping beer and watching the TV set mounted high on the wall. It was showing a bicycle race, with commentary in Spanish. Two of his bodyguards leaned against the wall of the narrow bar, watching the other customers and the two Colombian barmen.

The two bodyguards checked Williams and Tony Carmino the moment they came in. For a start, while Carmino might just have passed for a South American, with his olive complexion and his black wavy hair – he also sported a modest pigtail, in the tight, short style of the bullfighter – there was no way Elmore Williams merged in.

What was not open to question was that both men were cops of some kind. It was there in the way they carried themselves. Like, here were two guys who took no shit and had that great confidence which announced, don't fuck with us, you will only lose.

Trafficante ignored the newcomers, saying something inaudible to the barman, who was also his brother-in-law. Trafficante had married a Colombian girl.

Williams leaned on the bar counter right next to the Sicilian hood, ignoring the bicycle race. His gaze taking in everyone in the place.

Even Tony Carmino was horrified by what his partner did next.

'Hey, pal, you got a light . . .?' Elmore Williams had turned to Trafficante, holding a cigarette to his lips.

Trafficante ignored him.

Oh, Jesus, thought Carmino. Give him a goddam light. He made like he was scratching his lower lip with his right thumb, to facilitate a smooth, downward draw, for the two bodyguards now had eyes for nobody but Elmore and himself.

'Did you hear me, Dino, old buddy, old pal? I asked if you had a mutherfuckin' light.' And Williams thrust his face forward aggressively, trespassing on the Sicilian hood's private space. It's something that never fails to get some kind of reaction, in this case that the two bodyguards as if by magic had a mini-Uzi and a 9-mm Beretta respectively in their hands, cocked and held inches from Elmore Williams' head.

Dino Trafficante, on the other hand, continued to watch the bicycle race, unmoved.

'What is this?' asked Williams of the two armed wiseguys, gazing past the muzzles of their handguns, all innocence. 'Is this a black thing . . .?'

He looked so relaxed, Tony Carmino wondered for a second if Elmore had flipped. His own right hand slid under his coat and touched the butt of his pistol.

'Hey, asshole. Get the fuck away from him.' This from the one with wide shoulders, who padded like a cougar.

'Tell you what, guys. You don't shoot me, my partner will not blow the head off your boss, *capisce*?'

And Tony Carmino's 9-mm Glock was instantly trained, rock-steady, two-handed, a few inches from Dino Trafficante's neck.

'What the fuck do you want . . .?' Trafficante seemed genuinely irritated at being distracted from the TV bicycle race.

Now Carmino understood. This situation, the physical arrangement of the protagonists, was a textbook configuration they used to practise in the close combat gym, during agent training and refresher courses. And while 'on the beach', Elmore had been doing that all day, every day.

Williams had baited the Sicilian bodyguards away from the far wall and into his own space – his own reach. And Tony had the target man in his gunsights, ready to drop.

'We are Federal Agents,' he announced, taking the cue. 'You're under arrest. Drop the guns and lie face down on the floor.'

The two Sicilians exchanged amused glances, just as Williams had guessed they would, and he made his move, using right and left forearms simultaneously to knock the mini-Uzi and the Beretta apart and continue his big hands' forward thrust, fingers rigid-straight to clap their heads hard together, and as their pieces went off, BANG BANG BANG! and BRRRPP!, bullets blasting and ripping around the bar-room, all in the same movement Elmore stepped forward and his hands made talons, gripped each man by the throat in what he called his 'maniac grips', and proceeded to whack their heads together again and again, and even as he had started his moves, Tony Carmino had stepped past, behind him, just the one long stride, jammed his 9-mm Glock hard under Dino Trafficante's jaw and bundled the hoodlum into the corner of the counter and the wall, just beyond him, slugs from the two bodyguards being seriously beaten up by his partner finally stopping, on account of the guns had become empty.

The outside door burst open and the third bodyguard was framed in the doorway, a MAC-10 silenced Ingram sub-machine-gun held ready at his hip. Williams and Tony Carmino fired together, BLA-BLAM! and the guy crumpled where he stood.

Adrenalin coursing through his veins like crack-cocaine, Elmore Williams dropped on one knee, rolled his dazed opponents on to their bellies, and handcuffed them expertly.

Tony Carmino handcuffed Trafficante, hands behind his back, then frisked him and found a 15-shot Sig-Sauer P226

9-mm pistol, in a holster on his right front, butt facing across his body, which indicated he was left-handed.

'You have the right to remain silent, shit-for-brains,' gasped Williams, as the broad-shouldered one started to groan, his left temple and hair wet with blood. The other one just lay there, maybe unconscious, maybe not. From the street outside came the growing wail of approaching sirens.

Williams hauled himself to his feet and, breathing hard, tugged Trafficante roughly by the shoulder, turning him to stare into his eyes. It was a look Carmino had never seen before and, as he remarked later, it sure as hell made the once big Dino Trafficante flinch. Something nobody had seen before.

Trafficante tried to be cool, to collect the shreds of his mister tough guy reputation in front of the other wiseguys in the bar, who were beginning to emerge from underneath tables and far-away corners of the floor.

'Would it have made any difference,' he tried to smile sarcastically, but his nerves got in the way, 'if I had given you the goddam light?'

Elmore Williams seemed to consider this. Then he patted Trafficante's cheek patronizingly.

'Not really,' he said.

Dino Trafficante and the two disarmed and handcuffed bodyguards were handed into the custody of NYPD Sergeant of Detectives Jerry MacBeth (whose real name was Jerzcy, on account of his mother being Polish, but that's another story). MacBeth had not really taken Elmore Williams seriously when the Secret Service man had said he was no longer required on the stakeout, and he had sprinted from his unmarked Ford to the Hato Viejo on hearing the first sounds of gunfire. Which just goes to show how quickly something that seems to last for ever, lasts in real time. For he had arrived just as Dee-Sac Elmore Williams was saying 'not really' to the prisoner Trafficante.

The Sicilian hoods were taken to the 110th Precinct and locked in separate interview rooms. The fact that a joint Task Force was up and running provided Williams with access to the arrested men, subject to the approval of the senior local NYPD officer. That officer was Homicide Lieutenant Don Clancy and he gave his approval with some reluctance, for the story coming out of the Hato Viejo was that the government men had started the whole damn thing.

Also, he had a homicide to investigate – the third Sicilian bodyguard – and he was irritated that Jerry MacBeth, a good detective, was now tied up as Crime Scene Supervisor, over at Washington Heights.

Clancy had insisted on being present during the Secret Service interview with Dino Trafficante. He leaned his backside on a cold central-heating pipe and watched with grudging approval as Elmore Williams and Tony Carmino got to work.

'Okay, Dino,' Williams was saying, 'I guess you must be wondering what made us pick on you . . .'

Trafficante, sitting on a straight-back metal and canvas chair, hands still handcuffed behind his back glowered at the Special Agent.

He did not say a word.

On the way from the scene of the fracas to the Precinct House, Williams had explained to Carmino just how he wanted to play this confrontation. Tony Carmino began to see a cold logic in the violence and confusion of Dino Trafficante's arrest.

'Well, it goes like this. You were in Marion with Harry Cardona.'

'Harry got iced, you know that, don't you?' This from Carmino.

Trafficante gazed back with cold contempt, having recovered his sang-froid.

'And you were the guy put him inside. Tempting him with funny money.'

'I did not,' replied Trafficante, in Italian.

'Hey, come on.' Elmore Williams paced around the straight-back chair. 'The money you passed to him. The counterfeit stuff. Ten million bucks. You know we have your prints on it?'

'I never touched the fuckin' money.'

'Two Samsonite cases, Dino, we know you opened them.'

'Nothing to say.'

'Your prints are on three of the forty-eight parcels.'

'Bullshit.'

'Pal, we have the evidence.' Tony Carmino leaned close to Trafficante, his face real close to the Sicilian's.

'So I take the rap. So what?'

'I also hear you put the contract on Harry, while he was waiting trial in NY State. Why was that? Frightened he would pigeon you?' Williams produced a pack of Camel Lites from his pocket.

'I want a fuckin' lawyer.'

'Say what?'

'I got one phone call. Get my lawyer.'

'Dino, you ain't even under arrest.'

Silence.

Williams lit a cigarette, casting Trafficante a look that hinted he still had not forgiven him for refusing a light.

Clancy studiously ignored the huge NO SMOKING sign above Elmore's head.

Outside in the rubber-tiled, pale green walled corridor, murmur of male voices. Some guys, some cops, laughing. Footsteps. Jingle of keys.

More silence.

'What do you mean?'

'What?'

'What do you mean, I am not under arrest . . .?'

'Why, Dino, we ain't holding you here. At this moment in time. However, you can't just up and leave, because Lieutenant Clancy will shortly be charging you with possessing a concealed firearm, without a permit or lawful cause . . .'

'That's two to ten,' added Clancy, helpfully.

'Then there will be resisting arrest and accessory to attempted murder of a Federal Agent. Twice. There's two of us.'

'Eight to life,' contributed Clancy, who seemed happy to be in on the deal, whatever it turned out to be.

'Then there's accessory to counterfeiting . . .' Tony Carmino relaxed, resting his back against the grey wall.

'And the contract killing of Harry Cardona.'

Trafficante was not the kind of citizen who felt ill-at-ease in a Queens precinct interrogation room. It was like a home from home.

'Yeah, yeah, so do what you have to.' He shrugged. 'If this is leading up to some kind of a proposition, *mangiari stronza*!' which was Sicilian for no fuckin' way.

'Show him,' said Elmore Williams to Special Agent Carmino.

Carmino took a computer printout from his pocket. He held it for Trafficante to read. It was a list of Trafficante's several secret bank accounts. Secret even from the Cosa Nostra.

'Does Don Giovanni know about these . . .?' asked Tony Carmino, softly.

Trafficante lifted his shoulders and sneered. 'You think they worry about stuff like that? We are serious men, *signor*. We do not treat each other like . . . civil servants. Like clerks.'

'Does he know about these . . .?' Elmore Williams tapped a few entries on one of the balance sheets from a bank in the Cayman Islands.

He held the printout sheet so that Trafficante could read it clearly.

'That's US Government money, Dino. It's all regular, accountable, and recorded dollar payments. From the United States Secret Service to you. Look, Account 4088327, Grossischer Bank of Lucerne. Is that in Switzerland?'

Dino Trafficante remained silent. Now he was one worried wiseguy.

'I never took no money from the Feds. This is a frame-up. These are goddam forgeries.'

'But will the brothers in Sicily take the same view? That's what I ask myself. That's the big question, Dino. You want to take the chance? You sure must be in big with the *capo* . . .'

This was the heat the Task Force had always planned to put on Trafficante. The bank printouts were fakes, run up by an agent in the New York Field Office.

Williams had understood that the low-key arrest of Trafficante on a parking violation would not only fail to worry him, it would probably have put him on his guard against just such a move.

But the violence, confusion and humiliation of the bar-room arrest, the gunfire and the fact that one of his bodyguards was lying stiff in the morgue, on the other hand, conspired to convince Dino Trafficante that these men were deadly serious. And if they had been quietly paying funds into his account with the Grossischer Bank, in Switzerland, the Sicilian was not sure how Giovanni Favorito Noto, or his appalling *consigliere* Franco Cagliaro, would react.

For a study of Trafficante had revealed that his two brothers, Aldo and Freddo, had both been murdered, one by Cagliaro, the other, it was rumoured, by Noto himself, one fine morning in a farmyard near Corleone, at breakfast, shot through the head, just after the *becci a morte*. The kiss of death, planted by the *capo*, on both cheeks.

It would have puzzled Williams why the last surviving Trafficante brother still worked for the Mafia, had the Secret Service man not understood that the lust for millions of dollars in cash that attracted capable hoods like Dino to the arms of Don Giovanni and his Sicilians outweighed considerations of *vendetta*.

But the Trafficantes were clearly not the most trusted of Giovanni Favorito Noto's criminal family, and like in one of those old vampire movies, Dino seemed to age right in front of them.

Don Clancy folded his arms. It was nice to watch fellow professionals at work.

After eighty-seven minutes, Dino Trafficante announced they had only made him a fuckin' dead man and he asked if the Witness Protection Program would apply to him.

Elmore Williams said it most certainly would, and while he unlocked the handcuffs, Lieutenant Clancy put two chairs either side of a small table with a microphone and a small tape-recorder on it.

'Man, I'm hoarse,' said Trafficante, meekly. 'Any chance of a glass of water . . .?'

'Sure.' Williams glanced at Tony Carmino, who crossed to the door. 'In the meantime, tell me about the hit on Special Agent Elmore Williams, down in DC. Who ordered that?'

'I only put the package together,' replied Trafficante.

No kidding? thought Williams. It was always good when a lowlife started to sing. The great myth was that it did not happen. Elmore Williams knew it happened plenty. All you had to do was ignore the rules and scare the shit outa them.

'I can see that. Who gave the order?'

Dino hesitated. But Elmore had left the bank printout, which seemed as good as a death warrant, in clear view of the prisoner.

'Franco Cagliaro. He said this guy Williams had made a fool of the Mob, and he needed a lesson.'

'Thank you, Dino,' said Williams, gently.

And as Trafficante met his cold gaze, he somehow knew what his captor was going to say.

'We have not been introduced. *I* am Special Agent Elmore Williams. It's a pleasure, believe me . . .'

It had been four days since Alan Clair had taken David Jardine to the Treasury and introduced him to Counsellor Nancy Lucco. After the first meeting, Nancy had thanked Jardine and had spent the next two hours studying the SIS classified file he had lent her. She was impressed by the cold thoroughness of the British Intelligence Service. It was pretty clear that David Jardine knew much more than even the comprehensive information he had passed to her, about Davidov and his history since being kicked out of Mossad and his death being announced in Tel Aviv, including a funeral service in one of the more obscure plots on the Mount of Olives.

She had an able brain, and if she had been aware that Director Farley considered that in, say, twelve years' time, she might become a candidate for his own job, Counsellor Lucco would have been pleasantly surprised. But not astonished.

So, after four days and three more meetings with the English spymaster, who so disconcertingly reminded her of Eddie Lucco, yet was so very different from the wonderful big Wop cop, Nancy Lucco met Alan Clair in the CIA's Old Vietnamese Embassy office, just a short walk from the Treasury, and told him that number one, Jardine was hiding material evidence from them, and number two, the US currency was just too goddam important for some Limey spook to play dumb games with.

Clair nodded. He had paid great attention to David Jardine's briefing of Nancy, and the SIS man could not have been faulted. He answered her every question courteously and in as much detail as anyone could have wished. And yet Alan Clair had continued to have the feeling that his old friend was disclosing to the Treasury Counsel only what he wanted her to know.

Which was situation normal in any interchange between intelligence officials of different services – even under the same national aegis, let alone between foreign organizations. But when he attempted to explain how such things worked to Nancy Lucco, she just became tougher and more insistent that Jardine be made to tell all he knew.

'Hell, Counsellor, what do you want us to do? Sandbag the guy on his way to the Henley Park Hotel and fill him full of scopolamine?'

'Listen, have you really digested what this guy has been telling us? Have you . . . analysed what's going down here?'

'Sure, of course I have.'

'With respect,' Nancy Lucco took a deep breath, 'I suggest you have looked at the Danny Davidov case from the Agency's point of view. My service has to protect the US currency. That's the job. I've made a few graphs.'

'On computer?'

'On graph paper. The old-fashioned way. Starting with the very first Davidov scam.'

'The airplane fuel.'

'And working it on, tracking the development of each succeeding job. Each country. Each particular use of counterfeit and disinformation, to achieve success. And this is a goddam success story, Mr Clair.'

'And what do you find . . .?' Alan Clair did in fact, at this juncture, begin to wonder if his office had really done more than pay lip-service to David Jardine's information about Danny Davidov and some unidentified wiseguy who were burglarizing fairly stupendous amounts of money from targets chosen apparently at random, all over the world.

'Number one, each victim organization, or in the case of the Thais, country, could easily have been wiped out by what he did. He just happened to have been in a good mood, so far. Look at the St Petersburg Credex operation. They could've wrecked Credex worldwide. Did you read that the Thai Government had to recall and change its entire paper currency after Davidov hit them with 800 million dollars' worth of forged Thai notes?'

'Sure. Of course.' If I were to be honest, Clair mused, maybe I have only been looking at this from an intelligence point of view. After all, what's of military, political or economic interest in a crazy Israeli who has chosen to cut a swathe through the world's previously inaccessible money systems? If the guy was using his funds to support a hostile regime, or topple a government to our disadvantage, or obtain technology secrets from the USA, well that would change the pace of things. But so far, it hasn't happened.

'Has it occurred to you what would happen to the US economy if somebody released thousands of millions of perfect counterfeit dollars all over the world? Tens, maybe, of thousands of millions.' Nancy leaned back in her seat, watching him like he was a potentially hostile witness.

'That would take manpower, which we have no evidence of. And once he starts to recruit hundreds of people, his operations get leaky. We could soon track him down and, um, neutralize the guy.'

'Just like you did with Sadaam Hussein . . .?' inquired Nancy meekly.

Their eyes met, and Clair started to grin. He held his hands up. 'Okay,' he said, 'I'm listening . . .'

It was 4.24 on the afternoon of the 27th. Always a better time, the afternoon, reflected Danny Davidov, to enter a government building than in the dead of night, which was a mistake many people had made. Including, maybe, the Watergate burglars.

No jemmies, no skeleton keys, no hooded ski masks were necessary for Danny and his partner, Nikolai Kolosov, for they had proper identification as employees of the Bureau of Engraving and Printing, with their photos sealed in laminated ID passes clipped to their shirt pockets. And they were accompanied by a regular visitor, on official business, to the US Treasury Repository – James Thompson Fenwick, one of their recruited Operation Medusa agents whom they had met with that evening in the bar on 6th Street, near Washington Harbor. The other recruit was sitting by a telephone in the Bureau itself, on 14th Street, ready to confirm the bona fides of the three men, should anyone decide to carry out a check.

The United States Repository of Records was at the rear of the main Treasury Building. There details of every transaction ever made on behalf of the US administration were kept, some of them historic, going back to the first inauguration of Congress.

Records for the year 1865, which coincidentally was the year, during the Civil War, when the US Secret Service was founded, to protect the President and the US currency from counterfeiting, were kept in the dehumidified basement, in Sector B-12, locked in a long chamber, a maze of lanes of shelves on which rested annotated carton after dusty carton, each bound in pink tape and sealed.

Because there was considered to be a risk that such rare documents would be tempting to thieves, it was difficult to obtain entry, but once inside, only a clerk from the Archives Division would normally be present.

Fenwick was not unknown to the clerk who led them into B-12, for he was, among other duties, responsible for indexing the archives at the Bureau of Engraving and Printing.

Thus the atmosphere in the long, arid chamber was one of everyday tedium.

The cover story was that Davidov and Kolosov, using different names of course, were checking the records of 1923, for the allocation of funds to the Bureau for the purchase of materials, since they had found some in store and thought it might have some ephemeral value for the Bureau's museum.

It was no coincidence that records for the year 1865 were on shelves directly across the narrow passageway from those for 1923.

And while Fenwick engaged the clerk in conversation, asking if, while they were there, he could check out the new indexing system – something which Danny's research had revealed was this particular clerk's pride and joy – Kolosov, shielded from view by Danny, got to work.

The precise location of the carton holding files recording Treasury purchases on behalf of the War Department, for the month of April, was known.

Danny and Kolosov had practised, with exact replicas, cutting the pink tape, removing it, opening the box, locating the files for Week 14 and removing – nothing. It was a couple of additions that the two scoundrels were making.

A couple of little changes to the history of the United States' fiscal transactions, in April 1865.

The job done, while Fenwick, at the far end of the corridor, expressed impressed amazement at the proficiency of the new indexing system, Kolosov replaced the pink tape and seal with a replica, even to the age of the tape and chemical composition of the seal. And with sweat running down his temple, the Russian glanced at Danny Davidov.

'Perfect,' murmured the former Mossad man.

And inside the sealed carton rested two more documents, recording the purchase of 70,000 dollars' worth of gold bars from a private banker in the Ukraine, the order confirming purchase dated 11 April, and the internal memorandum confirming delivery, on the 29th of that month, to a recipient who was recorded only as 'Secret. War Department Submarine Research'.

The records had been forged on virgin paper milled in Connecticut in 1859, by the Nghis, using a variety of chemicals and expensive X-ray and infra-red equipment purchased in Europe by Danny Davidov and the Russian, in order not to attract the interest of any US investigators.

Such pristine old paper, unmarked, unwritten or printed upon, was an absolute essential in the fine art of real counterfeiting. Every paper has microscopic strands and idiosyncrasies within its fabric. The passage of time has a physical effect, depending on exposure to light, heat, damp, carbon dioxide, and so on. And at that time, not even the best forgers in the world, who at one time had been a secret team of about six people, four men and two women, who toiled in white-tiled, sub-basement laboratories in Moscow, beneath the Headquarters building of the Communist Party of the Soviet Union – not even the Disinformation and False Documents Cell, as it was called by the very, very few people who knew of its existence, had been able to reproduce 100-year-old paper.

The dried ink too was extremely hard to fake, because of

changes in its molecular structure over the decades, but this was something of a speciality with the Nghis, and the ink on those documents stood up to any scientific examination.

In fact, both Danny Davidov and his partner had noticed, with the pleasure of real players, that the colour of the counterfeit paper was the same as that of the sheets between which they had just been inserted.

For the first time in weeks, Kolosov felt a prick of excitement. He nodded, and smiled his pleasure. Only his eyes remained cold.

For the endgame had commenced.

13

Stone Dancer

DURING THOSE NEXT couple of weeks, Elmore Williams and his Joint Task Force arranged with the DA, one Tony Faccioponti, for charges against Dino Trafficante to be held on file. These included conspiracy to murder Harry Cardona, attempted murder of Elmore Williams, his wife Martha and their daughter Melanie, possession of a concealed weapon, trafficking in cocaine and trafficking in counterfeit dollars. And they still had, as Elmore remarked, the illegal parking of one Porsche, should all else fail.

Anyhow, Dino Trafficante was committed to the Witness Protection Program. They took him to a safe house, guarded round the clock, in Westchester County, and peeled the guy like an artichoke, acquiring more information than they ever had before on the workings of the Palermo Mafia, Giovanni Favorito Noto and, especially, on Franco Cagliaro.

And among the stuff that the Task Force interrogators were learning from Dino was that Cagliaro had persuaded Don Giovanni to hire the services of two Vietnamese counterfeiters, who had worked for the CIA in Vietnam, to some crazy wandering Jew and his Russian sidekick.

Dino even knew these were the guys who had hit the Banco di Calabria in Palermo, a couple of months back. That was interesting to Elmore, but at that time, on that precise day, he was not aware – how could he be? – that his guardian angel, Nancy Lucco, could have used such intelligence. So he pressed on with building a case against the man who called himself Cagliaro, for he was the lowlife who had ordered Elmore Williams' death. And for the Secret Service agent, that made it kinda personal.

Nancy Lucco shrugged into a pleasant silk dress by Karl Lagerfeld. She had soaked in the tub, with a wonderful oil of grapefruit, by Czech & Speake, from Barney's in Manhattan, and felt she smelled pretty good. As she bent her head to one side and put on tiny single-pearl earrings, she wondered what this David Jardine would be like socially. There was that dangerous quality she had recognized, reminding her of Eddie, and there was little doubt that he was relaxed and comfortable in the company of women.

Too damn comfortable, she mused. The man conveyed a relaxed, quiet, self-deprecating confidence that any sane girl would recognize as the smile on the face of the tiger. Jardine had good eyes. They said things that the rest of him, words and gestures, never hinted at.

She laughed quietly, knowing herself too well to duck what she was really and most privately wondering, and felt that Lucco, wherever he was, would be amused. For the truth was, just the once or twice, Nancy had caught David Jardine gazing at her in a, how could she put it, well, not in an entirely neutered, professional way.

But it was Eddie who occupied Nancy's thoughts, as she gazed at her face in the mirror. You might have imagined, she thought to herself, in fact to be 100 per cent selfish, you might have hoped, kid, that the pain would get a little less, each time. But it did not. The healing process had turned out to be completely different. For she had come to understand that the dumb Wop cop was never very far away. Wherever she was. Whatever she was doing. She knew that for sure.

So the Legal Counsellor for the US Secret Service took a deep breath and stepped out to see what supper with David Jardine would bring.

Well, it was okay, as things turned out. He was fun and friendly, with some riotous stories of espionage's more absurd and embarrassing moments. He looked nice in a pair of neutral-coloured linen trousers, navy blue cotton shirt and an unstructured fawn wool jacket which might have been Armani. In other words, nothing like the English gent's stuff he had worn to their four meetings at the Treasury.

'Where would you like to go?' he asked, after they had each had a couple of Manhattans at the round bar in the Willard Hotel, not far from the White House.

'Wherever,' Nancy replied.

'It's your town.'

'You're not a stranger here yourself.'

'Okay. Trust me.' And he shot her that look again. Amused but friendly, like 'I can bite, but I won't'. And they grabbed a taxi and went to eat in a neat little restaurant he knew of, in Georgetown, called Nathan's, which adjoined a bar of the same name. The tables had red-and-white-checkered covers, with candles in wine bottles.

Now Nancy was familiar with Nathan's, of course, but she was pleased the Englishman had not taken her to someplace really boring, with starched white and polished silver, and waiters in tuxedos.

They had a couple more Manhattans, and ordered some food. Avocado with Italian ham for her, Caesar salad for him, and they both went for Spaghetti Napolitana to follow.

'And a bottle of, um,' Jardine looked to Nancy Lucco, 'you prefer white or red, Nancy?'

She shrugged. 'Either.'

'Okay, let's have a bottle of . . .' he showed the menu to the waitress, 'this one.'

'The Zinfandel. Red? Coming right up.' The young

waitress turned like a drum-majorette and marched back to the kitchen.

'So,' said David Jardine, continuing one of his fund of outrageous stories, 'there he was, down on his knees, the bunch of peonies and mistletoe, stolen from the Ambassador's own garden, offered to Madame Ceaucescu, when the bedroom door opened and in walked the old tyrant himself.'

'Ceaucescu?'

'The very man.'

'Jesus . . .' she shook her head, quite sure Jardine was making the story up as he went along.

'Ask me what Ronnie did.'

'What did he do?'

' "Thank God you've arrived," he said, blurted.'

They were both laughing now. 'Oh, boy,' said Nancy, 'come on . . .'

'No, really. Thank God, Mr President, you have arrived. I was explaining to Madame Ceaucescu how deadly this berry can be, when I dropped my false tooth, ah, here it is.'

'Stop! Oh, boy. Come on, David. Jeez . . .'

They chortled, Jardine wiped the tears from his eyes, and that inevitable, brief instant, when their eyes met, his gaze was warm and . . . friendly.

'So how does it feel?' she asked him.

'How does what feel?'

'Job like yours. Every schoolboy's dream, every liberal's *bête noire*, every taxpayer's . . . hidden agenda. Every journalist's misconception.'

'It's a job,' he said.

'It's not the kinda job other people have.'

'You want the truth?'

Nancy grinned. 'Not if I have to be silenced afterwards, I saw the Watergate movie . . .'

'Sometimes it's the most enormous fun. You get to behave really badly, and you're quite right, the taxpayer pays. Other times? It can be so boring you wonder why you signed on. And sometimes it can be . . . chastening.'

'Frightening?' She watched him closely.

Jardine nodded. 'Terrifying. To be confronted with just what a shitty game it can be. Using people.' For a moment he seemed lost in thought, then he brightened up and smiled, even with those eyes of his. 'So. Tell me about the Treasury. How did you get there? They find you at Harvard?'

It took a moment for Nancy Lucco to reply, so struck had she been by the patent honesty of his reply to what had been essentially a flippant question.

'You can tell *me*, I'm sure,' she said.

'Really and truly, I couldn't. Alan told me you're a Harvard Law School lady. Your late husband was a highly regarded detective in New York, killed in the line of duty. And, um, folks in the business trust you.' He could hear an Aerosmith number, seeping through from the bar next door, for the two places were not completely separated by the wall between them. You could get round, through the back of the restaurant, by the cash desk. Jardine had checked it out the first time he was there, in June 1976.

Nancy Lucco was thinking, Eddie used to nod his head in time to rock music, just like that. Sure, lots of people did, but it was yet another similarity.

'He used to do that.'

'What?' asked Jardine.

'Nod his head.' She nodded her own head, to illustrate what she meant, in time to 'Janie's Got a Gun . . .'.

'God, was I? Drives my kids mad. Oh, Dad, they say, stop nodding your bloody head, you look such a nerd.'

'A what?'

'You know. Dickhead. Buffoon.'

'Last thing I would call you, pal.' Damn. Why had she called him that?

He smiled. 'Stick around.'

So they rapped, like that, and ate a very relaxed and pleasant supper. Nancy asked him about his kids and she told him about Judge Almeda, and how the Director, Jim Farley, had sent her on the Special Agents' training courses.

And about her job, and how she enjoyed it. And this part of town. How she was settling into Washington.

David Jardine noted that she had hardly mentioned her late husband, except very briefly. Yet he was sufficiently sensitive to understand how much she missed him. Lucky man, he must've been quite a guy. Then, while she was telling him about the culture shock of Washington after New York and their cramped apartment in Queens, he seemed to recall one lunchtime about eight million years ago, sitting bored out of his mind, in Le Palm Restaurant, when he had amused himself by trying to catch the eye of an attractive woman eating alone, across the room.

It might just have been Nancy Lucco. He had a good memory like that. 'You ever eat in Le Palm?' he asked, as the waiter cleared away the remains of their spaghetti.

'Sure, why?'

This is a dumb line to pursue, he realized. 'Oh, just wondered.'

'I sometimes lunch there. It's difficult for a woman to eat alone, even in the capital city of PC.' She meant Politically Correct. 'You get ogled by, what was that word . . .? By nerds.' She smiled and let her eyes wander around the room.

David Jardine was surprised to feel an emotion close to pleasure at being in the company of such a woman. The merest possibility of . . . something good, yet perhaps mutually risky, was just discernible, like mist forming wraiths on the surface of a lake

'I can see that,' he said.

They decided to pass on the coffee and sauntered out into the warm Georgetown air. David Jardine glanced at his watch. It was ten after ten.

'You like jazz . . .?' asked Nancy, swaying sideways as a Rastafarian on rollerskates surfed past, weaving along the sidewalk.

'I love it.'

She did wonder, cynically, if she had said do you like late night glove puppets or would you like to hear a cello recital of Stravinsky's *Rite of Spring*, if he would have given the same reply. But after ten minutes in Mister Smith's Riverside Jazz Club, it was obvious that David Jardine did indeed love jazz. Thelonious Sphere Monk was his favourite, he told her. 'Blue Monk' still sent shivers down his spine, when it was played right. And 'In Walked Bud'. Plus Monk's version of 'I Can't Get Started'.

So three Jack Daniels and soda later, by which time it was round about midnight, and the Tommy Sullivan Trio was well into a nine-minute improvisation of 'Blue Monk', and yes, Jardine's head was nodding in time to the music, Nancy Lucco leaned towards him and, when he looked at her, moved her mouth closer to his ear.

David Jardine felt a delicious tingle. Sometimes, Lord, you really are too kind to this old sinner.

'David . . .' she whispered, a slight huskiness in her voice, the aroma of fresh bourbon on her breath.

'Mmm-hmm . . .?' he breathed, nuzzling her hair.

'Why the fuck are you holding out on us?'

Round about the same time, in New York City, Nikolai Kolosov kept a rendezvous with a respected and able lawyer, Michael Mitchel, senior partner in Mitchel and Weintraub. It was late, because the story was Kolosov had just arrived off a plane from Europe. A hireling of the criminal pair had made the journey, using a passport which was now in the inside jacket pocket of the former KGB Colonel.

Mitchel specialized in contract and copyright law and government debt to individuals. He believed Kolosov was a Ukrainian American called Peter Topolsky, a one-time bit-part player and crowd extra who had returned to the Ukraine after the fall of the Berlin Wall and the collapse of the USSR.

There, the story went – and it could be substantiated all along the line, because Kolosov had indeed turned up in a small town near Vinitsa, with all the correct legend and papers, including US passport and Equity card, family letters and his mother's and grandfather's birth certificates – Topolsky had secured for his new-found relatives and kinfolk the return of the old Topolsky lands, which were considerable, and included a derelict big place, built in the Palladian style, now shelter for stray sheep and goats, with a hundred pigeons in the ruined roof.

But there had been a small town-house in Vinitsa, and a letter from Grandfather Topolsky to his daughter in America had enclosed a letter of introduction to a local lawyer and notary, who was keeping the family's most confidential documents safe, until after the 'problems'.

Well, the problems had turned out to be the Bolshevik Revolution, and over seventy years later, it was by dint of diligent research and the most amazing luck that the bit-part actor, Peter Topolsky, came into contact with the descendants of the lawyer concerned. And they, like many folk during the nightmare years of Communist dictatorship, had minded their own business, and kept the files of the old law firm wrapped in wax-paper in sealed metal containers and buried them in the ground.

Amid exchanges of mutual toasts in cherry vodka, photographed by a local newspaper team, the remaining documents of the family Topolsky had been handed back to the senior surviving member – Peter Andreyevich.

Peter had magnanimously signed over the lands and the town-house, the ruined estate and the land, to his new-found Ukrainian kinfolk, and headed back to the USA.

The original, pre-Revolutionary wealth of the Topolskys had come from a private bank founded by one Bogdan Topolsky in the eighteenth century. With branches in St Petersburg, Sweden, London and New Amsterdam, the bank had at one time been renowned for its power, its contacts among the New World's ship-owners and insurance pioneers, and its legendary discretion.

Which is why Mitchel's instinctively sceptical, not to say jaundiced, researches had convinced him that the United States Treasury had purchased in the year 1865, in conditions of great secrecy for it was during the Civil War, gold to the value of 70,000 dollars from the Ukrainian Topolsky family bank.

The gold was to be paid for in US Treasury Bonds and Topolsky's case was that the payment had never been made, despite the receipt with which he had furnished Mitchel, for the gold bullion.

The purchasing letter which Peter Topolsky had handed to Mitchel, in the presence of two witnesses, Jack Stevenson, for Mitchel, and a short, balding man, Phillip Messervy, for Topolsky, was sealed in plastic and bore the letterhead seal of the Secretary for the United States Treasury.

It was in effect an agreement between the Topolsky Bank of Kiev and the United States Treasury for repayment of the 70,000 dollars at a rate of interest of 1 per cent, compounding per calendar month, after delivery of the gold bullion, which should have been academic, if the Treasury Bonds had been paid on time.

And that would have been interesting but no more, if Topolsky had not also produced letters covering fifty years, noting that the US Government had failed to pay, and that the shrewd Topolsky family had simply been allowing the interest to pile up.

Until the Revolution.

And now, with the collapse of Communism and the restoration of the family's estate, Peter Topolsky was here to collect.

'The first thing I have to do,' said Mitchel, having taken possession, duly witnessed, of the document, 'is to have this authenticated. I'm afraid there are many forgeries of this kind of thing around.'

'How long will that take?' asked Kolosov.

'Not long. We have the ace on rare document counterfeiting right here in New York City.'

'In that case,' replied Kolosov, 'we are in your hands . . .'

And the two men shook hands and parted.

*

One oh six in the morning.

The Tommy Sullivan Trio was into the seventh minute of 'Caravan', it was that late and they just didn't care.

Nancy Lucco and David Jardine were both smoking. She had not paid any attention to the beat-up old brass Zippo. Now they no longer looked like prospective potential lovers. More like a married couple discussing the housekeeping budget, for they were much more intent on each other's words than something as inconsequential as sex might indicate.

Nancy's blunt question – why are you holding out on us? – had come precisely – at least, within two or three days – when Jardine had anticipated it. Indeed he had planned his game towards just that moment. And he was too experienced an operator to miss it.

'Because in order for me to do my best,' he had murmured back into her ear, which had the faintest hint of aromatic freshness about it, like clover, or oranges, 'I need some help from you people. Maybe from Alan and your Director. Some high-level . . . clout.'

Nancy had lingered close to him, cheek to ear, for maybe a smidgen longer than the exchange had required. But she was pleasantly intrigued with the answer. Number one, she had been right. He was holding something back. Something pretty damn vital, if he was suggesting some form of quid pro quo at Directorate level. At government level. Number two, it followed that, if they could accommodate this David Jardine, she would get the credit for having winkled it out of him.

And number three, she had ruminated, as she sat back and studied the British spymaster, if she got it wrong, it would be her ass and not Alan Clair's that would be in the sling.

'Explain,' she had said.

Jardine had told her that this Danny Davidov business was more serious than anyone realized. There was a strong possibility that the crazy Israeli's series of capers had been hijacked by a hostile Foreign Service. And that, at the very moment when Davidov's perverted near-genius had gotten the US currency market by the balls, just to show how good a player he was – and doubtless to extort a few billion from the Treasury – the dark forces that were using him would slit Danny Davidov's and the dollar's throats at one and the same time.

'Don't you think it's irresponsible to play dumbfuck games with that kind of information?' She was suddenly almost sober.

'I need to be in a position to access SIS files and compartmented, ongoing investigations which, being separate, are not making the right connections.'

'Gimme a break, David. You are a top man in the organization. All you have to do is ask and you shall receive. Come on, I know what kinda bizarre, broad-spectrum security clearance you have.'

Jardine had explained to her how his Firm worked on a strict need-to-know principle. There were secrets he was keeping that the Chief himself could never be told, there were current clandestine operations and plans the files of which would never be retained. In order to access all material concerning those vestiges of the old KGB and their present illegal foreign operations, conducted by what were known to the Russian Security Service as Mixed Ventures Soumestnvye Predpriyatiya David Jardine was going to need a special intervention at government-to-government level.

Nancy Lucco stared at him. The band had finally found a way to get out of 'Caravan', to the great relief of the couple of dozen people left in the jazz club.

Desultory clapping of hands.

He met her gaze, unblinking.

'The KGB . . .?' Nancy made a dismissive gesture. 'It's dead. The KGB was disbanded, back in ninety-one or ninety-two.'

'It may be dead, but it won't lie down.'

'You're serious.'

'Dead serious. But Alan's people know this. We all do.'

He stubbed his last Winston filter out in the crammed ashtray, not taking his eyes off her.

'Thank you, ladies and gentlemen. This is Tommy Sullivan and the Trio saying you've been a wonderful audience. Come again real soon. Thank you and . . . goodnight.'

Drum-roll and clash of high-hat symbols.

'Nine o'clock tomorrow morning,' she said, sober as a black hat, as Lucco would have put it.

'I'll be there.'

Jardine raised a hand for the check.

Outside, Nancy declined his courteous offer of an escort home, and as she started to get into the taxi, she turned and looked at him.

'Fuck you, David Jardine. I was just beginning to like you . . .' And she shook her head ruefully.

He grinned. 'I like you,' he said simply. 'Safe home.'

They lingered for a couple of seconds. Then she nodded.

'Great night. Full of surprises.' And she climbed in, pulling the door shut, and the cab moved off, up Wisconsin.

David Jardine turned and started to stroll towards M Street, hands in his trouser pockets. He started to whistle, and being almost tone-deaf, it sounded terrible. And as he strolled, sauntered almost, for he felt the evening had gone according to plan, Jardine wondered about the signal he had received from his office in London. Heather, of all people, his young and hopeful secretary, quite clearly had a reasonable idea of what, precisely, her boss considered to be of moment these days. For the signal contained the information that, according to Tel Aviv Station, the retired Mossad Director of Covert Operations, Nathan Zamir, who was terminally ill in a hospital in Haifa, aged seventy-four, had been found dead in bed. Cause of death, suffocation. A forensic detail was that minute fibres from the pillow which had been replaced under the dead man's head were found in his lungs.

What was niggling at the back of Jardine's mind was the connection between Zamir's murder, the mugging of Avvie

Eitels in Paris and the killing of Elena Constantinovna in Moscow. Because, if his theory was correct, each of those victims of violent death had been part of the unauthorized, illegal element lurking inside Mossad, which had accepted the corrupt millionaire Robert Maxwell's millions to service their own secret agenda.

A dark-featured man loomed out from a shop doorway, mean-looking, with a big leather Rastafarian cap and a T-shirt with 'Ice T Rules' in big letters on the front.

'Okay, man, gimme your wad,' he growled, with menace.

Jardine stopped and gazed into the mugger's doped-up eyes. Some instinct for self-preservation must have penetrated to what passed for the guy's brain, for he hesitated, keeping both hands by his sides.

'Don't be absurd,' said Jardine, and without a second glance strolled on, leaving a dumbfounded citizen staring after him, trying to figure out what the hell had just gone down.

The next morning, 7.10, the telephone beside David Jardine's bed in the Henley Park Hotel rang shrilly. Jardine, more than slightly hungover, reached across and lifted the receiver.

'Yeah?'

'David, it's Alan. Your nine o'clock meeting will not be at the Treasury. It's been moved forward to eight, and a car is waiting outside your hotel. See you in fifty minutes, buddy.'

And the line went dead.

It was to be predicted, considered Jardine, as he swung his legs out of bed, that one or two people were going to be extremely pissed off with him. But a spy had to make a living . . .

The car was a Lincoln from the Langley pool, the driver was an uncommunicative young CIA agent who grunted in reply to Jardine's cheery 'Good morning' and drove him back into Georgetown, to the safe house not far from Dumbarton Oaks where Jardine himself had taken the

Soviet defector, KGB Colonel Oleg Gordievsky, for his first Stateside debriefing with the CIA.

Inside were Alan Clair, Nancy Lucco, Jim Farley, the Secret Service Director, and the CIA's Director of Plans, Greg Jackson.

Nobody was smiling.

The room was upstairs. It was spacious and comfortably furnished, with American Indian rugs, big armchairs and two wooden rocking chairs. There were much-thumbed books on the bookshelves and a good-sized table round which folks could sit. Paintings on the walls were by Grandma Moses and someone whose name Jardine could not recall, who was famous in the USA for his paintings of bison hunts and Custer's Last Stand and heroic folklore subjects.

The others were sitting around the room. Jardine got the feeling they were watching him and ignoring him, at one and the same time.

Inside the safe house, a tall black CIA officer David Jardine had noticed before, on protection assignments, had opened the front door and led him upstairs. His name, Jardine knew, was Bob Devine.

When Devine had ushered the Englishman into the room, he retreated and closed the door.

'David, you know Greg.'

'Good morning, Greg.'

Greg Jackson raised a hand in greeting. He had a file open on his lap.

'And this is Jim Farley, Director of the Secret Service.'

Farley glanced up from reading a similar file. 'Pleased to meet you, Mr Jardine.'

Jardine nodded. 'Likewise . . .' He chose a comfortable seat, ignoring the one Alan Clair had been indicating, and crossed his legs, composed and giving the strong signal, here is a senior executive officer of the Secret Intelligence Service. Don't forget it. He wore a comfortable, sand-coloured linen suit he had bought off-the-peg from Brooks Bros in New York about three years back, a faded blue shirt from Armani and a navy silk necktie. Plus the faithful tan boots he had had made for him about eight years before, in Peru, and on his wrist the fake Rolex Oyster, stainless-steel, that had kept perfect time since the day he bought it for a few dollars in Singapore.

'Help yourself to coffee. We can have a cooked breakfast sent up if you prefer.' This from Clair.

'I'm fine. Let's cut the crap, shall we?'

Director Jim Farley nodded. 'Sure thing. Can I call you David? David, I asked for this early morning meeting because time really is of the essence, if your prognosis about the Israeli –'

'Former Israeli,' said Jardine.

'Okay. If you're right. So tell us what you need. I can't speak for the Agency, but the Secret Service is taking your report', he tapped the file on his lap, 'with the utmost seriousness.'

David Jardine inclined his head and glanced at Alan Clair and Greg Jackson.

They gazed back. Waiting.

'I believe, as a result of information which has been given to me by a protected source, even from my own service, that's the nature of the deal, that I am uniquely placed to represent SIS in this . . . investigation.'

'Well, we have no problems with that, have we, Alan?' Jackson looked around as if to say, is that all there is to this?

Alan Clair shook his head. 'No problems with that.'

'David, yesterday,' said Nancy Lucco – he noted she did not say 'last night' – 'you mentioned you could use some help from us in accessing certain SIS protected areas. To do the job right.'

Perfect, thought Jardine. Nicely put.

'Absolutely right,' he replied, and he proceeded, succinctly, to outline precisely the steps the US administration could take to help him to help them by being assigned the SIS end of a joint investigation. Together, he was certain, they had just a chance of nailing Danny Davidov and whoever it was that had hijacked his eccentric criminal operations.

When he had finished, the others made a few notes. Then Jim Farley nodded and Greg Jackson said, 'Okay. We hear you. David, would you step outside for a few minutes? Bob will make you comfortable.'

So David Arbuthnot Jardine, Director, Foreign Service Liaison, Her Majesty's Intelligence Service, was ushered downstairs, most courteously, by Bob Devine and he visited the washroom, splashed his face, wished he had taken an Alka-Seltzer for his throbbing head and flopped down on an easy chair, picked up a copy of the *Washington Post* from the day before and started to browse through it.

At ten past eleven, a smiling Alan Clair poked his head round the door, a much more relaxed man.

'Come on back upstairs,' he said.

In the upstairs room, the others had emptied the coffee pot and were standing in a corner, conversing easily, the earlier frosty formality almost gone.

'David, thank you for you candour,' Jim Farley said. 'My colleagues in the Company have made a few phone calls. I think we can do business . . .'

'Thank God for that,' replied David Jardine, frankly relieved. The others seemed to appreciate that. 'I need to be able to drop all other commitments and run this as a major operation. In complete cooperation with yourselves.'

'Nancy will be your point of contact, I have every confidence in her. And I am always there for you.'

'I appreciate that, sir,' said Jardine, and gripped Farley's hand as it was offered to him.

'I'm outa here,' said Farley. 'Good luck, you guys.'

'Thanks.'

And the Director was gone.

'Okay, David. We'll play ball,' said Greg Jackson. 'You're a known quantity to us and Alan convinced us, whatever your goddam motives and frankly I know a personal career boost when I see it, it will give you the strength you need. The . . . "clout"? Is that the word?'

David Jardine smiled, unperturbed by the Company man's perspicacity.

'It'll do,' he replied.

Thus it came to pass that over the next forty-eight hours cipher clerks at Langley and in the bowels of the United States Embassy in London's Grosvenor Square were kept busy. And at 9.41 the next morning, the United States Ambassador was visited by the British Permanent Under-Secretary at the Foreign and Commonwealth Office, to discuss an agenda arranged some weeks before. The Ambassador, at the end of the formal meeting, asked his secretary and Minister to leave and made an off-the-record request concerning an intelligence matter.

The same request was made by the CIA Station Chief, Ray Burton, to the SIS representative in the Cabinet Office, which distilled all intelligence and security matters and interfaced directly with the Prime Minister and the senior members of his Cabinet. And the Foreign Secretary himself was spoken to by the US Secretary of State, in Paris, where they were both attending a conference.

By five that evening, just as Sir Steven McCrae was getting ready to descend a couple of floors inside Century House, to chair the New Building Committee, a call on his secure line, from the Cabinet Secretary, presented him with a distillation of these several special requests which was couched in such a way there was very little the Chief could have done but agree, with as much grace as he could muster.

'And Steven,' went on the Cabinet Secretary, 'the cousins will make a substantial – substantial is the word they used – contribution to your operational fund for this one.'

'I don't see why they could not merely have signalled this office direct.'

'Probably because the US Treasury initiated this and you know how they like to pull out government-to-government stops. Inflated idea of their importance, perhaps, but the Minister has made it clear they are to have what they desire.'

'Oh, very well,' replied Steven McCrae petulantly, glancing at his wristwatch, for the New Building Committee would be waiting.

'There's just one thing,' said the Cabinet Secretary, a Wykehamist and Fellow of All Souls. *Very* close to just about everyone who mattered.

'What's that?' McCrae wondered if this might be a good assignment for Marietta, she had the experience.

'They specifically have asked for David Jardine to run it. And we have, I'm afraid, said okay. Foreign Secretary has. Hope that creates no problems.'

'My cup is full and runneth over . . .' replied McCrae, probably unaware he had learned this minor blasphemy from Jardine himself.

Eight minutes later, he walked into Committee Room 3, on the eighth floor of the Great Glass Box, with views across rooftops towards the Elephant and Castle roundabout and the Old Vic Theatre, and was less than delighted to see David Jardine sitting there, between Kate Howard and Marietta Delice.

'My dear,' he beamed to Jardine, as he took his seat at the head of the table, 'I thought we were stepping out in the colonies . . .'

'Popped back briefly, Chief,' smiled Jardine sweetly.

'We must have a word,' said the boss, and he struggled to control his apparent anger.

After the meeting, which was so dull it made J-WISC seem like the Gunpowder Plot, Steven McCrae shuffled his papers together and, with a pointed glance to Jardine, walked to the door and hovered by the three grey elevator doors.

As David Jardine came out, chatting with Tim Lewin, Director of Personnel, other committee members emerged from the room, avoiding eye contact with the boss, already mentally in their cars or on their bicycles or standing at bus stops, Going Home; for today was Friday and in the

Service that was called POETS day; Piss Off Early Tomorrow's Saturday.

'A word, Steven . . .' Jardine murmured as he reached McCrae.

In his inner office, where David Jardine noted the wicker wastepaper basket had been replaced by a standard metal one, Steven McCrae shrugged out of his expensively tailored, double-breasted, grey chalkstripe jacket and plumped himself down on one of the two old and much-used tan leather armchairs. He nodded, perfunctorily, at the other.

Jardine obeyed smartly, not presuming – being sensitive to atmosphere – to divest himself of his own suit jacket.

'Problems?' he inquired solicitously.

'David, you really are a total shit.'

'It's a point of view.'

McCrae fixed the object of his anger with a gaze unsettling in its coldness.

'Exactly what the hell are you playing at?' he asked in a disquietingly mild voice.

'Absolutely lost, sport. Please enlighten me.'

'Look, I run a very able Station in Washington. Don't you think I am aware of your . . . that you and the American Service have been living in each other's pockets, this last week?'

'It is actually my job, Steven. Liaison. I can hardly sit on my arse in the British Embassy, can I?'

The ornate Louis XV ormolu clock ticked quietly on the Chief's desk. His Meerschaum pipe lay beside it. Rain abruptly rattled against the blast-proof windows. Like a small declaration of hostilities.

McCrae continued to gaze at David Jardine, fairly intently. Jardine met his eye and, stretching his legs, crossed his ankles, relaxing.

'I have received a request. To cooperate in a joint investigation with the US Intelligence Service.' It was well known in Century that Steven McCrae had never used the term CIA, and over the years the most cunning attempts to lure him into saying it had failed. 'They want it handled by us because of its quote geopolitical ramifications unquote, and they want it to be run at Directorate level. And they specifically want you to run it . . .'

'How very rewarding.'

'Yes. We all know for whom . . .'

'Steven, it's good for the Firm.'

McCrae's eyes bored into the other man's skull. He can be quite a tough old bird when he puts his mind to it, mused David.

'Don't give me any bullshit, dear boy. Whatever you've been up to, you have somehow contrived to feather your nest. Well, here's the SP.' SP stood for Starting Price, it was a horse-racing expression and Sir Steven lost no opportunity to remind one that he owned, through his wealthy child bride, two middling good racehorses. 'They want you, specifically, for reasons which, when pressed, they declare are "US Eyes Only". Although it's clear you know every detail of the affair.'

Jardine tugged a pack of Camel Lites from his packet, then hesitated as a frown from McCrae dared him to light one. 'It's about an attempt by a criminal enterprise to destabilize the US dollar. I believe some very nasty Russians, the power-house behind the pro-Communist underground have infiltrated what was until then a straightforward law enforcement problem. When the Central Intelligence Agency, the CIA, Steven, asked me to tell all, I thought, hold the phone. Let's do the Office some good here, and hold out for a direct involvement. They have even offered to fund our end of the show.'

It was not unlike confession, reflected Jardine. He had obeyed Alice Hanson's dictum and told the truth. As much of it as he wished to burden the boss with.

'In other words, while you were in Moscow, and Beirut too, one suspects, and just recently in Washington . . . you kept to yourself all kinds of . . . information, of data, and proceeded to build up a picture of an old-guard, KGB operation.'

Jardine inclined his head. 'Just so. It is, if one might bring to your attention, Steven, precisely what we do, it's called Secret Intelligence Operations.' And he went on to brief McCrae comprehensively on the entire Danny Davidov operation, omitting only the identity of the KGB officer he believed to be dictating events.

In the silence that followed, McCrae was almost transparently going through all his options, from ignoring the Cabinet Office, which was his prerogative, to firing David Jardine on the spot, to agreeing to the Americans' request, but appointing someone else to head up the UK side of what might indeed become a prestigious operation to deflect an attack on the US economy.

Finally, he began to announce his decision. 'If the Israeli Davidov really has been . . . hijacked?'

'Hijacked is a good word.'

'And if Oleg Kouzmine's Staraya Zemlya group have succeeded in slipping a man under the wire . . .'

'Oleg who, Chief?' Jardine felt his plans turn to dust. This was his ace in the hole. Had Ronnie Szabodo taken Elena Constantinovna's microfilm straight to the boss? And if so, who could blame him?

McCrae smiled, except with his eyes. 'Believe it or not, David, there are some items of secret intelligence you are not party to. Oleg Kouzmine runs a clandestine and powerful group of revisionists, culled from the old Communist Party, the KGB and dispossessed or dissatisfied elements in the military and in Russian industry. They are funded by sections of the *nomenklatura* and by the Moscow Mafia. If your Davidov gang has been infiltrated by a former KGB colonel, he will be a creature of Kouzmine's, believe me.'

Jardine uncrossed his ankles and sat straighter in his chair. He felt guilty of arrogance and, worse, short-sightedness. Never begin to think you are the only spy in SIS, Ronnie Szabodo had admonished him, twenty years ago, when the squat Hungarian was training him in the arcane skills required for survival, or at best you'll cease to be taken seriously.

'As a matter of fact, Steven, I had just recently learned about Kouzmine. The existence of Staraya Zemlya, groups like that, of course. But I wanted more . . . collateral.'

'Of course you did, dear boy . . .' McCrae smiled his crocodile smile and went on, 'Kouzmine's is the most clandestine, the best funded, and the most dangerous to the future of the New Russia. If a cell of his is having a go at the dollar, they might just make waves.' He got up and poured two stiff tumblers of Ballantynes whisky, then ambled past Jardine's chair and handed one to him.

'David, you've got the job. Just try to trust us all a bit more. We are on the same side, you know . . .'

The desire to assault McCrae was such, David Jardine contemplated seeking professional counselling.

'I'll need to put liaison on the back-burner.'

'Of course.'

'Acquire personnel.'

'Speak to Tim. I want a draft of your plans on my desk by noon tomorrow, which is no longer Saturday. It's Day One. Speak to Housekeeping about a bigger space to work from. I want to be able to tell Cabinet Office that we are up and running from start of play on Monday. Anyone gets in the way, I'll sort them. Questions?'

Jardine considered. If one was to be fair, this was not the Steven McCrae he thought he knew. And maybe it was the adrenalin coursing through his veins, the fresh air racing through the dusty corridors of his mind, but he suddenly felt something not a million miles from the merest iota of grudging respect for the man's ability to shift with the wind.

'Not right now.' Jardine drained his scotch and climbed to his feet. 'I'll get on with it.'

'You'll need a codename.'

'I, um, dug one out of the computer. Just before the meeting.'

'What is it?'

'Stone Dancer,' replied Jardine.

14

A Little Murder On Wall Street

IN THE LEGAL Department at the State Department Building on the junction of C Street and 23rd, Counsellor James O'Connell, head of the Foreign Claims Department, sat gazing at a photocopy of the US Treasury letter, written in longhand in the Secretary of that time's own hand, countersigned by one Daniel Bogdanovich Topolsky and witnessed by two clerks, one of whom, John Wilkes, historical research had confirmed was on duty at the Secretary's Arlington home on the date in question – 11 April 1865. The other witness was a Ukrainian by the name of Tuminsky, R.

The accompanying letter, from Michael Mitchel, enclosed five authenticating affidavits, signed and countersigned by a battery of acknowledged experts, including Maximilian Eidelman.

If this promissory note turns out to be genuine, wrote O'Connell neatly, attaching his observations to the growing file, there is not enough money in existence to settle the debt which, it is alleged, the United States owes to Mr Topolsky and his family.

It is therefore in our interests to prove the original is a forgery and I recommend we obtain possession of same as a matter of urgency.

*

Jamaica Bay lies no more than three miles south-east of Central Park. It consists of the bay, a number of islands, and is flanked by Brooklyn Harbor, JFK International Airport, Rockaway Beach and the old Floyd Bennet Navy Airfield.

The SS *Sumaru* had discharged her cargo of bulk paper for the newspaper industry, and the Vietnamese counterfeiters were enjoying a game of poker with the ship's cook, a Mongolian by the name of Chan. Chan was the one indulgence Kolosov and Danny Davidov had permitted themselves. He had once been ship's wardroom cook in the Soviet Navy and had been personal cook to the Commander of the Frunze Military Academy, before the fall of the USSR. Thus the standard of prepared food in the small wardroom on board SS *Sumaru* was among the best on the high seas. Or on Jamaica Bay, as she was at that moment.

It was a half-hour before midnight. The other crew members were all on board, the radio operator on his bunk, reading *Playboy* and listening to his frequency scanner and the local harbour and coastguard channels simultaneously. If that seems to require more than average skill, the radio officer, whose papers and passport showed him to be an Estonian by the name of Reitel, had in fact served with a Russian Naval Special Forces Unit, 35th Spetznatz, with the rank of Lieutenant. He had experience of commando operations on the Kola Peninsula and in Afghanistan.

The First Mate's documents showed him to be Gunduz Ergan, a Turkish citizen. In fact he too had seen service with a Soviet GRU (Military Intelligence) vessel; a deep-sea 'trawler' whose mission had been to monitor NATO warships in the North Atlantic.

The engineer? A swarthy half-Pole half-Scot, Stanislav MacFarlane. But not really. He had eighteen years' experience as an engineer officer with the Black Sea Fleet.

The rest of the *Sumaru*'s crew, some orientals, some European, some Slav, were all former Soviet Navy marines or Spetznaz commandos. There were eight in all, and three of them had belonged to the elite Ninth Directorate of the KGB, the only men permitted to carry arms near the rulers of the Soviet Union, for they had been the bodyguards.

Did Danny Davidov feel secure, therefore? To be so well protected by a crew of combat-hardened Russian illegals?

Not really. Because he did not know. He was blissfully unaware that, since the time he had recruited Nikolai Kolosov two years before, and Kolosov had recruited the crew, he had been, to all intents and purposes, in the custody of the military–industrial complex's most clandestine, well-funded and ruthless cell: the Oleg Kouzmine Direction.

Even when operating abroad, when carrying out one of his brilliantly conceived deceptions, Davidov and his partner/custodian, Kolosov, were often under discreet surveillance, as we have seen. Those watchers were agents of the Oleg Kouzmine, as the group was known to the very few aware of its existence.

Their aim? Just as Elena Constantinovna had told Jardine. The destruction of democracy in the former Soviet Union and a return to Communist rule.

All this information was unavailable to the nine heavily armed Mafia soldiers of Giovanni Favorito Noto's Sicilian *famiglia*, as they waited on the deck of a small but fast launch, which quietly and steadily approached the *Sumaru*, on the side hidden from moonlight, its powerful engines professionally muffled, a skill acquired from fast, noiseless runs between the Florida Keys and Cuba.

Franco Cagliaro watched the *Sumaru* draw closer. Using lightweight Eurolook B-11 night-vision binoculars, he could discern the tramp-steamer's superstructure and cabin portholes. There was no one topsides and the small ship seemed to have shut down for the night.

Besides Cagliaro's two bodyguards there were six of Don Giovanni's top enforcers, drawn from New York City, Miami and Palermo. After the total fuck-up by the hoodlums sent on the Elmore Williams contract, Cagliaro had resolved only to employ the very best, and every man on board that launch had dozens, which was not hyperbole, of slayings and kidnappings to his credit.

In terms of armament, two of the six 'soldiers' carried AAI Close Assault Combat Shotguns, without butts. These weapons fired 12-gauge shell, each loaded with eight drag-stabilized 1-gram flechettes. Two of them had Heckler & Koch MP 2000 9-mm silenced sub-machine-guns, and of the remaining two, one carried a British Parker-Hale Model 85, 7.62-mm sniper's rifle with sound suppressor, and the sixth Sicilian cradled a Hawk 40-mm MM-1 12-shot grenade launcher.

In addition, each man carried pistol or revolver, knife or machete, according to choice.

Cagliaro wore a black flak-jacket over the dark green boiler-suits they all wore, for ease of identification between themselves. He and his two bodyguards had the almost traditional MAC-10 9-mm Ingram grease-guns.

'Who's on this goddam boat, *padrino*?' asked Vito Menfi. 'The entire US Marine Corps?'

The others laughed.

'It never hurts to pack a little extra heat, *paesano*. Just suppose one of those sailor boys has a little *pistola*, mmm?'

They grinned.

'Well, these guys are thorough. They will have some kind of muscle protecting their Saigon chickens. Overkill is the name of the game. We hit them hard. The Jew and the other one are ashore tonight. And when they come back . . .' Cagliaro raised his shoulders, 'their crew will be over the side and the two Viets will be gone.'

'*Andiamo* . . .' let's do it, they murmured.

'And one last thing, the Viets are like precious porcelain. They will come with us okay. Just don't hurt them.' He smiled. 'Or I will skin you . . .'

And they, too, knew he was not kidding.

Inside the wardroom, Chan held his cards perfectly still and listened. The Nghis glanced at him and they too listened.

It had been the merest, softest 'd-bump'. But it was not usual, and it came from the lowered companionway.

Chan lifted the mattress on a bunk beside him and eased an AKS paratrooper's assault rifle from beneath it. Then he opened the hinged lid of one of the steamer's internal communication tubes.

'Ai, ai . . .' he breathed.

Back came a clicking sound.

'Company . . .' he whispered.

And three sets of two clicks responded.

Chan swung round, AKS at his hip, as the steel door to the corridor outside opened. It was Ergan, the First Mate. He swiftly pushed the big door shut and slid two iron bars into place, securing it from the outside.

He swung to his right and caught a Remington pump-action shotgun, which Chan had lobbed across the cabin to him. The two Viets were moved from porthole to porthole; there were three of them, swinging the iron storm guards shut.

'Gas masks,' ordered Ergan, speaking in Russian for the first time since he had joined the ship's company. The Nghis exchanged glances.

Chan opened a locker and produced four gas masks, of a design used by US Special Forces. And as he handed one to Grandson Nghi, they heard the first shots in the battle of Jamaica Bay being fired.

Cagliaro had been terrified of the leap from launch to companionway. He was a brave man in many respects, but water and that thirty-inch space, that drop, between companionway and black Brooklyn water, was an almost insurmountable obstacle for him. He had pushed Joe Messina and Vito Menfi on, then gripped one body-guard's sleeve and forced himself off the comparative safety of the launch's forward deck. And slipped, and been hauled on to the companionway by the ever-faithful Messina.

That had been the sound Chan had noticed.

The six-strong Mafia team swarmed past Cagliaro and padded silently up the companionway. Just at that moment, after there had not been a soul on deck for about forty-five minutes, one of the engine room artificers emerged from a door below the bridge and strolled towards the rail.

The Sicilians waited, hardly breathing.

The artificer leaned on the rail, and gazed at the lights of Brooklyn. They could hear faint noises of traffic.

Then another man came out from the same door and asked, in English, if he had been on the companionway, for he had heard a bump.

The artificer turned to reply and the side of his face was gone, spinning across the bay. *Brraaarp*, and the man in the doorway spun to one side, a solid column of blood spouting from the side of his neck, and *Brraarp*, a second, nightmare spout of blood, from a totally different angle, as if coming out from his forehead.

The mafiosi padded on, at work now. This was what they were best at.

How were they to know others were even better . . .?

In the wardroom, Chan and Ergan listened to the clicks and soft whistling sounds coming steadily now from the intercom tube. It was a form of communication 35th Spetznatz had evolved during five tours in Afghanistan, when long periods behind *mujahedeen* lines made speech, even whispers, unwise. The message so far was that armed men were on board, six to twelve in number, two crew down, and response number three was under way.

Response number three had been planned and rehearsed many times. It was designed to counter an attack, when the protected targets were safely contained in the steel-enclosed wardroom.

Cagliaro watched his team split up and head for the bridge, the accommodation cabins and the engine room, as they had been briefed, from detailed observations made by himself and the two bodyguards, Messina and Menfi, during their several visits to the *Sumaru*, when it had been moored off Antigua, in the Caribbean.

The bodyguards remained close to him, their task different from that of the would-be kidnappers, for the protection of Franco Cagliaro was their sole function.

In the silence, in the darkest shadow beneath the bridge superstructure, Cagliaro was calm. His assassins and kidnappers gone now, disappeared into the fabric of the small ship, busy about their lethal work, he felt, as he always did on operations like this, like a ghost, a bogey-man. As an infant, Franco Cagliaro had been terrified of the dark. He could not sleep unless his mother or one of his five sisters was there in the room. He had been told gruesome stories of phantasms and demons by the old peasant woman who worked for them, and his tiny childhood world had been spent in paroxysms of terror at what might lurk in any shadow, beyond any darkened staircase.

But now, oh yes, Franco Cagliaro was the fearful thing in the dark. It had been cathartic, the first time he had crept into the home, the villa, of a wealthy Sicilian rancher who had crossed Don Giovanni (by writing a letter to a Palermo newspaper, condemning the Cosa Nostra) and had stood there, listening to the measured breathing of the middle-aged man and his wife, asleep in a big old four-poster bed. In fact, standing there in the dark, his silenced Beretta machine-pistol in his hands, that room had seemed quite scary. Until the twenty-two-year-old law graduate had realized for the first time he *was* the bogey-man. What blessed release, after all those years of being afraid of the dark.

He had shot them in the legs first. Then, as they screamed in anguish and dread, he had laid down the gun, and drawn his blade . . .

Ah, yes, and here he was, twenty years after, still surviving. A creature of the night. A man whom everyone, even, he guessed, Don Giovanni, was afraid of.

Vito Menfi turned abruptly, pointing upwards, and as Cagliaro followed his line of sight, a body was dropping, in mid air, from the bridge to the solid steel deck. It hit with a crumpled thud and lay still, blood flowing from its green boiler-suit.

Shit. One of ours, registered Cagliaro, and in the same instant he realized that Vito had not been pointing; his arm had been thrown upwards by the impact of the same bullet that had made him turn, and now he continued to turn, almost gracefully, until he hit the ship's guardrail, across which he collapsed and remained, like a body hung on barbed wire.

'*Don Franco!*' Joe Messina grabbed Cagliaro by the elbow and placed his body between the boss and the lifeboat station, from where spits of fire were flickering. Bullets cracked around them and ricocheted off steel bulwarks, splintering wooden hatch covers.

Together, Cagliaro and Messina returned fire, shooting from the hip, in short, controlled bursts.

A tremendous explosion from the far side of the superstructure momentarily cheered Cagliaro, for it was the noise of a grenade exploding, but Messina shook his head and for the first time glanced back towards the companionway.

It took the Oleg Kouzmine team of Spetznatz defenders eleven minutes to eliminate the opposition. As the last of the Mafia attackers was dragged, wounded in the pelvis and semi-conscious, into a cabin for what the Spetznatz euphemistically called 'battlefield interrogation', Luigi Messina, bleeding from an upper arm wound, hustled Cagliaro back down the companionway, and as the *capo* cowered back from the dark waters of Jamaica Bay, lifted him bodily and threw him on to the launch, which was manned by two Sicilian harbour workers.

Even as the launch backed off, twin engines growling with potency, two of the *Sumaru*'s team appeared at the gunwale of the tramp-steamer, armed with an RPG-7 rocket launcher.

Cagliaro could only watch, his teeth chattering from shock, as a third figure – it was Ergan – appeared and stopped his men from blowing the launch out of the water.

Even in his shaken state, Franco Cagliaro understood that far from humanitarian considerations, the ship's defenders had no wish to attract the attention of the authorities.

As the launch gathered speed and swept in an arc of foaming phosphorescence towards Canarsie Wharf, Cagliaro realized that the normally devoted Joe was looking at him coolly.

There was no way, he determined, that this faithful bodyguard, this sole other survivor of the *Sumaru* débâcle, could be permitted to live to tell Don Giovanni of the fiasco that had been Cagliaro's attempt to kidnap the two Vietnamese.

As he gazed into the man's eyes, it was clear, like the bull in the instant before the blade of Toledo steel went in, that the poor loyal bastard was aware of his impending fate.

'*Amico mio . . .*' said Cagliaro softly, and shot him eight times, in the heart and chest.

The two crewmen crossed themselves and one went forward to help. They rolled the cadaver in anchor chains and dropped it over the side, into eight feet of water and twenty of mud and silt.

And it was not until they had helped the sea-fearing Mafia lawyer and failed kidnapper to the solid safety of Canarsie Wharf that he killed them, and walked off into the night, his little murders helping him feel less of a coward, more like the bogey-man of his nightmares.

'Gather round,' said David Jardine. It was 9.55 on that first Monday morning. He and Ronnie Szabodo had been working throughout the Saturday and Sunday, putting the 'Stone Dancer' essentials together. Recruiting – poaching might be a more accurate word – case managers, analysts, disinformation and computer wizards, agent-runners and operations planners, together with communications, secretarial and security people. Preparing a 'Stone Dancer Eyes Only' dossier to bring everyone up to speed on the Danny Davidov 'footprints' crimes and the infiltration of his operation by revisionist elements within the former KGB and other disaffected groups.

By working seventeen hours a day, they had assembled the nucleus of a Grade 3 operational unit. Grade 3 gave them broad access to other sections' and departments' most highly classified intelligence files. It provided a budget for recruiting agents and setting up networks around the globe, for paying substantial bribes and for supporting black, offensive intelligence operations run by regular SIS deep-cover operators.

Present in the briefing room in the self-contained unit of offices on the north-east corner of the ninth floor, were Szabodo, Joss Hurley from Personnel, Bill Jenkins, his old Operations Manager from the halcyon days of West 8, and Kate Howard, Director of Security. Also Marietta, whom he had telephoned, then driven over to Prince of Wales Drive in London's Battersea district, to cajole and persuade in person to join his team.

Marietta was every bit as senior as Jardine and he had required all his powers of rational, unemotive argument before she had grudgingly agreed to run a major and vital part of the operation.

A map of the world was on one wall, with coloured tapes and pins to indicate where Davidov had struck, along with black crayoned numbers, denoting the rising value of each theft in US dollars.

There were surveillance photos of Danny Davidov and a blow-up of the small framed photo Jardine had stolen from Natalya Kolosova's apartment. Also photographs supplied during Jardine's weeks of intensive research, by local SIS Stations, of the exteriors and, where possible, interiors of the targets, and of the various personnel involved, along with background information on them and their families.

It was not bad, considered Marietta, who knew Jardine had only been given the job on Friday evening.

'You have all read the briefing notes?'

Nods and murmurs indicated, yes, they had.

'Okay. That's the tourists' guide to our problem. Now

permit me to lead you into some back-alleys and places we shall never speak about, except to each other.'

The others waited in silence. Comfortable. It was like a homecoming.

'Essentially,' Jardine went on, 'this operation has two tiers. They might find themselves running parallel, or we might in fact find one being abruptly taken over by the other.'

He was half-sitting on the window-ledge. If he had looked out, he would have just have been able to see the dome of St Paul's, behind, about two miles away on the other side of the Thames.

'First, it is an investigation. Detective work. We urgently require the answers to a number of seemingly disparate questions. Precisely who is the Danny Davidov gang comprised of? What is their precise, current criminal activity – what are they doing right now? Where? Also . . . let's not talk about this Oleg Kouzmine as if we know him, them. Or their methods, because we don't. So everything about the Oleg Kouzmine Faction. Staraya Zemlya. Preferably today.'

'Shall we try to place someone?' asked Kate, tapping the eraser on the end of her pencil against her ear.

'I don't actually know if we are going to have time.' Jardine met her gaze, aware that if his hunches were all correct, there was very little time left, but this was a high-class operational team he intended to use long after the Danny Davidov business was attended to.

She smiled, and returned to study the file on her knees.

Ronnie Szabodo imperceptibly shook his head and patted his jacket pocket, looking for his pipe, which he seemed to keep next to his denture.

As the assembled craftsmen in the business of espionage listened to David Jardine's succinct briefing, a shaft of sunlight filled the room, warming them with its touch.

Jardine was like that, reflected Kate Howard. He brought a little bit of magic into people's lives. Even to those of them stuck in Century House, he spoke as if they too knew what it was like to be stabbed in some beautiful agent's Beirut apartment, or kidnapped by the Viet Cong.

Then she was cross with herself for becoming so . . . fond of the big rat. She removed her spectacles with the crooked frame, and polished them on her cotton shirt.

'How close do we get to the Agency?' asked Marietta.

'As close as we want. It is, as I have written in the briefing notes, a joint venture. But let us dictate the level of propinquity. We should try to make an independent contribution first.'

For instance, he thought, now we can produce the name of Nikolai Kolosov, the mystery KGB element. That should keep everyone pretty chipper. Of course, Alan and Nancy would guess that was precisely what he had been holding back, in order to negotiate his own terms of involvement. But secret intelligence was currency, a commodity for bartering like any other, and Alan at least would understand.

He smiled and beckoned come in to Heather, who had opened the door tentatively and put her head round. She came in, pushing a trolley with an enormous pot of tea and another of coffee, along with more of those bloody croissants. He wondered if she had taken shares in that stall at Waterloo. 'Marietta', he continued, 'will run the Investigation Tier. Ronnie, Action. Bill, you make sure it all ticks like a Swiss watch, which you always do . . .' Bill beamed with pleasure. 'Kate, you and I need to speak about a security whizz who understands electronic counterfeiting and infiltration. And Joss, we are going to need some of your very best black personnel. Regulars who have never been near this Glass Box. Men and women on full pay, with experience and understanding of the word urgency. For immediate investigations on unfriendly territory and for acquiring and preparing safe houses at short notice.'

Because they had all done this kind of thing before, and because they had all worked together before, it took only just over twenty-four hours before the first piece of decent information was on David Jardine's desk. It came from Ronnie Szabodo, and concerned the death of Elena Constantinovna Ratanskaya.

'I can't understand it,' said the Hungarian. 'Word among the Chechens is she was killed by the Israelis. The scuttlebutt' – Ronnie loved to use words like that. Pronounced in his imagined upper-class English, murdered by Magyar consonants, there was an almost poetic richness to it – 'from Moscow Militia Investigators' Office, is she was silenced by the Mafia, and out at Yasenevo, at the SVR complex, gossip is she was murdered by SIS.'

'Who?' asked Jardine, incredulous.

'Us,' replied Szabodo, simply.

'Are they just incompetent or is someone putting out a smokescreen?' wondered Jardine.

Ronnie Szabodo sucked air and opened a slim, dog-eared diary. As if to refresh his memory. Pure play-acting. The man was clearly bursting to impart some gem of intelligence he had no doubt received from his quite illegal private espionage network inside the Moscow establishment and criminal fraternity.

David Jardine ignored him, refusing to entertain the charade, and went back to the impressive pile of files and updates from twin tiers of 'Stone Dancer'.

'Evidence has been filtering into the Prosecutor's Office', Szabodo remarked casually, crossing to the window and gazing out at the rooftops of Lambeth and beyond the South Bank to the City, 'that she moonlighted.'

'Doing what?' asked Jardine. But in his heart, he already knew.

'Callgirl.'

Oh, no, Jesus . . . can't this business ever leave somebody with just a touch of dignity? Of grace . . .?

'Go on.'

'Well, according to the current investigation, she worked two or three times a month. No foreigners. Only with Russians. Mafia bosses, couple of well-known politicians, old-guard *nomenklatura*. Some ex-KGB. As in, generals.

Colonels. And one special, so the story goes . . .'

David Jardine gazed at Szabodo. They had known each other for so long they hardly required to communicate out loud. He nodded. 'Oleg Kouzmine?'

'How is it that after never hearing this chap's name, David, suddenly it's on everyone's lips?'

'Well, it's not, Ronnie. It's on the lips of our Director-General. And now it's on the lips of your completely deniable sources inside the Moscow Prosecutor's Office.' David Jardine leaned back and stretched his aching spine, the legacy of too many heavy parachute landings and a fight for survival in some Cold War back-street. 'But isn't that the way? Some word you've never heard before suddenly crops up all over the place. It happened to me once with the word dithyramb. Even saw it chalked on the side of a bus, within hours of hearing it for the first time.'

'What does it mean?'

'Christ, I've no idea.'

'You won't, I think, David, find Oleg Kouzmine on the side of a bus.'

Outside, in Wonderland, a red London bus did in fact pass the glass building, one of those with the top missing, so that tourists can enjoy the rain and pigeons in equal measure. A New Orleans-style jazz band was belting out 'South Rampart Street Parade'. Its bass drum and reedy clarinet tones just about percolated through to Jardine's subconscious. But he was miles away, back there in that little café near the Stanislavsky Theatre, eating forkfuls of baklava and watching her sparkling, head-lowered glances, while she related the time she got shot. In a men's lavatory in some Moscow jazz club.

'What are you thinking?' inquired Szabodo.

'How very sad, Ronnie. That's what I was thinking.'

'Apparently she was, her . . . assignments –'

'Assignations.'

'They were arranged by . . .' The Hungarian consulted his notebook once more.

'Ronnie, enough is enough, please.'

'I was only going to say –'

'Natalya Kolosova. Five oh three, Yuri Gagarin apartment block, Ulitsa Samorodinka. Olympic Village.' David Jardine met Szabodo's hurt gaze.

'How did you know?' he asked.

'Like the same name cropping up, so do the same players in the same game. I think Jung called it "synchronicity".'

'So why don't I just get you a Ouija board and you can sit here and solve the whole bloody thing? Sir.'

David Jardine remained silent. Then he smiled. 'Come on, you toad, let's have it . . .'

Ronnie Szabodo bent to examine the Thomas Mudge carriage-clock. It was at ten before three. 'The investigator went to her apartment. She was gone. Madame Kolosova and the girl, you remember she had a daughter at school?'

'Yes.' He remembered very well.

'Natalya phoned the school, last Thursday morning. Said she was going away, her mother had died. Taking the kid.' Szabodo spread his arms and shrugged. 'Her mother died eight years ago.'

'You're saying she's disappeared?'

'Looks like it. Any theories?'

Jardine opened a drawer, took out a pack of Chesterfields.

'You do like to change your brands,' remarked Szabodo.

'To put pressure on Nikolai? Wherever he is . . .?'

'But they're divorced. You said she thinks he's a bastard.'

'People don't always tell the truth, Ronnie. Besides, maybe he loves the girl. His daughter. Maybe that's who is being used to apply a little . . . *prizhat*.' He meant pressure.

'Which means what, to us?'

Jardine took a cigarette from the pack. Then slid it back in again. 'It means that Kolosov is close to the move against the dollar, and somebody just wants to concentrate his mind.'

Ronnie Szabodo frowned. Then he understood.

'Oleg Kouzmine,' he offered. And Jardine smiled and put his cigarette pack away.

'Time to go west, young man . . .' is all he said, and lifted his passport from the drawer.

At the request of State Department Counsellor James O'Connell, the New York attorney, Mitchel, had parted with the original US Treasury promissory letter on a certified government receipt, along with a claim for the repayment to his client of 70,000 dollars, for gold bullion delivered on 27 April 1865, at monthly compound interest of 5 per cent.

The US Treasury had researched its archives for the period in question and had indeed found three documents confirming the purchase of bullion from the Ukrainian Topolsky family.

It could not, however, discover any record of payment, or, more worrying, precisely where the gold, for which the Treasury had issued a receipt, had been delivered.

Well, almost 130 years later, about 48,000 days at 5 per cent monthly compound interest, there was not enough money in the United States, including Fort Knox, Las Vegas and the millions of trunks and shoeboxes under old ladies' beds, to approach the amount needed to repay the US Government's debt to Daniel Bogdanovich Topolsky and his family in the Ukraine.

If one wanted to get academic, the figure calculated by some financial brain worked out at around 90,000,000, 000,000,000,000,000,000 dollars. More money, in fact, than there was in the entire world.

There was no hint as to what the loan had been for, and a thorough perusal of the President's diaries, private papers and all remaining government papers of the time revealed nothing.

Except for the word 'sparrow'.

It had been detected by the laboratory, using ultra-violet light and reversed televisual polarity, as a mere imprint on the back of the Treasury Secretary's purchasing letter of confirmation. Chemical tests then revealed it had originally been written on another piece of paper, probably in pencil, and its imprint had come through.

And there were cryptic references to 'sparrow' in three of the 16th United States President Abraham Lincoln's private diary entries, written in a form of code which he had used for personally sensitive entries. All between three weeks and two days before the date of the loan documents.

None of those diary entries had been available to the public, being locked away in the vaults of the Smithsonian Institution, in Washington, DC.

All those documents had been examined by the Treasury, and despite the scepticism of Counsellor O'Connell and his opposite numbers there, teams of US counterfeit experts, scientists, calligraphy laboratories and historians could not find fault with the paper, the ink, the distinctive penmanship or, indeed, the signature of the witness for the US Government, John Carradine Wilkes, a young official serving, ironically enough, with the United States Treasury.

Eventually, the Treasury's Legal Department held a meeting with senior officials, and things had gotten so far down the road that a 'substantial' settlement was being considered, when Nancy Lucco, reading an internal digest of monthly happenings within the Secret Service's Counterfeit Analysis Lab on Connecticut Avenue, learned of the letter and asked for a meeting with O'Connell, at State. James O'Connell told Nancy about Mitchelson's initial approach. They both knew the lawyer to be a tough nut, wily and devious, but at the bottom line, dead straight and reliable. If Mitchelson had guaranteed he knew the owner of the letter was a genuine Ukrainian, with genuine title to the letter and correctly authorized to represent the Topolsky family, then that was probably right.

If the Topolsky in the USA insisted on no face-to-face dealings, that the entire negotiation was to be conducted through Mitchelson, then he was being properly prudent.

Nancy Lucco returned from O'Connell's office strangely . . . elated. And she could not figure out why. Maybe it was her lawyer's instinct, for she had an excellent legal mind, which is what Judge Almeda had recognized. Or perhaps it was the training in detection and observation that the Director had insisted she went through on joining the Service. Whatever, by the time she got back to her own office, Nancy buzzed Toni and asked for the Stone Dancer file.

She sat late into the evening, a janitor cleaning up around her, just reading and re-reading both the copy of the promissory note and the file, which David Jardine had sent across in the diplomatic pouch with a handwritten note, 'bringing her up to speed', as he had put it. The naming of the until then unknown KGB man, suspected of having surreptitiously taken control of Davidov's activities, had not surprised Nancy. She had figured the scar-faced, Thelonius Monk devotee had been playing a little bit of poker.

The accompanying photograph was about six years out of date, judging by the height and age of the daughter, if she was now fourteen, but the information, on nineteen pages, was comprehensive and succinct. She could hear David Jardine coming through on every page, and she had to admit the guy knew his business. By the time she had re-read the Stone Dancer file, she knew more about Danny Davidov and Colonel Nikolai Kolosov than either of them would have felt comfortable with. It was kind of a thrill, to be party to the results of seriously expensive, and risky, secret intelligence-gathering.

Now she was beginning to understand what Jardine's job entailed. And she began to appreciate him, on a strictly professional level.

So, why am I sitting here when I could be at home reading *Vanity Fair* with my feet up and my hair in rollers? she asked herself.

I'll tell you why, Nancy. Because on the one hand we

have an outrageous demand against the United States, its government and people, for an agreed settlement which will probably be about a thousand million bucks, to include perpetual and universal discretion – for who knows why old Abe wanted that money? – and the document in question appears not to be a forgery. And on the other hand, we have Danny Davidov and Nikolai Kolosov, who have spent the last few years royally shafting banking and government institutions – and the Government of Thailand – with examples of counterfeiting so varied, so . . . immaculate, that their very excellence has become a signature.

Nancy Lucco sat back and smiled. 'Sparrow', in invisible ink. What a touch. Hats off, fellows. Now let's see if the US Secret Service can grab your bad asses before Mr David Jardine and the British MI6 get remotely close to you.

At which point, the Night Communications Manager knocked and came into her office. 'Classified memo just come in from the London Embassy. Working late?'

'No,' she answered, without a smile, 'I'm on California time . . .'

The Night Communications Manager considered this, then shrugged. 'Sure thing,' he said and ambled out, unperturbed.

The message was from SIS, delivered by hand to 'Gentleman' Jack Dempsey, the Secret Service Attaché at the American Embassy in London. It read:

> *Stone Dancer endgame imminent. Watch out for something imaginative and special. This in my judgement will merely be their lever to get at the target so be careful what you commit to Treasury computer data base, it might be a Trojan Horse for a virus. Arriving DC tomorrow.*

And it was signed, simply, 'David'.

Okay, make me feel guilty, Nancy Lucco reflected wryly,

reading his signature one more time. It had a quiet strength to it.

And she realized this was no time to play games, they would have to work together, if the march of time permitted.

Nancy lifted the phone and dialled Elmore Williams' New York number – he was staying in a rented two-room apartment off 8th Avenue, near Waverley Street – and while she imparted cryptic instructions to the undercover agent, she scribbled a memo to the Service's Intelligence Division asking them to obtain photographs of Colonel Nikolai Kolosov from the CIA's register of KGB personnel, present and future. Plus any biog details while they were at it.

And she ordered that the inquiry should not be traceable to the Danny Davidov investigation.

In New York, Elmore Williams had been lying on his bed, half-watching a TV Movie Hall of Fame re-run of *Serpico*, with Al Pacino, and half-catching up on some shut-eye.

He had received a phone call the night before, at 1.20 a.m. It had come from NYPD Homicide, who had just found two Italian harbour workers, down on Canarsie Wharf. They had each been shot, then their throats had been cut, and their tongues pulled through the bloody gaps. It was known in the trade as the 'Sicilian necktie'.

The lieutenant who phoned had heard Williams was on a joint task force, seeking some Sicilians who had put a contract on Elmore and his family. NYPD was like that, once a member of the fraternity, you had earned their respect and commitment. Williams had not even bothered to ask how the caller had gotten hold of his clandestine phone number.

He had hauled on his clothes and gone down to Canarsie, where the forensic detail were still at work. The ubiquitous Dr Henry Grace was stooped, rummaging around two gory bundles of extinct humanity. A search of the victims' pockets had revealed nothing, except the keys for a fast, thirty-two-foot launch which was found moored at a pier not more than fifty yards away from the derelict warehouse shed where the bodies had been found.

Homicide Lieutenant Ray Donnelly, the detective who had phoned, told Williams that a preliminary search of the launch, whose engine was still lukewarm, had revealed fresh wood splinters and eleven bullet-holes, three in the windshield, four in the stern and six in the hull.

'Fuckin' Sicilians,' Donnelly had remarked.

'Fuckin' crack merchants,' Elmore Williams had corrected him. He had some really good friends in the Sicilian Anti-Mafia Squad.

The night had been chilly and he had turned his collar up.

Henry Grace had reached out for a brown-paper-wrapped object and for a second Williams imagined it contained Grace's necessary quart of Jack Daniels. But when the pathologist shook the bag, out flopped a severed human hand, with a few inches of wrist and a very nice Patek Philippe wristwatch.

He had shuddered.

'Jesus Christ, Henry. You are a sick man, sick, sick, sick. Jesus . . .'

'Yeah, yeah,' Grace had replied. 'How good is your arithmetic, Tennessee?'

'Tennessee?' Donnelly had inquired, amused.

'Forget it, Ray.' Williams had frowned, and studied the two cadavers closely. Well, it did not need a certified public accountant to count there was one hand too many. For both corpses had a full complement of extremities with which to tie their shoelaces and pick their noses.

'So whose hand is it?' he had asked.

It seemed the hand had been found on the floor of the speedboat's open cockpit.

By eleven the next morning, which Elmore Williams had spent either with Homicide or down at the morgue at Bellevue Hospital, it had been established that the severed hand had been the result of a blast trauma and that the watch was genuine and would have cost about 12,000 dollars, if it had been bought and not stolen.

It was, of course, still working.

The hand had been found to be without the calluses associated with manual work and the fingernails had been clean and well kept. Both sides of the hand, the outside lateral base of the little finger and part of the wrist, however, had cultivated calluses, or hardened skin, which indicated a practitioner of karate or some similar martial art.

The fingerprints had been wired to law enforcement agencies and police and State Trooper offices nationwide.

Traces of human blood had been found on the forward deck, which did not match the DNA of either of the murdered men. Or of the extra hand.

Five spent 9-mm shell cases had been found on the forward deck and four on the ground inside the derelict warehouse.

So the consensus was that a shootout had taken place, probably with another speedboat. Probably some altercation over cocaine. It was a daily event in New York City. There had been reports of a couple of explosions from a nightwatchman on Canarsie and a Guardian Angel on his way home from subway patrol, near Playland subway station on the Rockaways. That was probably when the hand got detached from its owner. Then maybe the guy who had fired the shots on board – who had been wounded? – had for some reason killed the two harbour workers who had been crewing the launch. Or he had fallen overboard and the two Sicilian harbour men had been shot by persons unknown, after mooring the launch and walking through the derelict wharf area.

After a conference with Donnelly and the Harbor Police, Williams had agreed there was not much more they could do that night. He had gone back to the Waverley apartment and had written up a report which he filed under the carpet. Then he took a long shower and flopped down to grab some shut-eye.

He had only been awake twenty minutes, half-watching *Serpico*, when Nancy Lucco had telephoned.

What the fuck, he had wondered, is the point in having a secret undercover number when everybody and their dog can phone whenever they like?

And what did Nancy want?

Only for this dog-tired Special Agent to get his sorry ass on to the street, rustle up a serious surveillance team from Joe Pearce's NY Field Office, and stake out, with static and mobile surveillance, the home and office of one Michael Mitchelson, attorney-at-law, and take intense interest in anyone he contacts called Topolsky, or anyone who looks like one of two suspect photographs which might or might not be wired to the Field Office tomorrow.

Terrific. Situation normal.

David Jardine had taken a taxi from his Tite Street flat to Heathrow, to catch the early morning Concorde. So it was something of a surprise to him when he strolled into the exclusive atmosphere of the Concorde Lounge, enveloped in glass, with a sleek and not all that big supersonic dart of an airliner parked just outside, to see Ronnie Szabodo sitting in one of the leather armchairs, sipping freshly squeezed orange juice and reading the *Daily Telegraph* (what else?).

'Travelling with us today?' murmured Jardine as he sat next to the Hungarian.

'Read this,' replied Szabodo and, withdrawing two folded sheets of paper from his inside pocket, passed them over.

As David Jardine read, he felt a slight flush of too-late precognition.

Of course . . .

The first sheet contained a terse few paragraphs, written in Marietta's unmistakable no-bullshit prose. Its content was therefore very clear.

For Marietta had directed her considerable brain to something so obvious it made Jardine feel . . . well, dumb, for the first time in recent weeks, just when he had begun to think he was on top of things. She had used her formidable memory and matchless contacts to dig deep into the background of one Youssef Abdul-Fetteh, assassinated newspaper editor, and father of Alisha.

The second piece of paper left no doubt, because it came from a top secret Israeli Intelligence document, filched from Golda Meir's office many years before. Youssef Abdul-Fetteh was the workname of a deep-cover Mossad operator, who had entered the Lebanon from Morocco the same month of the same year that another Mossad deep-penetration officer, Eli Cohen, had been hanged by the Syrians for espionage.

Abdul-Fetteh was a Moroccan Jew, who had been taken to Israel by his parents in 1937 at the age of ten. He had been a member of Hagannah and was recruited into Mossad at the age of eighteen, sent to the USA and fed, by way of Morocco, into Beirut, where he studied at the American University and graduated in English and Middle East History in June 1961.

'Anything to do about this . . .?' asked Szabodo, quietly, gazing at luggage being loaded on to the slim aircraft just outside.

'Not at the moment. Thanks.'

And Ronnie Szabodo folded his newspaper and left. God knew how he had charmed his way into the departure lounge in the first place.

David Jardine let out a long breath and stared at the runways and a departing 747 in some green livery.

It made such sense. Alisha of the glistening thighs was the child of an Israeli.

A very brave Israeli. Marietta's concise note stated he had been a moderate, very much on the side of the doves in the Knesset, and his journalism had often urged the granting of some land and some autonomy – some self respect – to the Palestinians, in return for the PLO's recognition that Israel had a right to exist.

So, mused Jardine, if such a man had somehow learned of the extremist group which had, unauthorized, appropriated the Robert Maxwell millions for their own hidden agenda, then it was close to inevitable that he would have to be silenced.

Which explained, and even David Jardine felt a chill, why Reuven Arieh, the group's fixer, had arranged for the man to be murdered by the Druze in Beirut.

The resulting mayhem was a mere by-product.

Jardine sighed. The more he knew about Alisha, now functioning (less than regularly he had been aware) as Agent Mongoose, the more of an enigma the woman was becoming. For instance, had she always been aware that her father was a deep-penetration Mossad operator, or did she only learn – quite probably from Arieh, he was certainly capable of that – that her beloved father was an Israeli hero?

He picked up his old Colombian leather travelling bag and joined the group of passengers about to board Concorde Flight BA 01 to New York, some of whom he recognized. James Brown – the hardest-working man in showbusiness – Sir David Frost, deep in conversation with a US Senator whose name Jardine could not remember, and the tennis star Agassi.

One of the Concorde Lounge staff approached him. 'Mr Jardine?'

'That's me,' he replied, smiling his frankest I-have-nothing-to-hide smile.

'Telephone call. You can take it in that booth, just there.'

Inside the booth, Jardine lifted the receiver as the phone buzzed discreetly.

'Yes?'

'You're a hard man to track down.' Nancy's voice.

'I hope so,' he replied, pleased to hear from her.

'Thanks for your letter.'

'All on the same side, right?'

Slight pause.

'David, I gotta hunch. Why don't you stay in NYC and I'll fly up.'

Jardine considered this. With the sort of scam Danny Davidov had been working, New York, the financial capital, would be a better place to attack the dollar than Washington.

'Sure,' he said. 'My office will tell you where to find me.'

'I'll meet you at JFK,' she said. 'Time's wingèd chariot and all that.'

He smiled. 'I can't wait.'

'You behave yourself.'

And those two people hung up. And maybe they were thinking about more than the case as they went about their business, she packing a few things – it was ten after three in the morning, and she was back at her Georgetown apartment – and he joining the queue of passengers filing past the desk towards the enclosed gangway leading to Concorde.

He glanced at the morning papers. The dollar was taking a mauling on the Tokyo money markets but that was attributable to a difficult few weeks following publication of US trade figures and the country's very real struggle to keep Federal reserves credible in the light of the National Debt which, on paper, defied basic rules of solvency.

Jardine folded the newspaper and dozed most of the three-and-a-half-hour flight. Then, 64,000 feet over the Atlantic, at 3400 miles per hour, he suddenly woke with a jump, hit by a feeling it was all going to go badly wrong. His skin felt cold and his pulse quickened. It was not an instinct he ever ignored . . .

Despite the near-disaster of the attempted kidnap of the two Vietnamese counterfeiters, Danny Davidov was a happy man. As he read the financial newspapers and magazines of a score of countries from Tokyo to Argentina, with assiduously planted rumours of the US Budget deficit being almost double that admitted by the administration, he began to feel that he and Nikolai Kolosov had spent tens of millions of their illegally acquired wealth to good effect.

Over the last two years they had quietly hacked their way into the secure computer networks of eight major organizations, each one an important brick in the structure they had evolved to present, to the US Treasury, a deadly serious, and immediate, threat to the stability of the mighty dollar.

How immediate was at that moment known only to the two scoundrels and one or two of their faceless, unknown henchmen, recruited agents of Operation Medusa.

The SS *Sumaru*'s ex-KGB crew had disposed of the dead Mafia hoods through a standing plan which involved the ship's cook, some extremely sharp hacksaws and a tank of sulphuric acid, part of a consignment scheduled for delivery to a merchant in Lagos, Nigeria. The survivor (temporary) who had been brusquely interrogated using a combination of morphine, to deaden the pain from his wounds, and scopolamine, a truth serum, was by definition the last to die.

The *Sumaru* had left Jamaica Bay at dawn that morning and was soon ploughing through the Atlantic, unnoticed, at a steady eleven knots, on its way towards the West African coast.

The results of the unfortunate surviving Sicilian's interrogation had been communicated, by secure means, to Davidov. All the poor man knew was they were to kidnap two Vietnamese who were being held on board, without harming them, to kill all the crew, and to return to their regular criminal employ, with no questions asked.

He did not know the name of the *capo* who had summoned them to do his work, but it was known his two bodyguards were Don Giovanni Favorito Noto's men. If the man had spoken the truth, mused Danny Davidov, that meant Franco Cagliaro himself was behind the outrage.

Well, time would see to him, reflected Davidov, as he sat in the spacious, tasteful Park Avenue apartment rented in the name of Robert Bannerman, the persona he had adopted for the serious collector of rare manuscripts and documents.

Robert Bannerman was an identity Danny had begun to

create in 1983, some years before Mossad's accountants had caught up with him and, just as Elmore Williams was known to most people in Washington, DC as Joe Marcus, so the cosmopolitan residents of 509 Park had gotten used to the infrequent comings and goings of Mr Bannerman. Inside the apartment, a housemaid, burglar or curious stranger would find driver's licence, passport, Wheeling Lions Club newsletters, correspondence with business colleagues and family, fraternity pin from UCLA, discharge papers and four medals from enlisted service with the US Coastguard . . . in short, evidence of a regular American citizen.

There had been a real Robert Bannerman, who had died on 14 May 1983, while on a visit to a brothel in Cyprus. At the time Danny Davidov was running a Mossad operation to find and eliminate a cell of killers from Yasser Arafat's Force 17, the Palestinian's personal special force, who had murdered a Mossad team working under cover from a sailboat in the harbour at Famagusta. Danny had been paying the brothel-keeper for information on his customers, in an effort to find a red-haired anti-Semite from Manchester, England, who had found employ with Al-Fatah and who took an unhealthy pleasure in his work, which was currently the killing of Israeli agents in Cyprus and Beirut.

Well, the red-haired man soon disappeared. And the spin-off, for Davidov, was that when the American Robert Bannerman died of a heart attack, brought on by suffocation beneath and between the too-ample breasts of an athletic Serbian whore of Sumo-like proportions, he was asked by the brothel-keeper to dispose of the corpse discreetly, as a favour to the pimp.

He had gone back to the man's hotel room, at the palatial Lhedra Palace in Metaxis Square, taken all his belongings and checked out. There had been quite sufficient in the dead man's wallet – travel documents and a few letters – to bring joy to the Mossad man's heart. For Robert Bannerman had no living family except for a sister he had long ago fallen out with, few friends, and was self-employed as a modestly successful supplier of travel articles to a number of publishing syndicates.

Davidov had disposed of the body in a deep geological fissure, in the foothills of the Troodos Mountains, and by his skills in the art of deception, had continued the late Robert Bannerman's peregrinations around Europe and the Middle East, filing fewer and fewer travel pieces and gradually dropping from the memories of his few acquaintances.

Thus Danny felt reasonably secure in the Park Avenue apartment. And though he always harboured the commendable – for someone in his trade – paranoid suspicion that he was going to be denounced at any moment, it was not that which was causing him to feel an unusual degree of excitement and apprehension.

He was waiting for the arrival of a very rare, and very special, guest. His Chief Operations Director. The two men knew each other only as the Moor and the Nomad. They had met, face to face, only seven times in the last two years, but they had communicated, by satellite, in cipher, in short, low-frequency sound bursts, on a weekly, sometimes daily, basis.

This was the first, and only, time the Nomad was to meet Danny Davidov at the Bannerman residence. Danny judged this to be an acceptable risk now, because he had no intention of being there, ever again, after noon the following day.

Nancy Lucco was waiting for Jardine as he emerged from the Concorde flight at 8.29 a.m. JFK Immigration was working smoothly and with his diplomatic passport David Jardine was waved through, and he met Nancy in the Arrivals Hall nineteen minutes after touchdown.

They got into the back of the Secret Service Lincoln sedan, with driver, and headed for Queens and the bridge to Manhattan Midtown. Nancy briefed him on events. She told him about the Ukranian gold affair, which had grown to altogether different proportions with the discovery, just two days earlier, of apparently genuine documents in US Treasury Archives supporting the claim, and she passed him a file, recording strange events over the last forty-eight hours, along with a digest of financial and political columns from serious newspapers all over the world.

The gist of those stories was that the US Budget deficit was rumoured to be just about twice what the Government had admitted in its annual Presidential address.

'And check this out . . .' said Nancy.

She showed him about eight cuttings from papers like the London *Daily Telegraph*, the *Financial Times*, the *Wall Street Journal*, *France-Soir*, the Italian *Corriere della Serra* and *El Espectador*, published over the last three weeks and at first filed as 'silly season' stories. The nub of them was that the USA did not have sufficient gold reserves, in terms of actual, physical ingots of the precious metal, to match the number of dollar bills in circulation and meet their fiscal commitments to international trading partners.

Jardine read them carefully. Then he took off his reading glasses, leaned back and thought deeply.

'The problem is,' he remarked, 'once one becomes . . . aware, you can read so much into all kinds of stuff, which might just be coincidence.'

'David, we are talking here about the integrity of the US dollar. These stories that've been cropping up have begun to take on an . . . orchestrated look. If we agree that Danny Davidov is out to shake our tree, as you once put it, he could do worse than start his moves like this . . .'

Jardine frowned. He nodded. 'Maybe it would be sensible to assume you're right.'

She stared at him. 'Jesus. Are you patronizing or what?'

'I'm a total shit,' he replied blithely. And grinned.

Nancy Lucco could not resist a smile of satisfaction when she handed him two buff envelopes containing four surveillance photographs of Colonel Nikolai Kolosov and three of Danny Davidov.

'These might be of some assistance to you.'

'You see?' he said without a blush. 'Mutual cooperation at work . . .' Then, as he studied them, she passed him a green folder marked 'Top Secret US Treasury Eyes Only', which was the master file on the Mitchel/Ukrainian gold case.

Jardine whistled as he got to the impossible sum being sued for.

'Watch out for something imaginative, your memo said last night.' Nancy watched him carefully.

He inclined his head. 'And special. Yup. This really does fit the bill.' He shook his head in wonder. 'When you have the key, it's like a calling card.' He read on, scanning the reports and case notes swiftly, pausing occasionally. Then he turned and looked over his glasses at her. 'Who precisely is this man Mitchel?'

Nancy told him.

Then she said, just as casually as could be, 'I've probably broken some Amendment, but last night I put round-the-clock surveillance on him.'

His glance of respect was, she admitted, rewarding. He flapped the two envelopes of photographs at her. Outside, they had reached the Van Wyck Expressway, the graffitied walls of Queens becoming more prevalent. 'And you have doubtless furnished them with copies of these . . .'

'Furnished . . .?' She frowned. 'I passed a ton of them around our New York Field Office, if that's what you mean.'

David Jardine continued to pore over the various documents she had given him.

'Have you ever heard of a former KGB general called Oleg Kouzmine?' he inquired mildly.

An open carriage drawn by a somewhat moth-eaten horse clip-clopped through the stakeout area, which was on Fifth Avenue between 42nd and 41st, opposite the New York Public Library.

Deputy Special Agent in Charge Elmore Williams sat three feet from a window on the nineteenth floor of an office building, directly across the street from Michael

Mitchel's luxurious offices and one floor higher, so that he could look down into it. To one side was a bank of ten TV monitors, which had been installed in the course of the morning by a less than delighted Joe Pearce, from his stash of surveillance equipment in the Field Office store.

Joe had a larger budget and more agents than most Dee-Sacs, apart from Miami, Los Angeles and DC. But there were eighteen million souls in town, and NY Field Office was generally overstretched at any given time.

However, he had grudgingly assigned forty agents to work in two details for Williams, staking out attorney Michael Mitchel's Fifth Avenue office and his home about five blocks east of Central Park, on 67th.

Elmore Williams had not declared that the request for a stakeout came from Nancy Lucco, because as a member of the Service's legal staff, she had no operational authority. But number one, Elmore liked her, number two, he trusted her judgement, and 'C', as Eddie Lucco used to put it, if push came to shove, she would only get Director Farley to order it and therefore attract the Chief's beady gaze on the whole shemozzle.

So Joe Pearce was under the impression the Mitchel surveillance was part of Elmore Williams' remit to investigate the perpetrators of the attempted murder of Williams and his family, which had its origins in the disastrous counterfeit sting way before Easter, when Sammy the Nose had lost his proboscis.

Elmore knew that sooner or later he would have to bring the surveillance team into his confidence. He was just waiting for the right moment.

In addition to video surveillance at the Fifth Avenue stakeout, Williams' team had four unmarked cars and three motorcycles, eleven pavement artists and a control unit.

He had split his team into three details; one on the home, one on the office and one to travel with Mitchel, wherever he went. The control unit consisted of three Special Agents, communications and eavesdropping experts, who maintained constant contact with each detail and reported to Williams. They were fully mobile, if need be, and were established in the same room on the nineteenth floor of the office building where Elmore Williams was gazing through powerful binoculars into the lawyer's private office.

Tony Carmino was Williams' deputy and he studied the video monitors, which showed changing views of the street and side-streets, the entrance to the Fifth Avenue building, the lobby on the first floor, the four elevators that went as far as the eighteenth floor, the lobby outside the eighteenth floor, and long-range close-ups of the interiors of the Mitchel office suite, from the Public Library opposite.

All those cameras had a zoom/big close-up capability. Photographs of Kolosov and Davidov were pinned around the video sets.

'What've these guys done?' asked Carmino, which was a sly question and meant he did not believe for a second this had anything to do with Iro Sonson or the Sicilian hoodlums' lawyer/enforcer, Luis Restrepo Osorio.

This was Williams' chance to explain what was going down.

'It's a big confidence-scam,' he replied casually. 'Extortion from US Treasury.'

'Much money involved?' Carmino was less than interested. This was the kind of thing they did every day.

'Last I heard . . . about twenty billion dollars.'

Stunned silence.

The two men and the woman on the control unit exchanged glances.

'Well, excuse me,' said Tony Carmino and started to scrutinize the screens more closely.

Elmore Williams smiled. There, that had not been too bad.

In Wall Street, the New York Stock Exchange was beginning to buzz with activity. The dollar was under attack from a dozen different directions, and worse, computer gremlins were fucking up simple instructions to buy the US currency, worldwide, and adding the occasional zero or two to instructions to sell.

The atmosphere was hectic, and several dealers had considered suspending operations until such time as the international communications system was repaired.

Joe Pearce poured three cups of coffee from the vacuum flask on his desk. He was deeply thoughtful, for Nancy Lucco and the English guy, some kinda spook, had just briefed him on Stone Dancer, leaving out nothing of any importance.

'Sugar, anybody?' he asked.

'Just as it comes,' replied Jardine, who was reading a coded signal the SIS New York Outstation had just sent round to the New York Field Office by hand.

The gist of it, from his Stone Dancer team, was that Alisha Abdul-Fetteh and Reuven Arieh had flown out of Beirut on separate flights, but had been glimpsed together, the day before, in Rome, at the airport.

'Just milk, Joe,' said Nancy.

'There we go.' The big Irishman distributed the cups. As he sat facing them, he looked at Nancy. 'You hear what's going on at the Stock Exchange?'

'Today? No.'

'Place is going crazy. Dow Jones is in bad shape.' He meant the Dow Jones Index, which showed on a minute-by-minute basis how things were faring as far as US stocks were concerned. And he went on to explain about the computer errors and the chaos they were causing.

Jardine gazed at Nancy Lucco. 'Trojan Horse,' he said.

'Trojan Horse . . .?' She stared at him. 'What the hell are you talking about?'

He nodded slowly, closing the file on the Mitchel/Topolsky claim. 'This US Treasury gold purchase. Quite harmless, really.'

'Harmless?'

'Nancy, even if the letter was real, Mitchel must realize a settlement will take years to achieve. And for how much? Maximum of, say, ten million dollars. That's not going to break the bank, even if it is one of the moves on Danny Davidov's chess-board.'

Nancy and Joe Pearce stared at him. He sipped his coffee. Pearce was just waiting for the Limey spook to lift a pinkie and say 'delaytful'. But instead, David Jardine remarked, 'Unless he has used the letter as a Trojan Horse.'

'In what way?' asked Pearce.

'Well, if I was doing it,' replied Jardine, 'I would seed in a little . . . conundrum of some kind.'

'A conundrum,' said Nancy Lucco drily.

'Sure,' said Pearce, 'if this man's father is my father's son who took the hind leg off the donkey, you know the kind of thing.'

David Jardine blinked, then grinned. 'Exactly like that. Something to make you think. Nancy, is there anything this abbreviated report on the letter has missed out?'

'Um . . .' Wise up, Nancy, she thought, this is no time to play games. 'Does it mention "sparrow"?'

'Sparrow?' Jardine stretched his neck and opened one of the files she had given him, flipped it open. Then closed it again. He looked up. 'No. It does not mention that.'

So Nancy Lucco told David Jardine and Pearce about the word 'sparrow', and how it appeared in three entries of the 16th President's diary, in his form of shorthand. And how no one at the Treasury or at the NSA crypto-analysis labs had been able to make anything out of it.

'I mean, if the Secretary of the Treasury's purchasing letter is genuine, then he wrote "sparrow" on some other piece of paper and the imprint came through.'

'Or that's what we are meant to think,' said Pearce.

Jardine met his gaze. 'I agree. So what did some turkey, I mean bright investigator do? Probably some computer whizz. Doubtless one of the best brains in the Treasury. Let me guess. He or she fed the letters S.P.A.R.R.O.W. into the Treasury's secure computer systems, they tried the letters in every possible permutation, slotting other letters and numbers in between, above and below them. They converted the letters into numerals and the numerals into binary codes and they probably used higher calculus and, for all I know, standard Kanji. All attempting to wring some magic result from the poor old sparrow.'

He watched Nancy patiently. 'Tell me I'm wrong.'

She shook her head. 'I can't. For I was that turkey.'

'Well, if it is a Trojan Horse, dear Counsellor Turkey, and if I were Danny Davidov, one of those permutations, one of the thousands, will be a little electronic soldier. Unlike Achilles, I shall only need one soldier in my Trojan Horse. For he will be carrying one thing, to let me into the citadel.'

'A key,' breathed Joe Pearce.

'A key. To that vast electronic citadel which is the repository of all secrets and the conduit for all secret transmissions, transactions too, which is the US Government's cosmic secret access system between the Treasury, foreign Treasuries and other foreign government departments, the Treasury and the Stock Exchange, and every major banking, trading and economic system in the civilized, and sometimes not so civilized, free and not so free world.' David Jardine smiled and sipped more coffee. Then he took a pack of Winston cigarettes from his pocket.

'Anyone mind . . .?' he asked politely.

'Go right ahead,' replied Nancy.

'I quit in seventy-three, 'cept for a brief lapse,' said Joe Pearce, pushing a gas lighter across the table to Jardine.

Jardine lit the cigarette and waited.

'Why did they not think of that?' demanded Nancy angrily, of nobody in particular.

'I think, because it was a different kind of crime,' said Jardine.

'Yeah, he's right. You get a couple of wiseguys present this Mitchel with a letter, oh, not the old Treasury promissory note scam, say the guys at Head Office. Then they can't find a fault and they say, either this is genuine in which case we fight for a few years then make a settlement. Or it's a terrific fake in which case we stall and tail and tap everybody in the other team till they fall off the carousel.' This was Joe Pearce talking. He gazed longingly at David

Jardine's cigarette as the Englishman inhaled. 'But nobody who is not wise to this Stone Dancer pair would ever dream of a Trojan Horse caper . . .'

Nancy Lucco sighed.

'Maybe we start by putting a whole ton of agents on to Mitchel,' said Pearce. 'Plus all kinds of eavesdropping. I mean, the guy has to communicate with this Peter Topolsky, right?'

David Jardine found something very interesting about his left boot, as Nancy swallowed and said to Joe Pearce, 'Joe, that's what Elmore Williams is doing right now.'

Silence.

Pearce laid down his coffee cup and thought for a moment.

'Nice,' was all he said. 'That's real nice.'

Then he turned to Jardine and stretched out his hand. 'Gimme one of them fuckin' cigarettes . . .'

The Editor-in-Chief of the *New York Times* was busy discussing with his Financial Editor and his News Editor how to set the lead story for next day, which was of course the Wall Street business.

'How about', offered Tom Ringwald, News Editor, 'The Wall Street Hiccup?'

'As opposed to the Wall Street Crash. I like that,' said the Financial Editor, John Bird, 'it has a responsible ring to it.'

'And what if things get worse?' inquired the Editor-in-Chief, Harry Gershwin.

'Well, we did not help it on its way,' replied Renshaw.

'Fuck that. We are news reporters, not manipulators. Tell it like it is . . .' He reached for his indigestion tablets.

Ringwald and Bird frowned and thought hard.

'Maybe . . . Wall Street Staggers,' suggested Bird.

'More like it.'

At which moment Jean Andrews, Deputy Political Editor, came in.

'Jean, later,' said Gershwin. 'Front page conference.'

'I think you should read this.' She glanced around the room. 'All of you.' And she handed a letter to the boss.

It was typed on standard A4 paper, with the letterhead of the Bureau of Printing and Engraving, on Raoul Wallenberg Place, Washington, DC. The date was the previous day.

'It was delivered by hand.'

'To Reception?' asked Renshaw.

'Sure.'

'So we'll have a photo,' said Bird. A security camera retained photographs of everyone who came into the front lobby.

'It was a kid, some guy gave him a fin,' remarked Jean Andrews. A fin was a five-dollar bill.

But Gershwin did not hear that, for he was reading the letter. It said:

> Dear Miss Andrews,
> I have been a loyal servant of the Government for many years. Both in this Bureau, where we print the dollar bills, and Treasury Notes, and at Fort Knox, in earlier days, where we move, as I am sure you know, stacks of gold bullion around the warehouse floors, to cover transactions with foreign governments and major banking institutions.
>
> I don't know how to say this. My hands are shaking as I type. But three good colleagues of mine have committed suicide over the past two months, because something terrible is happening. Something rotten with our system.
>
> You see, the rumours that the Treasury does not have enough money to cover our debts is true. But it is even worse. *We do not have enough gold reserves to cover the dollar notes in circulation*.
>
> The three friends I mentioned have all killed themselves because they could not live with the lie. You see, much of the gold in Fort Knox is fool's gold. Thousands of lead ingots have been manufactured by

> the Treasury, in great secrecy, then gold-plated and brought into Fort Knox and stored among the bullion.
>
> As a nation we are more than bankrupt. We are corrupt.
>
> Please investigate and report as fearlessly as you always do.

It was signed 'A Patriot' and clipped to the page were three newspaper clippings, two from Kentucky, where Fort Knox was, and one from Wheeling, West Virginia. The stories were of three sudden deaths, two in auto accidents and one by drowning while swimming in the Kentucky River.

'What do you think?' asked Jean Andrews, who hated being Deputy Political Editor and had always wanted to be a frontline reporter where she could yell hold the front page.

'You would be surprised how many letters we get like this. Most are from cranks. I would not get too excited,' Gershwin replied, and smiled like a crocodile. So Jean Andrews left. But Gershwin held on to the letter.

He turned to his News Editor. 'Tom, check out those deaths. Johnny, speak to your contacts at Treasury. I want a denial from the White House by midnight. We'll run that side by side with the Wall Street story.'

In trading and banking throughout the world, certified bank drafts are used as standard currency. Just as Davidov and Kolosov used them to gain entry to the Banco de Antioquia's strongest vault, so entire shipping lines and entire crops of grain have been paid for by drafts drawn on the major international banking institutions.

In the case of the USA, Treasury Notes are issued, in batches of varying denominations, from 100,000 to a billion dollars. They are printed in limited batches and the serial numbers are altered with each batch. Thus, say one hundred billion-dollar Treasury Notes were issued, they might be serials 2556378 through 2556478. And if an inquiry came from abroad, asking if a Treasury Note with the serial number 2556415, for example, was within a billion-dollar serial group, back would come the answer, yes.

In order to protect against forgery, Treasury Notes are retained in book form by the administration. Registered Bearer Forms are issued, confirming that the holder has title to the Treasury Note corresponding to the cusip number and serial number on the form. The Registered Bearer Form itself is an impressively produced document, and alteration of the cusip and serial numbers, to lift them into a different serial batch, is extremely difficult.

Any serious person with fraudulent intent would probably go to the Golden Triangle, on the border of Thailand with China, or to Vietnam where, as Pablo Escobar and Danny Davidov knew so well, the best counterfeiters can still be found.

Such frauds do occur. In England not so long ago, an American very nearly succeeded in borrowing 500 million dollars from a major bank with, as collateral, a 700-thousand-dollar Registered Bearer Bond, which had been altered in Thailand, with an accurate cusip number, to become a 700-million-dollar Registered Bearer Bond. Even the US Treasury had at first confirmed it as genuine.

Thus, when on the same day as the Wall Street Confusion, an electronically secure, protected US Treasury computer transmitted a code to all of its European and Middle Eastern foreign government opposite numbers, suspending all dealings in US Treasury Notes and Bearer Forms until further notice, that was taken very seriously indeed.

And the result was a further severe blow to the credibility of the US dollar.

David Jardine and Nancy Lucco had set up an Operations Room just down the corridor from Joe Pearce's office in NY Field Office. They had TV sets with access to the major news channels, telephone, fax and satellite communications with the US Secret Service in Washington, the Treasury's Operations Room, the CIA at Langley, the Communications Security Staff at the National Security Agency, and with SIS and the Foreign Office/UK Treasury Liaison team in London's Whitehall.

Three of Pearce's brightest agents worked with Jardine and Nancy. They had set up a big blackboard along one wall and they were busy trying to chart events as they unfolded.

'Bad news?' asked Nancy, as Jardine replaced the phone, looking thoughtful. He had just been talking to Marietta, who had phoned from London.

'Let's just say . . . interesting,' he replied, with that shy smile she was coming to realize meant he had no intentions of discussing it.

The British intelligence man poured some lukewarm coffee from a flask, digesting this latest development. Just three hours earlier, Lieutenant-Colonel Anatoly Dzerzhinsky had been found dead in his apartment, in Olympic Village; cause of death alcohol and cocaine overdose. His wife and children had been at her mother's for a few days.

With the exception of Reuven Arieh and Danny himself, David Jardine realized, that just about wrapped up the potential scandal of the mislaid Maxwell millions.

And Alisha. Who had protested, that last time in Venice, that nobody ever told her much.

'Nancy, it's Treasury for you.' One of the agents waited till Nancy Lucco picked up her receiver, then switched the secure line through.

'Nancy Lucco,' she said, and listened.

David Jardine was on the line to Whitehall, speaking with the UK Treasury's man who monitored Stock Exchange dealings as they unfolded. It was clear that a worldwide assault on the US dollar was under way. And that it was taking many forms, some of them illegal disinformation of the sort the old KGB used to do so well.

'Thanks, Richard,' he said, and put the phone down. He loosened his necktie and undid the top button of his shirt.

Nancy hung up and shook her head. 'Oh, boy . . .'

'What now?'

And Nancy Lucco told him about the anonymous letter to the *New York Times* and the request from the Editor for a White House denial regarding the lead ingots allegation.

'What do you think? Coincidence or what?' she asked.

'Sounds like Danny.'

Nancy looked harassed. 'David, maybe this is going to work. For them.'

'We'll see. Look, today is obviously their big day. You didn't expect it. Neither did I. But it was on its way, so let's stop Danny Davidov in his tracks.'

Even the hard-assed agents glanced at this Limey.

'Okay, I'm listening,' said Nancy.

David Jardine tapped his pen on the desk. A phone rang and one of the agents lifted it, spoke quietly, and put the phone down.

'I think Davidov's using an access code he picked up when he conned you people into feeding every manner of permutation of the word "sparrow" into your computer systems. That's how he has managed to hack into the Treasury's security program and send out a code suspending all dealing in Treasury Notes.'

'Say, I go along with that . . .' Nancy was sceptical.

'Well, he obviously has several lines of attack. But we should deal with them one by one. You must have duplex systems of communication, am I right?'

'I wish,' replied Nancy Lucco. 'Are you suggesting what I think?'

'Ask Treasury and State to shut down every system into which they fed the word "sparrow". The Trojan Horse that let in Danny Davidov's little electronic soldier.'

Nancy suppressed a laugh. Maybe she was getting hysterical. 'Chaos,' she said, 'that would be chaos.'

But in the silence which followed, no one made any alternative suggestion. She shrugged. 'Okay, let's just suppose I can persuade the United States to close down about

12 per cent of its secure computer systems. Just for the sake of the argument.'

'Then, switch to alternative systems.' He noticed one of the agents, an attractive girl called Maggie Prosperus, was taking this down in shorthand. 'And have Communication Security at NSA wait and ambush each attempt to hack back in, using one or more of the "sparrow" permutations.'

'And each time he does', Maggie Prosperus had caught on, 'they shut down *that* path . . .'

'Just so,' replied Jardine. His hand was in one pocket of his jacket, which hung over the back of his chair. He found himself fiddling with the brass Zippo lighter, like it was some kind of magic charm. God knew he needed one. He met Maggie's thoughtful gaze. 'Can we try?'

'Sure,' said Maggie Prosperus. She glanced at Nancy, who shrugged, as if to say, what the hell?

'We'll speak to NSA and our own Electronic Security Staff.' Maggie turned away and lifted a green phone.

Elmore Williams stretched and yawned, and when he turned to look back into Mitchel's office, the lawyer was still dictating to a scrawny-looking secretary with thick spectacles.

'Now that is a man with a dull job,' he remarked to nobody in particular.

'How's Martha?' inquired Tony Carmino, who was casually scanning the array of video surveillance monitors, while trying to adjust the date on his wristwatch, for they had just passed a month with only thirty days and he had been one day behind since the previous Monday.

'She's recovering. Plenty of fight, but Jesus, man, it sure whacked her, those four fuckin' slugs. Down to seven stone four.'

'Shit. But you know . . .'

He meant, she could've been dead.

'Sure, sure. I know.'

And as each man sat with his thoughts, the way it goes

on surveillance assignments, the voice of Marty Socorro came through real clear on the Agents' Circuit.

'Say, ain't that the guy . . .? This is One Four, I'm on Sixty Third and Third.'

Williams and Tony Carmino looked at each other. Special Agent Marty Socorro was on the Mitchel Home Detail, more or less forgotten, while the target was working in his Midtown office.

'Which one?' asked Carmino tersely.

'Stone,' came back the reply, Socorro's voice slightly distorted by the radio signal.

'Well, you got the mugshot, pal . . .'

Silence. They waited, adrenalin hovering, waiting to go to work.

Then they heard a series of cryptic words of command and responses as the local team leader moved his mobile video, hidden in the hand-held telephone of a motorbike delivery rider, with 'Red Devil Express' on his leathers, into position.

Marty's voice again. 'Okay, I am now walking ahead of suspect and stopping, to cross the street. And . . . taking a good, close look.'

Elmore Williams found himself tapping the binocular tripod in time to some silent beat. It was probably his heart.

Muffled voice from Agent Socorro. 'Hot damn, we got a good make, repeat, the make is affirmative. Take over, somebody, I have to move on . . .'

And at that instant, on one of the ten video screens, second from right, lower bank, there was former KGB Colonel Nikolai Kolosov, looking just like the black and white twenty-by-sixteen photo stuck to the frame just two feet away.

'Stone . . .' breathed Williams. He had designated Kolosov 'Stone' and Davidov 'Dancer'. The names seemed to fit.

Elmore Williams grinned. 'Wild thing, Ah thinks Ah love yah . . .'

'Foxtrot, this is John Belushi,' said Tony Carmino, into the Home Detail microphone. His nickname was John

Belushi on account of he looked so like the late star of the Blues Brothers. He even wore a black fedora. 'Ten nine nine.'

Ten nine nine meant simply, tail the subject, and if you lose him, your ass is grass.

Two mobile video units, the motorcycle and an attaché case, hand-held, managed between them to keep Kolosov in sight. The other ten agents moved on foot and in two yellow New York taxi-cabs, constantly leaving the immediate environment and returning.

Kolosov was walking briskly, heading south. He moved west towards Madison, and for a while Elmore Williams and Carmino guessed the Russian was heading, at last, towards Mitchelson's office.

The second detail was detached from the Mitchelson location and sent the half-mile uptown to work with the Socorro team.

Thus Nikolai Kolosov was being kept under surveillance by twenty experienced Secret Service agents, who looked like everything from businessmen, through tourists, to scruffy vagrants, to delivery men.

As Kolosov walked, he was busy thinking. He had just come from the Robert Bannerman apartment, which he had gone over meticulously, checking that Danny had left no trace of his true identity, or of Operation Medusa.

You had to hand it to the Jew, thought Kolosov, he really had gotten them to this day. From the moment Danny had bumped into him at the swimming pool in Olympic Village in Moscow, off Prospekt Michurinsky, the man had delivered everything he had said he was going to do. From the aircraft fuel scam, through a half-dozen mounting successes to St Petersburg, a real masterpiece, then Bogota, an outrageous piece of chutzpah, and here they were. Judging by what he had seen on CNN, in the Bannerman apartment, all the devious little ex-Mossad operator's several prongs of attack on the dollar were coming to fruition.

And he reflected on the dumb Mafia attack on the *Sumaru*. That just had to be Cagliaro. He hoped the *rebyonok*, the bastard, had died in that fiasco. But if not, one day Staraya Zemlya would catch up with him.

No problema.

Danny Davidov . . . it seemed a pity, what was planned for him. Kolosov had come to like the guy. He smiled to himself as he remembered the night they had gotten drunk together. A real likeable fellow.

'Whadda you mean, smiling?' asked Elmore Williams to the microphone, as he watched four mobile surveillance monitors swing like drunken fools around Madison Avenue, trying without success to get Kolosov in the picture.

'He's smiling. God knows,' replied Marty Socorro.

In the Oval Office of the White House, the President sat behind his desk, reading the *Wall Street Journal*, and among the files there was a copy of the anonymous letter to the Deputy Political Editor of the *New York Times*.

Present in the room were his Chief of Staff, the Secretary of State, the Secretary for the Treasury and the Director, Central Intelligence.

'Well, I dunno,' the President said, 'but it seems to me whatever group of people out there are doing this, they are having a damn good run for their money.' His beady gaze lighted on each of his senior men in turn.

'Mr President,' began the head of the CIA, 'my Director of Operations tells me the prime suspect is a former Israeli intelligence officer who was booted out of Mossad, a few years back. Teamed up with a Soviet, former Soviet, to, I quote, shake our tree. Shake the dollar.'

'To what end, Douglas?' asked the President, almost too softly.

'Extortion, sir,' said the Secretary for the Treasury.

'Extortion?' The President turned back to Douglas Sheridan. 'And what do I have you people and the FBI for . . .?'

'Mr President,' said the Treasury Secretary, 'an attack on the currency is primarily the remit of the Secret Service, to protect.'

'Really,' said the President scathingly. It was a known

fact that he was not the Secret Service's greatest fan. 'And what are they doing about it? Please don't say, everything they can.'

The Secretary raised his hands and smiled thinly. 'At this moment we have a senior officer leading a major operation in New York, sir. The perpetrators are being fought every inch of the way and' – he glanced around, presumably to make sure nobody from CNN was lurking under a chair – 'we are hopeful of making arrests quite soon.'

'Soon enough to save Wall Street?' The President fiddled with a video monitor set into his desk which provided more data than the Oracle ever did. 'I see the dollar is down to point four two on the London market . . .'

'If my information is correct, sir,' Sherridan offered, 'the aim is not to weaken the currency permanently. But to give us a big enough fright to put us in the mood to do business.'

The President nodded, barely able to restrain his anger. In fact, he nodded quite a few times. 'Is that right? No kidding?'

'Sir, if I might suggest . . .' said the White House Chief of Staff.

The President turned to him, the glare cooled only slightly. 'Go on.'

'I think an address to the nation. Just, um, just tell people what's going down,' said the Chief of Staff.

People spoke like that these days in the White House, mused Doug Sherridan, they all spoke like Bob Dylan.

'Yeah. I was getting round to the same idea. Okay, set it up. And I want to know everything. Everything, understand?'

At which point the Director of the US Secret Service, Jim Farley, knocked and entered. He smiled courteously into the President's frosty gaze.

'Bad news,' he said gravely. 'When the ingot letter came in, I ordered a check on gold bullion stocks at Fort Knox. We have found three ingots which are lead, expertly plated in ten millimetres of twenty-four-carat gold.'

'Gentlemen,' said the President, 'there is no way I am going before the nation with this can of worms.' He stood up and arched his aching back. 'Get it sorted out or none of us will have a job by Monday. Or a currency worth a damn.'

Danny Davidov glanced at his wristwatch. It was ten after three and the sweat was trickling down his back, despite the air-conditioning in the room.

He sat at a desk with three computer consoles on it, and on either side, slightly in front, were two tables, each with four video screens. Their monochrome flickering was reflected on his perspiring face, as his fingers flitted over one of three keyboards. There was something slightly deranged about him, hunched over his electronic empire, sending arrows of destruction into the heart of the American economy.

A quick glance at one screen told him that three dollars were now worth just one English pound sterling.

He permitted himself to sit back and sip a glass of water.

The Nomad, his Chief Director of Operations, should be planting the next work of forgery by his magnificent Vietnamese, just about now.

And outside the locked door, Danny could hear, so acute were his senses, adrenalin flowing through his veins like crack-cocaine, he could hear two of them moving, his bodyguards, his soldiers, probably bored out of their minds. Unaware they were present at one of the greatest coups of criminal extortion of their time.

Of any time.

Of History.

And with a smile, Danny Davidov began to access the secure New York Stock Exchange to Tokyo path. David Jardine had been right about 'sparrow' being a Trojan Horse, and as the State Department and Treasury had fed in all kinds of permutations, including binary conversions, Danny had been right on their trail, picking up access code after access code, as computer program analysts had played with their electronic toys, from the presumed safe fastness of the US Treasury, the Secret Service and the State Department.

Well, they had presumed too much.

In retrospect, the hagiographers at Century and in Langley were surprised how so much had happened on that one day.

The fact that years of planning by the cast-out Israeli had gone before did not damp their reluctant admiration for the way he had contrived to batter Wall Street and international confidence in the US dollar to such effect.

At twenty-six after three, a fax machine in CNN's International News Department produced a remarkable document. It purported to be a copy of a letter from the Secretary of State to the President himself.

The text was dynamite and attached to the fax was a sheet that read, simply, 'The original is on your reception desk.' And sure enough, there it was, in a manila envelope marked 'The News Editor'.

The letter read:

> Dear Mr President,
> I do not believe we can keep the matter of inadequate gold reserves under wraps for much longer now. I believe that the Secret Service has discovered at least one thousand of the lead ingots at Fort Knox.
> In order to save the country from international disgrace and the total collapse of our economy, I urge you to join with me so that we can resign together, today, and face the criminal charges that a Federal Grand Jury will undoubtedly bring against us.
> Yours ever,
> John.

David Jardine and Nancy Lucco sat in their makeshift Operations Room watching CNN News on one screen. Don Gether, the anchor, was grilling a State Department spokesperson who was vehemently denying the authenticity of the lead ingot letter.

Maggie Prosperus put her phone back on the hook and turned to face them, pushing a stray strand of hair from her forehead.

'NSA have coordinated with Treasury and State,' she said. 'They're initiating "Sparrow Shutdown" as we speak.'

'That was good, Maggie. How come so quick?'

Maggie smiled. David Jardine recognized the symptoms of extreme fatigue, because even though the agent had only been on duty for about eight hours, the nervous strain of what she had achieved was taking its toll.

'They actually had a computerized directory recording everything they did relating to "Sparrow",' she said.

'Maggie, you're a star,' said Jardine. 'Now, why don't you take a rest?'

'Sir, I'll just hang on in till we see if it makes a difference. If that's okay.'

Nancy got up and poured some more black coffee. 'Sure you can.' And she turned to Jardine. 'And you quit ordering my people around, Limey.'

And as they all laughed, the red phone buzzed. Another agent lifted it. Jimmy Petrovsky. He listened, then covered the phone with his hand. The others watched him, no doubt wondering what the hell next.

'They have Kolosov in a thirty-two-man box, heading south on Fifth,' he announced. And the whoop of joy brought Joe Pearce hurrying along the corridor from where he had been running the rest of the Secret Service's New York problems, which were not few in number.

Striding up Fifth Avenue, towards the Empire State Building, Nikolai Kolosov was heartened by the newspaper blurbs he saw on the stands: 'Dollar Sinks to New Low' and 'Sec of State Urges President to Resign'.

He was still thinking about Danny Davidov, up there in a dingy building opposite the Prince George Hotel on East

27th. The man was among the best operators he had ever worked with. Methodical, painstaking and imaginative. He must have been quite a loss to Mossad.

Davidov's ability was probably close to genius, there was no doubt. And in his genius lay his doom. For when he had made his pitch to Kolosov, back there in Olympic Village, strolling past the twin small lakes of Samorodinka, Nikolai Kolosov had indeed been feeling betrayed, rejected and spurned.

He had been one of three Deputy Directors of Service A of the First Chief Directorate of the KGB, as it had been at that time, before Yeltsin hived it off and made it the Russian Intelligence Service. The wise men at Yasenevo had signalled he was in line for promotion to Chief Deputy Director, which put him in line for the Director's job in a few years, and also on the first rung of the *nomenklatura*, the privileged ones who enjoyed plots of land near Moscow, where they could build summer houses with misappropriated funds, shop at the best store reserved for the Party and important foreign guests, and all the other stuff that went with it.

Then jealousy had raised its deadly green eye, and his enemies in the KGB had raked through his entire past, trying to find something with which to discredit him.

It had been his adoption, by his father the General and Hero of the Great Patriotic War. For Nikolai Ivanovich Kolosov had been born a Pole, to a fine family of landowners and cavalrymen. And just as David Jardine had surmised, the three-month-old infant had been plucked from the smouldering ruins of a once fine estate, right in the path of the advancing 62nd Army of the victorious Red Army under General Vladimir Ivanovich Chuikov.

Thus, it was pointed out by some jealous commissar in Section S, the security arm of the FCD, Kolosov had untruthfully entered his name in his Positive Vetting forms as 'Russian'.

He had been told there was no future for him, and with the changed shape of the KGB already looming he had been given the 'opportunity to resign', two years short of qualifying for a half-pension.

So Danny Davidov had selected his prospective partner unwisely. Because Nikolai Kolosov had his own ideas about how to rehabilitate himself. And not being in the least bit eccentric or unstable himself, he had used his wife Natalya's friendship with that die-hard Communist stalwart of the old military–industrial complex, Oleg Kouzmine, to explain the mad Jew's plan to 'frighten' the US Treasury into handing over a few billion dollars.

Kouzmine had listened. Colonel Nikolai Kolosov had been secretly reinstated into the KGB, and his orders were simple. Go along with this man Davidov until he reaches his ultimate target. And when he has the US dollar tilted, on the precipice . . . kill him and push it all the way over.

That had been two years ago, and Kolosov, walking towards his victim, felt pretty bad. The little shit was quite likeable, really. But the future of the Party, the collapse of Boris Yeltsin's power base, the Yankee dollar, were a million times more important than the life of one mildly endearing Jew.

Besides, the bastards were holding his beloved daughter at a submarine base near Murmansk. That had probably been Natalya's idea. The slut.

As Kolosov reached East 27th Street and walked past his intended destination, checking for surveillance, David Jardine and Nancy Lucco were watching the banks of video screens portraying a kind of Star Wars saga of top secret, protected, once protected, computer program paths being shut down, like submarines diving for the deep. And after a few moments of deepest black decoy paths, free of the little electronic soldier from Davidov's Trojan Horse.

And sure enough, it did not take long for the quarry to start looking for its prey. A sequence of initial passwords and code numbers provided just enough entry to prove that whoever was hacking meant business, and knew his business. Then the defunct, shutdown entry code would be given. And the screen would signal, ACCESS DENIED.

So the hacker would try another way into the maze. And each time, the message ACCESS DENIED would appear again, until every screen was taunting him with the same message.

'Well done, Maggie,' said Jardine, much relieved and smiling. 'Good work.'

Maggie Prosperus beamed. David Jardine had a knack of making people feel special, but in truth, the kid had cottoned on so fast, she had probably saved the US dollar from plummeting even further.

'So where is Kolosov now?' asked Jardine, as he and Nancy opened the door to step out into the corridor. A big, good-looking guy, with skin a darker shade of purple, stood facing him, not that much shorter than David Jardine, which made him about six feet and an inch.

'You the English spy . . .?' asked Elmore Williams, examining him from head to foot, like a horse dealer.

'Look no further,' replied Jardine.

'David, this is Elmore Williams. His team are on the Kolosov tail.' Jardine noted Nancy was protective towards her own.

Williams spoke to Jardine, holding his gaze with a frank, untroubled stare. 'We got the guy in a brownstone near Madison Square Park. You know where that is?'

Jardine nodded. 'Sure.'

'I have a thirty-two-man team on him, he can't shit without us knowing.'

'That's exactly right,' said Jardine. 'No sign of the other one?'

'We ain't seen Dancer right now. But we stay on this guy's ass long enough, if they're real close we'll find him.'

'And why did Kolosov – Stone – go into the brownstone?'

'Beats me, my man. We were expecting him to go into Target One's office. Michael Mitchel's.'

David Jardine turned to Nancy. 'Can I help out here without getting it chewed off?'

Nancy Lucco shrugged. 'I'm not sure. Try it and see.'

Jardine turned to Elmore Williams. 'You were right not to crowd Stone in there. That could be the place they're operating from. Do you mind if we take a look?'

Williams shrugged. 'Be my guest.'

And the three of them went down to the street and climbed into an unmarked Oldsmobile sedan, driven by a young Special Agent. There was a full radio hook-up with the surveillance teams, and a small video monitor, showing the front entrance to the 27th Street building.

As they bumped across Manhattan South's potholed avenues, the car's springs protesting, the phone buzzed. Williams picked it up, pushed a button and grunted. Then he passed it to Nancy.

She spoke and listened. Saying uh-huh and yep a few times. When she handed it back to Elmore Williams, she looked more relieved than at any time since she had met David Jardine at the airport.

'They think it might be working,' she said. 'Stock Exchange and Treasury are squealing about the shutdown but it was not for long and it looks as if NSA could have shut the sonofabitch right out.'

Inside the 27th Street building, on the seventeenth floor, the elevator went no higher, and you had to climb the last three floors by way of an inner stairwell, from the dirty windows of which, on the eighteenth and nineteenth floors, parts of rooftops, air-conditioning vents and dead pigeons could be seen.

Danny Davidov's eyrie was on the top floor, in an office converted from a rooftop store-room. The windows had been painted black and boarded over from the inside. This was where the master-shafter of the United States dollar had his control room. His nerve centre.

There was a lobby outside, facing the elevator housing,

which frequently creaked and whispered as folk down below came and went.

There was a washroom and a small kitchen, plus a smaller room on the other side of the elevator shaft. That was where the four bodyguards, part of Danny's operational structure, rested, made coffee, and took it in turns to guard the door and the approach from the stairwell.

Inside the control centre, as Davidov had insisted on calling it, the Israeli sat, beads of perspiration running down his temples and chin as his fingers moved furiously over the keys.

Nikolai Kolosov sat on a packing case, watching his partner, without emotion.

'You have problems?' he asked, in Russian.

'Nothing we can't handle . . .' replied Danny. 'Some bastard's getting smart, that's all.'

Kolosov watched the screens as Davidov made his way rapidly, professionally, into a succession of protected government and banking computer programs. But each time, the message ACCESS DENIED would eventually appear.

Davidov's fingers flew even faster. Sweat stained his armpits and the back of the blue denim shirt he had bought just the day before, at the Banana Republic store off Lexington Avenue. He had become remote, withdrawn in concentration.

So, the sixty-four-zillion-dollar question, my little Yiddisher friend, mused Kolosov, is . . . are you going to make it? And he willed his friend, for that was what Danny Davidov had become, to succeed.

'Have you made our terms known?' he asked.

'What?'

He had never seen the little guy testy before. 'Have you given the administration your terms?'

Danny nodded, sharply. 'Sure. Ten minutes ago.'

In the Oval Office, the President was sitting chatting with

his daughter and two schoolfriends who had been evacuated some months before from Sarajevo. Both had American cousins, and since one was Croatian and one Moslem, it had been a symbolic gesture at the time, and one of the happier moments in that dreadful day.

There was a knock at the door and Alan Clair came in, accompanied by Jim Farley.

The President patted the kids on their shoulders and strolled over to one window of the office, gazing out at the White House lawns.

'I think we have him on the run, Mr President,' Farley murmured quietly. 'He's going crazy trying to hack back into the fresh systems.'

'Good work.' The President was not so easily assuaged. 'You know how many weeks it's going to take, to restore credibility to our currency?'

'At least we still have a currency, sir,' said Alan Clair.

The President turned to gaze at the CIA man. 'I will want to know how they got so close. It must never happen again.'

'No, sir,' replied Clair gravely. Thinking that was unfair, it was really a Secret Service problem. Or was he just feeling guilty at not paying more attention to David Jardine, sooner?

'And Jim.'

'Sir?' This made a pleasant change from 'Mr Farley'.

'I really want to know how those ingots got into Fort Knox.'

'Yessir, we're working on it.'

'When the dust settles, gentlemen,' remarked the President softly, 'I sure as hell am going to kick some ass.' And with that he turned, smiling, to the orphans and crossed towards them, the crisis averted.

Jim Farley still held in his hand the faxed demand note, impressive at the moment of arrival, for it had been remotely originated on the Treasury's own fax machine, in the Director's outer office. But now? Slightly pathetic. It read:

To The President of the United States

Sir,

As you will be aware, I am in the rapid process of destabilizing the US economy. By the time you receive this, the dollar will be worth thirty cents to the British pound sterling. By tomorrow, you will need $13.70 to match £1, and by mid-week, maybe $5.

All you need to stop this slide is to arrange for $20 billion to be paid into an electronic holding account.

Reply yes on any of your secure Treasury programs and I will stop at once.

Sparrow.

Farley did not bother to show it to the Chief. He crumpled the demand, the zenith of Danny Davidov's career in the international big-time, and left the room with Clair.

In the rooftop eyrie, the converted store-room, Nikolai Kolosov watched, without emotion, as screen after screen registered the message ACCESS DENIED. They seemed to be mocking Danny.

The Makarov jammed into his belt, silencer screwed on to the muzzle, seemed hardly necessary. There was going to be no opportunity to push the American economy over the edge. The other side had been smarter, in the final moments of the eleventh hour. Somebody had second-guessed Danny Davidov's most outrageous scheme.

The KGB Colonel knew he was supposed to kill Danny, for security reasons. It was standard operational procedure in his service. It would be correct and prudent. But what did Davidov really know? What could he ever tell? He had no idea that for the last two years he had been virtually in the custody of the Anti-Yeltsin faction.

Besides, nobody had succeeded in making Kolosov laugh the way Danny Davidov had done, with his absurd tales of that early marriage to an inexhaustible sexual athlete, or his deadpan wisecracks in moments of extreme danger.

The Russian, the Polish Russian, sighed. Maybe he was getting older, there had been so much killing.

He waited for a few more minutes. It was almost painful to watch Davidov seeming to age before his eyes. There was something undignified about the scene.

'I think I'll just grab some air . . .' said the Russian and he crossed to the door and unlocked it, letting himself out.

One of Danny's four trusted bodyguards glanced up as Kolosov came out from the nerve centre of Operation Medusa.

The KGB man pointed to the rest-room, where the others were relaxing, and with a jerk of his head, indicated it was time to go.

The five of them quietly slipped away, descending the dank stairwell silently, their departure unnoticed by the desperate man with his disconnected line to wealth untold.

Kolosov left his men to split up, so as not to draw attention to themselves. He took the elevator from the fourteenth floor, and as he stepped out into the street, felt strangely flat. Those last two years had been exciting.

As he started to walk away from the building, he registered someone across the street watching him. There was no rouge now on her aristocratic cheekbones. She looked good. And as she met his eye, just for a second he knew real fear, for the first time in years. For she seemed to be looking at a doomed man. And there was no pity in her eyes.

His life was probably saved by the sallow-skinned man, wearing a black fedora, who appeared at his side.

'Colonel Nikolai Kolosov? I'm with the US Secret Service, please don't go for your gun or my men will kill you.'

Kolosov allowed his arms to be pinned to his sides. He realized he was now surrounded by about ten men. And when he glanced across the street, the girl from St Petersburg was no longer there.

As Kolosov was led away, the Oldsmobile with David

Jardine, Elmore Williams and Nancy Lucco pulled up next to the New York Life Insurance building. A running commentary from a Special Agent who had gone to NSA's Operations Room had documented, blow by blow, the close-down of Danny Davidov's attempt to touch the sun.

They had heard also of the moment of Kolosov's arrest, although they remained unaware, and always would, of the sinister presence of the Oleg Kouzmine watchers, who had flitted like spectres around everyone connected with the Medusa affair.

'He's up there. Top floor.' Marty Socorro appeared as they climbed out from the Oldsmobile.

Williams pushed at his radio earpiece and glanced at Nancy. 'I really can't let you or our guest go in there,' he said, without much hope of success.

'Bullshit,' replied Nancy Lucco.

'Just so,' added David Jardine.

And the three of them walked down the street, which was now crawling with agents and undercover cops from the local precinct.

As they approached the entrance, across from the Prince George Hotel, the hair on Jardine's neck started to rise. And he glanced around the environment, alert and ready for trouble.

Sitting in a green Mustang, at the kerb near the hotel entrance, was, disquietingly, a man David Jardine recognized and was both surprised, yet not surprised, to find there, as the business which had started for him with a trap set in Beirut drew to its conclusion. The man used a number of names, as people did in that business which he and the Englishman conducted in the shadows of world events, quietly and without fuss. He wore a dark blue shirt, no necktie, and a sand-coloured raincoat. He ignored the clandestine activity in the street, although he must have been aware of it. He was Mossad's current Director of Covert Operations, a fact he would probably have been appalled to learn was no secret to Jardine.

The man sat there, cold as ice, and David Jardine had a

chilling presentiment as to how this business was being resolved, by the very people Reuven Arieh and his clique, now mostly dead, had dreaded finding out. The real, all-singing, all-dancing, three-dimensional, legal and fully authorized Mossad. The men upstairs, whom they had all imagined they could ignore. Nathan Zamir, Avvie Eitels, Anatoly Dzerzhinsky. All . . . dealt with.

Jardine marvelled at how utterly, ruthlessly, urgently determined a service used to fighting for its people's very existence could be. These people meant to survive.

The three of them took an elevator as high as it would go, and as they emerged, as the metal gates creaked open, he was somehow not surprised to see her.

Alisha Abdul-Fetteh waited politely as Nancy, Williams and Jardine emerged from the elevator cabin. Jardine left last, and as he did, their eyes met for a moment. He had a brief and unwelcome memory of her head thrown back in ecstasy, skin glistening, hair across her face.

And they had passed.

As the sound of the elevator hummed, diminishing, David Jardine kept his hand in his empty jacket pocket. He knew now, with a cold sense of having been royally used and manipulated, what they were going to find.

The ruthless inevitability of it left him short of breath for a moment.

It was still, inside the nerve centre of Operation Medusa.

He looked like a schoolboy somehow, slumped exhausted over his keyboard.

The bullets had made little mess, for Mossad tended to use reduced-charge .22 cartridges, with soft-nosed bullets, designed to remain in the target. In this case, the dreamer's head of Danny Davidov, aged forty-three.

One slug had exited. It lay, misshapen, on the desk beside the lifeless face, the eyes still open.

A trickle of blood had spread from one ear, to form a still wet pool beside a notebook which had charted the falling value of the dollar.

And every screen on the banks of TV sets had the same message:

ACCESS DENIED

Poor bastard, thought Jardine. And he resisted an unexpected wish to touch the man's shoulder, or his hair. So alive, one moment, so full of his strange dreams. What on earth would he have done with twenty billion dollars, for God's sake?

And Kolosov. He wondered what the Americans were going to do with him. Put him on trial? Where was the evidence?

He turned to Nancy, who was standing staring at the dead scoundrel. He realized no one had spoken a word. Tears were wet on her cheeks. He was struck by her compassion, and was not to know that the tears were for that big Wop cop, Eddie Lucco, who, she had just realized, must've looked like that when they found him. In a Bogota drainage tunnel. Nobody had used the word sewer.

'Here's another one,' said Elmore Williams, as matter-of fact as if he were picking up fallen plates.

And on the floor, beyond poor Danny's desk, lay the man whom David Jardine would always remember from their first encounter in a Beirut street, cloaked in beggar's robes, with surprisingly healthy teeth. 'Get in the car,' he had said. 'I'm double-parked.'

The look on his face was one of surprise. Somehow it robbed him of final dignity.

'Four slugs in this one,' remarked the laconic Williams, stooped and peering at the blood and hair. 'Kind of . . . excessive.' Then he straightened and looked directly into Jardine's eyes.

'Is this Nikolai Kolosov?'

'I don't think so,' Jardine replied.

'Do you recognize him?' Elmore was a good cop, David Jardine reflected.

'Salim Jaddeh,' he replied, expressionless, meeting the Secret Service man's stare. 'Arab. He's known to us . . .'

And Elmore Williams knew that was all he was going to get.

'Let's go,' he said.

Outside, uniformed cops from the 14th Precinct were arriving, taking plastic rolls of tape from their trunks to seal off the area of what was officially just another homicide.

As David Jardine emerged, with Nancy and Elmore Williams, he instinctively looked for the green Mustang. It was still there. The passenger door was open and Alisha glanced back, momentarily, before getting in.

The door closed and the Mustang moved away.

Nancy was watching him.

'Anyone you know . . .?' she asked.

David Jardine stared after the disappearing car.

'I'm not sure,' he replied.